Birding 101

Paradise Pond

Unillustrated

Novel 1 of the Antiguo Cuentista Trilogy

E. M. Williams

Willeimr Tales

E. M. Williams

Birding 101 Paradise Pond   1st Edition

FOR MATURE READERS AGES 18+

Cover photos and design by E. M. Williams

> Front Cover: Prothonotary Warbler, Paradise Pond
>
> Back Cover: Crested Caracara, Paradise Pond

ISBN: 978-1-943313-01-3

Willeimrtales@gmail.com

The Antiguo Cuentista Trilogy

By E. M. Williams

Novel 1:   Birding 101 Paradise Pond

Illustrated (FOR MATURE READERS)

Unillustrated (FOR MATURE READERS)

Abridged

Novel 2:   Dancing Flowers – Chasing Moon
(FOR MATURE READERS)

Novel 3:   Cruising for a Bruising

Epilogue: For Those Who Dance

Willeimr Tales

E. M. Williams

To

Margaret

CONTENTS

Acknowledgements

My hat's off to the State of Texas and everyone involved in the Great Texas Coastal Birding Trails and trail guides. They are dreams come true. The same applies to Port Aransas, Texas, and the organizations, sponsors and volunteers that make it such a superb birding and nature lover destination. Habitat improvements and nature trails provide great opportunities to see birds and wildlife.

I admire the foresight of those like the late Norma Friedrich Ward, who donated property in San Antonio for the *Emile and Albert Friedrich Wilderness Park*. That applies to those who protect and maintain it and the other birding, nature and sight-seeing jewels mentioned in my book.

Though some settings and venues changed before publication, I left them as originally written—snapshots in time.

Prologue
Beware the Birds of the Night

Sex for money. A lifetime of leisure worth of money.
Or is this another damned screw-up?
Sandra Perot downshifted, wheeled onto Beach Access Road 2, and stopped. Port Aransas, Texas, lay a few miles ahead. Corpus Christi sprawled twenty or so miles behind on the other side of Corpus Christi Bay. Home was San Antonio, a hundred-seventy-miles away.

Sandra's destination, a Mustang Island beach on the Gulf of Mexico, was less than a half-mile in front of her. It was just like her situation--so near and yet so far. All she could see were the dunes protecting the barrier island, the mountains between her past and future.

A man waited for her there. He was burly, had a bouncer's physique, but wasn't that tall—maybe five-nine. His handsome face sported a boyish grin and the bluest eyes she'd ever seen, nearly cobalt.

His mop of sandy-brown hair lightly streaked with gray suggested he could be anywhere from his forties to mid-fifties. At first his looks and flirty manner made her look forward to their tryst. The forbidden nature added to the excitement. She could play the hooker, a favorite fantasy. But now, late in the day, she had second thoughts.

A monster truck careened onto the narrow road and skidded to a stop inches from her car's back bumper. The driver waited patiently for five seconds before pounding his horn.

Sandra showed him what she thought of his inconsiderateness.

Enraged, the driver drove forward. "Fine, bitch, I'll move your piss-ant car for you." The truck's massive grill bumped her car, shoving it toward the ditch.

She glared over her shoulder and edged closer to the pavement drop-off.

The driver swerved around and cut her off. He stumbled down from his truck and tottered erratically toward her.

"OK, smart-ass ... Holy crap!"

Sandra tugged up uselessly on her neckline, then out her super short miniskirt that revealed her black G-string panties.

"Great tits and legs. Whatever you're charging, sugar doll, I'll pay it," he offered, leaning his forearms on the door. "Do y'all take credit cards?" His voice slurred, breath reeked of alcohol.

"Fuck off, cowboy."

Cowboy grinned and reached for her breasts. "Them little ole things sure are purty. Let's see how they—" His jaw dropped. "Hey, you shave—"

Sandra shifted into reverse and mashed the gas pedal, hoping to break his arms. She slammed her brakes when another pickup turned the corner.

"Screw you." Cowboy gave her a double middle-finger salute, staggered to his truck, and weaved toward the beach.

The second driver ogled, made an obscene gesture, and held up a bottle of tequila. Smiling crookedly, he nodded toward the beach and drove on.

"That cuts it. I'm through with immature, lowlife bastards." Sandra eased her car forward.

A sign beside the road warned of rattlesnakes. The weaving streams of windblown sand coursing through the winding pass between the dunes reminded her of them. Not a good omen. Neither was the wind tunnel effect whipping her hair and filling her convertible with gritty sand.

When Sandra cleared the dunes, she stopped and stared at the Gulf while raising the car top. Gigantic waves churned the usually clear, blue-green water a murky brown. Heavy clouds roiling in from the Gulf created a premature dusk, and the ocean mist coating the windshield added to her discomfort.

The dearth of people on the beach made her more uneasy, as did the pickup truck pervert on her left, pretending to fondle himself while beckoning to her.

The pavement ended at the beach, where thick mats of sargassum seaweed lined the shore. She turned right as instructed, and her car tires began to bury in the sand.

I don't need a damned sports car. I need shit-faced cowboy's dune truck.

The tires caught, pitching her car forward, and Sandra thanked God for cellphones. She could call for help if she became stuck.

A fisherman gawked at her tiny vehicle and pointed that she should turn around and go back. The few other fishermen she encountered sat braving the elements, watching the tips of their surf rods secured in white PVC pipes hammered into the sand. Their four-wheel-drive vehicles could be the source of a tow should her car bog down.

Within a half-mile, she was alone on the beach.

The blood-red sun lowered into the celestial crawl space between the base of the clouds and the tops of the dunes. Backlit sea oats drummed against those towering mounds. The beautiful, serene scene should have been comforting, but high waves and the incoming tide were constricting her path, making it more dangerous for driving and impossible to turn around. The gusty onshore wind rocking her vehicle added to her frayed her nerves. "Where is that van?"

Popping and crunching noises startled her. Seashells. Moving. She jolted involuntarily and hit the brake. Swerving around the fiddler crabs scurrying across the sand was out of the question. She would become stuck in this godforsaken desolation.

Her clothing added to her anxiety. Her neckline and pushup bra highlighted her delicate breasts that monster-truck pervo found so irresistible. Matching stiletto heels accentuated her long legs. Her G-string panties were courtesy of a Naughty Nancy Lingerie and Adult Novelty Shop, where just being there increased her excitement.

She visualized the crude pickup drivers. What if her car became stuck near the wrong fisherman? Her attire would certainly give a poor impression to the beach patrol and getting arrested wasn't part of her hooker fantasy.

If her husband, Edward, discovered her outfit, could she say it was for him?

The sun disappeared behind the dunes as an object loomed out of the mist like a haunted castle. It was the unmarked industrial van she'd been told to look for. Fishing poles with bells on their tips and lines extending into the ocean sat in PVC pipes. To a beach patrol, the van's occupants would appear to be night fishermen. No other vehicles were in sight, and the beach faded into dusk and mist.

"Shit. I'm out of here."

The sand looked firm, so Sandra nervously drove past the sinister-looking van. The howling wind muted her car's engine noise, but her shaking foot made the car lurch spasmodically. Bucking, shaking, it sunk to its axels in the wet sand. *Damn, damn, damn.*

Sandra debated walking back to the access road, but thought better of it, especially not on stiletto heels. Not barefoot, either, on a darkening beach covered with sharp shells and ghastly crabs accompanied by pissed-off, drunken monster-truck drivers.

Could she hide in the snake-infested dunes while waiting for a tow truck driver to protect her and extricate her car? What would he think of her attire? Worse, what would Edward think? She was supposed to be on a girl's outing in Rockport, thirty miles away.

The tow truck seemed her only choice. She located her cellphone in her huge purse and searched its address list for the auto club's emergency number.

A tapping sounded on the window, and the door opened.

Crap! I'm a dead woman.

"Hi, Sandra, I thought you might be lost."

She might be just that. The man's friendly face and calm, deep voice did nothing to soothe her rattled nerves. She held up an index finger. "Just a minute."

Chest heaving so hard she feared she would hyperventilate, she bent over the console and fumbled around the floorboard for her dropped phone.

Smiling oddly, the man grasped her arm. "You won't need that." He nodded at the car. "We'll take care of this thing later. Besides, it's hell out here. Let's go inside where we can relax."

It was her last chance. She would explain that she'd changed her mind and ask to reschedule to a different day.

"That would be good," she squeaked. *Good Lord.*

A smirk played about the man's mouth. Menacing—or appreciation of her makeup and clothing?

Her heels weren't designed for the soft sand. She would remove her shoes slowly, use any excuse to delay and hope for salvation.

"I need to take off my—"

No delay. No salvation. Sandra hopped on one foot as he pulled her from the vehicle and tugged her along. No one knew where she was. If she struggled, tried to run, she could be raped and murdered—her body buried in the dunes where it would never be found.

Panic became terror when she entered the back of the van. Shackles and torture instruments lined its carpeted walls. She shoved backward against her companion. It was like trying to move a living brick wall.

"We'll use those only if you agree to them," he said while snapping a padlock into the latch on the door.

Despite his pleasant demeanor, his grip hurt when he led her to a recliner beside a large mirror in the forward part of the van's cavernous interior. He shoved her into it and nodded at a wine rack above a small refrigerator. "Which would you prefer ... Merlot? Champagne? There's beer, too."

Ashen-faced, unable to speak, Sandra pointed at the champagne.

The man handed her a glass and smiled as she warily eyed the van's interior. "Like the décor?"

Sandra looked away, unable to hold his eyes and insidious smile. She would do or say anything to not upset him.

"It's exciting." Her flat, quavering voice belied her statement.

The drink might be drugged, so she toyed with accidentally spilling it. No, if she was going to become a victim, she might as well make it as easy on herself as possible. She took a sip. The bubbly wine was top quality.

They talked easily. It wasn't until her second glass that she realized the man wasn't drinking. But at least she was alive. Warm, she no longer trembled.

When the man pulled her neckline to the sides of her bra, she stiffened but didn't resist. Neither did she object when he exposed her breasts.

He murmured appreciatively and lifted her to her feet. Heady from the wine, she giggled and raised her arms. There went the dress and bra. She stepped out of her G-string and rotated full circle.

The man whistled. "My compliments to your chef, Sandra."

"Thank you, sir."

Cupping her breasts, with the flavoring she'd applied to her nipples, she mounded them, held them out, before losing her balance and clutching his arms. She was wobbly, woozy. Had he spiked the drinks? Or was it the wine? She didn't care. She steadied herself by gripping his shoulders as he accepted her offering.

She was quite pretty, if slightly overweight. Her lips were moderately full, and she had a cute button nose. Her breasts were small, super soft-looking, but pert. Buzzed, again gifting them to him, she gave him a flirty look.

The man accepted her offering and nodded his appraisal.

He punched a button on a CD player and sat in the feminine, velvet-flocked recliner. "Dance for me."

Sandra twirled on the thickly carpeted floor to the soothing music, tripped, and caught herself. "You spiked my drink, didn't you?"

The man shook his head but looked like he was lying.

She let her mind drift with the music. Dancing naked in front of a strange man worked its magic. She became excited—her mind on fire. Her abdomen twitched pleasurably. After all, it was in the contract. The man's appreciative gaze fueled her throbbing need.

When the music stopped, he beckoned. His trembling fingers traced her body, fondled her breasts, pinched her nipples.

Sandra couldn't control her hips. Whimpers escaped her lips. She pulled the man's hands back to her breasts.

"Squeeze them." He evoked fire. "Pleasure me." The relationship had changed. She was now in control.

She unbuttoned his shirt and pulled it off. But when she reached for his belt, he gripped her wrists with hands of steel.

"Try that again, before I'm ready, and I'll have to restrain you."

Further effort served only to tighten his grip.

She tried to jerk away. "I want you ... now."

"I've warned you, once. This is twice." The man nodded at shackles on the wall. "Three strikes and you're in."

She snapped with her teeth, dared with her eyes, shook her head slowly from side to side. "You can't. I'm too strong."

Smirking, he effortlessly spun her around, and carried her to the side of the van while she feigned an attempt to break from his hold.

Finding him strong, savoring his masculinity, she dropped the pretense and fought in futile fun to prevent him from confining her wrists and ankles.

Until he made a mistake. Although spread-eagled facing the van's carpeted wall, Sandra turned her head and bit him full on the shoulder when he reached around to fondle her.

The man grunted and jerked away.

She laughed delightedly at the sight of the tiny droplets oozing from the wound. "No part of your body's safe, you know."

"We'll see about that."

She gasped when his hand slid between her legs, stroked, and probed. Her knees buckled, thighs trembled, head lolled back. The bondage and waves of pleasure birthed fantasies unlike any in her life. "Damn it ... why are you waiting?"

He unlocked the clamps and carried her trembling body to a device hanging from the ceiling. "A love swing," he explained.

"I hope you're man enough," she taunted, hoping he wouldn't ruin the evening before he removed his clothing.

He gave a strange, crooked smile and removed the rest of his clothing.

Sandra's eyes rounded. She drew in a sharp intake of breath. Previous misgivings came flooding back. "No ... stop ... I've changed my mind!"

The man ignored her, positioned himself without comment.

The silence in the van became all-encompassing. All she heard was their breathing—no music, not the violent wind rocking the van. Someone immediately outside the door couldn't hear her.

Terrified by the monster's maniacal smile, Sandra yanked frantically to untwist her wrists from the hand supports. She screamed.

A feeble screech escaped her constricting throat as her world went black.

1

Odd Birds Out

"You want *sex*? At ten o'clock in the *morning*?"

Jim Smith knew his passionate kiss had an effect—Marsha's knees gave way, and her eyes glazed over. The hand clutching her chest provided another clue. But her wagging finger told him it wasn't going to happen.

Focusing on her plump bosom, he reached for the buttons on her blouse.

Marsha shoved her husband's hands away and scolded, in breathless exasperation, "Jim, we made love just the other day."

"It wasn't this week and it wasn't last. I can't remember the last time we made love."

"Then you're getting senile. Besides, Sarah will be here any minute to pick up Spud," Marsha spouted as she tottered away.

Jim shrugged, strolled to his recliner and perused their vacation checklist for perhaps the fiftieth time. It might have been many times more. A ringing phone interrupted his concentration. He glanced at the TV screen and saw their daughter Sarah's cellphone number. She was probably on her way.

Marsha answered after the second ring, but Jim had already refocused on the checklist. Everything was ready for their trip to Port Aransas, Texas. He set the list aside, cranked back, and visualized two fun-filled weeks with their friends from the Edmond Vagabonds RV club. He daydreamed about the camaraderie, the evening card games, the fishing, but most of all the birding. He would take great photos this year.

"Jim?" Marsha's hesitant voice broke his reverie.

"Yes?"

"That was Sarah."

"I know."

"She and Stan are going to a trade show in Las Vegas." Marsha chewed her bottom lip. "They want us to babysit, and I told her we would."

"So? That's no problem."

He and Marsha were always bouncing back and forth between grandkids, Anderson and Taylor, in Oklahoma City and great-grandchildren, Cindy and Buck Jr., in Kansas City.

Jim's smile faded. "No. Not again."

"They need us, sweetheart. You know how Anderson and Taylor don't like other sitters. And Sarah likes it that I always read to them and teach them manners."

"They like it that you clean their house, do the laundry, and perform every maid duty known to mankind. Our fifth-wheel is at the curb." He glanced at his watch. "We're supposed to leave as soon as Sarah leaves with Spud."

Marsha played the trump card. "Don't be mean. You know how Anderson and Taylor love for us to be with them. I told them you would play horsey and take them fishing."

Unable to speak, Jim lowered the leg rest, stalked to the back patio, and slumped onto the thick cushion on the lattice settee, Spud looked up from the bone he was gnawing, stood and stretched, front paws out, rump in the air. Tail wagging, he trotted forward and laid his head in Jim's lap.

White in the muzzle, the old retriever was roughly the color of an Irish potato and smelled all dog. He understood that his only purpose in life was to make his masters happy. When Jim didn't immediately respond, he licked his hand and nudged it with his cold, wet nose.

Jim cupped his dog's jaw and scratched behind his ears. Spud stared up with loving eyes.

Marsha made her way to the patio, carrying two glasses of tea. It was a warm day for March, but there seemed to be a lot of them these days. "There's no need to be moody, Jim. Family always comes before friends. Anderson and Taylor will be grown before you know it, and when they're teenagers, they'll ignore us."

"We cancelled last year's trip to babysit Cindy and Bucky at the last moment." He frowned. "Think about it, Marsha, we're well over the age hump. What're the odds we'll live to 130? Each year, we lose abilities. Our bodies, muscles, joints ... and brains ... deteriorate, so it's now or never for some aspects of our lives.

"Plus, you promised our friends we wouldn't miss this year, and we've already cut the trip three weeks short for the dental appointment you didn't move."

Spud turned sad eyes toward Marsha without moving his head, tucked his tail, and sat.

"Couldn't move," Marsha corrected, an edge to her voice. "And that's a good reason not to go. Towing a fifth-wheel twelve hundred miles for only two weeks and spending one week all by ourselves is ridiculous."

"But our friends are counting on us. Jeff says the fish are biting."

"So ... fish are more important to you than your grandchildren?"

Jim's eyes crossed. "Marsha...."

He pitched his tea into the flower garden. "Sorry Spud." He pushed the dog away and stood. "I promised the gang we'd go, and I'm going."

"Jim, Anderson and Taylor will be *crushed*."

"We've babysat them half this month. They won't miss me."

"You're going without me?"

"I don't think you'll miss me, either."

* * *

"Damn it to hell, Mother, you can't go with me. I have to do this by myself."

"Mary Elizabeth, if you're going, I'm going. That's all there is to it."

"Holy crap. You're most of the reason ... make that all the reasons ... I'm in this mess."

"Watch your language, Mary Elizabeth," her father cautioned.

She spun toward him. "Shut your damn trap, Frank. I'm twenty-nine. I can take care of myself. And you know I need to get away as much as she does."

"Don't call your father, Frank, Mary Elizabeth. It doesn't show respect."

"Fathers *rock* their daughters when they're little. They don't make them leave the room or sit in the corner." Mary Elizabeth glared. "How's this for respect?"

Frank Matthews gave his wife, Helen, a solemn look while their daughter gave them each the finger.

Mary Elizabeth's angry glare wilted under her mother's steady gaze, but she continued complaining. "Don is all *your* fault and getting the hell out of this mess is *my* responsibility."

"Now, now, dear, you're too upset for the situation. If you'll see Dr. Parkman, I'm sure he'll prescribe the meds you need to calm you down. I made you an appointment for next week, but I'll try to change it to tomorrow."

"Screw Dr. Parkman. You don't have any idea what I'm going through."

"Don't be disrespectful to Dr. Parkman, Mary Elizabeth. He's been so patient to reschedule your appointments."

"I'll never see the bastard, Mother, so stop making them for me. But I do have a reservation. It's at the Windward Dunes, and I'm leaving tomorrow."

"What does Port Aransas have that Kemah doesn't?"

"Birds, Mother, birds. It has Paradise Pond. And it doesn't have Don ... or you. You want me to be calm? Birding makes me calm. Photography makes me calm. You, on the other hand, make me want to puke."

Her father tried to interrupt, "Mary Eliz—"

She whirled. "I told you to shut the fuck up, Frank."

"Mary *Elizabeth*."

Mary Elizabeth picked up a flower vase, yanked out the flowers and hurled them at her mother. She then poured the water on the sofa and smashed the vase on the coffee table, shattering both it and glass tabletop.

Shocked by her actions, she strode to a wide oak staircase, and ran up the steps. At the end of the hall, she opened a door. An army of Madam Alexander Dolls and Cabbage Patch Kids stared with sightless eyes as she flung herself on a king-sized canopy bed and curled into a ball.

* * *

"I wish you wouldn't go, Jim," Marsha said. "I know something bad is going to happen."

"I'll be careful."

Pride prevented Jim from emptying the RV and returning it to storage. His friends gave him a sense of purpose. His passion urged him on.

"You dented the fifth-wheel two years ago at the rest stop in Waco when you cut the corner too short."

"I remember."

"And you tripped over your minnow bucket at San Luis Pass and broke two ribs. You couldn't breathe without pain for six months."

"That ... I don't want to remember."

"There was the time you scraped your leg on the barnacles and needed antibiotics."

"It was an accident."

"The log was three feet high and twenty feet long, sweetheart."

"Marsha, I get the picture. I'll be careful."

She looked dubious. "But you do it all the time."

"Not this time."

"Well, stay near the group," Marsha said anxiously, as if their six friends could somehow protect her klutz of a husband. "And listen to Maggie." Their friend

Maggie Saunders was different. Something of a seeress.

Jim nodded.

After making sure the RV's jacks were up, the antennas down, and the doors locked, he said, "Help me make sure the lights work."

Marsha walked to the back of the rig while he climbed into the pickup and started the clattering diesel engine. He switched on the lights, stepped on the brake, and worked the turn signals. She gave a thumbs-up to each and returned to the window, tears in her eyes. "You can still stay home, sweetheart."

Jim swallowed the lump in his throat. "I promise to be especially careful."

"Then call me every night at eight, no matter what."

The what was the nightly card game Pegs and Jokers. Or the ice cream social, bingo night, or movie night. She leaned forward for a kiss, worry-wrinkles lining her brow.

Jim lightly bussed her lips. "I'll see you soon, beautiful."

She had been once. Her face still was, but it was difficult to make out her body curves that took his breath away the first time he saw her. Time and food had taken their toll. With him, too. Both were obese.

Marsha moved to the sidewalk and stood crying as she waved goodbye.

He blew her a kiss and stepped on the gas pedal.

Waving frantically, hurried to the side window. "Did you remember to fill up the propane tank? It was nearly empty after the last campout."

He hadn't. "I'll fill it this evening." They always stayed the first night at an RV park near the Texas border to check everything.

"OK, don't forget." Even after reminding him, Marsha bet he would.

Jim settled into the RV campground three hours later and hooked everything up. By nightfall, he'd made sure everything worked properly. There was nothing to hold him back—other than his growing guilt. He swallowed. This would be a guilt trip. He wouldn't turn back.

As he settled into bed and turned off the light, he thought about the gamblers in the casino a few miles away.

How can people be so foolish as to risk their happiness?

* * *

Holding a sports magazine, Frank reclined against a bank of pillows as he waited for Helen to come to bed. He wasn't reading, and he didn't look forward to the discussion sure to follow—the continuation of their argument.

"So ... you're not going to help me keep Mary Elizabeth here and force her to get the help she needs?" Helen made the indirect demand as she walked from the bathroom.

"No, Momma, I don't think it's our call. And, I think she *should* go alone, for once in her life."

"You're being obstinate, Daddy. She could be hurt. Or hurt someone. You know how she is when she's having one of these episodes."

His wife was right about one thing. Their daughter became irrational this time of year. Like an annual event. It usually lasted until late June, and then she calmed.

Not this past year. Frank had both his suspicions and his doubts. Helen had threatened divorce if he let their daughter watch his programs or encouraged her to be in sports, like he had their sons Joshua, Dan, and David. "I wish we'd handled things differently when she was little. I could have rocked her and not encouraged her to be in sports."

"No. All you ever watched were ballgames, racing, hunting, and fishing shows. She wanted to be with you. Begged to. She even wanted to play golf," Helen snapped. "You had our three sons. I only had Mary Elizabeth."

"I could have watched little girl programs."

"But you *didn't*. And look what happened with the environmental programs I agreed to let her watch. All she wants to do is traipse through spider webs, sloughs, and brambles, taking pictures of snakes, birds, and animals."

Frank held his tongue. His wife objected to the only things that made their daughter happy. He was thankful he'd at least had his way on that but regretted cowing to his wife's other stipulations. What father wasn't allowed to hold his daughter?

One who'd been an alcoholic before she was born. Still was, although he could cite the day, thirty-five years earlier, when he took his last drink. Helen's threat to take their sons and leave set him on the path of righteousness, and she used that success to get her way with Mary Elizabeth, who was born eight years after their youngest son, David. Joshua, their eldest, had been fourteen.

"At least I wasn't the mother of a tomboy," Helen exulted. "God blessed me with a daughter, when I was forty-one, and I've kept her that way. I made Mary Elizabeth play with dolls, so she could learn to be a good mother when she grew up. I taught her to cook and sew and become an obedient wife."

"And she's none of those things, Momma. All she is, is unhappy."

"It's not my fault, Daddy, or hers. She's bipolar. I'm sure of it."

"You don't know that."

"And you don't know what you're talking about. *I'm* the one who's read all the books. *I'm* the one who did the online research and consulted Dr. Parkman. I know my daughter. I've been with her ... here for her ... all her life."

Frank caught the implications. He couldn't win this argument. Helen had managed every facet, arranged every step of Mary Elizabeth's upbringing. She was proud of her crowning achievement—the one he suspected was making their daughter miserable. And maybe crazy. "Yes, Momma, you sure have."

Helen's eyes narrowed. "Just what do you mean by that?"

Frank shrugged.

"So, you're not going to help stop her?"

"No, Mamma, I'm not."

2

The Roadrunner

The gray-brown farmland beside Texas Highway 35 matched Jim's mood—glum. The small town of Tivoli reflected in the pickup's rearview mirrors. He would soon be in Aransas Pass, the gateway to Port Aransas.

And he wasn't only being pressured by thoughts of Marsha. At the posted speed limit, a line of RVs and vehicles hounded him, shoved him along the road. He would pull onto the shoulder to let them pass, but it was cluttered and narrow for an RV.

The sight of a great egret and great blue heron stalking fish and crabs in a tidal creek improved his mood. His spirits lifted even more when he reached the pastures midway between Tivoli and Fulton, where long copses of trees, cropped flat on the bottom by grazing cattle, reminded him of caterpillars. He saw black vultures, turkey vultures, and crested caracaras feeding on a carcass in the field. Shoved along by the vehicles behind him, he missed the photo op, and the line was growing because the approaching traffic was too steady for anyone to pass.

Or so Jim thought.

His heart skipped when a black Chevy Tahoe appeared in his side rearview mirror as a motor home hurtled from the opposite direction. Reflexively, he hit his brakes and yanked the steering wheel toward the shoulder, dangerous or not, but he couldn't stop quickly. The tailgater behind might plow into him.

Miraculously, the motorhome avoided the roadside ditch, and the SUV squeezed through the gap between it and Jim's fifth-wheel. Heart pounding, riding the edge of the highway shoulder until he brought his rig to a stop, Jim praised God he was still alive.

Helen Matthews clutched her chest and began crying when her daughter pulled out to pass. "Mary Elizabeth, what are you doing?"

She couldn't believe it when the motorhome edged left and RV veered right enough to save their lives.

"Mary Elizabeth, we could have been killed. Praise God, we're alive."

If the near-miss of a potentially fatal multi-vehicle accident or her mother's uncontrollable crying had any impact, Mary Elizabeth didn't show it. "Stop bitching and mind your own damn business."

"But you could have killed a lot of people," Helen cried, wiping away tears.

"I didn't invite you along and don't want you along. And if you don't shut up, I'm going to put you out on the side of the road."

"You wouldn't dare."

"See what happens if you say another word about my fucking driving."

"You won't do any such thing," Helen commanded imperiously. Her daughter might complain loudly, bitterly, and with many an obscenity, but she would do as demanded. Eventually.

"Mary Elizabeth, you've been brought up in a religious home and you're directly involved in the church. I don't understand how you can curse the way you do." Helen did, but the nasty old man died years ago.

Mary Elizabeth resisted the urge to hit something. "Shut the hell up, Mother."

She passed a semi and then pulled to the shoulder as a Highway Patrol SUV, lights flashing and siren wavering, blew by, followed quickly by two more.

Helen wondered where the police had been when she needed them to pull over her daughter. Instead of being relieved at escaping what seemed like certain death, she found herself unable to stop crying and shaking until they reached Fulton, ten miles down the road.

When no one passed from either direction and the motorhome stopped on the opposite shoulder, Jim realized an accident had occurred. People were running toward him on the highway. He cautiously opened the door, stepped down, and stared behind him. The highway looked like a train derailment. Semis and RV rigs were jackknifed for a quarter mile. Two lay on their sides in the ditch on his side of the road.

The first on-rusher arrived. "What the hell happened?" he asked.

Jim was so shaken, he had trouble recollecting. "A black SUV ran me onto the shoulder."

"Is that what caused all this?"

He nodded.

A large group of onlookers gathered by the time a Texas Highway Patrol cruiser arrived. No one had seen the SUV's driver. No one had a tag number. The only information Jim could provide was that it was a black Chevy Tahoe. He didn't have the slightest idea which year.

He thought he remembered a screaming, blue-haired woman, but Tahoe's windows had been tinted, so he couldn't be sure. He withheld the information because he didn't want to get an innocent driver in trouble.

Being in the lead vehicle and unscathed, Jim was permitted to leave the scene after providing a statement, his name, address, and phone number.

A trooper gave him a card containing an emergency number. "If you remember anything at all, Mr. Smith, call this number. We need to find that SUV."

"If I get my hands on the maniac, I'll turn his life upside down."

The trooper frowned. "Leave that to us."

Jim nodded. "Don't worry, I want the idiot behind bars."

* * *

Mary Elizabeth stomped the gas pedal and peeled out of an Aransas Pass Stripes convenience store parking lot. She and her mother had made a rest break and bought bottled water for the seven-mile drive that could take up to two hours during spring break.

"Mary Elizabeth, the speed limit is thirty-five miles an hour." Helen prayed silently that her daughter would get enough traffic tickets to have her driver's license revoked.

Grinning, Mary Elizabeth increased speed. They topped the Intracoastal Canal bridge at seventy miles per hour and zipped down to Steadman Island at an even eighty—just as they passed a fifty-five miles per hour sign.

Downy clouds dotted the sky in the brilliant afternoon. Tall palms in the housing addition to their right swayed in the steady gulf breeze. The bays bordering the island were their usual, clear aqua-blue.

People camped along the shoreline wade-fished and crabbed in the shallows. A few watched water and shore birds, but most sat on lawn chairs, savoring the perfect day and enjoying the view.

An osprey, ripping a fish to shreds, perched on a utility pole beside the second bridge connecting the series of islands between Aransas Pass and Port Aransas. White sandwich terns, recognizable by their white-tipped black bills, preened on the railings.

Mary Elizabeth's troubled mind relaxed. She loved the serenity, the birds and beauty. Always had. She slowed.

"That's better, Mary Elizabeth. You should drive like this all the time."

She glared, glanced back at the road, and slammed her hands against the steering wheel. "Shit!"

Alarmed, Helen braced for a rear-end collision. But instead of a rapidly approaching car trunk or Texas State Trooper, she saw a scattered line of cars ahead.

Why do I ever ride anywhere with my daughter? Mary Elizabeth drove recklessly, sped, tailgated and cursed endlessly while weaving in and out of traffic. She risked their lives, sometimes only to gain a car-length over several miles.

Helen's concern for her daughter's sanity and brief fear of impending disaster gave way to a forced smile and sweetly voiced, "What's wrong, sweetheart?"

Mary Elizabeth's forehead furrowed. Her jaw tightened. "There's a two-hour wait for the ferry." She shouted an obscenity and screamed, "Spring break."

Peering over her shoulder, she prepared to make a U-turn and drive around Corpus Christi Bay.

"It's more than seventy miles to go around, Mary Elizabeth, and it will take even take longer because of the line of partiers headed to Padre Island and the beaches on a Friday afternoon."

Helen ignored her daughter's angry glower. "I thought this might happen, so I brought books for us to read." She looked hopeful as she slid one on the seat toward her daughter.

Her mother was right. As usual. Ignoring the shaken fists and gestures of angry drivers she forced onto the shoulders, Mary Elizabeth squeezed between the line they were in and a line of approaching cars.

She didn't ignore the clearly audible obscenities yelled by the drivers of the many vehicles she passed illegally by using the right-hand shoulder. She flipped them off. She did the same to the driver who tried to cut her off when she worked her way back into the line of traffic where cones blocked further travel on the shoulder.

Worried sick about her daughter, Helen struggled to comprehend. "Mary Elizabeth, how can you risk our lives and the lives of others by engendering road rage? You have a family to represent. A duty to uphold. Do you know what being arrested would do to our reputation?"

"I won't listen to this, Mother."

"Sweetheart, you have everything anyone could possibly want ... a nice home and family, people who love you, who shower you with attention. I've treated you special since you were born."

"Let it go, Mother. Or would you prefer walking to the ferry?"

"But don't you understand? You've had it too good to be like this. You *must* have a mental disorder, and a psychiatric evaluation will only take a week."

"I won't be locked up. If you think getting a ticket will hurt our reputation, think what a week in a mental facility would do."

Her mother shook her head. How could she get through to her sick child? "Mary Elizabeth, you have no reason to be ungrateful and spiteful and so reckless with your life. You didn't know Daddy when he was an alcoholic. You didn't witness his drunken binges that got him fired from four jobs. You've never known want or heard him scream at us for no reason. You didn't have to look for hidden bottles of whiskey, like Joshua Macomb and I did. One time, Daddy came home drunk and fell into the Christmas tree Joshua Macomb had just put up by the living room window. Did he apologize? No, he cursed him for putting it in his way. If anyone should be angry and depressed, it should be your brother. But he loves his daddy. He loves and respects our family."

"Screw it, Mother. I've heard this a thousand times."

"Oh, baby, can't you see you're on the verge of a nervous breakdown?"

"If you don't shut up, you're going to experience what a breakdown is."

"Don't threaten your mother, Mary Elizabeth."

Mary Elizabeth grit her teeth. *Maybe if I shut up, she'll give up.* She glanced at the book on the seat beside her. *Mood Swings.* Lowering her window, she tossed it in front of the line of oncoming traffic and smiled as vehicles smashed it to scraps beside a sign that read: DON'T MESS WITH TEXAS.

"Mary Elizabeth, you can be fined for littering."

"I didn't litter, Mother ... you did. You knew what I'd do when you gave me the book. Stop trying to control my life."

When her daughter turned to stare at the cars ahead of them, Helen sighed and pushed out another book.

Mary Elizabeth found it acceptable—a *Cat Who...* novel by Lillian Jackson Braun. She enjoyed the series, even though a murder or two occurred and the victims were often likeable people. Each book contained fun and interesting side stories that calmed her nerves. They also contained no sex. She hated sex. Anything resembling sex. Anything sensual.

She opened the book, but her eyes glazed as she again dwelled on her situation.

Damn, I hate my name.

She detested her mother sitting beside her. She hated life, period. This was her get-away, not her mother's. It was intended as a sabbatical for soul-searching, a time to reflect and find herself. Why had her mother invited herself along? Worse, why had she allowed it?

The latter question was easily answered. She was too weak to prevent it. As for the former, it was her mother's unending protectiveness. While a child, a stubbed toe meant a trip to the ER. Her mother had scrubbed an injured body part, dabbed it with hydrogen peroxide, blown warm breath on it, and applied a colorful Band-Aid. Followed by chicken noodle soup and a day sequestered from friends. *I've been a vestal virgin all my life.*

The line of cars inched forward. One mile to the ferry. She grimaced.

After what seemed an eternity, the line crept forward another hundred feet.

Mary Elizabeth stared at her baggy shirt and safari pants. They were her mother's choice of clothing, especially after the incident when she was fourteen. They'd made her an object of ridicule by all but a few close girlfriends who belonged to her religion.

She thought of her father. From the time she remembered until she was about seven, she'd tried to climb onto his lap for companionship, to be rocked and watch TV. He ordered her to leave the room. On rare occasions, he allowed her to watch nature programs, but not while on his lap.

She came to love those programs, especially the ones about birds. They warmed her, gave her pleasure. She wasn't squeamish. All birds were beautiful and necessary. If an accipiter hawk caught and ate a cardinal to death, well, it required nourishment, too. Nature required balance. Wasn't that what life was all about—the strong subjecting or destroying the weak?

The programs also provided relief from the boredom of playing with the dolls her mother gave her at every occasion. No Barbie Dolls. Those produced unrealistic images in a young girl's mind. Her mother's list of approved dolls fostered healthy ideals. It worked—no one could have mistaken her for Barbie. She'd eaten her way to more than two-hundred pounds by the time she was a senior in high school.

But the incident when she was eighteen changed all that. At five-feet-eleven-and-a-half, she now weighed a hundred fifty-five pounds. She hated her curvy figure but considered it a necessary evil. *Thank goodness for my church's dress code.* Her unruly hair was another plus. One she enhanced by not using make-up.

"Mary Elizabeth, we need to move."

She looked up. "Miracle of miracles, Mother, the ferry landing's in sight."

A ferry line handler waved them toward another handler who directed them into a line that held sixteen vehicles, the capacity of the Port Aransas ferry headed toward their dock. Hers was the middle vehicle in the lane. She shut off the SUV's engine and fell back into thought.

Even now, while trying to take a respite from the necessities of her life, who sat beside her? The trip had been holy hell, and they'd left Kingwood just six hours earlier.

She recalled the near miss when she passed the crappy pickup with the lumpy fifth-wheel. Picturing the driver's face in her rearview mirror, she scowled.

"What are you thinking about, sweetheart?"

"Old fart face."

"Who?"

"That damned winter Texan we passed who was creeping along." She shook her head. "Something should be done with those idiots. They should be retired from driving when they become senior citizens, especially assholes from Oklahoma. We beat them in football last year, so you'd think they'd be too embarrassed to set foot in our state.

"And if everyone left such large distances between themselves and the cars in front of them, no one would ever get anywhere. We were going in reverse in that line."

"But, sweetheart, he was going the speed—"

"Shut up. We need to board the ferry."

A handler wearing a bright-yellow safety vest waved them onto the ferry. Another directed them to the right front and chocked a wheel. Soon, the boat surged forward, and Mary Elizabeth's mood improved.

Brown pelicans and sleek white terns plummeted head-first into the clear, blue-green channel to catch fish and minnows. A family of dolphins rolled in front of them, puffing fine mist in the air. She pointed them out to her mother, and both watched expectantly for them to reappear.

When they did, Helen clapped her hands. "It's a good sign, Mary Elizabeth. We're going to have a nice time."

Mary Elizabeth winced. We *shouldn't be having a nice time.*

The ten-minute ride seemed all too short. They were soon driving past the colorful row of fishing shops, restaurants, and condominiums beside the harbor. A right turn, a left toward the beach, and a right into the Windward Dunes Condominiums.

What the hell am I doing here with Mother?

3
Ruffled Feathers

Marsha played with granddaughter Taylor, age five, while keeping a close watch on the clock. They had to pick up Taylor's sister, Anderson, age seven and in the second grade, in an hour. They were her youngest granddaughters, even though their mother, Sarah, was the older of her two daughters.

Sarah married Stanley, Stan, Hughes, a hard-working high-school dropout, a year after meeting him on a blind date set up by her sister, Deena.

They waited fourteen years to have children, just as Marsha decided they wouldn't become parents. The reason for their delay was their desire to establish a thriving landscape business. Sarah provided financial management, using her master's degree in business administration, and Stan did the landscape work. They now had a staff of twenty, which allowed them to be the parents they wished to be.

Taylor tired of playing and took a nap, leaving her grandmother with only her thoughts. Marsha's premonition that something bad would happen to Jim filled the void. He hadn't called, and her calls went to his voicemail. She knew the person to talk to, Maggie Saunders, a member of the group of friends Jim was traveling to meet. Maggie looked something like a witch, albeit a beautiful one. Her prognostications were uncanny, and some of the things she did, or made happen, downright spooky.

"Hi Marsha. No, Jimmy isn't here, yet."

The greeting confirmed Marsha's suspicions. The woman was clairvoyant. "How did you know it was me?"

"Caller ID."

"Oh. Did you say Jim hasn't arrived yet?'

"Haven't heard from him."

"Maggie, I'm worried. I sense he's in danger."

"I told you I'd look after him. He'll be okay."

"Do you think he's been in a wreck? He should be there by now."

"He hasn't been in a wreck." There had been one, but Maggie knew Jimmy wasn't in it. There were aerial photos, and his rig was too recognizable. "Marsha, like I told you the last four times you called, he's staying at a Walmart parking lot, so he won't have to fight the spring break line at the ferry and arrive after dark."

"Then you're sure he's okay?"

"Bad news travels fast."

"Maybe he had a heart attack. He's growing old."

"Marsha, if you're so worried about Jimmy, you should have come with him. Sip a glass of Crane Lake Chardonnay and play with your grandkids."

"My grandchildren need me. And I don't drink."

"Well, you should. You two had this trip planned for two years, and Sarah knew it. A trade show doesn't happen on the spur of the moment. She and Stan didn't have enough respect to tell you they wanted to go, months ago. They waited until the last minute because they knew you couldn't say no. No offense, Marsha, but you need to decide who you love best … your children or your husband."

"No, Maggie, *you* don't understand."

"Oh, I understand very well. Your husband's fine, and he'll be better when he gets here. I'll call if I hear anything."

The conversation ended—neither woman happy.

Anderson and Taylor fussed from the time Anderson jumped into the car at school. It didn't lessen when they arrived home. Marsha felt like a World Wrestling Federation referee. Taylor started each fight, and her older sister invariably overreacted. Until Marsha managed to turn their attention to a large doll she brought for them to play with. She found it a week earlier in a closet—forgotten for years.

"I got Dolly when I was seven. She was the next to the last doll I received as a present when I was growing up, and my only birthday present that year."

She stood Dolly and tilted her backwards. "See how her eyes open and close? You girls need to take care of the presents your mommy, daddy, and I give you, so they'll last like Dolly."

She purposely left out grandpa as a gift-giver. That wasn't his gift. He left it up to her to purchase all the children's presents and send birthday and holiday cards.

The truce proved brief. Taylor tried to yank Dolly out of Marsha's hands.

Anderson chastised her and grabbed for the doll, too. "I'm the oldest. I get to hold her first."

Marsha feared that Dolly wouldn't survive the afternoon. At least her limbs wouldn't. "Don't fight—"

Taylor sunk her teeth into Anderson's arm. Anderson slugged back, and the girls ended up in different corners of the room. With the TV off. Otherwise, they couldn't hear the lecture. It worked—after Marsha stopped their face and tongue bickering by giving each child a mild swat on the bottom.

After dinner she continued explaining the value of gifts and why it was necessary to take care of them. She often complained, mostly to Jim, about the many presents her grandchildren and great-grandchildren received for their birthdays and every holiday, and how they abused them. They tossed down each toy and gift as soon as the gift bag or box had been greedily ripped apart.

Marsha would pick up the discarded carefully-selected, colorful tissue, wrapping paper, and hand-curled ribbons that had concealed each treasure, regardless in whose house the party was held. She then collected the forgotten gifts, took them to the child's room, and organized them on their desks, shelves, and dressers.

"You girls need to take care of your presents. Do you know how old Dolly is? She's nearly as old as me."

Taylor stared at the doll then up at Marsha. "You're prettier, Gramma."

Marsha smiled. She had to admit that Dolly showed her age. She might not have wrinkles, but she no longer said, "Waa," when laid on her back. What was left of her hair was frizzy and uneven. It was difficult to tell that Dolly's dress was blue and white gingham. But other than those blemishes, grime, and a few nicks on her face, arms, and legs, Dolly was in pretty good shape.

Anderson brought Marsha back to earth. "She looks just like you, Grandma. Only she's not fat."

Marsha ruefully realized that she'd used the wrong example to press her point about treating presents with respect.

* * *

Jim was still trembling when he arrived at the Walmart in Aransas Pass. He might have flipped into the ditch and been severely injured. The motorhome could have swerved into his path and killed him. Marsha would have been right—something impossible to live down.

It was late. His near accident and the delay while the highway patrol made their investigations and questioned him took the entire afternoon. He couldn't continue to Port Aransas. The line of spring breakers would delay his arrival for hours, and the park office closed at six.

Jim obtained permission from the store manager to spend the night in the parking lot and felt much better while consuming a super-sized meal.

A woman in her early twenties caught his attention. She looked so much like Marsha at that age, Jim thought it uncanny. *How can women be so beautiful*?

He studied his belly. How had he and Marsha let themselves go and become so obese? He snuck another glance at the woman. He'd held a body like that once. It created a longing to do so again. And a prayer requesting forgiveness for thinking the evil thought.

His stomach growled. He patted the round mound and yielded to temptation. As he pushed away from the table to go order the second meal, he realized the same held true for Marsha. Her days living with a hard-bodied man were also well in her past.

Later, back in the fifth-wheel, he tried to read a novel. No luck. He relived the potential tragedy, chewed antacids, and went to bed.

* * *

Once Anderson and Taylor were in bed asleep—invariably much later than their parents' instructions—Marsha usually performed the duties of housemaid. Tonight, she made a cup of green tea and picked up a novel, but her mind dwelt on Jim. Why hadn't he called?

She called Maggie, even though Maggie promised to call if anything changed.

"No, Jimmy still hasn't arrived, and you wouldn't want him to, Marsha. It's dark, and he'd put another lump on your dinky old rig. I told you, he's at Walmart."

Marsha tried to contact her friends eight more times. The first time, Maggie answered. When the next call went directly to her voicemail, Marsha called her other two friends, Patsy Warner and Nadine Danielson. Those went to their voicemails, too. She tried to reach Maggie one more time, sent a text message to each of her friends, and cried herself to sleep.

4
Bird Calls

Jim slept fitfully. The fatty foods he'd consumed sorely tested his antacid tablets. He should become a distributor. It would save a lot of money.

When he awoke, he was tempted to sleep in, but the sunlight flooding through the windows and overhead vents forced him up. Satisfied the stubble on his face was in the acceptable range, he went to breakfast. A couple of Egg McMuffins, double order of hash browns, a Big Hotcake Breakfast, several coffees, and three antacid tablets later, he climbed into the rig and drove to the fuel pumps.

As he removed the spout, the man on the other side of the pump did the same for a shiny motor home. Large and rotund, each weighing the same, they smiled at each other like blood brothers. "Where 'ya from?" he asked.

"Benny Ingram from Detroit. You?"

Their hand sizes matched.

"Jim Smith. Oklahoma."

"An Okie, eh? Where in Oklahoma?"

"Edmond."

"Hey, I have an aunt and uncle there, Dave and Janice Packard. You heard of them?"

"Afraid not. Edmond's a pretty large town these days. "How long have you been here?"

"Since October. It's been a hell of a trip ... fishing, learning how to country and western line dance with my wife, playing cards with friends, visiting the Valley to bird and buy Mexican junk. We can't wait 'til next year. You coming, or going?"

"Coming." Jim resisted the urge to blame Marsha for arriving late.

"How long you going to be here for?"

"Two weeks. I didn't want to miss the spring bird migration and sheepshead fishing. My fishing buddies in my RV group have been in Port Aransas three weeks. They say the sheepshead practically jump on the jetty. All we have to do is scoop them up."

Ingram chuckled. "I'd like some of what your friends are drinking. Other fish are biting, but not keeper sheepshead. Where you staying?"

"Palm Gardens."

"Then you know about Paradise Pond. It's great this year. There are a pair of kiskadees and least grebes."

Exciting news. "I haven't seen those. I'll need to check my bird book this evening."

"They're good birds for the area, and they've been here since we arrived. The kiskadees are large flycatchers with brown bodies, yellow bellies, and black and white heads. They have a yellow crest they sometimes flare up. There's nothing else like them. The grebes have a nest back in the willows, but they're so tame they'll swim right up to you.

"And be sure to go to Hazel Bazemore Park in Corpus," Ingram advised while pulling his credit card receipt from the pump. "It's a good place to see green jays, golden-fronted woodpeckers, and hawks. Blucher Park's great, too. It has everything … warblers, woodpeckers. The catbirds and chats are gorging on mulberries there, now."

"Where are those places?"

"Bazemore's on the west side of town. Take I37 to 77 South and take the first exit right. Look for an irrigation ditch about a half-mile down and turn right. Blucher's right downtown, off Tancahua Street."

The two men shook hands.

"See you round, Benny. Thanks for the info."

"Don't mention it, Jim. Hope to catch you next year."

The rig that took Ingram's place looked similar to Jim's, dent-wise. Its owner appeared from around the rig and shuffled to the pump.

"Hey," he said, sticking out his hand. "I'm happy to see a rig in worse shape than mine. You have a nice touch with duct tape."

The man matched his rig. Both showed a lot of miles. A weathered, wrinkled tan, he listed to one side. And, Jim had to admit, his RV was tape-free.

Jim stuck out a paw. "Hey." He felt like repeating it when Mr. Wrinkles gripped his palm in a vise-like grip.

Wrinkles echoed Ingram's comment about keeper sheepshead. "Spanish mackerel, gafftop, redfish, and pompano are biting like mad. I'm taking home a freezer-full of redfish and pompano filets." He gave instructions and listed the baits and lures to use.

Jim thanked him and left, mulling over what he'd heard. Twice. Legal-sized sheepshead weren't biting.

He stared longingly at the bay beside the string of islands between Aransas Pass and Port Aransas. The water couldn't be clearer and more beautiful. Ospreys perched on utility poles, surveying their domains. One was devouring a fish breakfast. Great blue herons proved as proficient but didn't grip and rip their meals. They gulped them down.

The short ferry line didn't surprise him. Spring breakers generally weren't early birds. A handler waved him onto a ferry. Another directed him to straddle two lanes due to the size of his rig. A couple of cars were tucked behind him, and the rest sent to the other side of the small ferry to balance the load. While waiting, he watched bottlenose dolphins leaping in the bow wave of a heavily laden tanker traveling through the ship channel toward the open water of the Gulf of Mexico. *I'm home.*

After the quick ferry ride and a few short blocks, he entered the Palm Gardens RV Resort. It was like driving into a botanical garden. One couldn't see the office from the street. The view was blocked by a hedge of short palms that provided a leafy backdrop for a row of pink oleander bushes not yet in full bloom. Blooming shrubs interspersed with bougainvillea periodically lined the drive. The final row of palms was so tall that only the roofs of fifth-wheels and motorhomes could be seen from the surrounding streets.

Most of the park was well-hidden. The exceptions were a fence near the boat storage, the trash dumpster area, and a row of cabins bordering a side street exit. The fish-cleaning hut was near the dumpsters so prevailing winds would sweep unwanted smells away from the resort. Their location also helped muffle the early morning banging made by trash trucks.

An opulent bathhouse and Olympic-sized pool flanked by hot tubs marked the park center. Screened by palms and tropical plants, it made one feel like being on a Caribbean island. Water cascaded into the pool from an impressive waterfall. Lounge chairs graced thatched cabanas. A bougainvillea-draped fence hid a hot tub reserved for adults. The grand clubhouse's large bay window faced the pool deck, but the hot tubs were obscured by tropical plants.

The clubhouse contained a dining area, library, TV lounge, and an alcove filled with billiards and foosball tables. An electronic game room satisfied the younger at heart.

The dining room was the site of park-hosted ice cream socials, bingo, and movie nights during the winter months. It was also available for pot-luck suppers. October through March, the park hosted a monthly fish fry—the fish donated by fishermen guests. The dining room also served as the card room.

Palm Gardens' seclusion, tranquility, and numerous amenities allowed the park to charge the highest prices in south Texas. It took most of Jim and Marsha's annual vacation budget, but they thought it worth it.

Before he could park in front of the office, an exotic beauty in her fifties, who could grace short shorts, stormed up and peered into the cab, hands on her hips.

When he got out, she stepped through his comfort zone and shook a slender finger in his face, her ebony eyes smoking. "Forget something, Jimmy?"

Maggie Saunders was more imposing than her five-and-a-half-foot trim build would suggest. She ruled the roost of their RV club. Of French, Cherokee, and mixed descent, she took pride in the diverse blood coursing through her veins. She could relate each of her ancestors' involuntary relocations—Canada to pre-U.S. Louisiana, Eastern U.S. to Central U. S., Africa to the Americas.

"Someone's scared sick." Maggie folded her arms across her chest and impatiently tapped her foot. "Marsha's called at least fifty times and she's demanding we call the police, the Texas Rangers, and National Guard. She even requested the FBI, DEA, and Homeland Security."

Jim smacked his forehead and flushed bright red. "Marsha. I forgot to turn on my cellphone. You didn't contact the police, did you?"

"We would've, if you hadn't arrived by noon."

How could he forget to call Marsha? He'd promised to call every evening. Maybe the near-wreck erased his memory.

Maggie read his mind. "By the way, how did you cause that mess near Fulton?"

"How do you know about that?"

"It had your signature. But why anyone would want to avoid running your piece of junk off the road is a mystery to me. It would be a community service."

When Jim started to explain, she cut him off. "You're in big trouble, Jimmy boy." She bounced a fingertip against his chest. "Get on that phone. *Now.*"

Whirling, called over her shoulder as she strode away on long, trim legs that Jim said a prayer for admiring. "We're in site 45, the Danielsons are in 107, and the Warners in 302."

An added example of her clairvoyance was that she'd somehow known he had arrived even though it was impossible see the office from the RV sites. When he'd asked her about it once, she gave credit to her tiny, pipe-smoking, Louisiana arrière-grand-mère, Maw-maw Maude Fontenot. Then chuckled. "There's no such thing as psychics, Jimmy. It's all calculations and deductions."

While checking in, he noticed the Wi-Fi code. He'd also promised to e-mail Marsha every day. He briefly considered chickening out and sending an e-mail apology, but a living hell didn't seem a viable option.

The first thing he did after parking in his slot was pull out his cellphone. Dreading the upcoming experience, he hesitantly turned it on and poked his home number. He would soon feel like the hapless fish he saw being pecked to death by the osprey beside the bay.

* * *

Mary Elizabeth awoke with a start and struggled from a sound sleep. Everything looked wrong, out of place, unfamiliar. *Where am I? Oh yes, the condo bedroom.*

Light from a thin crack between the thick curtains dimly lit the room. She squinted at the clock: 10:30 a.m. "Crap."

Her plan to visit the birding center and Paradise Pond in the early-morning light favorable for photography was already flushed down the commode. She'd screwed up the first day of her all too short escape from reality. She moved unsteadily to the bathroom and splashed water on her face.

She entered the condo's combo living and kitchen area fully intent on bawling out her mother for letting her sleep late, but all was silent. No coffee aroma, either. Her mother couldn't be up if coffee wasn't brewing or warming.

Still upset, she stormed to Helen's bedroom door and opened it. The room was as dark, cool, and conducive to sleeping as her own had been, and she heard soft snoring. She thought about silently closing the door and going birding without her mother but lost her own debate. There would be hell to pay, and she couldn't fight her mother. Why? Why couldn't she do that?

She hated her controlling mother and hated herself for her inability to resist, even more. She shook her head. *I'm a fucking masochist.*

"Mother." The light snoring continued. "*Mother.*"

Helen rolled and stared with the same sleep-dulled eyes Mary Elizabeth had when she awakened. "Is it time to get up?" she asked sweetly.

"It's way past time. After ten."

Helen thought it nice but highly unusual. "Thanks for letting me sleep late, hon."

"The stupid alarm didn't go off."

* * *

Marsha sounded frantic when she answered the phone, disappointed when she discovered that Jim wasn't in a hospital, then angry when he confessed that he'd wanted to avoid a long ferry line and spent the night in a parking lot. He didn't mention the near collision.

"You forgot to call me?" she asked incredulously.

The remaining conversation wasn't pleasant.

"I've apologized at least a hundred times, Marsha. I'm sorry."

Each apology made her madder. "You worried me, sick. You're not only forgetful, you're an inconsiderate idiot."

"You're right, I'm sorry."

"Plus, you made Maggie, Patsy, and Nadine mad at me for calling them so often."

"I'll tell them it was all my fault and apologize to them, too."

"Don't forget to call me, tonight," Marsha shouted, and hung up.

5
Bird Town USA

Sipping coffee, Mary Elizabeth and Helen gazed across the tall, wide dunes bordering the beach. Ragged lines of white-capped waves fringed the iridescent blue-green water beyond. Fishermen dotted the rails of the Horace Caldwell pier in the distance. The almost mile-long south jetty, with the possibility it provided for seeing unusual birds, such as western grebes and ocean-going pelagic birds, could be seen beyond the pier. What caught their attention, however, were brown pelicans smacking into the Gulf.

Port Aransas was a birder's Zion, a Mecca. A myriad of shorebirds, raptors, and land birds awaited them on Mustang Island's twenty-five miles of beach, prairie, ponds, and dunes.

On the bay side of the island, the city had created a twelve-hundred-acre nature preserve they named Charlie's Pasture in honor of Charlie Bujan, a rancher who grazed cattle in the area in the 1940s and 1950s. It bordered the picturesque ship channel and contained an endless variety of birds—raptors, warblers, doves, wading birds, ducks, swallows, and sparrows.

Miles of nature trails were being extended each year. They weaved through marshes, beside tidal pools, lagoons, and storm wash-over ponds. Near the condo, Wetlands Park, opposite the Post Office, was sandpiper and plover heaven when it contained water. Those were on their agenda, but today's destinations were the Leonabelle Turnbull Birding Center and Joan and Scott Holt Paradise Pond—premier world-renown birding sites on any birder's bucket lists. Or should be.

The fluffy clouds, waving palms, cooing doves, and cool, breezy morning lifted Mary Elizabeth's spirits. She agreed to go to the Island Café for brunch and the birding center afterward, despite the harsh noon light that made it difficult to edit photos.

"Mother," she growled, forty-five minutes later, "if you don't hurry, it'll be dark before we leave. How can it take you so long to get dressed?"

Her own clothing included baggy, lightweight sweatpants and a T-shirt with the picture of a whooping crane emblazoned on the front. Its back read: CELEBRATION OF WHOOPERS AND OTHER BIRDS. She'd purchased it a few years earlier at the annual Port Aransas whooping crane festival.

She'd bound her breasts flat, wore no make-up, and had slathered her face and exposed parts of her body white with maximum SPF sunscreen. She restrained as much of her unruly hair as possible with a hair band and held in her hand a floppy, wide-brimmed hat for additional sun protection. It featured cords, she secured under her chin in strong winds, that allowed her to flip it back without losing it when she took pictures.

Helen couldn't be rushed. "It'll only take a minute, Mary Elizabeth."

Her short, gray, blue-tinged hair was wet from her shower. It took little time to fluff it into a presentable manner, but she wouldn't skip her ritual for preventing wrinkles for anyone. That included St. Peter, himself, when that time came. Wash. Rinse. Apply the special-formula cream. Remove the cream and apply a foundation containing sunscreen.

Dressing was as fastidious. There wouldn't be a birding lady her age within a hundred miles—the entire Gulf coast—more fashionable.

Mary Elizabeth once wondered if her mother's beauty procedure was intended to please Frank, but eventually realized it was an addiction. Arguments could be entered into for argument's sake, but she would be the only one who suffered anguish.

At eleven-thirty, her relatively quiet annoyance reached its limit. "Get your ass in gear, Mother. I won't wait until tomorrow."

"Don't be rude to your mother, Mary Elizabeth. You're always complaining about how the middle of the day is a terrible time to take pictures."

"And whose fault is *that*? You take half a day to get ready." Mary Elizabeth threw her arms in the air.

"Maybe we should wait until later this afternoon," Helen suggested.

"Damn it to *hell*, Mother." She stomped from the condo.

"Thank God, you're finally beautiful, Mother dear," she said sarcastically, thirty minutes later, when she returned to the condo after roaming the grounds and gardens searching for birds. She'd found nothing unique or picturesque, but it killed time and lowered her stress level.

More than ever Helen believed her daughter was on the verge of a nervous breakdown. "You needn't be so vulgar, Mary Elizabeth. And I believe it best that we go birding later. You're upset. We should talk."

The walk in the palm, bougainvillea, and flowering shrub landscaping had endowed Mary Elizabeth with a measure of patience. "You're the reason I'm upset, Mother, and the problem isn't just today, so arguing will just frustrate us both. Let's eat."

"It's your irritability, Mary Elizabeth. I'm the one trying to make you see reason. We need to return to Kingwood, so you can get psychiatric help and get your life back in order."

Mary Elizabeth rolled her eyes. "I'm leaving, Mother. I'm hungry."

"Do you have your binoculars, sweetheart?" Helen asked. "What about your fanny pack ... bird books ... camera bag...?"

Floppy hat in hand, Mary Elizabeth stalked out the door.

* * *

Jim was assigned to the overflow area, which he preferred. The bathhouse, pool, and clubhouse were nearby, hidden behind a screen of bougainvillea.

The fish cleaning facility and cabins provided an energetic walk in the opposite direction, and he was equidistant from his friends' rigs scattered throughout the large campground. Each stroll would be beautiful and peaceful, through scented gardens filled with bees and butterflies.

By the time he connected the hoses and cables, opened a propane bottle valve, turned on the refrigerator, and added treatments to the holding tanks, it was noon. Sweaty, he grabbed shorts and a T shirt and strolled to the bathhouse.

CLOSED FOR CLEANING—a midday routine accomplished when most campers were out and about the island.

Jim stared. *First Maggie, then Marsha, now this.*

He detoured to the fish-cleaning hut, found it full of men and women cleaning fish, but his buddies weren't among them. The happy occupants cleaning their fish confirmed Benny Ingram's and Mr. Wrinkles' comments—sheepshead were plentiful but below the minimum length. His friends must be doing better, he thought. They wouldn't lie to him.

His friends weren't at their RVs, and he should have remembered. Corpus Christi for lunch and a dollar movie was a Saturday afternoon tradition. Sundays were church, dining afterwards, and sightseeing or relaxing.

A note on Jeff and Maggie Saunders' motor home door gave timing and instructions, but he'd taken so long begging for Marsha's mercy it was too late to join them.

His growling stomach directed him to the Dairy Queen. He would visit the IGA later to purchase groceries for most of his stay.

Returning to his RV, he took his digital camera out of its case, made sure the memory card was empty, and checked the battery charge. All was ready for Paradise Pond, a few blocks away. Suffering heartburn, despite four antacid tablets, he walked to the pond, hoping to pass gas, and he needed the exercise.

* * *

Mary Elizabeth bristled. She was a kidnap victim in the Island Café. No one but her mother could spend an hour eating fish and chips, no matter how much or delicious.

Now after one, her day was slipping away. She swore she could hear each French fry snap as Helen daintily nipped off each miniscule bite. She sipped water and simmered while her mother slowly crunched her milkshake, too.

She was at wit's end with her life situation. Her mother thought she was going nuts, and maybe she was. She must have been to let her mother come with her. Helen was the major contributor to her problems, thus couldn't help with the solutions.

It dawned that her mother was eating even slower than usual. "Mother, you're taking ten minutes to eat each French fry."

"Mary Elizabeth, one is supposed to chew their food, not gulp it down whole like you do."

Helen wouldn't budge until she finished her last bite of food, last sips of regular cola and chocolate milkshake, and the final drops of water that rinsed the food from her teeth. Besides being habit, doing so helped her think. Having long ago diagnosed her daughter as bipolar, she contemplated how to force her to see a psychiatrist. The longer treatment was delayed the direr the prognosis.

Scowling, Mary Elizabeth stood and headed toward the checkout counter. "See you later, Mother. I'm leaving."

Helen grabbed her hat and purse.

They passed the town's athletic complex on their way to the birding center. It contained a swimming pool, skateboard park, and baseball field surrounded by a walking path.

A half-mile later, they turned right into the birding center parking lot located next to the city's sewage treatment plant—the center's life blood. The treated effluence supported the aquatic life necessary to attract birds year-round. Other

Mustang Island ponds and lakes dried during times of drought.

A chain-link fence separated the parking lot from the treatment tanks, which were adorned with beautiful bird and pond-scene murals. A tiny, striped ground squirrel, chewing seeds off a grass stem, watched apprehensively while they parked in front of it.

"We're here."

Mary Elizabeth excitedly exited the Tahoe. It was a gorgeous day. Puffy, white clouds passed overhead toward the mainland, providing photogenic shade. Flowering coral bean trees, adjacent to the parking lot, were havens for hummingbirds and orioles. A flower garden graced the left edge of the sidewalk. Beside exotic plants, it contained honeysuckles, trumpet and confederate vines, and bottle-brush plants. Their bright flowers attracted butterflies and colorful anole lizards stalking insects. Small metal plaques provide the names of some of the flowers, shrubs, and vines.

A cattail marsh obscured by mulberry trees, sweet acacia, black willows, and invasive Brazilian Pepper trees began about fifty feet to the right of the sidewalk. The vegetation provided refuge and sources of food for migratory birds such as warblers, vireos, grosbeaks, and tanagers. It teemed with resident birds—wrens, rails, sparrows, and red-winged blackbirds. Water-filled depressions beneath the trees provided excellent opportunities to see least bitterns, small chicken-like sora rails, and sometimes, Virginia, king, and clapper rails.

Mary Elizabeth put her hands and arms through her binocular straps, fitted the binoculars to her chest, and donned her hat. She grabbed her camera with its telephoto lens. "Ready, Mother?" She left without waiting for a response.

"Yes, sweetheart," Helen called softly after her.

They stopped at an information box, at the edge of the sidewalk, that contained pamphlets, entitled Birds of Port Aransas and Mustang Island, Texas. They listed—in bird guide, not alphabetical order—every bird species confirmed seen on the island. Loons and grebes headed the list. The house sparrow ended it. A key identified which birds were residents, which were migrants, the seasons of the year to expect them, and whether they were common, rare, or in between. It also listed Specialty Birds—those birds everyone wanted to see and where to find them.

Taking a checklist, Mary Elizabeth gushed, "Texas is the best birding state in the nation."

Helen was pleased that her daughter's attitude for the day seemed to be mellowing. "I told you it would wait for us. And it's the middle of the day, many birds will be hiding."

Her comment received a slit-eyed glower.

Helen trailed behind as Mary Elizabeth eased along scanning the flowers, shrubs, and trees for the brilliant birds migrating northward through Texas during spring. Sweet chirps, songs, and calls abounded. Small birds flitted in the willows and pepper trees to her right. She could hear the constant harsh calls and chatter of coots, moorhens, and rails in the cattails beyond. Raucous gull calls and duck quacking came from the lake obscured by pepper trees and cattails at the end of the sidewalk.

Helen heard her daughter exult, followed by the rapid click of a camera. A five-inch long, yellow-green bird with a black-hood and bright-yellow face hopped about in search of insects.

"A hooded warbler." No matter how many times Helen saw these jewels of God's creation, they took her breath away. They also seemed to keep her daughter at least partly sane. "Isn't it lovely, Mary Elizabeth?"

She watched her daughter take another burst of photos, wait for the bird to move to a more photogenic location, and fire again. The process repeated itself many times.

After more than a hundred pictures of the constantly moving bird, Mary Elizabeth lowered her camera and fixed her mother with a broad grin. "Let's move on."

They left the tiny warbler to feed in peace.

A sign at the end of the sidewalk warned of the center's resident alligators. It contained the picture of an alligator head with a hole between its jaws where people could insert their heads for photos.

They smiled at the sign and followed the sidewalk to the boardwalk that extended approximately a hundred yards into a shallow lake, perhaps one or two feet deep, enclosed by cattails. Stopping, they gazed expectantly at the watercourse that curved under the boardwalk and disappeared into the marsh, hoping to see a rail, bittern, or marsh wren searching for food in the cattails. Occasionally snakes and snapping turtles could be seen.

Today they saw none, so they examined the water toward the main pond, perhaps ten to twenty acres in size. A myriad of shallow, brackish lakes, ponds, and pools in the birding center were home to waterfowl and both freshwater and saltwater fish, as well as other marine life. It was impossible to tell how many pools there were due to the impenetrable cattails.

The near-constant water level supported minnows, fish, crabs, worms, aquatic insects and animals, and vegetation that provided food sources for wading and swimming birds. Those, in turn, provided the center's exceptional birding opportunities. This was especially true during the fall, winter, and spring months. Ducks, shorebirds, and other migratory birds spent the winter at the center, too. Resident birds, like roseate spoonbills, herons, egrets, neo-tropic cormorants and black-necked stilts, feasted year-round. Barn swallows nested under the boardwalk during late spring and summer. Raptors perched in trees and on utility poles to pick off hapless prey.

With the knowledge that seeing the birds was a near-certainty, local experts hosted a weekly bird watch that drew thousands of bird-watchers to Port Aransas each year.

Seeing nothing exciting, Mary Elizabeth pointed at the boardwalk's twenty-foot-tall observation tower and courtesy telescope. "Let's go up there."

When she and her mother strolled onto the boardwalk, they noticed a crowd of people pointing smartphones and cameras over the railing.

"Boots," they said in unison.

* * *

Jim daydreamed about Paradise Pond during the short walk from Palm Gardens. He envisioned the wooden boardwalk that zigzagged into the pond and visualized the myriad of tiny birds of many colors flitting through the willows.

Recalling Benny Ingram's mention of the kiskadees, he picked up his pace in anticipation of seeing those and other flycatchers darting from limbs to pick off flying insects. He could picture night-herons sleepily human-watching from the tangle of trees while awaiting the call of night.

It was past 2:00 p.m. when he reached Cutoff Road. A minute later, he reached the small sign with a picture of a green heron that marked the entrance to the pond. He turned right and strolled past the San Juan Restaurant. Despite the discomfort churning in his gut and heartburn stressing his chest, the savory smells wafting from its kitchen made him hungry. Maybe he would go there for supper.

At the end of the short gravel driveway between the restaurant and a motel, the pond's small parking lot overflowed with cars and a tour bus—a sign of a great birding day.

Several butterfly and hummingbird gardens abutted the parking area and sidewalk to the pond. Jim perused a sign showing butterflies common to the island, but the first butterfly he saw—a large white one—wasn't on it. It might be rare.

He stalked it unsuccessfully for five minutes before abandoning his quest. It wouldn't sit, fluttered erratically from flower to flower with seemingly no purpose in mind, and seldom landed.

The reason for failure was his digital camera. Its shutter delay foiled every attempt. After achieving focus, a second expired before the shutter released. By that time the butterfly was elsewhere. The pictures were interesting, though. If one found beauty in leaves, petals, and plant stems.

The tall willows in the wedge-shaped entrance to the pond were sometimes excellent places to see birds. Pyrrhuloxias, tufted birds that resembled cardinals, occasionally rested on the wooden privacy fences separating it from the housing area on the left and the motel on the right.

He scanned two catch-water pools beside the housing addition fence while he eased along the sidewalk toward the pond. No birds, but he took a couple of pictures of red-eared slider turtles with red and yellow stripes on their heads.

In the tangled mass of tree limbs beyond the fence, he heard the constant chatter, whistling, and chirping of unseen grackles.

He couldn't see the pond until he arrived at the right-angle bend in the sidewalk. Much of the eastern side of the pond was obscured by heavily-foliaged, dark-green Brazilian pepper trees.

His anticipation grew as he took pictures of six white ibises foraging in the pond in front of him. His excitement peaked when he reached the pepper trees. House wrens, Lincoln's sparrows, and gray catbirds skulked in the twisted morass of limbs and dead leaves at their base. His mood dampened at the impossibility of taking their pictures.

At the edge of the boardwalk, he obtained a courtesy copy of the island bird list to use for his checklist. He surveyed the chalkboards attached to the motel fence. One contained a list of birds seen that day. The other was scribbled full with names of birds seen the previous day.

He happily noted that the kiskadees and grebes were still there. A litany of warblers, vireos, orioles, grosbeaks, buntings, woodpeckers, and flycatchers were listed, as were herons and egrets. Even a pyrrhuloxia.

He stepped enthusiastically onto the boardwalk.

6
Trouble in Paradise

Mary Elizabeth and Helen confirmed their assumption when Helen excused their way through the crowd. Boots the alligator—at least ten feet long—lay sunbathing in all his or her mud-covered splendor. Its wide, toothy head appeared capable of swallowing a child whole. In the tea-colored water, the reptile, its mouth forming a natural grin, seemed at peace with the world.

From a few feet away, shorebirds and ducks cast wary glances in its direction. Boots appeared to care less. The same applied to the adoring people standing two feet above its head.

When past the gawkers, Mary Elizabeth pointed at blue-gray egret with a shaggy, rusty-purple neck and head prancing about in the shallows on the opposite bank. It spread and flapped its wings as it hopped and whirled.

"Hello, Mrs. Reddish Egret," Mary Elizabeth mumbled. "I'm going to shoot you even though it's a waste of card space." She had hundreds of pictures and videos of the picturesque egrets' pirouetting ballets while chasing minnows and fish through the shallows, yet her camera clicked continuously. "Ballerina gone wild, Mother."

"Maybe you'll get some good shots," Helen offered hopefully.

"No, it's too far away and backlit by the sun, but it beats nothing." She motioned to the birds around them. "Most of these are teal and northern shoveler ducks. I have a lifetime supply of photos of them."

More than an hour later, they returned to the parking lot. The hooded warbler still fed, oblivious to the fifteen people watching it, some with tripods supporting twenty thousand dollars' worth of photo equipment.

"Time for Paradise Pond," Mary Elizabeth announced.

* * *

Paradise Pond was a vestige of Eden for birds and bird-watchers alike. Perhaps two hundred feet in diameter, depending on the season, much of the pond's perimeter extended into a forest of Brazilian pepper trees, willows, and tall trees Jim couldn't name. If the cacophony was an indication, the unseen areas of the pond teemed with birds and ducks.

The pond was one of the few sources of fresh water surrounded by trees on Mustang Island. It was home to the insects, aquatic animals, and vegetation necessary to help nourish birds on journeys as far as South America in the fall and the Arctic Circle during spring.

The thick trees and brush provided a refuge from gulf and winter storms. Five species of resident herons, two egret species, four species of doves, and the ever-present sparrows, grackles, starlings, and cardinals could often be seen foraging and nesting. The great variety of birds and ability to see them up close and personal made Paradise Pond a U.S. birding hot spot.

A gray catbird in the shadows under the pepper trees captured Jim's attention. The secretive, black-capped bird sat motionless for a moment before flushing, and Jim was able to make out the rusty red beneath its tail. Although satisfied to have seen it, he might have taken a nice photo with the right camera.

Behind the privacy fences to his left, were homes where people were playing games, visiting, and grilling hamburgers and steaks. The aromas heightened Jim's preoccupation with food.

The boardwalk in front of him was comprised of three sections, each about seventy-five feet long, with its own observation deck. The first section veered directly away from the motel fence. The second right-angled left and the third back right.

Halfway to the first observation deck, an Inca dove nested eight feet above the water on a snapped off treetop. Not more than twenty feet from the boardwalk railing, the small, golden-brown dove with scaly-patterned feathers provided a great photo op. Jubilant, Jim had a spring in his step after the successful encounter.

A group of people looking to their right lined the first observation deck railing. He eased forward. "What do you see?"

"Least grebes," said a plump gentleman wearing a wide-brimmed hat. "They're unusual for this area, but they'll probably stay for the summer, now that they've nested."

Jim rose on his tiptoes and peered over the crowd. A small, dark bird with orange eyes and a fluffy white rump swam unconcernedly several yards away. "Where's its nest?"

"You can't see it from here." The man pointed. "You have to go to the end of the boardwalk, but you'll need a spotting scope to get a decent look."

Jim thanked him and turned to leave. Inches above the water, a five-inch-long blue and gold bird perched momentarily on a large fungus that looked remarkably like a crust-filled pizza. It plucked insects from a partially submerged tree trunk and flitted on. "*Wow*. Was that a *prothonotary* warbler?"

A lady smiled at him. "Yes. But it's pronounced pruth-*on*-otary." When Jim blushed, she added, "It's a common mistake. And by the way, it's been called the golden swamp warbler."

He thanked her, and she turned back to the grebe.

The golden warbler, with a yellow-green shawl of feathers on its light-blue back returned, but rarely sat still as it searched for food.

"Stop. Sit. Whoa." Jim looked like a two-handed conductor while attempting in vain to train his camera on the constantly moving bird.

Giving up, he noticed a tall, pleasant-looking woman in baggy clothing step onto the boardwalk. She was accompanied by a lady about his age. After the brief glance, he strolled onto to the second section of boardwalk.

Six feet from the railing, a four-inch-long multi-colored dervish fed on insects in the willows. Blue, white, olive-green, and yellow, its yellow breast appeared splattered with red. White semi-circles rimmed it eyes. Jim thanked God for creating the marvel and blessing man with the ability to see colors. Fumbling excitedly, he raised his camera before the bird could flit out of range. Its rapid movements frustrated him. "Why don't these birds sit still?"

"Because they fucking like to eat," drawled a deep, feminine voice with a strong Texas accent.

Jim winced at the curse and prayed for forgiveness for having heard it. Turning, he was startled by gray-blue eyes level with his. The young woman he'd seen entering the boardwalk stared intently at him, and he was as uncomfortable with her proximity as with her vulgarity. He gulped. "What ... is it?"

To calm himself, he glanced at her companion who was peering at the bird through binoculars even though it wasn't more than eight feet away. Why did she need them at such close range? His couldn't focus at that distance.

She was about Marsha's height, but trim. Silver-blue hair extended from beneath her wide-brimmed hat. Her cupid's-bow mouth puckered attractively as she concentrated on the bird. It gave her a sweetly benevolent expression. She had fewer wrinkles than most women her age—if she was as old as he thought or hadn't had a face-lift.

Mary Elizabeth instantly disliked the old pervert but answered him anyway. "It's a northern parula. Isn't it a cute little shit?"

Jim found her slightly nasal, deep voice pleasant. *A flat-chested angel who talks like a sailor. Probably raised in a dysfunctional family.* "It's beautiful. Are they rare?" he said while scanning the bird list. Embarrassed, he did it too quickly. Shaking hands didn't help. "I can't find parulas listed."

Frowning, Mary Elizabeth took a burst of pictures of the tiny bird. "Try warblers."

As it flew to greener willows, Jim located it on his list and patted his pocket for a pen to check the box and enter the date.

A slender, lightly-tanned hand tapped his nose with a pencil. "Have you ever birded before? You're unprepared as hell and dumber than dirt about common birds."

"Mary *Elizabeth*," Helen reprimanded, feeling chagrin for her daughter's attempt to humiliate the fat, homely senior. "Can't you see this man doesn't like your language? Or your unwanted comments? He winces every time you speak."

Mary Elizabeth's eyes narrowed wickedly, her mouth widened, and she fixed Jim with the most penetrating, unblinking stare he'd ever experienced. Her smile changed into an exaggerated pout. "You don't mind my crappy language, do you, Pops?"

Blushing brightly, Jim swallowed. His voice cracked. "Frankly, I do mind. I don't like curse words." He was immediately sorry he'd admitted it.

"Well suck it up."

"Mary *Elizabeth*."

Helen turned to Jim. "You *don't* have to pardon my daughter. She seems to enjoy upsetting people these days."

Mary Elizabeth stared at her mother and back at the trembling man. "Would you mind if I ask what that little thingy is you were pointing at the parula?"

"My camera?" Jim squeaked, before realizing the girl was baiting him. Heat radiated from his face. Sweat soiled his shirt's underarms.

"*Mary Elizabeth.*"

Ignoring her mother's objection, she bored a hole in the man's skull with her eyes. "If that's what it is, you can't use it on warblers. They don't stop and pose on command ... one winglet against the sides of their heads, the other on their tiny hips. The only thing that piece of shit's good for is taking pictures of things that sit and smile. Like the yellow-crowned night-heron over your right shoulder.

Otherwise, you might as well shove it up your ass."

Without thinking, he turned and saw nothing. The girl was horrible, cruel. "Why are you doing this to me?" he asked, his voice high-pitched and pleading.

"I'm not doing anything to you. You're screwing yourself." Mary Elizabeth scowled. "And you didn't see it, did you? Look at the base of that willow tree."

Jim wouldn't be fooled twice. He started to walk away.

"Don't you *dare* leave, butthead." Mary Elizabeth grasped his shoulder and whirled him facing the heron.

Helen's face went white. She clutched her chest. The old man seemed nice, but her daughter was crossing all bounds of decency. *Mary Elizabeth has finally snapped.* She opened her purse and fumbled for her cellphone to call 911.

Jim recoiled. The woman's touch shocked him, made him hot and weak. Her powerful grip hurt his shoulder. He started to jerk away, then caught himself. He was responsible for his emotions—not her. Despite his growing hatred, he looked where the girl pointed.

And there the heron perched, looking much like a gargoyle as it napped and whiled away the daylight hours.

Mary Elizabeth released her hold, shuddered, and stumbled backwards. *What the hell?* She felt breathless and weak, as if she'd touched a live wire. "See, I didn't lie," she croaked.

"Thanks ... for ... pointing it out to me," Jim gasped. Disoriented from the girl's assault and nearness, he lifted his binoculars to study the heron in more detail. They weren't much help. He had to focus each lens manually, and focus was difficult to achieve, resulting in a double-image. It was still better than without them. The heron sat in profile, hunched with its head on its shoulders. Its coloration and the similarly-colored tree bark accounted for not seeing it his first try.

Night-herons were aptly named. They normally left their roosts at late dusk to hunt during night. One of the pond's attractions occurred moments before dark, when more than a hundred black-crowned night-herons materialized as if by magic in the trees surrounding the pond. They then flew away, one-by-one.

This heron sat in profile, hunched with its head on its shoulders. Its coloration and the similarly-colored tree bark accounted for not seeing it his first try. The head stripe that gave the heron its name appeared dirty white more than yellow. Its heavily lidded yellow-orange eye indicated it was about to nap or had just awakened. The thick, blunt bill made it look like a thug, one you wouldn't want to meet it in a dark swamp if you were a crayfish.

For the first time since the girl spoke to him, he smiled. He was glad she'd forced him to look at it.

Mary Elizabeth used the quiet time to recompose herself. "What the devil is that thing you're fidgeting with?"

"Young lady, what is your problem?"

Helen wondered the same thing. Mary Elizabeth had seen thousands of people using inadequate equipment. There were several gathered around them now. Most non-birders owned inexpensive binoculars and cameras incapable of capturing crisp images of flitting birds.

Mary Elizabeth smiled sweetly. "Those binoculars must be expensive, huh, Pops? Twenty bucks, you suppose?" She didn't give him time to respond. "You're one cheap bastard."

Going for the jugular, she punched the picture display button on her camera and magnified the picture. Pinning the man to the railing with her body, she held it within inches of his eyes. "See this?" She had trouble breathing. "It's a hooded warbler I ... saw a few minutes ago at ... the birding center. She scrolled to the next picture. "And ... here's ... your parula."

Too weak to lift her cellphone, let alone call 911, Helen sagged against the railing.

Jim flushed at the body pressing against his stomach and legs. Another warm wave surged through his body. *What's wrong with me*? He petitioned God for salvation.

Concentrating on the camera, he leaned backward. He needed his glasses at this distance but couldn't take them out of his shirt pocket without brushing his hand against the girl's chest. "Good picture," he mumbled. "What camera are you using?"

"A ... Canon 7D, a DSL..." Mary Elizabeth lost her breath. She wanted to admonish the bastard for thinking a good camera was all someone needed to take good pictures, but the heat of their bodies.... Dizzy, she stepped back and sucked in a deep breath.

Helen couldn't catch hers. Her chest ached. She might be having a heart attack.

The respite allowed Jim to realize he'd insulted the young lady by implying good pictures depended on the camera. "Sorry I insinuated you weren't a good photographer, young lady."

The man was nice enough to apologize after the verbal and physical beating administered by her daughter, so Helen found her voice. Maybe she could entice her wayward daughter away from the ridiculous situation without being arrested. "Mary Elizabeth, do you realize what time it is? We need to get back to the condo, so you can edit your pictures."

"Not yet, Mother."

Startled, Jim studied the older woman. She was the girl's mother, not her grandmother as he'd thought. What, then, was the source of her daughter's problems? Drugs, maybe? This sweet lady couldn't be part of them.

He heard himself say, "There's a pair of least grebes you might be interested in." *Why did I say that when the girl's mother is trying to drag her away?*

Helen started to protest, but Mary Elizabeth cut her off. "Where?"

"Back near the first bench, but it's too crowded there. They say you can see them from the last observation deck. That's where I was headed before I was so rudely interrupted."

"Then let's move it, Pops."

The crowd that had gathered to watch the confrontation began to disperse, but two women continued to hold their cellphones in case of an emergency.

Jim allowed the young woman and her mother to go first. The girl's mother intrigued him. She was everything Marsha wasn't, when it came to taking care of herself. She probably hadn't eaten a French fry or drank a milkshake in her life. He gave a short prayer requesting forgiveness for what might be lustful thoughts. It could also have been pure admiration. He wasn't sure which.

"Shit!"

Jim and Helen jolted.

"The nest's too damn far away for a good picture even with a tripod. Maybe the grebes will swim closer."

They watched the birds, without success.

"We need to go," Helen insisted, for perhaps the tenth time.

"You're right, Mother. We'll come back tomorrow."

Mary Elizabeth startled Jim again. She held out her hand as if they were old friends on the best of terms. "It's been fun talking with you, Pops."

Jim took it, completely bewildered both by the events that had transpired and his willingness to shake her hand. It felt good, and he involuntarily let it linger. He didn't know if it was because his gadfly was leaving, or if he somehow enjoyed the encounter. Either way, he would avoid the women in the future. The girl was violent, and her mother generated undesired thoughts. He gave a prayer of thanks they were leaving.

What is it with butthead? With me? Mary Elizabeth fixed the man with a perplexed stare before reluctantly withdrawing her hand. "See ya round, Pops."

When the women left the boardwalk, Jim meandered back to the people oohing and aahing over the nearly tame prothonotary warblers.

The birds hopped about around the feet of the gawking people as if they weren't there. Even Jim managed to get a decent photo of one that appeared to be reading an information sign.

7
Birds Haveth Charms

Fearful the man might follow and overhear what she had to say, Helen waited until they were in the SUV before scolding her daughter. "Mary Elizabeth, you embarrassed me to death. People stared at us like we were the plague. What on earth did you have against that poor little old man? It was senior abuse—" She ran out of breath.

"The old fart's a dumbass and a cheap bastard. I was helping him out."

"Helping? That was a mugging! You shoved him into the railing. What if it had broken and he'd fallen into the pond? We'd have been sued. Did you think of that?"

Mary Elizabeth hadn't, but she didn't respond.

"We might still be. You couldn't have hurt that poor little old man any worse if you'd poked him in the eye with a sharp stick."

Her daughter raised an eyebrow at her mother's cliché.

"If he thinks about it, he'll have a case. He seemed nice but wait till a lawyer gets ahold of him. I think we should go straight home, so he can't find us."

Helen became frustrated when her daughter didn't speak. "Are you listening to me? Why don't you say something?"

Mary Elizabeth wondered why she'd lost her composure. What was it about the old shithead that made her so mad? *He's Frank's age. Maybe older.* But the odd sensation when they touched—was she going nuts, like her mother insisted?

"Mary Elizabeth, I started to call 911. What would it have done to our family if the police arrested you? The publicity? Why can't you think before you act?"

Without a response from her daughter, Hellen felt like she was pounding her head against a wall. Was it time for a family meeting to have her institutionalized?

There was a long silence when neither spoke. Mary Elizabeth kept going over the event in her mind.

Helen began crying. "Please, speak to me, sweetheart. Do you want to go to the emergency room and get help or medication? I want to help you, but I feel so helpless."

"I'm okay, Mother. I just need time by myself to sort things out." Mary Elizabeth reached out and gave her mother's hand a squeeze. "I know you love me. You've helped me all my life, in everything I've done, but maybe it's time I did something by myself."

She parked the SUV. "We're back at the condo."

They walked to their unit in silence. Inside, Helen sat heavily in a recliner and stared at her daughter. She opened her mouth to speak. Closed it. It would be wasted breath.

Mary Elizabeth moved to her laptop, downloaded pictures, and started editing them.

* * *

Jim relived the afternoon's confrontation as he panted his way back to Palm

Gardens. He couldn't see a reason to tell his friends about it. They might not believe it anyway. They would believe he was terribly out of shape, though.

He went from rig to rig, visiting with his friends who had returned from Corpus Christi. Being ice cream social night, there would be no card games that evening, and the couples had other desires.

Charles and Nadine Danielson were sports buffs who rarely missed a University of Oklahoma ball game. The March madness of the NCAA Basketball Tournament had begun, and the OU women's team was in the Elite Eight. "We can't play cards, tonight, Jim. Our girls should make the Final Four," Charles said.

He was a tall man, an inch or two above Jim's six feet. Although he was seventy-one and four years older, he was in much better physical condition. At two hundred pounds, he weighed more than a hundred pounds less than Jim and had an envious head of thick gray hair.

A perfectionist, no one could accuse him of not being opinionated or not having a temper—much to Jeff Saunders' and Bill Warner's delight. They looked for every opportunity to get his dander up. It was often up to Jim to smooth over the situation.

"I baked some cookies," Nadine offered, knowing Jim couldn't resist them. "And there's decaf to go with them."

A couple of months older than Jim, she was one of those serious people who fretted over every situation, probably due to her life-long marriage to her perfectionist husband. She stood five-foot-eight and was slightly overweight but pleasing to look at despite her perpetual frown-smile. With the exception of Marsha—a close call—she was the most reluctant of the group to entertain new thoughts, go to new places, or do new things. Yet each time Jim saw her, she wore a different hair color. This time it was a short, sandy-blond.

"Nadine, your hair's beautiful. It makes you look years younger."

He received a large walnut and raisin-filled oatmeal cookie from her special stash.

All his friends looked nice for their ages. Maggie, Charles, and Bill, a diabetic, worked to keep fit. Jeff, Patsy, and Nadine were overweight, but none were fat like he and Marsha. And he was the worst by far.

He found his friends Bill and Patsy Warner in their usual good spirits.

"Hey, Jim, we're going to early-church, tomorrow, why don't you come along?" Patsy said.

"I'd like that. Is that good piano player still there?"

She nodded.

"You need to come to the ice cream social with us, too," Bill added. "I need to bring you up-to-date on the fishing."

"It sounds like it's been great," Jim said.

Bill winced. He was in the middle range of the men in the group in height, but they were all so close in that regard that they could be the four amigos. At seventy-three, he was the oldest but the trimmest due to his daily three-mile walks. His once dark hair was now more salt than pepper. Like Charles' it was nice and thick.

Bill and Jeff were the group's pranksters, Bill the more willing to pick on Jim. Jim didn't mind the ragging. It was what friends did.

Maggie usually egged them on. "Jimmy," she'd say, "you're too obedient, good-natured, and forgiving for your own good."

What did that mean by that? Didn't she believe in do unto others?

Patsy sweetened the offer. "I'll bring some no-sugar-added ice cream for you."

He respectfully turned her down. "I like to support the park."

At seventy-four, Patsy was the oldest in the group. Slightly more overweight than Nadine, she was pleasingly plump. Her curly brown hair had turned silvery-white years earlier, and she liked it that way.

She considered herself the group's leader, a misconception fostered by Maggie. Patsy managed Nadine and Marsha fairly well, and if anyone ever had their way over Maggie on a matter such as a restaurant, movie, or shopping mall, it was Patsy. But more often, Maggie didn't care what they did on that occasion. And Maggie was always game to try exciting things with new possibilities, so if a suggestion suited her purpose, she quickly seconded it.

When Jim knocked on Jeff and Maggie's motorhome door, she wouldn't let him in. "Have you called your irate wife yet, Jimmy?"

He nodded.

"Then come on in. I didn't want to be struck by lightning. Care for some tea?"

He nodded again.

"So ... how was your trip?" Jeff asked.

Jim recognized the trap, by his friend's silly grin. "I didn't cause the wrecks."

"Don't believe him, Jeff," Maggie called out while filling Jim's glass with ice. "I'd be willing to bet your life that he was poking along, pissing everybody off, and someone passed when they shouldn't have."

Jim blushed, and Jeff struck. "Why can't you drive like a human, Jimmy? Nobody drives the speed limit."

"His crappy pickup couldn't go faster if he wanted it to, Jeff," Maggie said as she handed Jim his tea. "You should stay on back roads and drive on the shoulder, Jimmy. Someday that junk heap will get you in a whole lot of trouble."

"Don't listen to her, Jimmy. It's a lot more fun this way." Jeff laughed. "You set a Texas state record for the number of vehicles demolished in a single wreck on a clear day."

Jeff was a perfect complement to his discerning, mischievous, and adventuresome wife. Twelve years older than she was and as calm-natured as Jim, he tolerated her controlling nature and was game to try most everything she dreamed up. At least he claimed he did.

Then, again, Maggie had a knack for getting most men to do what she wanted, Jim mused. She did it without flirting, and normally, without them realizing it.

Jeff's naturally blond hair was mingled with gray. He wasn't bald as Jim, but his thin, light-colored hair gave the illusion that he might be. The crow's-feet lines radiating from his blue eyes gave him a perpetual Crocodile Dundee smile. He could pull off practical jokes every bit as well as Bill Warner, and the two were usually in cahoots.

Before Jim could leave, Maggie patted his belly. "Wait a minute." She sauntered to their refrigerator and extracted two plastic containers. "Here's some baked chicken and a salad. Stay away from the San Juan Restaurant. I told Marsha I'd keep you safe."

"But—"

"No buts."

Back in his RV, Jim called Marsha and related the day's events. He briefly mentioned the incident at Paradise Pond, being careful not to mention the girl's mother's shapely figure. That would have put his ears in traction when he returned home. Marsha didn't like hearing about thin people—or her eating habits.

"I had a nice day birding at Paradise Pond. There were lots of birds and some tame prothonotary warblers. I also saw a yellow-crowned night heron and some least grebes."

"Don't we have those grebes in Oklahoma?"

"No, we have pied-billed grebes. We have prothonotary warblers, though. I looked it up in my bird book."

"I don't remember them. Are they pretty?"

"They're gorgeous ... blue and gold. I took a picture of one."

"Was the picture nice?" she asked.

"*Anderson*, leave your sister, *alone*."

"Sorry, Jim, what were we talking about?"

"*Taylor*, you can't hit your sister just for pestering you."

"Hold on, hon, the girls are fighting over Taylor's doll."

"*Anderson*, I'm putting you in time *out*."

"I have to break the girls apart and finish supper, hon," Marsha explained. "They've been terrors. I don't know how much longer I can put up with babysitting."

Please Lord, let it be sooner rather than later.

Jim knew the conversation was over. "I'll let you go, love," he said. "I'm tired."

He meant it. He felt miserable without Marsha, and he would be sleeping alone for two weeks for the first time since they were married. "I love—"

A loud wailing was followed by Marsha yelling, "*Taylor*, no *biting*. You're in time *out*, young lady."

"I have to run, Jim. Love you. Call me, tomorrow. And e-mail me photos of the pretty birds."

After the call, Jim made a ham sandwich, layered with tomatoes, lettuce, spinach, and onions, to go with Maggie's chicken and devoured everything. It tasted delicious, and because he was famished after the long walk and battle at Paradise Pond, he made another, larger sandwich.

* * *

Mary Elizabeth needed to reflect, and there was only one way to make that possible. She went into her room and replaced her breast wrap with a broader, tighter one. Being a couple of hours before sunset, she re-applied a liberal amount of sunscreen to her face and hands despite the dimming light. She refused to take chances with skin cancer.

"I'm going for a jog on the beach, Mother. I'll be back in a half-hour ... maybe longer ... then we'll go out to dinner."

At least her daughter hadn't changed her routine. Dr. Parkman had said that was a good thing and to call him if she changed it. Helen wondered if the horrid scene at Paradise Pond counted. "Okay, sweetheart."

Mary Elizabeth didn't turn heads when she strolled through the lobby, but her sunscreen-pasty face and hands raised eyebrows. *Good.*

Outside, she stretched first one leg and foot and then the other, walked to the sidewalk, and jogged slowly toward the beach. By the second block, she was drenched with sweat from the humid, late-afternoon air, but not breathing heavily.

A hazy mist rising from the ocean dimmed the sky. The sun, though still high above the horizon, was a dull, reddish globe behind her. It felt like she was running into dusk.

Dwelling on the incident at Paradise Pond, she was oblivious of the houses and people around her. *I was a turd.*

The old shit had seemed nice enough. He'd certainly changed after seeing the night-heron. It was he who apologized and mentioned the grebes, then escorted her and her mother to the end of the boardwalk to see them.

What was it about him? He had to be older than Frank and was cauldron-bellied. His sagging breasts appeared larger than hers.

She smiled and shook her head when she recalled her mother calling him a little old man. The guy was tall as her and weighed four hundred pounds, a mountain gorilla.

Something inside her stirred. *His touch...*

She automatically turned left at the beach and ran toward the pier. Something, perhaps larger fish, had baitfish trapped against the shoreline. Brown pelicans soared above, pitched downward, folded their wings at the last second, and plunged bill-first into the surf. Some bobbed in the water, pouches down, slowly draining the water to prevent their catches from escaping while laughing gulls sat on their heads, attempting to steal a meal. The heads and bills of other pelicans jerked skyward as they gulped down fish. Meals consumed, the pelicans flapped laboriously back into the sky to locate more prey and repeat the process.

Some pelicans had stark red pouches that contrasted with the brownish-green tint of their pink-tipped bills. The rest had mixed green and red, or green pouches. But the avid bird photographer jogging along the beach didn't take notice. Her heart wasn't in it.

The heavy sand filling her shoes made running difficult. She picked out an umbrella on the beach in front of her and determined to turn around when she reached it.

When she did, she kept going. Endorphins had flooded her brain. She moved in a rhythm, breathing heavily, exhilarated. She continued past the Horace Caldwell pier and enclosed playground and swimming beach beyond, before jogging to the water's edge. She no longer cared what the sand and water did to her socks and feet. Her heavy, water-soaked, sand-encrusted running shoes didn't slow her. She could have run to Corpus Christi or back to Kingwood. A smile creased the corners of her wide mouth. Gulping air, she picked up the pace.

When she reached the pelicans, she slowed to a walk, then stopped. The birds, waves, clouds, and sky mesmerized her. She didn't mind missed photo-ops. They were serendipitous, these times when she was alone and only she could truly appreciate the majesty around her. When she'd begun birding, her attempts to evoke the same thrill in others usually failed, so now she just mentioned the encounters, how they warmed her heart and calmed her spirit.

Why am I so alone when I'm always surrounded by family? Other than her sister-in-law Becky, no one cared to share her experiences. Shrugging off pangs of emptiness, Mary Elizabeth admired the pelicans' and gulls' antics for long minutes before heading back to the condo.

She jogged slowly, at first, then regained her former pace. She experienced the surreal when she stared directly at the sun resting on the horizon. She found the view breath-taking, the work of the Master's hand. She marveled that the late afternoon haze allowed her to view the two-toned orb without it harming her eyes. Her memories of the fat old man were replaced by those of the birds she loved. The hooded warbler, the dancing egret, the diving pelicans, and thieving gulls.

Nearing the condo, she slowed to a walk. Soaked to the skin, lumps of sand filling her shoes, she loved it. The run, birdwatching, and cool-down lasted more than an hour. Her mother would complain, but it had been worth it.

Barefoot and smelly, she smiled at the people in the lobby. She wished she were returning to an empty condo, but that wasn't to be, thanks to her mother. She frowned. That would be blaming the wrong person.

"Dinner will have to wait, Mother," she said, when she entered the condo. "I need to do some toning exercises."

"You look like a drowned rat. Wouldn't you rather clean up and rest? Besides, too much exercise is bad for you."

"It's better than a psycho lockdown."

When her daughter reached for the door, Helen made a final, imperious attempt to stop her. "You've done enough today, Mary Elizabeth. Come on, shower so we can eat."

Still on her runner's high, Mary Elizabeth walked out.

The well-equipped fitness room relaxed her even more. Her addiction to tight abs and toned arms and legs played a role, too.

When she returned, Helen greeted her with another command. "Donald called. You have to talk to him."

Mary Elizabeth set her jaw and headed to the bathroom. "No, I don't."

By eleven that evening, she was sleeping like a baby.

Helen wasn't.

* * *

At the social, Jim consumed two large bowls of ice cream, one chocolate mint and the other strawberry, while visiting with Bill Warner. His Aransas Pass gas pump buddies had proved right.

"Bill, why did you guys tell me you were catching sheepsheads?"

"We were."

"Yeah, but how many do you have in your freezer?"

Bill flashed a sheepish smile. "You know Maggie."

"What does she have to do with fishing?"

"You'll have to ask her that."

"Oh, for Pete's sake," Patsy fussed. "Jim, Maggie didn't want you to cancel your trip. She predicted, when Marsha kept her dental appointment, that either Marsha or one of your kids would try to keep you from coming. She warned us not to tell you the fishing was bad, and we weren't about to cross her."

Bill and Jim nodded.

Back at his RV, Jim found nothing worthwhile on TV. Not a basketball fan, he spent the evening editing his dove, heron, and warbler pictures and e-mailed them to Marsha.

8

The Fledgling

The alarm went off at 7:30 a.m. Mary Elizabeth rose groggily and pulled back the curtains. The Windward Dunes courtyard, beach front, and sea beyond were hazy with humidity, but the sky above appeared clear.

She ambled to the door, opened it, and sniffed the beckoning aroma of coffee. No gurgling sounds, so it was ready. She pulled off her night shirt and pulled on a T-shirt with a screen print of a prothonotary warbler on the front. It was a gift from Becky, Joshua's wife, who attended a birding festival in Fairhope, Alabama, the year before.

Becky shared her love of birding but didn't care to take photos, saying it slowed her down. She focused on lifers—birds she hadn't seen before—and her life list contained more than seven hundred species. A member of both the local and National Audubon Societies, Becky attended birding seminars and took birding classes. She had a bird App on her smartphone that she used to lure birds into viewing distance when it didn't harm the birds. She didn't use it on migrating birds foraging for life-sustaining food, or in National Wildlife Refuges and other sites where it was banned.

Mary Elizabeth loved birding with Becky, who became as exasperated as she did with her ever-present mother. They'd tried to escape unnoticed several times during the two hours minimum it took Helen to get ready, but without success. Frustrated, Becky would ask, "Helen, what are the odds of running into friends at Brazos Bend State Park? Who are you going to see at Anahuac National Wildlife Refuge? People will be looking for bitterns and rails, not you."

Mary Elizabeth pulled on calf-length cargo shorts, knee-length socks, low-cut hiking shoes, and walked to the dinette table, where her mother sat sipping coffee and reading the *Corpus Christi Caller-Times*. "It's nice to find you up ahead of me," she murmured while pouring a cup of coffee.

It smelled and tasted perfect, like it always did, regardless where they were and the brand of coffee. This time the package read Breakfast Blend from The Equal Exchange, a United Methodist project that supported farmers on small, organic coffee farms in Central America. It wasn't their church, but her mother occasionally surprised her.

Helen appraised her daughter. Mary Elizabeth looked rested. According to Dr. Parkman, that was another good sign. Not sleeping would be bad. "Do you feel well this morning, sweetheart?"

"There's only one way that could happen, Mother."

Mary Elizabeth changed the subject. "I saw a beautiful sight, yesterday. Hundreds of pelicans were diving into the surf a few yards offshore. It was incredible. We'll check to see if they're still there this morning."

"That will be nice, if it makes you feel better."

Mary Elizabeth's mood was too good for a retort. "Anything interesting in the paper?" She blew on the steaming coffee and tentatively touched the cup lip with the tip of her tongue.

Helen stared awkwardly for a moment. "Yes, they're having a special service at the Presbyterian Church."

Mary Elizabeth wondered why her mother didn't mind going to the Presbyterian Church. It was so different than theirs, and she refused to attend any other churches.

"The pre-service music begins at ten-thirty, so we'll have to leave early."

"Bull crap. We missed birding yesterday morning because we overslept. We can skip one day of church in twenty-nine years. We're going birding."

"Mary Elizabeth, it's the Lord's Day. Please, no cursing. And we can skip birding this morning. Four hours won't amount to a hill of beans."

"I'll go without you."

"You won't be back in time to take me to church."

"Call a taxi. Or take the trolley. It only costs a quarter and stops everywhere in town."

"Mary Elizabeth, you *will* take me to church. It's your last chance to keep from going to hell ... if that's still possible."

"I can't believe this!" Mary Elizabeth screamed, but she'd lost the argument. Her mother was right about the four hours. And despite her language away from home, she held a strong belief in God. It was the reason she excluded the damning curse from her vocabulary, asked for forgiveness for even thinking it, and constantly praised Him praise for the beauty in the world.

Her mother's silly cliché relaxed her. She loved her old sayings. The same went for Grandpa Craig on Frank's side of the family. He only spoke in clichés. And four-letter words. How she missed him.

Despite her daughter's loud ejaculation, Helen recognized the defeat in her eyes as clouds heavy with humidity rolled in from the Gulf and darkness swept in. "See, Mary Elizabeth, even God is telling you to go back home and get help."

* * *

At 9 A.M, Jim drowsily sipped his coffee. He'd stayed up late editing his few photos and hadn't wanted to get out of his comfortable bed. He wished he could have deleted all but a couple of photos to save time, but each was a little different. When with Marsha, he let her do the choosing. She intuitively selected photos with the most appeal. That usually meant rejecting the ones he thought best. He missed her terribly.

His cellphone trilled. Who would call this early? *Please, Lord, don't let anything be wrong.*

"Hi, Pee Paw," granddaughter Anderson said, when he answered.

"Hi, honey, what's going on?"

She giggled. "What are you doing?"

"I'm getting ready to eat breakfast and go to church. What are you doing?"

"I was helping Grandma make pancakes, but now Taylor is, so she told me to call you. She said, if I didn't, you might sleep late and miss church. Wait a minute. ... Grandma wants to know if you were already up, or if you were asleep."

"Tell grandma that she's right. I was asleep. Grandma's pretty smart, isn't she?"

"Yes. She knows how to do everything. Guess what kind of pancakes we're making?"

"Spinach?"

"No."

"Broccoli?"

Anderson giggled again. "Pee Paw, you're silly."

"Okay, I give up. What kind of pancakes are they?"

"Animal pancakes."

"Yuck. They aren't made of puppies, are they?"

"Pee Paw! They're not *real* animals. They only look like them. We have turtles and birds. You like birds, don't you?"

"Yes, I do. Guess what I took a picture of yesterday ... a yellow-crowned night-heron."

"Taylor wants to say hi."

The phone went silent for a moment. Taylor wasn't precocious like Anderson, who'd spoken complete sentences from the time she left the hospital nursery. Seemed to, anyway.

"Hello," Jim said. "Hello? Hello? Taylor? Are you there?"

There was a short giggle and a soft, hard-to-hear, "Hi, Pee Paw."

"Hi, Taylor, are you helping grandma?"

"What?"

After the fourth what, Jim heard Marsha tell Taylor to hold the phone to her ear.

"I hear you're making turtle and bird pancakes," he said. "Which one is prettiest, Taylor, honey?"

"Love ya, bye." The phone went quiet.

He was ready to tap it off, when Anderson was back. "Grandma said she'll call you later. I love you, Pee Paw. Bye."

That was it.

Marsha, what would I do without her? Jim gave a prayer of thanks for God bringing her into his life.

After a huge breakfast, he relaxed with another cup of chewable coffee while savoring what he considered a Coastal Bend pleasure, Catholic Public Radio Station, KLUX, that played the soothing music of his youth. At the moment it featured a prelude to a church service. Why didn't they have stations like this in Oklahoma, he wondered.

A light tapping on the door was followed by pounding. "Hey, Jimmy," Bill Warner called out. He usually dropped in after his daily walk when they weren't going fishing.

Jim opened the door. "Come on in."

"Can't, I'm dripping in sweat. Patsy told me to remind you of the church service. The Danielsons are going with us."

"You'll have a full house in that pickup, so I'll meet you there. Save me a place."

"Will do. And there's a special service, so be early."

At eight-thirty Jim drove past the church's overflowing parking lot. He had to park two blocks away. Sweating and puffing heavily when he arrived, he spotted his friends sitting on the next-to-back pew. They evidently hadn't arrived early enough, either.

Uh-oh. To the left, four rows nearer the front, were his tormentor and her mother. He squirmed into the pew and buried himself among his friends.

Pre-service piano music put the church in a grand mood. Resounding amens accoladed a honky-tonk version of "Victory in Jesus."

The minister asked visitors asked to introduce themselves. When the lady and her daughter stood, the mother introduced them as Helen and Mary Elizabeth— was Matthews—from Kingwood, Texas.

Jim didn't introduce himself despite the elbow from Patsy Warner. When she asked why, he whispered "I have my reasons." To be safe, he slouched lower into the pew.

After the service Patsy announced that the group was going to the San Juan Restaurant for lunch. "Jeff and Maggie are meeting us there."

Jim waited until his nemesis left, before leaving the sanctuary. Outside, he glanced fearfully in each direction and hurried to his pickup.

* * *

Mary Elizabeth's bad luck held.

"Take me to the San Juan Restaurant," Helen demanded. "I can't go looking for birds on an empty stomach."

Seething, Mary Elizabeth held her tongue. Almost. "Can you try to not take three hours, this time?"

Helen smiled sweetly and turned on her cellphone. A buzz and vibration announced a voice-mail. She punched the icon. "Hello?"

"Mary Elizabeth," she gasped, "Daddy's been hit by a car." She grew ashen. "We have to go home immediately," she wailed.

Mary Elizabeth's heart skipped. "Frank isn't dead, is he?"

"I don't know," Helen bawled. "Davey says Daddy's in the hospital and that I need to call as soon as I got this message. I could tell he's holding back bad news."

Mary Elizabeth calmed slightly. "The part about the hospital's good news. It's not likely he's dead, if he's there. Call David."

"I can't. If Daddy's dead, it'll kill me."

Mary Elizabeth pulled into a wide spot beside the road and held out her hand. "Give me the phone." She sounded braver than she felt. Heart beating rapidly, she called her brother. "It's me, David, mom was too scared to call you. How's Frank?" She listened. "That's good." She asked some questions, told her brother to tell Frank she hoped he'd get well soon and that she'd pray for him.

She handed the phone toward her mother. "Frank's okay."

Helen reluctantly accepted the phone with a trembling hand. "How's Daddy?" Her face relaxed in partial relief. "That's still bad, Davey. How badly is it broken? ... That badly? ... Therapy? How long? ... Of course, we'll come home. We'll be there this evening. ... Sedated but can talk? Of course, I want to speak with him."

"Hi, Daddy. What's this I hear about you getting run over? ... Backed into? Whatever. Davey said your bone was smashed and that bone fragments will have to be removed and a pin put in."

They spoke for a minute before Helen said, "Oh, Daddy, we'll be right home to take care of you."

She covered the phone with her hand and turned to her daughter. "Daddy's leg's been smashed, and they need to put a pin in it."

"I heard, Mother. But it looks like Frank will be okay."

Mary Elizabeth waited until the conversation ended, then continued to the San Juan Restaurant and pulled into the parking lot. "We're here."

Helen's eyes widened in surprise. "No. We're going to the condo to get our things." She raised her voice. "We have to go home immediately."

"Calm down, Mother. We need to eat first. We'll discuss things as we eat."

"I can't eat," Helen sobbed. "Daddy's an old man. He might not make it through the operation. We have to leave for home, right this minute."

Mary Elizabeth sighed. Frank was in his early seventies. Some seemingly healthy people that age went in for minor surgery and left the hospital in a hearse. "You're right, but we won't be leaving, only you. I wish you'd eat, but I know how you—"

"What do you mean only I will be leaving?"

"We're going to the airport to see if there's a charter to get you home as soon as possible. You need to be with Frank. I'll pack up at the condo and follow."

"No, Mary Elizabeth, we're going home together. We'll cancel the rest of our reservation and have someone pick up our things."

"Mother, I'll be all right."

"Helen's face filled with indignation. She became loud and domineering. "Mary Elizabeth, you won't stay here by yourself. I won't hear of it."

Thinking about her immediate future, Mary Elizabeth tuned out her mother's cajoling and demands. She stopped for a red light on Alister Street, turned right onto Texas 361, and drove to the airport.

"I won't go to Kingwood without you, Mary Elizabeth. Take me back to the condo, right now."

The airport appeared vacant, but Mary Elizabeth parked in front of the terminal. The door was locked. Heart sinking, she knocked anyway, and sighed with relief when she heard shuffling.

A crack appeared, and a sleepy-eyed young man peered out. Instantly awake, he gulped and stammered, "What can I do for you?"

""My mother and I need to charter a flight to Houston. It's an emergency."

"There's no one here."

"Am I imagining you, or are you a hologram?" Mary Elizabeth resisted adding you dumb fuck. "And if you *are* real, do you have a name?"

"Um ... Austin."

"Well, Um Austin, is there a charter available?"

"Uh, there's Addi Thibodeaux," he drawled, "but she's fishing at Wilson's Cut with Mark."

"Would there be any way I can speak with her? Is it possible she owns a cellphone?"

Gawking and blushing, Austin sputtered, "I'll get her for you."

He left the door open, without inviting her in, and disappeared into a room in the back of the building.

Peering into the waiting room, Mary Elizabeth saw two chairs, a sofa, and a table with a laptop and magazines on it. She turned and beckoned. "Come on, Mother. No use standing out here."

"I'm not leaving without you."

"Fine, we'll leave the car here, and I'll pick it up later ... without you."

"We'll send Davey for it."

Mary Elizabeth shrugged.

After listening to drawers open and close and papers being shuffled for what seemed like an hour to the worried Helen, the young man returned. "I thought you might like this while I call Addi." He handed Mary Elizabeth a business card. SPEEDY DESTINATONS – Your flying dreams come true.

It gave her second thoughts.

"Addi's not answering," he said, looking apologetic.

Mary Elizabeth used her mother's phone to call the number on the card. It transferred to Voice Mail. Peering at her mother, she said sarcastically, "This is Helen Matthews. My daughter and I need to be flown to Houston immediately. My husband was badly injured in an accident, and he'll be in surgery this afternoon. Please call me back."

Worried about the prospect of having to drive six hours back to Kingwood on an empty stomach, she gave her mother's cellphone number and clicked off.

Soon after the call ended, the phone chimed. She tried to hand it to her mother, who withdrew like it was a flaming match. Placing the phone in speaker mode, Mary Elizabeth answered. "Hello?"

A deep voice much like her own drawled, "Hullo, this is Addi Thibodeaux. Is this Helen Matthews?"

"It's her daughter."

"Y'all sure sound alike. How soon do y'all need to be in Houston?"

"I thought I said immediately," Mary Elizabeth snapped. *Oh shit.*

"Y'all think alike too, huh?" Addi chuckled. "It took me a while to find my phone in the tackle box. That, and I had to hand my rod to Mark. My first fish of the day, and it's a big 'un. He's still fighting it.

"We'll be there in about twenty minutes, but it won't take long to file a flight plan and get going. I always leave my plane ready for an emergency. That was true, wasn't it? It's an emergency?"

"Yes," Mary Elizabeth said icily.

"Hang on, then."

While waiting they learned Austin's last name was Churchwell. The more they spoke, the more relaxed he became, and the more anxious Helen became. Just as she felt she couldn't wait a moment later, a pickup wheeled into the parking lot and skidded to a stop. A sandy-haired beauty and muscular young man, both with sun-bleached hair, hurried into the waiting area.

"I'm Addi," the woman announced. As pretty as her voice, she looked to be about five-three, and her halter top and miniscule shorts proved her as solid as her hard-bodied husband.

Mary Elizabeth introduced herself and her mother and explained their situation.

The pilot gave a toothy grin that looked at home on her tan face. "This is my husband, Mark." She giggled. "He about got us a ticket getting us here so fast. The trooper's probably still trying to put on his hat. Our slip stream spun his SUV around in circles," she offered while gazing lovingly at her husband.

Mark smiled, appraised Mary Elizabeth unabashedly, and thrust out his hand.

"Glad to meet y'all."

Mary Elizabeth hated his deep masculine voice. *Definitely an alpha male.* The gentleness of the handshake despite his steel-hard hand surprised her.

Helen didn't hold out her hand. She dabbed her eyes with a tissue from a box Austin had located for her.

Addi pointed at the wall. "Those are my credentials, in case you're wondering."

Mary Elizabeth had examined them. "I noticed. Cost is no object."

Addi grinned. "In that case, I'll have to check on the weather and find a Houston airport. It shouldn't take me more than twenty minutes, tops, this time on a Sunday."

"Mind if I come in with you?" Mary Elizabeth asked."

Addi's smile flickered. "Uh … sure."

When they left, Mark addressed Helen. "I heard your husband was in an accident. Was he hurt bad?"

She gulped back the sob in her throat. "His leg was smashed."

Mark frowned sympathetically.

After explaining her husband's accident, Helen told him why they were in Port Aransas. "I came on a week's retreat with my daughter. Mary Elizabeth's … not well. She's moody. Coming here to see birds seems beneficial, and my husband and I don't believe a woman should go anywhere by herself. It's too dangerous."

Helen felt more relaxed, now that she was getting her fears off her chest.

Mark continued to make small talk. "Port Aransas is a beautiful place. I've lived near here all my life, but other than herons and spoonbills, I don't notice birds much. Show me a huge fish, though, and you'll sure get my attention."

Addi, with Mary Elizabeth a couple of steps behind, reentered the room. "Ready to go, Mrs. Matthews? It'll only take a couple of hours, and Mary Elizabeth's already called your son to tell him when to pick y'all up."

Mark assisted Helen into the plane and prepared to help her daughter, but Mary Elizabeth shook her head and whispered, "Hurry, close the door."

Looking puzzled, he complied.

Helen was startled when Mary Elizabeth didn't enter behind her. "Miss, Miss," she implored of Addi, "wait. My daughter has to get on the plane, but your husband shut the door."

"She decided not to go, Ma'am. She said she needed time alone. She'll call you this evening to see how things are going. Please sit back and put on your seatbelt."

"No. I won't leave without her."

"Then I think it will take y'all about a day to get to Houston. Your daughter sure seems to have her mind made up."

"Open the door. Now. She'll listen to me."

"Can't, the engines are running. If I shut 'em down, you'll have to pay for the charter, no matter what. Not that I like it, but I stopped what I was doing for a supposed emergency. It *is* an emergency, right? Do we fly or stay?"

Her daughter's rebellion flustered Helen. She could make Mary Elizabeth change her mind, but Daddy was in the ECU. Any delay, and she might not be there if anything happened. "I don't like this conspiracy, young lady."

Addi stared over her shoulder. "Which is it? If we go, you need to buckle up."

Her husband came first. Helen would take care of other matters when she arrived home. She clicked her seatbelt. Peering out the small window, she saw Mary Elizabeth waving.

"Why aren't you going?" Mark inquired.

Mary Elizabeth stared at him. The handsome man appreciated her looks, and she found it unnerving. "It's a mother-daughter thing. Just a mother and daughter thing."

"I got that opinion while I was talking to your mom. She's seems like my mother was with my sister ... a real mother-hen type." He winked. "Well, it's time to have your fun."

Mary Elizabeth wondered if he was flirting. *You're wrong, shit head.* "It's not that way at all," she protested.

"Yeah, right." He laughed, then sobered. "Take care of yourself, beautiful. Here's your chance to do your own thinking. If you're like sis, it won't be all that easy for a while."

After watching the plane take off and circle, Mark glanced at his watch. "Gotta run. Old speck's waiting back at the boat."

He gave Mary Elizabeth a hug that she didn't expect and strode toward his truck.

Uncomfortable with his stares and shocked by his hug, she stood immobilized. "Addi, you won't have any problem with your man straying. You're one lucky lady."

She turned to discover Austin smiling at her.

"You're right, there, ma'am. Sis married the pick of the litter. My parents love him, and he treats me like a brother"

Blushing, Mary Elizabeth bet Austin was who Mark warned her about. "Thanks for your help."

She received a warm smile. "Y'all take care. Your mom will have a good trip. Sis is the best there is. And I hope your daddy will be okay."

She thanked him again.

In her SUV, she realized she still had her mother's cellphone. She called Becky and explained what happened.

"Good for you, M. E., take care."

Mary Elizabeth looked at her watch. It was only one-thirty, but it felt like hours since they'd received word of the accident.

She felt strangely lost.

9
A Penny for Your Thoughts

A black Tahoe pulled out of the San Juan parking lot and turned right as Jim wheeled onto Cutoff Road. *Ridiculous. The odds would be astronomical.*

His late arrival proved a mixed blessing. His friends had just been seated, but he was met by an inquisitor.

"Fess up, Jim. What's the real reason you didn't introduce yourself at church, this morning?" Patsy asked.

He blushed. "A young woman jumped me at Paradise Pond for using crummy equipment. She was there, and I didn't want her to see me."

Maggie's eyebrows shot up. "*Oh-ho.* Bill and Jeff picking on you isn't good enough. You have to insult a professional."

Patsy laughed. "You coward."

Jim was glad he'd mentioned the incident to Marsha. She was going to get an earful from her friends.

After a long lunch, he detoured by Paradise Pond. No luck with the least grebes, but a pied-billed grebe treated him with a preening display. The grebe was so named for the black ring that made its bill two-toned—or pied. The name was a mystery to him. Other birds had ringed and two-toned bills, but he couldn't recall a pied-billed gull or pied-billed gallinule.

The small, brown grebe posed—arched its long neck over its back and touched its head to its raised wings. Jim wished he had his camera, but it probably would have caused more frustration. The thought brought the young woman to mind, and he shuddered involuntarily.

When he returned to the park, he and his buddies enjoyed the breeze under a tall palm.

"This is my worst year," Charles confessed. "All I've caught were baby sheepshead I had to throw back."

Bill nodded in agreement. "If it weren't for Spanish Mackerels and Pompanos, fishing would be a bust. I watched fishermen on the surf side of the jetty catching mackerel, so I tried it. Man, they fought like wildcats. They leapt out of the water and sometimes bit through my line. We ate a couple for dinner last night, and I don't know if I was fish hungry, or what, but they were the best fish I've ever tasted."

Charles sneered in disgust. "I'd never stoop so low."

Jeff elbowed Charles and addressed Jim. "Guess who's going home with an empty freezer?"

Jim cocked his head. "Why did you all tell me the sheepshead were biting? I thought you were my friends."

"Messing with Maggie is worse than messing with you," Charles shot back. "Did you know she makes voodoo dolls?" He glanced nervously at Jeff. "Seriously, there's one of each of us sitting on the shelf over their dinette window."

"Yours is the easiest to recognize," Bill added. "It's the only one that's round."

Jeff grinned. "She only uses them for Pegs and Jokers." He lifted his hands.

"Hey, she swears the dolls are for good luck ... to keep us safe." He tugged on his shirt collar. "And speaking of that, I'd better go. I'm in church clothes, and it's like a sauna. Maggie might send them to the cleaners ... with me still in them."

The friends agreed to meet at seven-thirty the next morning to go fishing at the jetty. Jim would take Jeff, and Charles would take Bill.

Back in his fifth wheel, Jim turned on KLUX and relaxed in the air-conditioning. He resolved to go to the birding center at four, but the recliner and pleasant music lulled him to sleep. His loud snort awakened him at ten till five.

* * *

Mary Elizabeth sat in the SUV for a while before leaving the airport parking lot. Although she was responsible for the birding itinerary when her mother was with her, she was now confused, unsure what to do next. She hadn't eaten, so she returned to the condo for a snack.

She ate more than she intended, and her full stomach made her lethargic. She sat in a balcony recliner and stared at the palm tree-lined courtyard and swimming pool shaped like a crab—if one looked at the hot tubs and kiddy pools just so.

She felt a pang of guilt about her mother, but this might be her last chance to work out the complexities in her life without truly suffering a breakdown. She couldn't have had an unhappier past year—last eleven years—and she suspected that Frank would come through his operation fine. He'd had a TURP, a prostate reduction operation, a year earlier and acted like it was no more than getting a tooth filled. His exercise and inclination to eat healthy foods made him strong.

Fighting the urge to nap, she decided to clear the cobwebs by birding. The late afternoon sunlight was perfect for herons and egrets stalking fish in the shallows, and stilts, snipes, and dowitchers probing the mudflats for worms and crabs. Sora, least bitterns, and marsh wrens were often visible in the cattails late in the day. She flattened her breasts, slathered on sunscreen, and headed to the birding center.

Boots again basked beside the boardwalk. The impressive giant's hide could probably make a shop-full of boots and purses. She scowled at the children aiming coins at its head. Most of the children were parents setting bad examples.

Mary Elizabeth forced her way through the crowd, climbed the tower, and scanned the lake through the courtesy telescope.

Only the usual suspects—roseate spoonbills, northern shoveler ducks, and hundreds of teal, mostly green-winged and blue-winged, with a smattering of cinnamons. Cormorants and brown pelicans rested on two sets of railings in the lake. Black-crowned night-herons roosted in the cattails.

Mary Elizabeth eyed the dainty black-necked stilts and snowy egrets wading in the shallows and wished they were nearer the boardwalk. A few dowitchers and stilt sandpipers probed the small pockets of mud flats being crowded out by cattails, but they were on the wrong side of the boardwalk for the lighting. She smiled wistfully at three American white pelicans swimming majestically at the far end of the lake, outside the range of her telephoto lens.

Arriving at the birding center, Jim searched the pools under the pepper trees for sora. He didn't find any, but a hooded warbler fed in front of a picnic table. He attempted to take better pictures of it than the photo the young woman showed him at Paradise Pond but gave up in disgust after fifteen minutes.

He stared pensively at a family taking pictures of their son with his head sticking through a hole in a sign bearing the picture of a toothy alligator. It read: 80 REASONS TO STAY AWAY FROM ALLIGATORS. He wished Marsha and his grandchildren were sharing the moment with him.

On the boardwalk, he saw a large group of people leaning over the railing. Some were dropping coins and candy wrappers. Others were laughing. *Must be tormenting poor Boots.*

To his left, at the edge of a narrow channel of water, humpback-shaped sandpipers with bills a third the length of their bodies fed in the flats. He guessed they were long-billed dowitchers. He'd heard they preferred fresh water. Their rapid probing reminded him of sewing machines, which again made him think of Marsha.

He took several blurry pictures before moving on to Boots. The beast appeared unconcerned about the coins bouncing off its hide. Jim recalled that Jeff and Maggie constantly complained about not seeing the huge gator. This would be their chance.

Mary Elizabeth spotted Pops. He stared at Boots for a few seconds and left. Since she couldn't reach him in time, she resolved to apologize to him the next time they met.

Climbing down from the tower, she eased her way to the end of the boardwalk where Ruddy ducks chasing fish underwater made muddy trails through the light-green water. Though not on her must-shoot list, she never passed up the chance to take pictures of males in breeding plumage. During winter, they were dull gray, brown, and black. Come spring, their bodies magically changed to ruddy red, and their breasts and heads became shiny black. Their pièce de résistance were their pure white cheeks and sky-blue, purple-tinged bills. She focused her camera at the head of a trail. When the duck popped up, it was the male she'd hoped for.

* * *

The door to Jeff and Maggie's motorhome was open despite the warmth and humidity.

"Knock. Knock."

"Get in here, Jimmy," Maggie said. "You bumming ... or what?"

"I'm a geek bearing gifts. Want an alligator?"

The parking lot was full when they arrived at the birding center, so Jim dropped them off at the entrance. "You two go on. I'll catch up."

By the time Jim reached the boardwalk, Jeff had entered the Boots bombing contest, and Maggie was his cheerleader. He shook his head disapprovingly. His close friend was littering and endangering wildlife.

Jeff exulted above the roar of the crowd. "Did it. Got him right between the eyes."

Maggie bounced while capturing the event with her small digital camera. She gave an ear-ringing whistle and yelled, "*Yee*-haw."

Jim froze. Mary Matthews was at the end of the boardwalk. He didn't see her mother, but that didn't matter. Her mother couldn't control her. How could he escape?

Jeff and Maggie acted goofier than the teenagers, when he reached them. "Did you see me?" Jeff yelled, reaching out for a fist bump.

Jim hesitated, then complied.

"Do you realize we've been coming here for five years, and this is the first time we've seen Boots up close and personal?" Jeff gushed. "What a monster. You're a great buddy to stop birding to come get us."

Maggie stepped well into Jim's personal space and shoved her camera display against his nose. Déjà vu. Only she didn't pin him to the boardwalk railing.

"See the penny between Boot's eyes?" It was off to one side and slightly behind the eyes, but on the gator's head.

"Are you aware those pennies and coins might harm the birds and other wildlife in the pond?"

"Sorry. I wasn't thinking, Jim," Jeff said. "It's so great to be up close to a twelve-foot alligator that I guess I got caught up in the action." Smiling broadly, he didn't appear the least contrite. "But my coin stayed on its head."

Jim glanced anxiously at the other end of the boardwalk. "Um ... it's closing in on six, and I'm bushed. Let's go back to the park."

"Oh, my gosh," Maggie said. "Marsha called. She told me to bawl you out for not having your cellphone turned on." She giggled, euphoric at taking a photo of a lifetime. "Consider yourself soundly scolded, Jimmy."

"Oh, no. I use it so seldom when I'm home that I don't take it anywhere. Or even turn it on. Now, I really have to get back to the park."

Pleased with her pictures of the ruddy duck, Mary Elizabeth saw Pops speaking with a man and woman on the other side of the alligator groupies. Her chance to apologize having arrived, she started toward him.

Then frowned when he glanced in her direction, said something to the couple, and they exited the boardwalk. *Is butthead avoiding me?*

She ran briskly up the boardwalk, elbowing her way through the crowd. "Coins can kill the birds." She glowered at the adults. "You stupid idiots should know better."

By the time she reached the parking lot, Pops was gone, so she drove to Paradise Pond. When she didn't find him there, she felt disappointed. And drained. Out of the mood for taking photos she returned to the condo. Depressed and weary, she stumbled to the bedroom, pulled the curtains closed, and dropped on the bed.

She had vivid dreams about the old man. When she tried to apologize, he turned his back on her. Cursing loudly, she kicked the jackass in the rear.

* * *

Vowing to make it a habit, Jim turned on his cellphone. In addition to a call from Marsha, there was one from his youngest daughter Deena, a successful mystery novelist.

He took a soft drink from his refrigerator, cranked back in his recliner, and called her first. "Hey, Deena, what's up?"

"Just checking in. Are you catching fish and seeing bunches of birds?"

Marsha must have put her up to it to force him to keep his phone with him and on, but it was nice to have a long chat with his daughter. She filled him in on what was going on in her family and her latest book. They spoke for thirty minutes.

Afterwards, he ambled from site to site visiting with his friends about fishing. When he returned to his RV, he expected to have a long talk with Marsha, but she was tired and exasperated.

"Taylor's been a toot all day. Anderson was okay but not helpful. I guess I'm getting old." She essentially repeated what she'd said the night before.

Wishing she would prioritize him higher, Jim told her he loved her, but he knew he was more problematic to her than the grandchildren. She accused him of demanding too much of her time even though the two of them were seldom alone together.

Showered, refreshed, and listening to his beloved elevator music, he fell asleep dreaming of a record sheepshead fish on his line.

* * *

"Stop screaming, Mother."

Helen screamed several times before Mary Elizabeth realized it was the condo phone. She groped about on the nightstand without turning on the light. "Hullo," she said softly, her head spinning.

"Mary *Elizabeth*."

"Yes, Mother?"

"How could you? You have no respect for me, your father, or anyone. You couldn't have hurt me more if you'd stabbed me in the—"

Mary Elizabeth shook off her stupor. "Does this mean Frank's okay?"

Helen sputtered at the insult of having been interrupted. "The surgeon told us Daddy came through the operation fine, but he may be in recovery for a long time ... no thanks to you. If he'd known you stayed alone in Port Aransas, he'd have been so worried there's no telling what might have happened. You're a hateful child. Do you realize you're the only one not in the waiting room? And why can't you call your daddy father instead of Frank? That's unheard of."

Her mother was correct, as usual. She should be sitting in the waiting room, worrying with the rest of the family. But, right now, she couldn't move. And they'd argued about why she refused to call her father by a more affectionate term since she was six. "I'm glad to know he's all right. I am, too, just tired."

"Why aren't you on your way home?"

Mary Elizabeth didn't answer.

"Well, between worrying about your father and you, the flight was the worst time of my life."

"Addi wasn't a good pilot?" Mary Elizabeth tried to focus attention anywhere but on her.

"She was fine," Helen said grudgingly.

Mary Elizabeth knew that meant the flight was uneventful and that Addi evidently did her best to buoy her mother's spirits.

She eventually spoke with everyone in the waiting room, including some who might not have been family, she reflected afterwards.

Her mother hadn't been forthcoming. David was there, as was his family, but neither Joshua nor Daniel were. Becky was there. So was Daniel's wife, Melinda, and a couple of grandchildren. All asked when she was coming home, probably at Helen's insistence. She gave vague promises.

Only Becky understood. "We'll see you when you're ready, M. E.," she'd whispered.

After the phone call, the listlessness returned. Mary Elizabeth didn't jog, exercise, or eat supper. She pulled up the sheet and comforter in the cold air-conditioned room and drifted into a troubled, oft-waking sleep.

The phone rang again and didn't stop ringing. She turned on the light and answered. "Oh, it's you, Don. I'm tired, worried about Frank, and want to be left alone. Don't call again."

She hung up, like one did to a phone salesman, and glanced at the clock—8:30 p.m. She considered doing what mother said and going home in the morning.

Anything would be better than this.

10
Party Birds

The elated woman nodded her head and tapped her fingers on the steering wheel to the song strumming through her head. She had a date with a most handsome man, one who promised her happiness. He had a funny, lopsided grin. Sexy as hell. She wouldn't have turned him down regardless of the offer. In fact, she'd made it.

She was on the bridge over Redfish Bay, between Aransas Pass and Port Aransas. Being dusk, visibility was rapidly deteriorating, but her destination was in sight. Her soon-to-be paramour was camping somewhere on the tiny island in front of her. She searched for the large industrial van, spotted it, and became so excited her hands shook.

Immediately beyond the bridge, she steered right onto a sandy trail that wound through low brush onto to a strand of beach beside a narrow channel of water. The many tents and recreational vehicles parked nearby enhanced the forbidden nature of the tryst. Sex with a stranger, and no one would know—not family nor friends. Not even those camping right beside her. Heart fluttering, she parked beside the van and hurried to the door. It beat faster when the door opened.

The burly man smiled down at her. "You look beautiful, Monique," he said, extending his hand.

She took it and skipped up the steps. "You, too, handsome, I've wanted you all month."

Her heart caught. Breath hitched. A tiny, naked woman laid on the floor—blindfolded, mouth taped, hands and feet hogtied behind her back. The walls, floor, and ceiling.... *Shit, the truck's a fucking dungeon.* Hearing the lock click, Monique whirled.

The man blocked her path. His grin didn't reach his eyes.

"Let me the hell out!"

He shook his head.

Her anticipation changed to fear. "What the hell is this?"

The man's expression didn't change.

She stared again at the woman lying on the thickly-carpeted floor. Was she dead? No, she was breathing. Monique turned to the man. "For God's sake, let me go. I won't tell anyone."

"The bitch screwed with me. You don't have anything to be afraid of."

Oh, yes, I do. "What did she do?" Monique asked.

"Something she knew not to," he said, as if a naked woman lying painfully hogtied on the floor was perfectly natural. "Would you like something to drink?"

Monique wasn't about to say no.

The champagne was top notch, but the man sipped sparkling grape juice. A second glass of wine relaxed her. Plus, she was taller than the man and just as muscled. The thought loosened her tongue. She nodded at the implements and trappings on the walls, those hanging from the ceiling, the ones neatly arranged in clear plastic containers on shelves under the mirror on the front wall. "Did you buy out a Naughty Nancy's ... or decide to own a franchise?"

The man finally chuckled. "You like?"

"I'm used to travelling tamale wagons, but this is ridiculous." She stared. "Are these things served hot, or do I have to put in an order?"

"You're a smart-ass, aren't you?"

Monique nodded. No longer concerned about her safety, she worried about the little woman rocking in discomfort and straining to breathe through her nose. The bitch wasn't young, but she had youthful features—some quite magnificent.

"What do you plan on doing with Little Bit?"

"You want her?"

She studied the man's face. "You did this for me?"

He frowned and shook his head. "Not really."

The man knew more about her than her family did. What would her husband, eight-year-old son, and twin teen daughters think if they knew how she earned their clothing and new car money?

"You're one sick son of a bitch," Monique said, grinning mischievously, "and I like how you think." She nodded toward the shelves. "Those legal?"

"Be my guest."

The night would be even better than promised. "Then help me hang her."

They removed the small woman's bonds and shackled her on the wall—weight supported by her outstretched arms and balls of her feet. The man then sat in a recliner to watch.

Monique stripped to her black leather teddy, put on a mask, and selected the implements she desired. She yanked on a crop on the wall. "Why can't I get this loose?"

"You have to know the combination."

She shrugged, studied the shelves and plastic containers, and selected the tools with the most bang for her buck. She removed the woman's blindfold and held up a ball gag. "Open your mouth."

The woman leaned her head forward compliantly.

Monique fixed the her with a penetrating stare. "You know what I'm about to do?"

A nod.

"And you're good with it?"

This bob was accompanied by a quirky, misty-eyed smile. The woman's mouth closed around the gag. She dipped her head and waited patiently for the strap to be buckled.

There's more here than meets the eye.

The woman reinforced Monique's opinion by staring pointedly at the man throughout her ordeal. She didn't complain, not once, even though the mistreatment ran longer than Monique preferred due to the man's urgings.

She finally balked and glared at the man in the red velvet recliner. "Enough?"

"Yeah, I guess."

"Then it's time for you. Stand up. I want you naked."

"Wait. Let's turn our observer to the wall."

True enough, the woman peered eagerly. Revenge? Anticipation? *Weird,* Monique mused.

He discovered him to be older than she'd imagined—graying hair, a paunch around the gut—but he had firm pecs and muscles. She kneeled to satisfy her curiosity. He was an eyeful.

Her close attention made the SOB embarrassed. He tried to cover himself with his hands.

Monique grabbed and stroked. Raked his firm buttocks and muscular thighs with her long fingernails, drawing involuntary shudders and grunts. "*Wow.* Stay just like that."

When she dished out equal treatment to him, he gasped, cried out, and squirmed.

"Geez, beer gut, Little Bit took it like a man."

Moving to her purse, Monique removed the foil packets, and her night of wanton abandon began.

The man was incredible. The perfect dance. He led, she followed, trying to keep up. Masterful, strong, knowledgeable of what both wanted, he positioned her as if she were twenty years younger and weighed a hundred-fifty pounds again. At times, she was disoriented—didn't know whether she was up, down, somewhere in the middle.

Am I being spun in a sling?

In the first hour, she opened three packets. Was it more? One time she saw a blinking red light. A video? *I'll buy it.*

Little Bit turned out to be something of a contortionist, managing to twist her body sufficiently to watch the encounter. Instead of a turn-off, Monique found it erotic.

Having temporarily quenched the man's appetite, she moved to their wall decoration to ensure Little Bit's safety. It was time to release her. But first, a neck and shoulder rub—and a slap on her surprisingly firm rump.

"You work out?" Monique asked, unbuckling a wrist restraint.

The woman nodded. When her gag was removed, the corners of her mouth curved up. She flicked her eyes toward the floor.

"You mean what I think you mean?"

Little Bit smiled and reclined in the thick carpeting.

Monique joined her and gazed at the startled man. "Come on, Hoss, there's always room for one more." When he shook his head, she shrugged. "It's your loss."

The tiny fox was creative, adventuresome, and she frequently shot looks at their companion, as if daring him to join them. Or trying to prove a point.

The man reached his tolerance limit. He yanked the women apart, hogtied, blindfolded, and gagged his captive, and dragged her on her stomach to the corner of the truck.

"Stop it, asshole, you're giving her carpet burns," Monique growled.

"The hell with her. I'm ready for you." He dropped the tiny woman and appeared pleased when she bounced on the floor, grunted, and gasped through her nose.

Pissed by the man's brutality, Monique shook her head. "*Screw,* you. You had your chance. I'm beat."

When the man walked over and mashed her breasts with his foot, she wished she'd kept her mouth shut. Played possum. Though no longer ready, not in the mood, she had signed the contract.

It wasn't a pleasant rest of the night. Her domineering date treated her roughly. It became an endurance contest.

When she awoke at eleven the next morning, Little Bit was missing.

The man shocked her one last time. "Come on, Monique. I'm treating for breakfast."

She freshened at the wet bar, but he didn't allow her much time before taking her to the Bakery Café in Aransas Pass. She followed in her car, actually.

Despite a superb breakfast, with biscuits and gravy, she felt in no condition to return home. She drove to a park overlooking the bay and Intracoastal Canal to assess herself. Her hair, face, and rumpled clothing were a mess. Sore, reeking of B O, she called home. "Hi Paul. My retreat has an optional meeting I want to attend. I'll be home tomorrow. Can I say hi to the kids?"

After their conversation she checked into a motel, paid cash, and reflected on her experience. Though parts had been intensely fun, it had been dangerous as hell and money wasn't worth her life.

She reflected on Little Bit. What did the elf do to make Mr. Insatiable's hit list? She hadn't spoken even when she could, nor complained when the mistreatment crossed the line. Why not? Mute? Threatened with harm?

Monique now wished she hadn't been the instrument of abuse. She hoped the man hadn't killed the woman but considered it unlikely. He seemed content making the woman suffer. Then again, it might not have taken much. At times his face—eyes especially—were frightening. Homicidal. She felt fortunate she hadn't crossed him.

A disquieting thought wormed from her subconscious while she showered. Could he be involved in the disappearances of the women in the area who advertised online to be massage therapists but proved otherwise? Should she report him using the hotline number? No, he might figure out who did it. And if he wasn't guilty, she'd lose everything.

She scrubbed forcefully to rid his smell from her body.

11
A Tern for the Worse

Monday morning broke clear and dripping-wet. Jim rolled out of bed at six-thirty, took his blood pressure and cholesterol medications, an adult low-dose aspirin, and turned on KLUX. He made coffee, sipped it, and shuddered. *Where's Marsha when I need her?*

The music relaxed him. It would be a great day. He and his friends would catch their limits of record-sized sheepshead by noon, and he'd have all afternoon for birding. The thought generated mixed emotions. Not the fishing. Birdzilla was haunting his favorite birding sites. Jim found the memory disquieting.

After gagging down half of a second cup of coffee, he dressed. He selected a safari style shirt with button-down pockets to secure his cellphone. Marsha wouldn't believe it an accident if it tumbled into the water. He put on shorts he'd bought at one of Port A's city-wide garage sales several years earlier and rotated in front of the floor-length mirror on the bathroom door. *Not half bad, if I do say so myself.*

At seven-fifteen, he placed his fishing gear in the back of his pickup, along with a backpack containing storm wear. Sudden storms weren't unusual this time of year. He squeegeed heavy condensation from his pickup windows and outside rearview mirrors and drove to Jeff's motorhome. His friend added his backpack and fishing gear and climbed into the cab.

"Morning, Jeff."

The morning sunlight appeared about to make Jeff sneeze. His eyes squinted shut, nose wiggled from side to side. When tears welled in his friend's eyes and his face ran the gamut of expressions, Jim thought it might be allergies instead.

"Nice shorts, Jim."

"Thanks." Suspicions confirmed. They'd been a good buy.

They joined Charles and Bill at the Port A bait shop to buy live shrimp.

"Any idea where we are, Jim?" Bill asked, when he and Charles arrived at the shrimp tank, bait buckets in hand. Their faces looked curiously like Jeff's had earlier.

Jim thought it a strange question. "We're at the Port A bait shop."

Bill rubbed imaginary sweat off his brow. "Whew. I thought I'd fallen into Wonderland."

"Wonderland?"

Jeff couldn't retain his laughter any longer. "You look like Tweedle Dum, Jim."

Jim blushed. "That bad, huh?"

His friends laughed uproariously while he pretended to.

"What do you weigh now?" Jeff asked.

"About three-ten, but I plan on exercising when I get back to Oklahoma." It was time to start, now that his friends were making such a big deal of it.

After catching their breaths, they debated how much shrimp to buy. "With four of us, I think we need at least a quart," Charles calculated.

"If they bite as good as they have been," Jeff retorted, "we ought to spend our money on Snickers Bars to munch on while we watch Kemp's ridley sea turtles. They're endangered. NASA is incubating some of their eggs to protect them from things like oil spills, plastic bags, and shrimp nets."

"How the heck do you know all this?"

"Maggie told me."

"Are those the sea turtles we see while we're fishing?" Jim asked.

"Beats me, but some lay their eggs here and on Padre Island."

Bill looked curious. "Why do they call them *ridley* sea turtles?"

"Are we going fishing, or what?" Charles grumbled, clearly unimpressed.

They didn't park their trucks close to the beach. High surf and tidal surges sometimes washed sand from beneath parked vehicles and left them bottomed out or sitting in holes.

They stepped up on the concrete bulkhead bordering the ship channel. The clear blue water in the channel made Jim even more confident he would catch his limit.

As they made their way toward the surf, they had to duck cautiously under the lines of fishermen fishing for redfish and black drum weighing forty or more pounds.

Not far beyond the shoreline, the danger increased. The concrete ended, and the jetty became a jumble of unevenly cut and spaced granite boulders. Stepping up and down a foot or more and across gaps up to two feet wide while carrying fishing rods, nets, and bait buckets weren't the only dangers. Moss, especially black moss, made slippery by rain, humidity, waves, and wakes from passing ships dropped even wary jetty visitors. Some fishermen purchased special white boots with improved traction, or attached clip-on cleats, but when they saw black, most walked around.

Vacationers tended to use flip flops, walk barefoot, and not pay attention. Despite warnings from fishermen, they usually flopped—sometimes more than once—on the hard, slippery surface. Teens would get up laughing, though obviously in pain. Small children and adults tended to sit or kneel where they fell and cry until the pain subsided. Sprains and broken bones weren't uncommon, and fishermen were diligent in warning pregnant women and people carrying infants.

His hands filled with fishing rods, bait bucket, and the dip net, Jim cocked his head at small sandpipers skittering over the boulders. "Ruddy turnstones. Aren't they beautiful?"

The orange-legged, dark-bibbed birds alternately raced to feed in the bright green seaweed exposed by wave troughs or to flee oncoming waves.

"Are we going fishing or birding?" Charles groused.

Jim followed him across the boulders, but Jeff held Bill back a few steps. "What?" Bill asked.

"Jim's gained at least twenty pounds. We need to make sure he doesn't tumble. You know how accident prone he is, and he's so fat he might have a heart attack."

"That's mighty neighborly of you. What if he takes the best fishing spot?"

"What best fishing spot? And Maggie will kill me, if he kills himself."

"Jeffrey, you're as pussy-whipped as he is."

Jeff winked. "Hey, Jimmy," he called out, "watch out for the black moss."

At the half-way mark, four-tenth of a mile out, Charles stopped beside an outcropping that extended thirty feet into the ship channel. "We've had our best luck here, Jim."

Breathless and wheezing, Jim was grateful they didn't have to go further. Lugging the twenty pounds of fish he planned to catch back to the pickup would tax his energy reserve even more.

"Looks good to me."

* * *

"Mansfield Investigative Services."

"Hello? May I speak with Mrs. Mansfield?"

"Whom shall I say is calling, please?"

"Helen Matthews. From Kingwood."

"Is she expecting your call?"

Helen held her tongue. "No, but I have a matter of utmost urgency."

"Is it all right if I place you on hold for a moment?"

"If you must."

After a brief pause, Helen's limited patience was rewarded.

"Good morning, this is Edith Mansfield. How may I help you, Ms. Matthews? Or is it Mrs.?"

"Mrs. You were recommended to me by Jane Batts."

"Janie? Yes, go on. Wait a minute. Would you mind if I tape our conversation? It'll save time, if I accept your case."

"Fine, but let's get on with it."

Mansfield engaged the recorder. "Shoot."

"My daughter's bipolar."

"My condolences, but what does that have to do with me in Corpus Christi?"

"She's having an affair."

"How old is your daughter, Mrs. Matthews?"

"Twenty-nine."

"Then she can do whatever she wants."

"Not my daughter, she can't."

"Well, since you already know she's having an affair and she lives in Kingwood, I can't help you. It's too far away, and I don't have a permit to shoot playboys or philandering husbands."

"That's just it. I don't know who her lover is. I haven't seen him."

What am I missing? "Then how can you be sure your daughter's having an affair?"

"She tricked me into leaving her behind in Port Aransas. She wouldn't do that for any other reason, and she's been acting strangely this past year."

Matthews wasn't making much sense. "So, you want me to find out *if* your daughter's having an affair?"

"If you insist in putting it that way, yes, but she *is* having an affair. And I want to protect people. She's dangerous. She attacked a poor little old man at Paradise Pond two days ago."

"Mrs. Matthews, how long does your daughter plan to stay in the area? I need to tell you, up front, that I won't follow her to Kingwood. I have all the work I need here, and there are plenty of private investigators in Houston."

"She'll be there until Friday. And money's no object, I'll pay whatever you require."

Now, the woman's talking. "That doesn't leave much time. It will be difficult to rearrange my schedule, and I may need to bring in an associate."

"I said I'd cover all costs."

"Mrs. Matthews, I need your daughter's full name, where she's staying, and all the particulars. And ... please ... don't leave out anything."

* * *

Jim positioned his five-gallon bucket on a concrete platform just beyond the outcropping and sat on its padded lid. The spot protected him from splashing waves and ship wakes, except when the wind and tide were unusually high. Jeff sat a few feet away. Their bait buckets between them remained essentially unused.

The two fishermen relieved their boredom by observing the scenes around them. Dolphins surfed and leapt in the bow waves of freighters and tankers travelling through the channel. A small dolphin played with an escaped beach ball. Sea turtles rose to the surface, took quick glances in the fishermen's direction, and paddled rapidly back into the depths. Hundreds of blue-purple Portuguese Man of War jellyfish-like organisms floated past. Large flocks of gulls and pelicans trailed returning shrimp boats. Ten tugboats towed a huge oil rig platform into the Gulf.

The sights were interesting, but Jim's premonition that they would catch their limits quickly didn't materialize. He and his friends hadn't caught a single fish.

Fishermen on the other side of the jetty were catching large Spanish mackerel, and Jeff caved. "I've had it, Jim. I'm chasing the mackerel."

He was immediately successful.

Jim held fast for fifteen minutes, but he should have followed Jeff. So many sheepshead fishermen had become mackerel fishermen, by then, only one boulder was left. It was difficult to reach, and rogue waves splashing it made the footing difficult. He stepped warily over the wide gap and began to fish.

His hook snagged in the rocks on his first cast. Bracing as best he could, he heaved back on his rod. The heavy line didn't break, and the hook didn't come loose. He debated cutting the line but not much remained on the spool. He took a short dowel rod from his pocket, wrapped the line around it several times, and pulled.

A group of pelicans and terns began plunging into the surf in front of him, plucking up bait fish panicked or cut in two by the feeding mackerel. Gulls joined the fray. The wondrous sight evoked a heartfelt prayer of gratitude from Jim, but his hook and sinker were still caught fast. For leverage, he straddled the gap between the boulders, and heaved—just as a majestic, black-crowned, light-gray sandwich tern wheeled ten-feet in front of him and plummeted into the surf.

Distracted, Jim lost his footing and slipped into the chasm between the boulders. Searing pain burned his shins as they scraped the ragged-edged granite. His palms stung when he caught the front boulder to keep from cracking his skull. Driftwood between the two boulders prevented him from becoming wedged at the base of the boulders—in water that rose and fell up to three feet in the surging waves.

Hands and bulging belly pressed painfully against barnacles, eyes tightly-closed, Jim waited for the pain to subside. As it numbed, humiliation kicked in. It would be tough to pretend he planned his tumble. The realization he could be injured followed. Breathing deeply, he opened his eyes and gazed up at Jeff and two other fishermen towering above him.

Jeff's eyes bulged with concern. "Are you hurt, Jimmy?"

Jim took a quavering breath and reached out his hand. "I'm not sure. Can you help me up?"

Jeff and the fishermen pulled and grunted without success. The slippery footing endangered them, as well, and Jim wasn't extracted until Bill, Charles, and additional help arrived.

"Ooh, Jimmy," Bill said, when he saw raw, mangled flesh on Jim's left shin and blood streaming into both sneakers, "Marsha's not going like this."

Jim gulped. Marsha had been right. Fat chance he'd ever live this down.

Jeff blanched. "Looks like you need some water and a bandage for those shins, Jimmy. You're bleeding like mad."

Jim looked down and wished he hadn't. His left shin looked like someone pasted a six-inch-long, two-inch-wide piece of raw hamburger meat to it. His right shin and calf were scraped, but not as badly. And, as Jeff had noted, his shins bled profusely.

Bill poured water on his left shin, and Charles pressed a paper napkin to the wound to stifle the blood flow.

Nauseated, Jim covered the gash on his right shin with his handkerchief to keep from looking at it. "I'm going to the clinic on Alister Street to have my legs treated."

"I'll take you," Jeff said.

"I'm fine. I'll be back as soon as they clean me up."

"You sure you can walk?"

His friends stared dubiously, amazed he hadn't broken a leg or an ankle on the granite boulders.

Jim put his full weight on his legs and took several steps. "Yeah."

Bill held out Jim's mangled fishing equipment. "You broke your rod and reel, old buddy."

Trying not to think about his wounds, Jim joked, "In that case, they're yours." He pointed at his net and five-gallon bucket. "Can you take my things back to the RV if you catch your limit before I get back?"

"Sure thing," Bill said, looking like he didn't expect him back on the jetty that day.

Jim didn't rest as often as he usually did when leaving the jetty. Heart pounding, neck pulsing, adrenaline pushed him on. People gawked, but few commented.

Finding the emergency clinic closed, he decided to return to his RV to clean his wounds. Thoughts of Marsha, if he developed an infection, changed his mind, and he drove to a hospital he'd seen in Corpus Christi.

The check-in nurse in the Emergency Room scowled at his legs. "Those look awful." She took his medical information and logged him in at nine-thirty a.m.

The triage nurse examined him about ten, told him it would be a few minutes before a room was ready, and sent him back to the waiting room.

At one p.m., she returned from lunch. "You still here?"

A few minutes later, she poked her head out the door and beckoned. She led him through her office, down the broad hall, and into an examination room.

Ten minutes later, a young man entered and introduced himself. "I'm Jim Edwards. How are you doing?"

Jim automatically said, "Fine," then felt foolish.

Edwards examined his legs, hands, and stomach. "Let's get these wounds cleaned up."

He bathed them and applied antiseptic. "The jetties are contaminated with fish blood and bird poop, and the water isn't clean to begin with, so you did the right thing by coming in."

Thirty minutes later, four hours after he'd arrived at the ER, a doctor walked in complaining that the ER was so full of patients he hadn't had lunch yet.

Jim nodded. *Welcome to the club.*

"That's quite a scrape on your left shin," the doctor noted. "The right one looks much cleaner."

He poked around the wounds, while Jim struggled to keep from crying out, then marked the edges with a permanent marker.

"Nothing appears broken, Mr. Smith, but shin wounds don't get much blood flow and can take forever to heal. Keep your leg elevated as much as possible and come back to the ER if the redness spreads." He stared pointedly. "You need to stay away from the jetties and out of the Gulf until these heal."

Jim clenched his teeth. His stupidity had ruined a major purpose for the trip—fishing with friends.

The doctor ordered a tetanus shot, wrote a prescription for an antibiotic, and left.

After the shot, Jim expected to leave, too, but he had to wait until two more doctors repeated the first doctor's procedures and comments.

"You're free to go, Jim. Follow me," Jim Edwards said, after applying bandages, reading the medical instructions to him, and giving him a copy.

Jim drove to a nearby Walmart to fill the prescription. Remarkably, no one acknowledged his bloody socks, shoes, and bandages except a girl about three.

"*Ooh!*" she exclaimed, throwing herself against her mother and wrapping her arms tightly around her mother's leg. "Look, Mommy, Shrek has a boo-boo."

"It's not polite to point," her young mother whispered.

The girl's comments gave Jim pause. He knew he was fat. Was he also green?

The pharmacist added more bad news—no iron, antacids, or dairy products within two hours of taking the antibiotic. Twice a day.

Jim frowned at the thought of restricting his diet that many hours. He liked to eat and eat well. Sometimes that required a Tums or two, and occasionally a daily regime of Omeprazole, but the taste was worth the discomfort.

Traveling back to his RV, he pondered his upcoming conversation with Marsha. *I'm a dead man.* It had been seven hours since his injury, and he hadn't had the presence of mind to call her. By now Maggie and the girls would have informed her of his injury. Aware of that, he did the logical thing. Waited until he reached his RV to call her.

"Hey, Marsha."

"I heard you hurt yourself ... this morning."

The I-told-you-sos came frequently throughout the rest of the conversation.

"You need to come home, tomorrow," Marsha insisted. "I have to take care of you."

Jim didn't find the thought of being around two energetic grandchildren appealing. Marsha would demand help, and there would be no keeping his legs elevated. No rest, either, based on past experiences. He pictured the twelve-hour drive home with his legs down and blood leaking into his shoes.

"I have to keep my legs elevated, and I want to rest a day or so to make sure the bleeding stops. It's soaking through the bandages."

Marsha grudgingly agreed. "Do exactly what the doctors told you. And let Maggie help ... she's a healer."

"I'll be fine."

After the call ended, Jim swallowed a tablet with a glass of water. Afraid of what he could or couldn't consume, he decided to wait two hours before eating. He showered, changed, and hobbled to the game room.

Maggie nonchalantly lifted her eyes from her card hand. "The mountain goat returns."

"Look at those bandages," Patsy said. "Marsha's going to throw a hissy fit when she finds out."

"Somebody already told her," Jim said accusingly.

The guys looked relieved, and he realized their wives must have brow-beaten them for not taking him to the ER.

Charles was first to speak. "How'd it go? Ya gonna live?"

"We'll find out when I get back home."

Jim saved the worst news for last. "The doctor said no more jetties till the wounds heal. I can't even get near the water."

"*Ouch.*"

"How'd the fishing go today?" he asked.

Nadine rolled her eyes. "Men. They fall off the jetty, go to the ER, and the first thing they want to know is if the fish bit."

Maggie didn't take her eyes off her cards. "A nincompoopery if I ever saw one. Come on, let's play. I'm winning."

His friends' banter lifted Jim spirits. He received a chortle when he told them about the girl calling him Shrek.

Limping back to his RV, he reflected on how much he loved making this trip with such good friends. He wished Marsha could see it that way, too. Their children could find suitable babysitters. But his wife was doing what she loved best and what their grandchildren needed. The day was approaching when she would no longer have the energy required to care for them, and their grandchildren would be too old to want her around. He missed her terribly.

His stomach growled in sympathy.

12

Lonely Birders

Mary Elizabeth changed her mind about going home but spent Monday moping around the condo. She called her mother mid-afternoon to find that her father was doing well and was in relatively good spirits. They had a pleasant chat, the best since she'd turned eighteen.

The experience energized her enough that she went jogging on the beach late in the afternoon. It was disappointing only in that she didn't see a repeat of the pelican adventure. But afterwards, her energy level was insufficient to work out in the exercise room.

What happened, she wondered. She'd been so psyched earlier. She went to bed without eating and struggled through a second restless night.

* * *

Jim slept fitfully. His injured legs ached whenever he rolled over, regardless of the care he took. Several bathroom trips contributed to his agony, and each time he returned to discover more blood on a mat he'd purchased to prevent it from soaking into the mattress.

He felt so sure he couldn't sleep that he was surprised by light filtering through the roof vent when he woke up. He stayed in bed for a long while deciding how to spend his day. He couldn't permit the injury to keep him down, and walking should promote blood flow in his shins when he wasn't keeping them elevated. He planned to divide his time between Paradise Pond and the birding center, where he could rest his legs on observation benches.

It was only six-thirty a.m. Unable to go back to sleep, he rose and started the coffee. It reminded him of his food-restrictions and that he hadn't eaten since nine the previous evening—crackers, popcorn, and a soda pop. His usual late-night snack of a glass of milk and bread contained dairy products. Plus, heartburn would require the antacids he'd been warned about.

He washed down his antibiotic pill, blood pressure med, and low-dose aspirin with a large glass of water.

Was coffee legal? Taking a risk, he poured a cup but didn't add the non-dairy creamer. Easing into his recliner, he cranked the leg support high and relaxed to the music. He would go birding, later, then eat. It should be safe by then.

* * *

Mary Elizabeth awoke to a golden dawn. Heavy dew had turned the Windward Dunes' landscaping into a sparkling wonderland.

Hungry, she prepared a full breakfast and consumed the meal on the patio. A mistake. The people in the pools and hot tubs for early-morning dips and soaks generated emotions of emptiness and homesickness.

Grackle chatter and Eurasian collared-dove cooing filled the early morning air. The beige-colored doves cooed loudly, over and over. They might be describing her. She probably was coo-coo, like her mother kept telling her.

If the sunshine held, she could utilize the colors created by the early morning sun for decent photos. If not, the earlier she went birding the better. As she dressed, she had a fleeting thought. *I wonder what crud head's doing, today ... besides avoiding me.*

There were several people at the birding center ahead of her. Based on their Swarovski and Leica spotting scopes and binoculars, most were serious birders, not casual observers who called grebes ducks.

She took pictures of a green-winged teal paddling vigorously in an upright posture for short distances while spraying glimmering droplets in all directions.

A tri-colored heron in full breeding color took her breath away. Its vivid, two-toned blue back appeared dusted with wisps of amber-colored feathers. Its bright belly provided a contrasting white, as did the short, shaggy plume on its head atop its serpentine neck. Reddish legs, a strikingly blue, black-tipped bill, and blue-ringed, blood-red eyes completed its ensemble.

The heron plunged its bill into the water and captured two wriggling, silvery minnows. In the few seconds the bird contemplated how to swallow them both, Mary Elizabeth took twenty photos. The lighting was perfect, and she was as exhilarated as she'd been the first afternoon of her trip.

* * *

Jim limped along, his binoculars slung from one shoulder, camera dangling from the other. He'd changed his mind about driving and was walking the four blocks to Paradise Pond to pump blood to his shins. The bright morning sunlight warmed him, and the throbbing pain reminded him to be more careful in the future.

The breezy southeast wind and cloudless sky bode ill for encountering migratory birds. Without strong north winds or a storm in the Gulf, they often flew across its four-hundred-mile expanse in continuous flight.

Adverse conditions drove them from the Gulf in massive flocks. They saturated protected areas, such as Paradise Pond, in what was called a fallout. Jim joked to his friends it was because tiny birds, like warblers and hummingbirds, weren't strong swimmers, but it was no joking matter. Their lives depended on such oases for protection, rest, and nourishment.

He'd once witnessed a fallout and found it spectacular. Beyond belief. Birds of every size, color and shape flit about on most shrubs and tree limbs. Occurring before his birding days, the event had ignited his passion for nature photography. It also proved to be a mixed blessing. He raced back to the campground to invite his friends to see the incredible display of beauty, only to discover that most weren't interested. Had it been tiny alligators hanging from the limbs instead of the Joseph's coat of birds of many colors, he would have been trampled in the rush.

The day was so nice that Jim couldn't help being enthused even with painful, swollen legs. He pressed on, limping more, huffing more, second-guessing his decision to walk with each step. As it did for migrating birds, the pond would serve as his place of rest and recuperation.

* * *

Mary Elizabeth capped her camera and prepared to leave the birding center boardwalk, when a short, plump, attractive lady hailed her.

"Miss? Miss?"

"Me?" she asked, after glancing behind her.

"Yes, you. Can you help me identify a bird?"

Mary Elizabeth considered putting the woman off, but her mother ingrained the need to be respectful to matronly ladies—other than her mother.

"Which one?"

The woman pointed at the tri-colored heron. "That one. It keeps catching little fish. I know it's an egret, but I thought they were white."

Correcting the lady's misconception about color, Mary Elizabeth explained that egrets and herons were quite brilliantly-feathered during the breeding season.

The woman took her hand and patted it. "Thanks for setting me straight, sweetie. I'm Edith Mansfield."

She explained that she was a retired elementary schoolteacher who'd had her fill of volunteer work and was discovering the joys of bird-watching. She had eight grandchildren—three grandsons and five granddaughters—she visited when her children invited her. "What sucks is that they treat me like a slave baby-sitter and maid service."

The pretty ex-schoolteacher's use of colorful language startled Mary Elizabeth. At the same time, she knew the sensation. She also knew that the tiny woman wasn't as interested in looking at birds as in having someone to talk with. She kept trying to edge away, but the woman was on a roll.

"My husband, Tuck, short for Tucker, passed away four years, ago. We were grade school sweethearts even though he was in fifth grade and I was in the first. We married when I was sixteen, after my parents realized we were meant for each other. It's like that when they catch you in bed together." She described her marriage in explicit, eye-widening, ear-reddening detail.

The conversation had taken a turn Mary Elizabeth wanted to avoid. Help arrived. Another widow worked her way into the conversation.

The candidness of the mature ladies shocked Mary Elizabeth. Fibbing that a person was waiting for her at Paradise Pond, she excused herself. Only a little after nine, with daylight savings time, the early morning sunlight should provide vivid photos for at least two more hours.

* * *

Exhausted and aching, Jim stumbled to the first bench on the Paradise Pond boardwalk. When the pain decreased and his breathing approached normal, he hobbled to the third observation deck to start with the least grebes and work his way back.

The effort drained him, and the grebes showed no inclination to swim in his direction. Warblers and vireos flit overhead in the willows, but he lacked the energy to photograph them.

The same applied to the heavy-lidded yellow-crowned and black-crowned night-herons perched near him. At night they would make life miserable for crawfish and other aquatic life, but for now, they understood the meaning of life much better than he did.

Giving a prayer of thanks, he felt a longing and wished Marsha were sitting beside him. Such moments needed to be shared.

The birds and serenity filled Jim with peace. How could anyone be upset or depressed in such a bucolic setting while watching God's most beautiful creatures?

13
Birdzilla

A pterodactyl, clutching a four-foot-long branch, rose majestically over the tall trees to Jim's left. The head and neck of another extended from a mass of limbs, examined the offering, and accepted it. Awed, Jim took several pictures of the nesting great blue herons that reminded him of the dinosaurs.

Glancing back at the boardwalk, he jolted. Birdzilla stood at the first observation deck, still mother-free. He slouched, hoping the vulgar young woman wouldn't see him.

Mary Elizabeth spotted Pops as she scanned the pond through her binoculars. Something akin to happiness fluttered in her chest. She hurried to him.

Jim's heart beat with apprehension. He flinched when she thrust out her hand.

"I'm sorry about the other day," she said.

Surprised, Jim stared without speaking.

"I'm trying to apologize, you dumb fart."

"Young lady, can't you leave me alone?"

"Well, screw you."

Mary Elizabeth whirled and stalked away. Her steps faltered. She returned. Teary-eyed, she again held out her hand. "Why won't you let a person tell you they're sorry?"

It wasn't what Jim expected. He recalled the Lord's Prayer and took her hand. "I'm sorry, too. That was rude of me. Your apology's accepted. Will you accept mine?" He was surprised by the tears in her eyes—and the warmth surging through him.

Mary Elizabeth choked back the knot in her throat and nodded.

For the first time, she noticed his bandaged legs. "What the hell happened to you? Oops, please forgive the curse word."

Jim grinned. "Guess a tiger can't change its stripes."

The cliché reminded her of something her mother might say. "But this tiger will try. What happened?"

They spoke for more than an hour. She learned about Marsha's premonition, Jim's disaster on the jetty, and his travails at the ER. She told him her father had been struck by a car and had had an operation.

Finally tiring of Pops and young lady, Jim said, "Mary Elizabeth is a mouthful. Do you have a nickname?"

"Isn't it the most horrible name in the world? It sounds like I'm always being called down. Most of my childhood friends have sensible names ... like Jennifer, Lara, Betty, and Faith. All except for those with moms in my mother's circle, who chose to name them Mary something-or-the-other, too. My friends and cousins refused to be called by dual names, but Mother ignored me when I complained." Mary Elizabeth beamed. "So give me a nickname. Please."

"How about Mare?"

Mary Elizabeth chortled. "Oh lord, no."

"Mary's good, the mother of Jesus. So's Liz, the mother of John the Baptist. How about one of those?"

"I'd prefer Liz. I've heard Mary enough to last a lifetime."

The girl was trying hard to be friendly. "I'm Jim, but you can call me anything you want ... as long as you call me when it's time to eat."

"How corny. And mom-ish. Can I be your friend, Jim?"

"Of course, Liz."

She glanced at her watch. "Then, Jim, since you like to be called when it's time to eat, how about a snack? I'm treating." When he started to protest, she shook her head. "I won't take no for an answer. Your legs must be killing you. And you're squirming. Does you back hurt, too?"

The woman was perceptive. "Yes, but there's no way I'll let a lady treat me. I'm old school."

"We'll see about that. Besides, I couldn't live with myself if I let you walk all the way back to your RV."

Liz grabbed his arm just before they stepped off the boardwalk.

Jim's discomfort flooded back at the memory of their first meeting—and her touch. "What is it?"

"A white-eyed vireo," she said, pointing her camera at a five-and-a half-inch-long bird. "Note its yellow spectacles ... that usually means a vireo ... though not always. The hooked bill and white eyes give this little guy away. Otherwise, the olive-green back, yellowish sides, and distinct wing bars could fit several birds.

"My sister-in-law, Becky, who's an avid birder, attended a bird banding in Alabama. She said banders don't like them. Or maybe it's the other way around. White-eyed vireos give serious bites."

Her eyes rounded as she swung her camera upward. "It's our lucky day, Jim. Look at the American redstart above the vireo." She breathed heavily while taking its photo. "Incredible colors. I need to hire you as my guide."

At the parking lot Liz noticed the ex-schoolteacher stepping out of a Honda and waved at her. Meeting or seeing the same people at the various Port Aransas birding sites was common. Many spoke with foreign accents and carried expensive birding and photography equipment, which attested to the city's renown.

Jim noticed lights blink on a black Chevy Tahoe when Liz pressed her remote. He argued with himself and won. The odds that Liz was the driver of the SUV that forced him on the shoulder and caused the chain reaction of accidents were next to nil.

He climbed inside and sat uncomfortably, legs throbbing, despite the leg room. Could he be getting an infection? He would remove the bandages and look when he returned to the RV.

Liz backed up abruptly, then gunned the motor. The large vehicle fishtailed, showering the cars parked behind them with gravel.

"Whoa, this is a little fast, isn't it, Liz? What if the gravel chips the paint on these other cars?"

She looked surprised. "I hadn't thought about that." She smiled. "At least you didn't scream like Mother would have."

Her statement conjured up the image of the screaming blue-haired lady. Jim couldn't keep his suspicions to himself any longer. "Liz, I have a story. On my way down here, a Black Tahoe passed me near Copano Bay. The driver ran me onto the shoulder and barely missed a motorhome coming from the opposite direction. You didn't have any excitement like that, did you?"

Liz's eyes narrowed. "So, you're the shithead. Slow assholes like you shouldn't be allowed on the road. You backed up cars for miles behind you. You were a fucking menace."

Jim scowled. "The tiger bares her teeth. I see it the opposite way."

"Sorry about calling you a shi— You wouldn't move over for the guy behind you, so why would you have moved over for me?"

"The shoulder was too narrow for my rig. And slanted. Plus, we were near Fulton, where the road expands to four lanes."

He voiced a thought. "Do you know you started a chain reaction accident that wrecked thirteen vehicles?"

Startled, Liz gawked.

"I'm supposed to turn you in to the Texas Highway Patrol. An officer gave me his card."

Liz pulled into the car wash ramp at the bend where Cut-off Road became Avenue G. "You're telling the truth, aren't you? You're not making this up."

"Didn't you see it on television?"

She shook her head. "I haven't watched TV since I've been here. Or read a paper." She seemed perplexed. "Mother did, but she didn't mention it." Liz's hands trembled on the steering wheel. "So ... are you going to turn me in?"

"You could save me the trouble by doing it yourself."

"I'll think about it."

She drove around the car wash and turned toward Avenue G.

When they arrived at the Windward Dunes, Jim wondered if there was a restaurant in the condominiums. He didn't see a sign for one.

"Wait here." Liz disappeared through the lobby doors and returned pushing a wheelchair.

Jim opened the door and started to protest.

"Shut up. I'm in charge. Sit."

Jim reluctantly obeyed. His body pressed against the seatback as she shoved him toward the condo. "Reckless driver. Can't resist the urge to speed, can you? Please, for my sake, watch for oncoming traffic before you pass anyone. I'd hate to cause a thirteen-wheelchair pileup."

"Gutless old fogey."

The desk clerk and people in the lobby stared.

"My grandpa," Liz explained. "He broke both legs in a bar fight."

Jim blushed and closed his eyes.

In the condo she made him lie on the sofa and elevated his legs with pillows. "Brunch in ten minutes. And, FYI, I'm thinking about the wreck."

She turned on the radio.

Jim heard KLUX's soothing music. "This is the same station I listen to."

The music put him at ease and immediately to sleep. He didn't feel Liz's hand on his forehead.

He awoke an hour later to the smell of an omelet like his mother used to make—with green peas and onions. Had he died and gone to heaven?

"Well, well, Rip Van Winkle awakens. Get up, old fart. Stop pretending you're hurt." Liz feigned a sheepish look. "It is all right to call you an old fart, isn't it?"

"I guess, but I prefer Jim. It's shorter. By the way, where did you learn to make a Spanish omelet? My mother made them the same way."

"It's something Mother taught me. An old family recipe. I know it's not a lunch item, but with her gone, I need to get rid of the extra eggs."

Liz helped him to his feet. "You need to exercise. You're way out of shape."

Jim's body ached. "Thanks for the help. I guess I hurt myself a little more than I thought."

Liz leaned into him. "My pleasure," she teased. But was she was teasing? Something about Jim made her do things she didn't understand—like desiring body contact.

She felt flustered. Was he a surrogate father, something she missed? Something more? He was the first stranger she'd been alone with for an entire morning. The first man with whom she'd taken such liberties.

They ate on the patio, enjoying the courtyard view. When Jim commented that her omelet tasted exactly like his mother's, she beamed.

Their conversation turned to birding for the first time. She downloaded the photos from her camera into her laptop.

Jim admired the teal splashing across the lake. The spectacular colors of the tri-colored heron affected him as much as if he'd been standing beside her when she took the pictures. Captivated, he said, "You sure have a nice camera ... Unh."

The elbow poke in his ribs masked his leg pain.

"A photographer gets up early to use the best lighting. She positions herself to capture the subject, makes sure her lenses are sparkling clear, uses the proper settings, and all you can say is nice *camera*? Jim, you're a turd. Oops, sorry," Liz said unapologetically while winking.

"I guess I don't appreciate a true artist when I see one. I mean it. You're good. Great even."

"You say the sweetest things."

When she laughed, Jim noticed her lips. Full and wide, they appeared soft. When she stared quizzically, he blushed and returned his attention to the photos on her laptop monitor.

The pleasant afternoon passed quickly, and the time for paying for the crime arrived. "Liz, are you turning yourself in, or will I have to do it?"

She fixed him with an unblinking stare. "You will."

"But you caused an accident that put people in the hospital and cost them a lot of money."

"Jim, you were as responsible for the accident as I was."

"But—"

"You didn't wreck. And you told me the woman driving the motorhome didn't, either. That means the people behind you were tailgating and driving recklessly. You and I didn't have anything to do with that."

"But if you hadn't passed in a no-passing—"

"It wasn't a no-passing zone."

"But it was unsafe to pass."

"I didn't hit you or the motorhome. I made it around."

Jim knew he'd have a hard time with the card on his dinette table that evening. "I need to return to my RV. My friends will check on me, and if they think I'm dead or unconscious, they'll call Marsha and there'll be hell to pay."

"My, my, looks like zebras *can* change stripes, Mr. Potty Mouth."

Both laughed, Jim in spite of himself.

Liz let him walk to the SUV. When they passed through the lobby, the clerk noticed. "Is your grandfather feeling better?"

Liz interlinked her arm with Jim's, leaned into him, and winked at the clerk. "He does, *now.*"

"Are you trying to embarrass me to death?" Jim whispered out of the side of his mouth.

Liz giggled but reflected. *Why on earth did I say that?*

On the way to the resort, she asked if he would go birding with her the next day. Jim thought he shouldn't but said he would.

Maggie stood at the door to Jim's fifth-wheel when they arrived. Her eyes narrowed, and Jim turned brilliant red. "Maggie, this is Liz..." *What's her last name?* "Matthews," he recalled.

"Liz, this is my friend Maggie Saunders from my RV club."

Maggie's voice was pleasant, when she and Liz shook hands, but she looked suspicious. "It's nice to meet you, Liz, but what are you doing with Jimmy?"

"Giving him a ride home from Paradise Pond. He walked when he should have driven."

Maggie nodded. "Figures."

"See you tomorrow, Jim." Liz hugged him and then held out her hand. "It's been nice meeting you, Maggie. We'll see each other again."

She waved out the window as she drove away.

"What was that all about, buster?"

"You wouldn't believe me if I told you, Maggie."

"Try me."

"It's the girl I told you about, the one who mugged me at Paradise Pond Saturday afternoon. She came up, apologized, and took me out to lunch."

Maggie glanced at her watch. "You left about nine this morning, and it's almost six. Regardless of when and where she took you, that's a pretty long lunch. You'll have explaining to do tonight. To Marsha too. I called her when you didn't answer my knock and your pickup was here. We thought you might be unconscious, and we might've been right. You were smiling before you saw me, then blushed like the proverbial fox in the chicken coop."

She started striding away. "See you in the game room at seven .... unless Marsha's still tongue-lashing your ears."

Jim climbed into his RV. He hadn't planned to stay long at Paradise Pond, so he hadn't taken his phone. "It wasn't my fault I was kidnapped," he whispered with a smile.

The phone wasn't turned on, and he was afraid to do it. He had good reason.

Marsha was crying. "Jim, I was beside myself."

He received his third browbeating in four days. So much for good omens. He needed to become better at taking care of himself—and keeping her informed. "I'm sorry, Marsha, I promise to—"

"Well, see that you do."

"I promise. I love you, darling."

"I love you, too, you big dumb idiot."

It was the best Jim could hope for.

After taking his evening antibiotic, drinking a large glass of water, and laying on his sofa with his leg elevated for an hour, he limped toward the game room to face the inquisition. He hoped he would survive. His carelessness-induced starvation, too. He'd have to set up an eating schedule and get on a routine.

His friends should have been well into the first game of Pegs and Jokers when he arrived. Instead, they were talking and laughing. The laughing stopped, and they put on thoughtful faces. Or maybe faces fighting back laughter.

"Hi, Jimmy. Have you called Marsha, yet?" Maggie needled. "You didn't accidentally forget to call her, did you?"

"That's what took me so long," he said, a tad too defensively.

"What's this about you hiring a nurse?" Patsy couldn't maintain a straight face.

"I cut my pinky cleaning fish," Charles said. "You have her number? From what Maggie said, any fee would be worth it."

Nadine didn't appear convinced with Jim's first response. "Are you sure you told Marsha the whole story? I hear Ms. Liz doesn't look anything like a nurse."

Jeff winked and nudged him in the ribs. "You, sly dog."

Bill eyed him up and down. "Looks can sure be deceiving, Jim. But maybe some women like bald headed, beer-bellied, gorilla-sized Neanderthal types."

"Didn't Maggie tell you?" Jim protested. "She's the woman who roughed me up at Paradise Pond on Saturday. She apologized and took me to lunch."

"A six-hour lunch," Maggie said, as matter-of-factly as if she was filing her fingernails.

Charles whistled. "A six-hour lunch? Hey Bill, maybe that's why Jim's belly looks a bit full."

"The girl isn't pretty. She's a photographer and wanted to show me her—"

"Etchings? Sure," Patsy interjected. "Anyone want to buy my bridge in Havasu, Arizona?" She laughed. "And from what Maggie told us, if you think Miss Liz is plain, heaven only knows what you think about us. A dusky blonde, with legs eight feet long, an hourglass figure, and a swing a man would want on his porch? Someone, hand me a cellphone, I'm calling Marsha to set the record straight."

"Where did you see these photos?" Maggie asked.

Trying to explain made things worse.

From that point on, she questioned him like a lawyer, and things went downhill, ribbing-wise. Jim was glad that his friends knew his character.

At the nine o'clock intermission, Maggie made it up to him.

"I figured you wouldn't have time to eat before coming to the clubhouse, so I baked you a chicken breast." Patsy and Nadine had brought dishes and dessert for him, too.

After the unmerciful teasing, Jim limped back to his RV, not too much the worse for wear. He showered before going to bed. The swelling on his left shin was bloody, but within the marks the doctor had drawn.

He fell feverishly asleep listening to KLUX.

* * *

Liz jogged three miles and exercised an hour. After showering and eating supper, she spent several hours editing photos to show Jim the next day. She hoped her pictures would provide him the incentive to upgrade his equipment. She wanted to impress him, too. Satisfied and happy, she slept soundly for the first time in three nights.

14
Joining the Flock

The previous evening, Jim's brain had decided to take his antibiotic pills at six in the morning and six in the evening. This morning, his body mutinied. Stiff and sore, he could barely roll out of bed. Bracing against the wall, he staggered past the radio he left on all night and slumped heavily in a recliner. The bandages weren't bright red, so his legs may have stopped bleeding. When he removed the bandages, the wounds were damp from antibiotic cream, and he decided to forego re-bandaging them. The air might do them good.

He chased his medicine with a full glass of water, reset the alarm to 7:45, and drifted off to sleep.

He rose with a start. Liz had said they'd go birding but didn't say when. He knew where she lived but didn't have her phone number, and she hadn't asked for his. Maybe she'd fulfilled her mission of apologizing, and he wouldn't see her again. That would be a good thing.

Jim mulled their situation. She'd been more pleasant, the day before, but it would be best if they didn't see each other again. Old enough to be her grandfather and injured, he'd just tie her down. More importantly, he was married and shouldn't go birding with an unmarried woman.

In addition, Liz had issues. He recalled her pinning him against the Paradise Pond railing and shoving her camera in his face—her mother on the verge of calling for a straitjacket. Liz was a proven curser and reckless driver who might have a death wish—like when she passed him near Fulton. Why did she call her father Frank? Was that part of her problem? Some type of abuse, perhaps? A knot formed in his gut. He still had to turn her in for causing the wrecks.

She might even be one of those fatal-attraction types. Pleasant-looking, but deadly—after trying to seduce him for money. Some older men were suckers, that way.

But what about her tears when she asked for his forgiveness? The way she treated him as if she was a mother hen and he her hurt chick?

He hoped she wouldn't come.

No longer sleepy, he pulled on a gray T-shirt he purchased in Cozumel during a Gulf cruise he and Marsha had taken a couple of years earlier. It had a picture of a large green iguana on the back. He bet it would make the birds nervous, although he'd heard somewhere that iguanas were herbivores.

Deciding it didn't matter what his friends called him, he put on tan cargo shorts to allow his injuries to get air and returned to the recliner.

He heard a light tapping on the door and realized he'd fallen asleep. Leaning forward, he unlocked it. It was probably Maggie or Bill wanting to check on him. "Come on in."

Liz bounced in, wearing a baggy, long-sleeved blue sports shirt, pants that resembled doctors' scrubs, and a concerned look. "How's my patient?" She bent for a closer examination. "Not good ... looks like someone tied a wildcat to your leg. You sure did a number on yourself, at least a ten in damage." She frowned. "It's still badly swollen. When are you supposed to go back to the ER?"

"Tomorrow."

"I'm worried about you. I'll pick you up at seven."

"One of my friends is taking me," Jim said, disgusted by his lie.

Liz studied his face. "I'd play poker with you anytime. If I played cards ... which I don't. I'll be here at seven, no matter what. If your friends show up, we'll caravan."

Jim blushed deep red. Despite his lie, she hadn't become mad. Maybe the tiger *was* changing her stripes. "I'm sorry I lied. I'm uncomfortable being with you and feel like I'm taking advantage of your hospitality."

She chuckled. "I'm your mentor. You pissed me off Saturday, but I know you want to photograph birds. I'm going to make sure you get some decent equipment and give you a few pointers. *Then* I'll get out of your life." *But why do I not want to be out of it?*

"How many friends did you say were here with you?" she asked.

"Six. Maggie and her husband, Jeff, Bill and Patsy Warner, and Charles and Nadine Danielson."

Liz didn't explain her request. "Ready to go birding?"

"I haven't had breakfast yet, and I can't eat for two hours before or after taking my antibiotic. I took it at six."

Liz glanced at her watch, as he looked at the clock over the door.

As if on cue, the alarm chimed in the bedroom. Liz laughed, found the clock on the bookshelf over the bed, and turned it off. Returning, she held her nose with a thumb and forefinger. "When was the last time you changed your bed linens?"

Jim looked guilty. "I'm not sure about the bedding, maybe yesterday."

Liz scrunched her face. "You're in serious need of bed-etiquette training. And getting your mouth washed out with soap. Now, where's the food, and I'll make breakfast?

"By the way, you're just like my mother. She always makes me wait before we go birding ... sometimes for hours."

"There's some in the cabinets over my head, some in the refrigerator, and canned goods in the pantry beside the stove."

Purposely leaning against him when she searched the cabinets, she shivered involuntarily.

Jim did, too.

"We've already had omelet. Hmm, this looks legal." She pulled out pancake mix and found syrup in the pantry. "Where's an apron?" At Jim's blank stare, she murmured sarcastically, "Thanks for the help," and began opening kitchen drawers.

She was stirring the pancake mix when another knock sounded on the door. Jim jerked, feeling guilty as sin for ogling her swaying hips.

Maggie poked her head through the door and held out a sack. "A little something for the invalid." She gawked.

Jim didn't know what to say.

Liz smiled cheerily. "Hi Maggie. Between you and me, we'll fatten Jim up in no time ... him being anorexic and all ... but we probably should make a schedule, so we can have some meals off."

Maggie appeared caught off-guard for the first time since Jim had known her.

Her mouth opened and moved, but no words came out.

He blushed. "Remember? Liz and I are going birding today. She showed up early and volunteered to make breakfast for me. How's that for a birding friend?"

Looking skeptical, Maggie found her voice. "Jimmy's wife, *Marsha*, will be happy to know you're taking such good care of him, Liz. I'll tell her he's in good hands."

Liz's expression didn't change. "I don't know about the hands part, but I'll make sure he eats right, doesn't bird too long on those legs, and learns a little about photography." She nodded toward the bed visible through the open doorway. "And learns he needs to make his bed every day."

Maggie peered at the rumpled bed and then at Jim's legs. "Oh dear." She'd known the wounds were worse than he let on, despite his unusual willingness to take himself to the ER. "I don't like the looks of these, Jimmy."

"They don't hurt, and I'm going back to the ER, tomorrow."

She stared dubiously.

Liz changed the subject. "In case Jim hasn't told you, I was here on a week-long birding trip with my mother. She went home due to an emergency, and this old fart," she flicked her eyes in Jim's direction, "seems safe to me. Especially since he has nice friends like you. I dislike birding by myself. It isn't safe these days."

That satisfied Maggie. "Jimmy, you're a lucky old geezer."

Turning, she and Liz acted like they'd been friends for years. "I have bacon and biscuits in this bag, Liz. I'll help."

Forty-five minutes later, after eating their fill and consuming a pot of Maggie's delicious coffee, Maggie invited Liz to play Pegs and Jokers at the clubhouse that evening. "We need six or eight to play, and Jimmy's the odd man out. You can be Marsha, tonight." Her inner sense hummed softly. "You can be Marsha today, too. Keep a close eye on him. He tends to fall off jetties."

Jim rolled his eyes.

15
Spooning

"Put on sunscreen and change into something more sun-safe," Liz commanded.

"I want my wounds to get air," Jim countered. When she didn't budge, he relented. "I have some clothes like yours. We can be twins."

Liz flashed a false frown. "My, you're corny. I can't believe you'd think of something like that. Or even suggest it." She moved to the other recliner to wait. "Do it. People will think I'm your doting granddaughter."

"Granddaughter?" Liz's father was seventy-four. Helen seventy. He was only sixty-seven. "Your parents are older than I am."

"But they look ten years younger." She cocked her head. "I'm going to have to work on that."

"You only have one more day. Your week's up Friday."

"I may have to do something about that, too." Liz said, so quietly Jim couldn't hear, but he was already on his way to the bedroom.

When he reappeared, she pretended to poke a finger down her throat.

Once again Jim noticed her long, lovely fingers. Limping to the sofa, he picked up his binoculars and camera, hung them on his shoulders, hobbled to the door, and held it open. "Let's go. I can't suffer this humiliation without a goal in mind."

"You haven't forgotten anything, have you?" Liz asked innocently.

"No."

"You're absolutely positive?"

Jim checked his equipment, felt his wallet and keys. "I give up."

"*Men.* Or, maybe it's just you." Liz pointed at the table. "Your cellphone. What if Marsha calls? Or one of your friends worries that I'm doing something bad to you?"

Red-faced, he stared at his cellphone—turned off as usual. He contemplated the distance. "Could you bring it to me? For a tiger, you're great to have around."

Liz laughed and blew him a kiss—a first for her—and retrieved his phone.

"Where would you prefer to go this morning?" She watched anxiously as Jim painfully eased his bulk down the RV steps.

"There's a small pond behind the ballpark. I've seen spoonbills and ducks there."

"I've been to Port Aransas many times, and this is the first I've heard of it. But Mother takes hours to get ready and doesn't like long walks, so I rarely bird the nature trails."

"I heard it mentioned at the birding center, a couple of years ago. It's not bad."

"Okay, it's worth a shot. I'm always on the lookout for birds in pretty surroundings."

They parked on the north end of the parking lot, next to the baseball field. When Jim groaned while exiting the Tahoe, Liz told him she'd brought a wheelchair."

Pride refused to let him be treated like an invalid. "I'm fine, and it's not far."
"Bring it on yourself."

A hundred yards later, Jim wished he hadn't been so macho. His left leg burned. Every muscle ached.

Liz frowned at his pronounced limp and grim expression but didn't say anything. He could save face—for now.

The path encircled the ball field and skateboard park. Half-way around, it intersected with another trail. A cattail-lined pond abutted the intersection. A benchless gazebo graced its far bank.

From the gazebo, the trail meandered a mile through native bush and grassland to Charlie's Pasture Preserve Pavilion near the ship channel. Nature trails from the pavilion extended for miles alongside ponds, bayside lagoons, desert landscapes, and marshes.

Gasping, Jim sat heavily on the second bench they encountered and pointed at the pond. "Spoonbills."

Liz had noticed, but Jim's difficulty and labored breathing worried her. "Where do you hurt?"

He gave a pained expression. "All over my body, more than any place else."

She laughed. "You are a dear. You rest while I get the wheelchair."

When he started to protest and stand, Liz raised her hand. "Sit." He settled back. "Stay." He looked sheepish. Leaning forward, she softly grasped the sides of his head, tipped it forward, and kissed his bald spot. "Good Boy."

Trembling, Liz wondered why she felt the need for physical contact. Why did it make her so...? She flushed and hurried away. It was the first time she'd been bold enough to kiss a man, a male, anyone, in such a manner.

Jim wondered if she might be a prostitute and the woman with her the first day her madam. It fit. Get his attention by roughing him up. Befriend him. Get in his knickers for a ton of money.

Impossible. She'd seen his pickup and fifth-wheel. And her tears, when he ignored her first apology, were real. He prayed for forgiveness for not trusting her. And for the sensations that had swept through his body when she caressed his cheeks and pressed of her soft lips against his head.

When she returned, Liz watched Jim fiddle with the eyepieces of his binoculars. "May I see those, please?"

He looked up. "Sure."

She replaced them with binoculars attached to a harness. "These are Mother's. Hold out your arms ... lean forward."

Jim did as she ordered, and she slipped the straps around his arms and over his head, glad they reached around his body. She showed him how to adjust the straps. "Fit them to your chest until they're comfortable. You won't even feel them after a while, and they won't interfere with your new camera."

"You brought me a new camera?"

"No, you're going to buy one. Tomorrow."

The heft of the binoculars impressed him. Though larger than his, their weight didn't cause the harness straps to bite into his shoulders. His lower jaw dropped when he peered through them. A brilliant new world burst into view, and he didn't even have to adjust the focus. It was automatic. The colors were vibrant. "These are great. How much do they cost?"

"A couple of thousand or so."

Jim choked. "Did I hear you right?"

"What's a hobby worth? These are Swarovski's." Noticing Jim's disappointment, she quickly added, "But you can get some decent ones for a fourth that much."

Liz ordered him to sit the wheelchair. Ignoring his protest, she dropped his binoculars in the first trash can they passed.

The roseate spoonbills waded in the shallow water, working their bills from side to side.

Liz moved slowly, trying to not flush them. Aware that birds ignored cattle and horses, she decided that pushing the wheelchair could be helping. The spoonbills might believe that she and Jim were a four-legged animal, not two humans. Whatever the reason, the birds ignored them.

Except for their bald heads and gray-green, spoon-shaped bills, spoonbills would be contenders in a bird beauty contest. Adults were a riot of color. Their bills looked scaly, almost reptilian. Their eyes looked like pieces of Red Hots candy stuck to yellow-orange teardrops. A thin band of feathers resembling runny black paint separated the birds' heads from a splash of red and pink at the top of their necks. The rest of their necks and first half of their backs were white that gradually faded to pink. Feathers at the base of their neck were blood red. Orange feathers outlined their wings and graced their tails. Their shoulders appeared to be dripping blood, and their red legs had black feet.

Although Jim had seen spoonbills many times before, he soaked up their beauty. "Aren't they fascinating, Liz. The world's best graphic artists can't match the Lord's imagination and artistry."

"Did you know that spoonbills' colors are diet-related, Jim? First-year spoonbills are mostly white, and adolescents mostly pink."

He shook his head and examined the younger birds. Their bills were gray and pink, without the scaly appearance. They weren't yet bald. Birds didn't get any cuter, no matter their bill shapes.

Though small, the pond contained an island. Liz grabbed Jim's arm to get his attention. "See the pair of ducks sleeping at the left tip of the island ... the beige ones with the striped sides? You would see their blue bills, if they weren't tucked away."

Her touch made him self-conscious, but he didn't draw back. Peering where she pointed, all he saw were tawny, purplish-brown mounds streaked with white.

"What are they?"

"Fulvous whistling-ducks. Here, take my camera and shoot the spoonbills. I've put it on program, so all you have to do is point and shoot. It's in the multiple shot mode, so it'll take pictures as long as you hold the button down. And be sure to support the lens rather than the camera." She demonstrated cradling the heavy lens. "Have at it."

Jim appreciated Liz's strength and stamina. "I'm impressed. How do you carry this thing around all day?"

She made a muscle with her right arm that Jim couldn't see through her baggy shirt. "You get used to it."

He looked through the camera's viewfinder and pressed the shutter button half-way down like he did on his camera. This camera focused immediately. He pointed at a pair of brilliantly-colored adult spoonbills, pressed the button all the way down, and heard several clicking sounds.

The ability to continually see the birds amazed him. On his old camera, the screen went blank when he pressed the shutter button. A lighter touch allowed him to take single photos of a first-year spoonbill staring at a great egret.

"Rats," Liz muttered. "The ducks flew away."

Her excitement returned when a small flock of black-bellied whistling-ducks landed in front of them and two became embroiled in a fight. She held out her hand. "Quick, the camera."

She took photos of their fight below, on, and above the water while the rest of the flock scattered in all directions. Her camera purred until one of the combatants fled.

One of the fulvous whistling-ducks returned and swam sedately in front of the cattails. Liz gave an exclamation and captured its image, too.

She looked ecstatically in Jim's direction and was taken aback by his flushed face. "It's time to go back to the condo. You need air-conditioning."

He didn't complain and sat in the wheelchair without being asked. When they reached the SUV, he climbed in stiffly and reclined the seat as far as it would go. He fell asleep before they left the parking lot.

When Liz reached Alister Street, she didn't turn left toward the condo. She turned right toward Corpus Christi.

16
Chirping the Blues

Liz gently shook Jim awake. "We're here."

Looking around, he became confused. They were in a parking lot but not at his RV or her condo. As he regained alertness, he realized they were at the ER entrance. "Why are we here? My appointment isn't until tomorrow."

"I'd feel better if you got checked out."

"I'm fine." Jim touched his forehead. "I don't think I have fever."

"Humor me. Get in this wheelchair."

He felt dizzy when he stepped out of the SUV. Maybe the ER was a good idea after all.

There was no delay in the waiting room, this trip. When the check-in clerk saw him, she told him to wait at the window. The triage nurse's door quickly opened, and the clerk escorted her out. "What do you think?"

The nurse didn't hesitate. "Come with me, young man."

She noticed Liz. "Are you family? When Liz nodded, she led them to an examination room.

Jim Edwards, the EMT from Jim's first visit, entered. "Back so soon?"

He eyed Liz. A smile curled his lips as he held a thermometer to Jim's ear. "And you are?"

"His god-granddaughter."

Edwards cocked his head, peered skeptically.

Jim questioned both their motives for pretending she was family, but he wouldn't prevent her from being with him. There was something comforting in her presence. He looked at Edwards, nodded, and introduced her.

Edwards checked the thermometer. "102.5. It might not be related to your leg, but I'll bet it is." He handed Jim a hospital gown and told him he only needed to remove his pants, shoes, and socks.

He turned. "You'll need to return to the waiting room, Liz. I'll notify you when he's ready."

Dizzy, Jim wondered what twisted mind conjured up such a diabolical wisp of so-called clothing. Clinging desperately to the examination table, he managed to pull it into a sufficiently modest manner in front of him, but he couldn't stretch it far enough around his body to tie the straps. That was when he realized one was missing. He used a cross-tie, but his backside detected a draft in the chilly room. By the time Edwards knocked and asked if he was ready, Jim muttered, "As I'll ever be."

Edwards inserted an intravenous needle in Jim's hand, taped it down, handed him a warm blanket, and left to get Liz.

They were talking about Liz, when they returned. She sat in the only chair in the room and winked when Edwards turned his attention back to Jim.

Jim wondered if that meant Edwards had inquired more about their relationship, or if he'd asked her for a date. The young man wasn't wearing a wedding ring.

A doctor, in her late thirties or early forties, entered the room and shook Jim's hand. "I'm Dr. Adams. Let's see what we have, here."

She glanced at Liz. "You're Mr. Smith's granddaughter?"

"Yes."

"You did the right thing by bringing him in. Has he been taking his meds regularly?"

Liz suspected he had. "Absolutely."

Adams poked and probed the same areas the three doctors examined two days earlier. "Nothing unusual, but we'll X-ray your leg to make sure there isn't a bone chip."

When Jim returned from X-Ray, Edwards connected him to an IV bag containing an antibiotic and took his temperature again.

"What's grandpa's temperature now?"

"The same, but he'll be fine."

Ten minutes later, while Jim thanked Liz for the twentieth time, Dr. Adams returned. "No bone chips, but I'm concerned about your fever and lab results. I'm going to admit you for observation and further tests."

Jim fought the urge to decline and nodded—despite knowing Marsha would be upset to leave Anderson and Taylor to come nurse him back to health.

An hour and a half later, after calling Marsha at Liz's insistence and lamenting having to spend the night in the hospital, Jim watched an orderly arrive with a mobile bed.

"You'll be in room 2036, Mr. Smith," the orderly announced. He eyed Liz appreciatively and asked her to bring Jim's clothing and personal effects.

Jim reconsidered his opinion that she was plain. First Jim Edwards and now this orderly seemed to think she was worth their time. And after spending a couple of hours in a room with her, he had to admit that Patsy had correctly described her hip motions.

He studied Liz out of the corner of his eye. Her face was pleasant but nothing special. Her lips were fuller than his first estimate. And wider. They tended to turn down at the corners in a perpetual frown.

Her eyes were round, more than oval, and since their confrontation at Paradise Pond, sleepy-looking. Her eyebrows were lighter-colored than her unruly light-brown hair, making them hard to see. Similarly, her eyelashes were so lightly colored as to appear nearly invisible.

Her nose was straight and narrow, cheekbones high, cheeks a bit hollow. She has a firm jaw line. If anything, her face was slightly masculine—nothing like her mother's very feminine face—so she must resemble her father.

Liz slouched, and her flat chest made her upper body appear small relative to her full hips. He found it difficult to tell. He hadn't seen her in anything but baggy clothing.

An hour after arriving in his hospital room, he talked her into leaving. He wanted to think. The call with Marsha hadn't gone like he'd expected. He'd presumed she would ask Sarah and Stanley to cut their trip short or find another sitter. Instead, she felt confident their friends could care for him. It disappointed him so much he didn't eat much supper. A first for him.

At seven fifteen an orthopedic surgeon strode into the room. "I'm Dr. Gutierrez. I'll be your physician until we get you over this infection." Although he appeared Latino, he didn't have an accent. "You need to beware of the jetty monster, Jim," he said, peering over his glasses. "We see some nasty wounds from there. Do you take a backpack when you fish?" When Jim nodded, he advised, "Put a spray-bottle filled with soapy water in it and bathe every nick and cut."

"Don't worry, doctor, I will from now on."

"If your temperature's back to normal tomorrow and your labs are normal, I'll release you."

The comment soothed Jim's spirit.

* * *

Marsha's refusal to come help concerned Liz as much as it did Jim. She'd wanted to snatch the phone from him and yell at her, but Marsha wouldn't have understood her involvement. For that matter, she didn't understand it herself.

The ER doctor's diagnosis was cellulitis—a potentially life-threatening infection. It could spread to the lymph nodes and bloodstream and course throughout his body. If Liz understood correctly, it could spread to the deeper layers and become the so-called flesh-eating bacteria. She'd read horror stories about that.

She remembered the sign beside the examination room door about MRSA. When Jim asked about it, Edwards hadn't pulled any punches. MRSA was methicillin-resistant staphylococcus aureus, a bacteria highly resistant to antibiotics that could be fatal. It appeared to be associated with hospital stays, so Jim could be more susceptible. In addition, seniors were more vulnerable and tended to be more severely impacted.

Liz wouldn't leave it up to Jim to inform his friends he was in the hospital. She didn't know their site numbers, but Maggie had invited her to play cards that evening, so she drove to the clubhouse.

"Maggie, I'm glad I found you. Jim's in the hospital with a bad infection."

"I expected it. He looked terrible, this morning. I'm glad he decided to go to the hospital. What's the diagnosis?"

"Cellulitis, but the doctors think he'll be okay. And he's grumpy."

"Sounds like Jimmy." Maggie felt an inexplicable unease. "Did he tell Marsha?"

Liz nodded. "But she refused to leave the grandchildren in someone else's care."

"And that sounds like Marsha. I'll call her, too."

Liz raised the topic she came for. "Jim's down in the dumps. It might be nice if y'all visited with him this evening."

She steeled herself for her next comment. She felt a desperate need to be with Jim and wondered how Maggie would take it. "Maggie, if Jim's released tomorrow, I'll pick him up and take him to my condo to keep an eye on him."

Smiling, Maggie patted her arm. "That would be sweet, and I can't think of anyone nicer to keep that old preacher in line."

Liz blanched, raised her hand to her chest. "Jim's a minister?"

"No, that's just what we call him, sometimes. He's a straight-laced old fogey, so we have him give the prayers and say the blessing at meals and our club functions."

"But he's not a preacher?"

Maggie shook her head while mulling over Liz's discomfort. "Jimmy has a penchant for making his life miserable, so keep an eye on him. If he's better, tomorrow, he won't be inclined to follow the doctor's orders." She gave a sly smile. "But I'm sure he'll follow yours."

They spoke for a few minutes before Liz excused herself. "I have to return to Kingwood on Friday, so I need to pack. Why don't you and your friends come to my condo tomorrow evening? We can play cards, and you can bring Jim back to his RV."

"That a wonderful idea." Maggie winked. "I think the rest of our group would like to meet Jimmy's nurse."

Liz gave Maggie the cellphone number, directions to the condo unit, hugged her, and left.

She'd intended to go running and workout in the condo's fitness center when she arrived, but troubled, opted for a light supper and a warm bath instead.

Liz then spoke with her mother and father. Conversations with her father were something she now looked forward to. After Jim's experience, she couldn't delay seeing him while he was in danger from post-op infection. At the end of the call, misty-eyed, she said, "Father, I love you."

Had she been able to see her father, she would have seen tears in his eyes. "I love you, too, Mary Elizabeth."

After hanging up, she thought of her upcoming chore and scowled. Her mother's clothing filled every closet in the condo. She would have to shoehorn it into the Tahoe, like she had before they left.

She was editing the pictures she and Jim had taken that morning, when she received a phone call. Holding her breath, she prayed it wasn't bad news about Jim. It wasn't, and she didn't answer.

Drained, she started to turn off her laptop, then decided to edit one of Jim's pictures. She picked out his best. Fighting sleep and her nagging discomfort, she manipulated it until she felt he would be pleased. Satisfied, she fell asleep before nine.

* * *

Jim found the TV programming disappointing, and he couldn't learn much about his roommate—other than he was Sam Pickard, a retired cabinetmaker from Ingleside. The man struggled with chronic pancreatitis and didn't feel like talking. Just as well.

Jim turned off the TV, but before he could turn out his light, a knock sounded at the door.

Led by Maggie, his friends trooped in.

"We heard you were going to have your leg amputated and thought you might like some company," she said.

Bill saw that his old friend needed cheering up. "It would make better sense to amputate your head. That way there would be room in here for all of us."

Jim chuckled. "You'd think I was on my deathbed or something. But I am glad to see you guys. I was feeling sorry for myself."

Despite his earlier sour mood, Jim's spirits lifted rapidly. The gang might pester and tease him—unmercifully at times—but they were always entertaining and had loving intentions. It was part of what made the trip fun and anticipated each year.

As Bill commented, the room was too small to hold them all, so Maggie and Jeff took the first shift. Ignoring his blush, Maggie kissed his cheek. "I heard Marsha decided to stay with the grandkids. You and I know that she's first and foremost a grandmother. Besides, I think she knows you're ornery enough that a bug can't keep you down for long." Her hand lingered on his arm. She stroked it absently.

Jeff gave her a quizzical look. "Exactly what did the doctors tell you, Jim?"

"They say I have cellulitis. I'm not sure what that is, but they haven't smiled much. How'd you do fishing, today?"

Maggie shook her head.

The conversation essentially repeated itself two more times as Bill and Patsy, then Charles and Nadine, followed. Jim felt sad when the latter said, "See you, later," and the group left for Palm Gardens. Although it seemed like each couple only visited a few minutes, it was nearly ten.

Between nurse checks, that night, he dreamed of arguing with Marsha. He accused her of loving their grandchildren more than him.

Liz hadn't returned, so he wondered if she'd gone on a date with Jim Edwards or the orderly. That shouldn't upset him, so why did the thought nag him as he drifted off to sleep for what seemed like the tenth time at 2:00 a.m.?

17
A Whale of a Rail Tale

Liz awoke at 5:00 a.m. feeling better than she had the previous evening but sensing a vague uneasiness. *The fitness room might help.*

Forty minutes later, she showered off the sweat and slipped into a frilly, one-piece bathing suit her mother purchased for her. Life became better. Being the only one in the pool, she swam fifty laps. Refreshed, she again showered and ate her favorite breakfast of oatmeal with walnuts, almond slivers, and blueberries.

With plenty of time, she stopped by the birding center on the way to the hospital. The morning humidity was thick—not the best for photography—but another photographer near the end of the boardwalk was peering in the direction of the cattails.

A bobbing warbler feeding in low vegetation beyond a small channel beside the boardwalk attracted her attention. It wasn't a waterthrush or ovenbird, two other birds that shared the characteristic. It had a yellow rump but couldn't be a yellow-rumped warbler. They didn't wag or have red foreheads. She took an identification photo and moved on.

The sun burned through the clouds by the time she reached the other photographer. He was peering intently through his viewfinder at the cattails nearest him, but all she saw were the usual suspects—northern shovelers, teals, and coots.

He smiled, as she passed, and she experienced a stirring in her breast akin to when Jim looked at her. She smiled shyly and continued to the end of the boardwalk.

There, she peered through the courtesy telescope, searching for birds and, she had to admit, Boots. No alligator, and the same old ducks, grebes, and night-herons returned from foraging. She glanced at her watch. It was nearing hospital visiting hours.

When she reached the photographer, she spotted what he was looking for—a bird on her list—either a clapper or a king rail. Rails' thin bodies enabled them to slip through dense vegetation. If someone was as skinny as a rail ... well, one got the picture.

It was slipping along the water's edge to the right of where the man was looking. She turned on her camera and eased toward him, admiring—but not craving—his professional rig. Its twenty to thirty-thousand-dollar price tag wasn't the reason she didn't use something similar. The camera, tripod, flash, and 500 mm lens were excellent for birds that moved slowly and sat for long moments, but the combined weight if the rig made it impractical for birds that flit constantly in heavy brush, especially if one had to enter that habitat to find them. The Fresnel lens in front of the flash boosted the range and illuminated backlit and distant subjects, but it often made the subjects' pupils look unnatural. Like red-eyes in family photos. She could fix them but preferred her photos to be as natural as possible. It was exactly times like these she enjoyed her more mobile camera and lens.

She took two long-range ID photos and hurried to intercept the rail. The photographer accidentally backed into her as she passed him.

"I'm sorry," she whispered, chagrined that she hadn't given him enough space. Her heart thumped in her chest. She had trouble breathing.

"No problem."

She pointed. "The rail's ... over ... there."

"Thanks."

While he lifted his bulky equipment, Liz murmured an excuse and ran down the boardwalk to near where she saw it disappear.

"Voila." She was ready when it crept back to the water's edge, hesitated a few seconds, and slipped back into the morass of cattails. She took a burst of pictures and called it a morning. She was capping her lens when a resonant voice made her jump.

"How'd you do?"

The other birder was a few inches shorter than she was. His muscular body wasn't one non-birders would associate with birding. He could be an ex-wrestler, football player—someone who would safari in Africa to shoot Cape buffaloes and wild animals to place on his den wall. Maybe kill them with his bare hands.

But the conceptualization was changing. Recent surveys revealed that forty-six million people participated in the sport of birding—more than any other but fishing. And sport the activity had become. Texas sponsored birding contests with substantial prizes.

The incredibly handsome man elicited a clenching deep within Liz's abdomen, and she didn't have the slightest idea how to react. *Damn, he makes me nervous.* She pondered her newfound freedom. She found it both exciting—and foreboding.

The man grinned, asked again. "How'd you do?"

"I haven't checked, but I think I took some decent photos." She turned on her camera, pressed the picture button, and studied the display. "They're dark, but I won't know how good they are until I download and edit them." Her hands shook when she pointed the display toward him.

"So true." He leaned against her to study the picture.

Liz hoped her heartbeats weren't audible. The man smelled masculine—alpha-male—and didn't share her level of discomfort. He seemed quite at home pinning her body against the railing. She glanced at his bare ring finger.

He smiled knowingly and stepped back. "I've been after that rail all winter. I'm pretty sure I took a few good shots, too, before you arrived."

He was ogling her. Her in her baggy clothes and stupid hat. Liz felt like the rail under his unabashed gaze.

He held out his hand. "I'm Jack West." He motioned at her camera and lens. "It looks like you've done this before."

West was the most beautiful man Liz had ever seen, regardless of age. His crooked smile made her imagine that he might want to put a mark beside her on his lifetime bird list. Or spread her like a bear skin on his den floor. *Why the hell did I think that?*

She trembled while trying to decide how to derail his thoughts—her thoughts. She swallowed to keep her voice from quavering. "Which rail is it?"

"A king. There's been a pair here all winter, and they're difficult to find on Mustang Island."

When Liz didn't take his hand, West disrobed her with his eyes, slowly, one area at a time.

She felt a throbbing in her groin. Her body's unexpected response startled her. It became difficult to speak in full sentences. Even think. ""How ... can I tell the ... difference? As I recall, they ... look similar ... in the guides."

West launched into a subject he was obviously passionate about. "Well, the guides, especially Sibley's and Kaufmann's, are usually right-on with their pictures and descriptions. While there are regional variations, king rails' necks and breasts are more rufous and the black and white stripes on their bellies more distinct."

He resembled Becky, with his tutorial, and his friendly manner and hypnotic voice captivated her. He elicited the information that she preferred photography to straight birding. "I'm here on a short vacation with my mother and grandfather," she said, in self-defense.

The man's eyes crinkled at the corners when he smiled, and her heart skipped. She wondered how she was coherent enough to lie to him and why she felt so uneasy. On the one hand, he made her weak in the knees and generated a throbbing in her groin. On the other—he frightened her.

Déjà vu. Something in his eyes. From long ago. She shuddered and glanced at her watch. "Thanks for the information, Mr. West, but I have to run. I'm on my way to visit my grandpa in the hospital. Maybe I'll see you again sometime."

They exchanged names, and West gave her his card. "Call when you need company, Liz. My friends and I know most of the birding hotspots, and we monitor state birding hotlines and online sites, like Texbirds and Birds of Texas."

He recommended Hazel Bazemore Park. "A scientific hawk count in progress there will last through April and end with a Big Sit bird count the first Saturday in May. Hans and Pat Suter Nature Park on Oso Bay, and Sunset Lake near Portland have interesting birds, but it's difficult to get close enough for good photos. A tripod and high magnification lens are best."

He stroked her arm. "Do you have a card, Liz, so I can contact you if I hear of any rare birds while you're here?"

She braced her other hand on the railing. "I ... don't carry ... business cards."

West released her. "You can write your number on the back of mine."

Regaining control of her senses, Liz smiled apologetically. "Sorry, I can't." She wasn't the least bit sorry and would toss his card at the first opportunity.

"Don't trust me, huh. I appreciate that. A woman can't be too careful." He again offered his hand.

His comeback calmed her slightly, and she accepted it. When it wrapped around hers, her breath caught, but the sensation wasn't electric like Jim's. "Maybe next time."

In the parking lot, she couldn't believe how quickly time had passed. She wouldn't reach the hospital before ten. She called Jim.

"Hello?"

His voice warmed her. "It's your favorite granddaughter. How are you this morning?"

Jim felt relieved, genuinely happy, like a weight had been lifted from his chest. "Great. Well, not so great, but refreshed. I had a decent night's sleep, considering the interruptions."

"I'm glad to hear you're better. Have you heard anything from your doctor?"

"Not yet. But my nurse told me I'll soon be back to normal."

"Great, I'll be there in thirty minutes. It would be ten, but I'm going to pretend you're in the car with me. You're a party-pooper, you know."

"I hope you're serious. And thanks again for all you're doing for me." The smack Jim heard in the phone jolted him.

When Liz started her car, she noticed Jack West putting his equipment in the back of a Toyota RAV 4. Strange that he would give up so soon after stalking a bird all winter, she thought as she pulled out of the parking lot. But perhaps it only appeared early in the day, and the boardwalk was now becoming crowded with bird-watchers and sight-seers.

Twenty-nine minutes later, as she'd promised, she knocked on the door to Jim's room.

"Come in."

The voice didn't sound like his. When she entered, she saw his bed vacant. "Hi," she said apprehensively to his roommate. "Do you know where my grandpa is?"

The man stared. "Boy, you're beautiful."

Liz's concern changed to annoyance. "He's all right, isn't he?"

The man groaned, rolled carefully onto his side, and introduced himself. "I'm Sam Picard, and your grandpa's okay. He wanted a real bath, and our nurse is humoring him."

Like Jack West, Picard seemed to see through her dowdy attire and rangy hair. "You're a looker, Liz. I'll bet you're the pick of Jim's litter of grandkids."

She reddened. "I'm glad he's doing better."

The door opened and a petite Asian nurse wheeled Jim into the room. They were laughing, so they must be having a fun conversation.

Lord he's beautiful. Oblivious of his obesity, Liz concentrated on the set of his jaw, his lips, and the light reflecting in his uniquely-colored eyes. The unfamiliar clenching in her lower abdomen returned.

Jim winked. "Hi, hon."

"Hi, Grandpa."

"Sarah, Sam, this is my granddaughter Liz." *We're both going to hell.*

Sam shifted and groaned. "We've met."

"Liz, this is my nurse, Sarah Curtains. Her dad met her mother in Hawaii. She's sweet and helpful."

Sarah smiled. "It's very nice to meet you, Liz. Your grandfather thinks a lot of you. He says it's wonderful when a grandchild has the same avocation their grandparent has. My grandpa in Victoria says the same thing."

She busied herself helping Jim back into bed, told Liz again how nice it was to meet her, and excused herself.

Thirty minutes later, Dr. Gutierrez entered the room, holding a chart. "I'm going to discharge you, Jim. We'll load you up with one more IV and turn you loose."

Heady about being able to leave the hospital, he pumped the doctor's hand. "Thank you so much, Dr. Gutierrez."

Gutierrez glanced in Liz's direction and smiled appreciatively. "Is this the granddaughter you've been raving about?"

Liz was surprised that Jim had told everyone about her—in glowing terms.

The doctor stuck out his hand. "Hi, Liz. Keep on taking good care of your grandfather."

When she accepted his hand, it wrapped about hers much like Jack West's had. It pleased her that the handsome doctor didn't affect her. Evidently, only certain men wielded that power.

After lunch, nurse Curtains returned with discharge paperwork and instructions. She directed Liz to bring the car to the entrance and told Jim he would be leaving in a wheelchair. He complained, until told it was hospital policy.

Liz was surprised to see Jack West standing near the information desk in the hospital lobby. And just as surprised by the breathlessness and tingling she felt.

"I thought you'd be long gone, by now, Liz."

"My grandpa was in the hospital overnight," she choked out. "What are you doing here, Jack?"

The surprised look on his face was replaced by one of sadness. "One of my cousins had an appendectomy, and I need to check on him. He came through surgery okay, but he's not feeling well."

His face grew sympathetic. "How's your grandpa? Not too serious, I hope."

"No, he's been discharged. I'm on my way to get the car. Thanks for your concern, though. I hope your cousin will be fine soon."

"I'm sure he will. Nice meeting you again, Liz. And be sure to call me when you want to go birding."

"I reserve birding for my grandpa," she said, trying to close the matter.

What a small world, she thought as she hurried to her SUV.

18

When Birds Collide

Jim sat mute as they crossed the JFK Causeway between Corpus Christi and North Padre Island. Eyes unfocused, he idly chewed his bottom lip. The euphoria of introducing Liz and being released from the hospital had been short-lived. His friends would return home that weekend. Under a doctor's care, his activities would be curtailed by the difficulty of driving with two injured legs. Marsha wasn't coming, and he faced a week alone. It would be like living in solitary confinement.

The bay was a light aqua, and birds were everywhere—preening in flocks, swimming in pods, wading the shallows in search of food. The beauty of it made Liz wonder why Jim was quiet after being so happy in the hospital. When he ignored an osprey on a utility pole, she broke her silence. "What're you thinking?"

Jim's head drooped. "Marsha called this morning. She asked if I was getting better, and I couldn't lie. Then she accused me of having Maggie and Patsy try to lay a guilt trip on her.

"I could sense her relief over the phone. She loves her grandchildren, even when they hurt her feelings and wear her out. And when I get home, she'll take her frustrations out on me."

He mentally kicked himself for sounding like the proverbial husband whose wife didn't understand him. "If I tell her she's enabling them by providing free housecleaning and rushing off to babysit whenever they ask, she'll become upset. If I refuse to listen to her, she'll say, 'Does this mean I can't discuss our grandchildren with you ever again? Do I have to keep these things to myself?'"

Liz knew the feeling from Marsha's perspective. And from Jim's. She reached over and squeezed his hand sympathetically.

"She's already mad because I didn't cancel this trip to help her." He sighed. "But I've done that so often, and the years are flying by. I'll be sixty-eight in a month.

"She warned me I'd hurt myself, and I have." He glanced heavenward. "Or maybe I'm being punished for not staying with her."

Liz waited while he discussed his concerns. When he finished, she spoke. "I know what you mean. All my life I've done or tried to do ... or tried to resist doing ... what Mother wants me to. I can't seem to please her, even when I try to do exactly what she wants. I took the lessons she arranged when I was a child ... piano, voice ... while all I ever wanted to do was experience nature."

She chuckled a throaty laugh. "FYI, those lessons were complete busts. I've always been jealous of my father and brothers. They're the outdoorsmen I wanted to be."

Jim thought it interesting that she called her father something other than Frank, but it was his turn to let her reflect.

"They were always out hunting and fishing while I stayed home disappointing Mother. I've always been ungainly. Hell, I was born to fail her. I grew out of beautiful baby and little girl clothes within weeks." She gave a shake of her stringy hair. "How bad was that?

"Mother was especially protective of me. She told me what was lady-like and what wasn't. There were things a girl didn't do ... with either boys or girls. Things I shouldn't do by myself. I couldn't even pick my boyfriends. How many mothers arrange their daughters' blind dates?" Her eyes glazed. "Course, there weren't many ... as in one." She glanced at Jim. "And she won't let me go anywhere by myself, like this trip. I'm twenty-nine years old and ...." She trailed off.

What a strange world, Jim reflected. Liz's mother wouldn't leave her alone. Marsha didn't seem to want him around except to help babysit. Liz needed relief from her mother's hopes and dreams for her, and he wanted someone with whom to share his.

While wondering why Liz allowed herself to become enslaved to her mother, he realized he and Marsha were no different. He felt remorse for being on this trip and was so lonely he ached.

"Lately, Jim, I've had a hard time dealing with all this. I felt like I was going crazy ... like Mother keeps telling me."

Liz chuckled sadly. "This was supposed to be a sabbatical to find myself, and would you believe it, Mother wouldn't let me come alone. Lord, what does that say about me? Mother's the one I need the relief from." She gently pounded the steering wheel. "I'm so screwed up ... oops ... sorry, but she pisses me off."

She didn't apologize for the second curse word, and Jim imagined she didn't realize she'd said it. It was common on TV these days.

Liz smiled. "But we're going to change all that, starting right now. I think it's fate. Dad broke his leg, you hurt yours, and I found you again. We're going to do some birding and be ourselves if it's the last time it happens."

She patted his thigh. Although she made the touch seem natural, the act presented a difficult milestone. A wave of endorphins flooded her brain, and a surge of heat filled her belly. But their time together would be short. She would have to head home the next day.

"Yeah, two misfits having fun," Jim said. The thought warmed his spirit but troubled his soul. "By the way, I couldn't help noticing that you haven't mentioned your father's name the last couple of times you spoke of him. Is that part of this change?"

"I hadn't thought of it, but it is. We've had some wonderful conversations since he was hit by the car. He asked me to go hunting with him on his next trip to the hill country. I can take pictures of him hunting and the birds and game we see from his blind. Isn't that great? I probably can't prove it, but I bet Mother had something to do with my relationship with him."

Jim broached a subject, one that gnawed at him, made him uneasy though he wasn't sure why. "Did you have a late night?"

"No. I was worn out and went to bed early. I didn't even jog or exercise like I usually do."

She smiled sheepishly. "Yesterday, when I left you, I went to Palm Gardens and found Maggie. I asked her to check on you and call Marsha."

"So, you're the reason behind the call that made me feel so bad. Well, it's not so bad, now that I know why. And you seem to know me pretty well for someone who's only known me a couple of days."

Liz nodded. "I was late this morning, because I felt so good that I exercised and swam in the pool. After breakfast I had some time, so I went by the birding center, saw a couple of new birds, and time got away from me." She saw no reason to tell Jim about Jack West. Besides, her thoughts of Jack were—perplexing.

Jim believed she was telling the truth. She had no reason to lie. Besides, she was young and could do what she pleased. It was none of his business.

"By the way, you're spending the rest of the afternoon with me," Liz said. "Your friends will be over around six. We'll have a potluck dinner and play that Pegs and Jokers game you told me about." She faked an apprehensive look. "You're corrupting me. Playing cards is against my religion.

"Afterward, if you don't mind, your friends will take you back to your trailer." Liz smiled impishly. "I know what a great chauffeur you think I am, but they're probably safe drivers, too. Most old and decrepit people are."

Jim pondered foul-mouthed Liz's claim to be religious despite seeing her in church. He laughed at her joke. "We don't bet on our games. And thanks for setting things up."

"I'm learning I can think on my own. Thanks for the opportunity." Liz risked all and blew him a kiss. It made her heart pulse rapidly.

"Thank you, too."

Jim spent the rest of the drive explaining the rules and nuances of the Pegs and Jokers variation he and his friends played. There were many. The card game was played using a board and pegs. Their boards were designed for either four or six players, and they played as teams—women against men.

"It's something like the game Sorry. Each player has a starting area, and a home area, five holes to the right. We each have five pegs that we move from hole to hole, the object being to move them into the home area. The first team that gets all their pegs in their home areas wins.

"The game may seem simple, but it's complex. There are many strategies ... just what seniors need to keep their minds sharp. Some players like offense and some defense. Some are cautious, others more rambunctious." Grinning, he said, "Mostly, I'm plain stupid."

Liz laughed but listened intently. It sounded intriguing.

They stopped by the IGA to purchase the items for the potluck dinner.

At the condo, she cooked, edited bird pictures, and flipped through her field guides.

"Hey, I took a picture of a palm warbler this morning." She made a checkmark on the island bird list. "It's a nice bird for the island. In case you haven't seen one, it looks something like a yellow-rumped warbler, but has a reddish cap and bobs its tail. This is my first picture of one." She shrugged. "Unfortunately, it's not a good one." She turned her laptop toward Jim.

He thought it a cute little bird, although dull for a warbler. He assumed it was in winter plumage.

Liz hummed constantly while editing pictures and cooking, but most of the time Jim didn't have the slightest idea what the songs were. She'd been truthful about Helen wasting money on voice lessons. Or was it some of that hip-hop or rap he'd heard about?

Her cooking, on the other hand.... "Whatever you're making smells delicious."

"Remember, I'm my mother's daughter when it comes to cooking. It's the one way I didn't disappoint, and it's my other love. This is baked chicken, covered with sliced apples and carrots, in a little water. I'm also baking sugar-free oatmeal cookies for Bill Warner. Maggie told me he's diabetic."

"You're a jewel, Liz. You'll make a great wife, someday."

She clenched her teeth, whispered inaudibly, "I wouldn't bet on that."

She was removing the last tray of cookies from the oven when Jim's friends knocked on the door. He rose stiffly and opened it.

It wasn't ladies first. Bill, Charles, and Jeff jostled to be the first to see his nursemaid.

Jeff won. "At last we meet your guardian angel. We about decided that you and Maggie were making the whole thing up." He whistled. "Talk about a great-looking angel."

Liz blushed. She wasn't wearing make-up, but she'd brushed her hair. She wore a bra instead of a breast wrap, a short-sleeved blouse, and slacks that weren't baggy like her birding outfits.

For the first time that day, Jim took a good look at her and silently whistled, himself. He'd been so easy in her presence and interested in their conversations, he hadn't noticed the change.

The men sat on one side of the room talking fishing, and the women sat on the other, discussing intelligent topics. Jim noted humorously that his friends frequently sneaked glances at Liz, and that Maggie also corralled her at times.

Always direct, Charles lowered his voice. "Jim, Liz is a beautiful woman. You may be lucky she's taking care of you, but I can't help thinking she might have an ulterior motive. Be careful. We old horses are susceptible to scams where pretty women are concerned."

Jim nodded. "I've wondered the same thing, but I think she's okay. And she's going back to Kingwood tomorrow, so that'll be the last I'll hear from her. Unless she responds to the thank you card Marsha's sure to send her."

Bill Warner chuckled. "I'd give anything to be in the girl's hands, no matter what her motive. Heck, even if she's Hansel and Gretel's witch and wants to fatten me up to eat me."

Jeff envisioned what he'd do given the opportunity.

When the topic returned to fishing, Jim suggested an alternative to the dismal luck they were experiencing. "Why don't you go birding with me, tomorrow? The warblers and tanagers will take your breath away."

He received the usual responses—a raised eyebrow from Charles, a frown from Jeff, and a, 'Too bad they don't have qualified brain transplant surgeons in Corpus,' from Bill.

The food was great. Compliments flew in all directions. The ladies shared recipes, and the games began.

It wasn't long before Bill and Jim realized they didn't need to baby Liz. She proved to have a good memory for both rules and strategy. Although the men won, she and Patsy kept the game close.

Charles and Jeff won their game against Nadine and Maggie on a separate board, and Maggie's eyes hardened.

The players switched. Jim paired with Charles against Nadine and Liz, and Jeff and Bill played Maggie and Patsy. Charles and Jim struggled. Nadine was a defensive player, and Liz preferred offense. Charles played conservatively and hated to lose, so Jim suppressed his tendency to take risks when partnered with him. It didn't help. The ladies won, and perfectionist Charles became as unhappy as he was when an Oklahoma University team lost. Liz, not expecting his temper, stared quizzically at Jim and decided to not rub it in.

Each Pegs and Jokers games took up to an hour, and the evening grew late. After the final game, Charles broke the news. "More than forty rigs are leaving April first, so Bill and Patsy and Nadine and I are leaving Saturday."

"We're still leaving Sunday," Maggie said, ignoring Jeff's frown.

"I have to stick around until Thursday," Jim said plaintively.

Maggie knew if it weren't for the arduous, two-day drive back to Oklahoma, with bum legs and towing a rig that required a mid-way stop in Waco, he'd leave with them. He might try, anyway, and she wouldn't let that happen.

Before leaving, Jim took Liz aside. "I can't tell you how much I've enjoyed meeting you and getting to know you. And you saved me from a long stay in ICU, so I wish you'd let me repay you for all you've done for me."

"It was my pleasure, Jim. I love your company. You can't know the freedom it's given me."

He extended his hand for a handshake, but she stepped into him and gave him a strong hug. She wanted to kiss him. "Thanks for your patience with me. I really will change for you."

While they hugged, Bill, Jeff, and Charles lined up behind Jim, and their wives winked at each other. Liz treated them like family. They told her to drive safely on her way home. She told them the same and the evening ended.

Jim had a lump in his throat during the ride to the resort with Jeff and Maggie. Parting from his young companion of the past two days was proving difficult. He wiped away the tears in his eyes. He hadn't asked for her phone number or address, despite needing to send her a thank you note.

"Are you seeing Liz off tomorrow, Jimmy?" Maggie asked.

"No."

"Why not?"

"I didn't get her phone number."

"That's no excuse. You know her condo number."

"It's best this way. I don't think our relationship is right for Marsha."

"There's no fool like an old fool. The girl may have saved your life, and you've provided her something she needs right now."

"Why would you think that?"

"Because we women don't sit around talking fishing all evening. You gave her a project ... nursing you back to health ... and she told me she enjoys sharing her love of nature with you. How can you turn down heartfelt TLC and a chance to indulge yourself?"

Jim mulled her words.

"Jim, Maggie should have been a lawyer," Jeff said. "She can worm information out of a rock. And you know she always gets to the heart of the matter, so listen to her."

Jim's resolve caved. "So, Maggie, what should I do?"

"You're right that Liz has problems, but she's not psycho. She's as hen-pecked by her mother as anyone I've met. You've given her the opportunity to act independently and make right and wrong choices without posing a threat to her psyche.

"She says you remind her of a late grandfather, although you're the opposite of him. In fact, I mentioned your nickname, yesterday, and she appeared startled. I explained you weren't a preacher, just as nice as they come. Goofy, maybe, but honest and trustworthy. And forgiving. You treat others as you'd like to be treated, regardless of how they treat you. You're perfect for her. You accept things that would tick Jeff off so much, he would tear his hair out."

"Forget what I told you about listening to my wife, Jimmy," Jeff muttered. "She's not making any sense tonight."

"You know what I'm talking about, Jimmy," Maggie continued. "You let Marsha get away with murder. Patsy, Nadine, and I have grandchildren, but we put our husbands first. We didn't marry our children and grandchildren and promise to honor and obey them.

"And Liz gives you the opportunity to do what you like to do best, chase birds without worrying about anything." She cocked her head. "I can't picture any old geezer not being flattered to be around a beautiful young woman who shares his passion and who's willing to help him get better at it.

"There, you don't need to take my advice, but I've gotten my unprofessional opinion off my chest."

Jim remained silent the rest of the trip, thinking about what she said.

Upon entering his RV, he took the highway patrol card off the table and tossed it in the trash. Liz was right. She might have been reckless, but those who crashed broke the law. And how could he turn in someone who'd saved his life?

19

The Bird Whisperer

At 8:00 a.m. Jim's cellphone rang. He hadn't resolved the issues Maggie brought up the previous evening, so arose slowly from the recliner, hoping the phone would stop ringing before he reached it.

"Hello?"

"I gave up and decided to call you. I can be humble, too."

"Liz?" Jim said unnecessarily. "I'm sorry I didn't—"

"Don't apologize. It'll ruin my he-man image of you. Besides, Maggie told me to call you."

"She did? Did she call you this morning?"

"No, last night. She said you'd get cold feet."

"To be truthful," Jim said candidly, "I thought it best if I didn't call you. I worry that what we're doing is somehow wrong to Marsha and that I'm interfering in your life by keeping you away from your father."

"Maggie said you'd say that, too. You know, Jim, I don't think I've ever met someone like her. She says what she thinks and doesn't hold anything back."

Liz didn't give Jim a chance to respond. "How are you this morning? How's your leg?"

"Not bad. I was afraid the games last night might not be good for it, but the swelling seems down. The redness is about the same, though."

"I worry about you, Jim. Why don't I pick you up for breakfast, so I can see for myself? I'll cook here in the condo. I don't have to be out until eleven, and I still have a little food left."

Jim sighed. "I can't fight fate ... or Maggie ... or you."

He decided to be up front. If she was taking him for a fool or misreading his intentions, so be it. "You own a part of my heart, Liz, and I think that's what worries me the most."

"That is *so* sweet. You'll be in mine forever, too. You give me freedom, accept me for who I am, and seem to like what I do. See you in ten."

It was closer to fifteen minutes. "I did the speed limit and stopped at stop signs. Ya happy?"

"I'm impressed."

Jim glanced in the back as he slid into the SUV. Its back seats were folded flat and the cargo space filled close to the roof. "All yours?"

"Mother's. She can't go anywhere without taking an entire closet and chest of drawers. She has to look perfect, no matter what. The backpack and camera bag in the seat behind you are mine. I came to bird."

She changed the subject. "You aren't limping as much, this morning. That's a good sign. But I wish you'd worn shorts, so I could see your left leg."

"Don't worry, my pants are baggy. I'll pull them up to my knees when we get to the condo. Besides, I look like Tweedledee in shorts." He found her deep laugh charming.

She made oatmeal with almonds, walnuts, and blueberries for breakfast.

"Did Maggie tell you this is the way I make it?" Jim asked.

"She's not guilty this time. It's just how I do it." Liz reached under the small table and patted Jim's thigh, gave it a squeeze. It could become a habit. "Our meeting must be fate."

They made small talk before she came to the point. "Maggie asked me to stay with you until after your appointment next Thursday. She—"

"What? She's playing us like marionettes."

Liz looked startled. "You don't want me to come back?"

Her disconsolate look didn't seem fake. Tears welling in her eyes made them sparkle. *You have so many problems.* Jim mused that if he didn't have time for her, after what she'd done for him, it would be wrong. "I can't think of anything I'd want more."

He both meant and feared it. He didn't want to be drawn into a situation where professional help might be the better course of action—for both of them.

Deep sobs wracking her body, Liz moved around the table and hugged him.

Jim recognized them for what they were, tears of happiness. He held her close and patted her back until she stopped shaking.

In the remaining two hours before check-out time, they talked photography. She showed him the roseate spoonbill photos he took two days earlier.

"I edited this one night before last. I intended to show it to you yesterday, but you needed the rest and the time went by too quickly. I hope you'll like it."

She peered expectantly over his shoulder while massaging his neck. Another first, another triumph. Her successes were becoming much easier now.

Jim's jaw dropped. "The picture's beautiful. The colors... A good camera sure makes a difference, doesn't it?"

"There you go again. The camera and software contributed, but you recognized an unusual event. The baby spoonbill staring at the great egret is a great shot. There were closer spoonbills with more gorgeous colors, but you chose it."

She squeezed his head against her breast and kissed his bald spot. *Um. Much easier.*

"It reminds me of you and me. I'm the spoonbill ... wondering what you are and if you'll be good to me. You're the egret ... suspicious of my intentions and wondering what you should do about it."

When Jim peered at her teary-eyed, smiling face, his loins stirred for the first time since he'd left home. It was a good thing he was sitting at the table. Passion bred passion, and crying women always engendered his. Liz was being nice, and he idiotic. He gave a quick prayer and concentrated on the photo to quash his unwanted lust. "I didn't put that much thought into it."

"Intuition's a good thing. Go with your gut impressions. If something seems strange or beautiful or funny, it could be a winner."

Liz closed the picture, clicked on the original photo, and pointed at the computer screen. "Now, for the second part of your editing lesson." She indicated with her finger. "You don't see all this background when you look through the viewfinder. Unless you're a pro, all you see is your subject and center it. Especially, if your camera is in auto focus mode, which is normal for this type of photography where you have only seconds. When you download the photos and evaluate them for the first time, you think, 'boy, the bird sure looked bigger in the viewfinder.'

"That's where editing comes in. We use a rule of thirds to improve pictures, and some editing programs even grid the screen to make that easier. At the same time, I've seen award winning photos with the subjects on thirds that seemed weird to me. But who am I to judge?

"Regardless, start with that. Crop your pictures with your subjects centered in the most appealing third, considering the background, and go with your instincts. You'll mentally frame your photos in thirds with experience."

She paused. "Uh-oh, look at the time. We have to be out of here in fifteen minutes."

They double-checked the condo and went to the front desk. The clerk was the one who'd been on duty when Liz brought Jim to the condo the first time in the wheelchair. He took her key cards and smiled. "Did you and your grandfather have a nice stay?"

"You can't imagine."

At his RV, she told Jim to expect her the next day, but it might be Sunday. "I want to spend time with Daddy, and there's Mother and other problems to deal with." She made a face but didn't elaborate. She gave him a strong hug. "I'll miss you."

Jim again wondered what he'd gotten himself into. "Good luck, but don't hurry back ... too much. I want you safe and sound."

Liz kissed his cheek. "Don't worry. You're rubbing off on me."

She drove away waving happily out the window.

When he turned to enter his RV, Jim saw Maggie and Patsy standing in front of the clubhouse's bougainvillea hedge. They waved and strolled up. "I'm glad you took my advice," Maggie said.

Jim winked at Patsy. "She called me. Said you advised her to last night."

"God works in strange and mysterious ways. When will she be back?"

"Why do you think she's coming back?"

"I told her to. But that's neither here nor there, she would have anyway."

Jim laughed. "She said tomorrow or the next day."

"Fancy that. Guess you'll be eating with Jeff and me for the next two days. Three-handed Pegs and Jokers is out, so maybe you won't mind going to the dollar movie with us instead."

Patsy, smile fading, shook her head. So that's why Maggie and Jeff weren't caravanning back to Oklahoma. *The sorceress is at it again.*

* * *

"Your daughter left on schedule, Mrs. Matthews. The only man's she been alone with is the one you claim she attacked at Paradise Pond. How about him?"

"Don't make me laugh. He's a pig."

"He's a rugged old razorback, all right, but some eccentrics look like paupers."

"Mary Elizabeth doesn't want for money. And surely you don't think that little old man could be anyone's lover."

Little old man? "No, but she took him to her condo twice ... the day I followed her to Paradise Pond and the day she picked him up at the hospital."

Helen paused. There must be an explanation, but she couldn't think of one. "Is there any way you can put a listening device on her?"

"I told you, I won't go to Kingwood. And since you've met him personally and I've sent you several photos, you have something to provide a local investigator. If, as we both believe, he isn't your daughter's lover, you need to hire someone there. You can help them plant a listening device on her. Perhaps in her purse."

The suggestions made sense, Helen thought. Mary Elizabeth's lover probably lived in Kingwood and was coming back at the same time. He might even be a member of their church. Must be. It was the only time Mary Elizabeth was out of her sight or unaccounted for.

"Mrs. Matthews?"

"I'm thinking."

Helen searched the recesses of her mind for who could be her daughter's lover. She couldn't recall Mary Elizabeth speaking with any man, but she did spend time with some of her life-long girlfriends.

Helen clutched her breast. Her face drained of color. The girls slept over at each other's houses all through high school. Most still weren't married. "Oh, *please*, God, don't let my baby be a homosexual," she prayed aloud.

"What's this about a homosexual?" Mansfield feared she'd missed an opportunity.

"Just a silly thought. Now, what was it you wanted to speak about?"

"My invoice."

"Oh, yes. How much do I owe you?"

Mansfield thought she heard her client sob.

20

The Pelican Place

Jim was resting comfortably on his recliner, feet elevated, when Maggie called. "Hey, Jimmy, the gang's going to the Big Fisherman. Let's go."

A long-time fixture between Aransas Pass and Rockport, on Tuesdays the restaurant served all-you-could-eat meals for $2.25—if one liked chicken livers, chicken gizzards, or chicken fried steak. Many winter Texans stopped fishing and shopping before noon, and the waiting line at the restaurant grew long. It was a tradition for Jim's group. He'd always liked gizzards, and Bill and Jeff always debated how the restaurant could stay in business with the number of servings he consumed of the chewy morsels. Although it was a Friday, delicious meals were available to fit everyone's taste and budget.

"Sure. What time?"

Jeff and I will pick you up around noon."

Jim started to say see you but stopped. Pelicans were the one bird she liked to see. "Say, Maggie, two years ago Marsha and I found a great place to photograph pelicans near the Big Fisherman. I can be your guide, if you like."

"Be still my beating heart."

After the call, Jim turned on the air conditioner to combat the morning humidity, propped back in his recliner, and reflected. Liz had bared her soul to him. Maggie was right, it was too bad he hadn't initiated the call. And speaking of calls, he needed to see how Marsha was doing. Anderson would be in school, so it should be a good time to talk while her day wasn't hectic.

She answered on the sixth ring, sounding exhausted. "Hi, hon."

"Hi, sweetheart. Everything okay?"

"As well as can be expected with two hyper and sick children. I know it sounds like an oxymoron, but it's the truth. How's your leg?"

"Better, I think. The swelling seems down. What's up with the grandkids?"

"Anderson threw up all night. I called Sarah, and she said to call Dr. Moore's nurse. The nurse said there's a bug going around and called in a prescription to keep Anderson's food down. She's already better and watching TV, but I'm worried Taylor will get it next. I didn't sleep last night, and these children are a chore even when they're being nice."

She called away from the phone. "Anderson, why is Taylor crying? Taylor, what's wrong, sweetie pie?"

"I wish you'd find someone to baby-sit them and come on down here," Jim said. "I have to stay until next Thursday, when I go in for a final checkup."

Silence indicated Marsha wasn't listening. It was several minutes before Jim heard her speak.

"Sorry, Anderson took Taylor's doll away and wouldn't give it back. Honestly, you'd think she'd treat her little sister better. She's definitely getting over the bug. "I wish—"

"Taylor, why are you crying?"

"Hold on a minute, hon. I have to see why Taylor's crying again."

"I'll have to call you back, Jim," Marsha said, minutes later. "I placed Anderson in time out and need to make sure she stays there. Love you."

"Wait, I have to tell you that we're—" The line went dead. "I love you, too."

Marsha would be hard to live with when he returned home.

Due to too much traffic for the express lane to the ferry landing, Jim and his friends were shunted into the auxiliary lane that looped into Robert's Point Park. The half-mile long park, situated between the shipping channel and the marina, contained a free fishing pier and a pavilion that served as the site for meetings, fishing tournaments, and the Ecumenical Easter sunrise service.

On the marina side, the friends could buy the freshest shrimp on the Texas Gulf coast right off the boats at great prices. The harbor was also home for the large catamaran shrimp boat, Polly Anna.

To kill time, the group admired the many pink and white oleander bushes they didn't have back home in Oklahoma. They watched palms swaying in the island breeze, children playing soccer, and single-file convoys of brown pelicans skimming the water in the ship channel. The men scanned the pier and ship channel bulkhead to see if fishermen were catching tasty sheepshead or the three-feet-long redfish and black drum prevalent this time of year.

"Look, dolphins!" Maggie alerted, pointing at several leaping in the bow wave of a passing tanker ship's bulbous front tip. She tried unsuccessfully to take their photo.

Across the channel they saw an abandoned structure called the Fina Dock. Although it posed hazards, such as chunks of falling concrete, fish could often be caught there when nothing was biting at Robert's Point or the jetty. Jim and his friends often talked about bringing a boat to fish the dock. After this year, they might.

At the Big Fisherman, Maggie and Jeff, the only imbibers, ordered small, dollar Margaritas to while away time in the waiting line.

Once inside, everyone kept up a lively chatter. They wouldn't be together again until the next monthly club meeting in Oklahoma.

Bill and Jeff kept the gang in stitches, and Jim didn't mind being the butt of most of their jokes. Even Charles laid it on pretty thick about Liz, since she was returning. Only Maggie didn't participate in the ribbing, which was unusual for her.

After the meal, Charles and Nadine and Bill and Patsy went shopping for last-minute items for the trip back home.

"Okay, Jimmy," Maggie said, "where's this pelican heaven? I'm dying to see them."

Within ten minutes they arrived at a public boat ramp and fish-cleaning shelter on a channel that led to the Intracoastal Canal. Jim laughed apologetically. "Now that I've talked the place up, there probably won't be a pelican in sight."

Two fishermen were cleaning redfish in the shelter, so he crossed his fingers. He sighed with relief when he and Maggie peered over the edge of the steep embankment. White and brown pelicans competed for the fish remains being tossed into the channel. The lighting was perfect, and Maggie ecstatic.

The afternoon sunlight painted the channel a deep blue and highlighted the white pelicans' feathers. It cast a glow on the brown pelicans' brown-tinged gray feathers and their red and green bills. Maggie pointed her camera first one way, then another, taking photos of every pelican in sight. Jim snapped a few pictures before stopping to appreciate the birds' shapes and colors through Helen's binoculars.

White pelicans had subtle shades of white. Their back feathers appeared pure white, but those on their wings and parts of their breasts looked sandy-tinged. Feathers out of the sunlight appeared light gray. The feathers on their necks bore a pinkish glow. Was it a refection from their pink bills?

Some had yellowish humps two-thirds of the way down their bills—something to do with the breeding season, no doubt. An upside-down, yellow-orange teardrop ran from the pelican's bills up and around their brownish-gray eyes. Their pouches appeared more off-yellow than any other color.

Chuckling at their shaggy punk-rock crowns, Jim felt fortunate to see them. White pelicans were winter Texans. They spent their summers in the northern U.S. and Canada. This spot in Rockport afforded his best opportunity to see the majestic birds from within a few feet. It was even better than at the pelican festival when they migrated through Oklahoma.

Jim noticed Maggie's cheap binoculars giving her fits and held out Helen's. "Here, try these."

Her raptured face glowed. "I know what Jeff's giving me for Easter." When Jim told her how much they cost, she said, "So?"

"The brown pelicans aren't so much brown as silvery-brown," she observed. "And some have chestnut necks. Others have white. Do you think the white and brown pelicans are cross-breeding?"

"It's probably the time of year. I think I read that their necks change from mostly white in the winter, to chestnut in the spring, then to black during the breeding season."

"This is so fascinating," Maggie said. "Some have blue-gray eyes encircled in red, and others have eyes encircled in blue and pink. I couldn't see that with the piece of junk I was using."

She pitched her binoculars into the channel and caught her breath when the pelicans raced for it. It sunk to the bottom before they could reach it. Relieved, she scolded, "Jimmy, if you ever tell Jeff I did that, I'll hex you."

His mouth dropped open.

"I'm *kidding*."

Maggie's eyes widened. She grasped his hand and gave it a squeeze. "Besides, I can think up more pleasurable ways to punish you."

Jim laughed nervously. Maggie was being so out of character. *Is it the Margaritas?*

To hide his embarrassment, he studied the brown pelicans. Their crowns were butch-feathered. The feathers around their faces and down the fronts of their necks were tan, tinged with amber. Some bills were red, mottled with colors that ranged from light brown, to gray, to greenish-brown, to blue-black. Some pouches were Marine Corps green and red, but most were green.

Maggie grasped Jim's arm, clasped it against her side, and nodded in Jeff's direction. Jeff and the fishermen were in their boat. He sat at the center console, turning the steering wheel from side to side. His new companions stood beside him, explaining the dials, knobs, and controls.

"Don't you wish you were a kid, again?" she asked. "That's why I love him. He'll be a child until the day he dies."

With his arm pressed so snugly into Maggie's side that he felt the curvature of her breast Jim's comfort level was being sorely tested. He found himself sending the most unusual prayer requests heavenward these days.

"Come on, Jimmy. Let's drag Jeff away from his toy so we can leave."

Jeff objected, and Jim played the peacemaker. "Have you seen the Rockport cemetery this time of year? It's covered in wildflowers."

Although late in the season, the hallowed grounds were a riot of reds, pinks, purples and blues, but mostly yellows. Butterflies, bees, and insects fluttered and buzzed in abundance.

Maggie took photos with the same enthusiastic abandon she'd exhibited at the Pelican Place. She posed Jeff and Jim in the flowers, beside unique tombstones, monuments, and wooden crosses. The serenity placated Jeff's annoyance as she pointed out coreopsis, Texas bluebonnets, and daisies while Jim posed them and took their pictures.

Back at his RV, Jim turned on the music, took his evening antibiotic pill, and relaxed on the sofa. He was nearing sleep when he recalled that Marsha hadn't called him back, so he called her.

When she answered, the background sounded exactly like it had earlier. She would call him back after the grandchildren were in bed. "Love you," she said, in a weary voice.

"Love you, too." He smooched into the phone.

He dwelled on Liz as he drifted to sleep. Since their reconciliation, she'd been a loving, even fawning person at heart. He envisioned her reunion with her mother. Difficult, he imagined. The one with her father should prove much better. And the problems she mentioned. What were they?

An hour later, refreshed by his nap, he edited his pelican pictures. *Not bad. Wait till Liz sees these.*

When he retired for the evening, he realized Marsha hadn't called him back.

21

Guilty Pleasures

Saturday dawned cloudy and dull. Jim took his antibiotic pill at five and went back to bed.

When he awoke at seven, he donned baggy shorts and selected a T-shirt that had a picture of Virginia shaped like a running shoe. It was from his running days and ridiculously too small. *How did I lose control and gain a hundred thirty pounds?* He tossed it in the ragbag and put on one that fit.

Bill and Charles were readying their RVs for the trip back to Oklahoma. The park was a hive of activity, and many rigs had already left. Jim went to Bill's rig first. "Hey, Bill, I appreciated the jokes. They let me make the most of a trying time ... jetty-wise."

"Same here. But the best part was letting Liz mug you, so I could meet her." Bill laughed and shook his head. "How on earth can a puffin-stuff like you rate such a great-looking nurse?"

Wondering the same thing, Jim chucked his friend on the shoulder. They shook hands, and he left Bill to the finishing touches. He suspected the line of RVs on Cutoff Road reached all the way back to the San Juan Restaurant, so his friend didn't need distractions.

Patsy was in a jovial mood. "Ah, the invalid. You better not let Liz see you walking like that when she comes back, or she'll know you were pulling her leg."

She became serious. "Jim, please be careful. The girl seems safe and sincere, but one can't be sure. I've seen men get taken by young women who seemed sincerely interested in their welfare, only to discover it was their own welfare and the men's money they were sincerely interested in."

"If she's after my money, Patsy, all she'll get is a dollar and twelve cents."

Patsy didn't return his smile. "There are other things to be careful about, too."

"I know, Patsy. Trust me." They hugged, and he headed to Charles and Nadine's rig.

His perfectionist friend was his grumpy leaving-day self, but he gave Jim the same warning Patsy did. Then he groused. "Twelve rigs have already left, and this is only one campground. Nadine's no help. All she wants to do is talk to Maggie. If she doesn't hurry, we'll be the last ones to the ferry."

As Charles noted, Nadine and Maggie were engaged in animated conversation. The women hugged, and Jim met Nadine as she returned to her rig. "You two have a nice trip. I'll be praying for you."

"Thanks, Jimmy. You be careful, too. Don't take any chances with those legs. Promise me you'll go to the doctor if they get any worse."

"I promise."

There was more concern in Nadine's face. "And do be careful ... about everything."

Although she wasn't specific, Jim knew what, or rather who, she meant.

They hugged, and he ambled to Maggie. "Sorry you and Jeff aren't leaving with them?"

Maggie gave a smug smile. "Everybody wanted to beat the rush, so they created a worse one. Tomorrow, there won't be a line at the ferry when Jeff and I leave. As for you, we're leaving for lunch and the dollar movie at eleven."

"Sounds good. What are we going to see?"

"Who cares? We'll find out when we get there."

After his friends left to join the caravan to the ferry landing, Jim limped back to his RV. It was eight, and he'd been on his feet too long. He pressed his luck by making breakfast and washing the dishes before staggering to the recliner.

He opened his laptop, chose a photo containing both a brown and white pelican, and e-mailed it to Marsha and the girls.

Now, for some rest. He positioned the footrest as high as he could and drifted to sleep.

He jolted awake at ten. He still hadn't heard from Marsha. He called but didn't receive an answer. Not even from the answering machine.

His phone chimed soon afterward. "Sorry, hon, I couldn't get to the phone in time. The girls and I are making animal pancakes. Thank goodness they slept late this morning. Yesterday was the day from Hades. The girls fought all day long, then Taylor threw up all evening. I'm glad she came down with the bug so soon. Maybe it's run its course .... Uh-oh. I put some batter in the skillet and asked Anderson to watch it. I don't see her ... just smoke. Love you."

The line went dead before Jim could say he loved her, too.

At ten-fifty, he decided he would save Jeff and Maggie a stop at his rig. He was walking toward the drive, when his cellphone chimed. Marsha calling back, he thought happily.

A husky feminine voice greeted him. "Hi Jim. How ya doing? Legs better?"

"The right one is, Liz. And the left one doesn't throb as much when I stand. The swelling is about the same though. How's your trip coming?"

"Fantastic. Daddy's already in a therapy unit. Oh, Jim, we hugged and cried. He told me how much he loved me and how bad he felt for not showing me affection all those years. I asked his forgiveness for how I treated him. A huge weight's been lifted off my shoulders."

"That's great. I'm happy for you."

"He didn't give me the reason, and it doesn't matter. It's how we are now that counts."

Jeff and Maggie's pickup entered the overflow area and headed Jim's way.

"Jeff and Maggie are here to pick me up. We're going to Corpus for lunch and a movie, but we can go on talking. I'm not driving."

"No, that's fine. I'm at Josh and Becky's, where I spent the night. I'll head your way right after lunch. I had a nice visit with my brothers and sisters-in-laws. They're supportive of me taking care of you, by the way. See you sometime this evening."

"Be careful and drive safely. I ... I'll be looking for you." Jim's urge to say I love you disturbed him.

"I'm driving like you, now, so don't expect me early. Love ya."

When Jim climbed into his friends' SUV, Maggie asked, "Marsha or Liz?"

"Liz. I spoke with Marsha earlier. Liz said she'll head this way after lunch."

"Is her mother coming with her?"

"I didn't ask. I suppose she is."

"Did she sound happy or sad?"

"Happy. She reconciled with her father and seems overjoyed by it."

"She's coming by herself," Maggie exulted. "Good for her."

* * *

They selected the movie *Charlie Wilson's War*.

Jim recalled his war with Liz at Paradise Pond. Why had she become so angry with him? But where would he be if she hadn't assaulted him? Most likely in the hospital. Had he survived, he'd be moping around the campground for most of a week. Instead, he would share a pleasant and leisurely few days with someone who enjoyed nature photography as much as he did, who would help him select a camera and improve his photos.

During the movie, the early morning haze and clouds had given way to a bright afternoon, and the return trip was under fluffy clouds floating in a baby-blue sky. Cloud shadows dotted the landscape, giving it a surreal touch. The bay wasn't as clear as it had been a week earlier, but it made a peaceful backdrop on the trip back to Mustang Island.

After crossing the Packery Channel—a man-made waterway between Laguna Madre Bay and the Gulf of Mexico that divided Mustang and North Padre Islands—Jim spotted a pair of American oystercatchers in a narrow pool beside the highway. He made a mental note to tell Liz. Hopefully, the birds would stay in the area.

He saw a myriad of other birds—gulls, curlews, herons, egrets, and terns. A great egret that broke with tradition made him curious. Instead of stalking fish, it chased them about.

Jeff interrupted his reverie. "You sure like birds, Jim. I thought you would get whiplash at the channel, back there. What say we go to Mustang Island State Park? I bet Maggie would like a walk on the beach. It's okay if you walk on the sand, isn't it?"

Jim wasn't sure. "I'd better sit at one of the picnic tables." He wished he had Helen's binoculars to watch the birds near the shore.

When they arrived, his companions took off their shoes in the parking lot. "See you, later." They walked, holding hands, across the wide expanse of beach, turned left, and disappeared behind the tall dunes paralleling the shore.

They returned as they'd left—holding hands.

"That didn't you take long," Jim said.

Jeff cocked an eyebrow. "It's been more than an hour. We worried that you were getting bored."

Jim was stunned when he looked at his watch.

"You should've seen the birds, Jimmy," Maggie said. "There was a tall gray crane standing beside a fisherman like he was a long-lost fishing buddy."

Jeff laughed. "Yeah, every time the fisherman turned his back, that sucker stole mullet out of his bait bucket."

Jim didn't correct their misconception that the great blue heron was a crane.

"We also saw some black and white birds flying along the edge of the beach with their pretty red bills in the water." Maggie gave a false frown and leaned into Jeff. "My big baby joined the kids chasing them along the shore."

She lifted her lips, closed her eyes, and Jeff broke with RV club precedence by bending her double with his kiss.

Jim looked away.

Maggie sighed and gave him an odd look. "Most people stayed here on the beach. If we'd been young again, we'd have gone skinny dipping."

That's when he noticed their wet clothing and saw Jeff blushing.

No way. Jim reconsidered. Maggie might do anything, pull any stunt, given her sporting disposition, and she wasn't one to be shy.

Maggie linked arms with Jeff and grabbed Jim's arm, pulling him against her as firmly as she had at the Pelican Place. Sandwiched between two men, she ignored her husband's questioning glances as they returned to the pickup.

Jim blushed when Jeff gave him the same inquisitive look. Maggie was pulling a stunt. But what? And why? She must know it made both him and Jeff uncomfortable. He considered it worth a prayer requesting forgiveness, although for what, he wasn't sure.

They stopped at the visitor center—set on concrete pilings to protect it from hurricanes and tropical storm surges—to purchase souvenirs.

While waiting for his friends to shop, Jim leaned his forearms on the concrete ramp railing to survey the surroundings. Directly in front of him were two ten-foot-tall flowering yucca plants back-lit by the sun. Their clumps of purple-capped off-white flowers reminded him of candelabras. To his left, he watched a snowy egret shuffling its bright yellow feet in the shallow water of a pond beside the parking area. The motion startled minnows into the last movements of their lives.

The lovely scene tugged on Jim's heart. He thanked God, even as his face grew sad and wistful. He needed Marsha with him to share the beauty, but she was doing what she loved best. The knowledge that she was wearing herself out doing that and he wasn't there to help created guilt for doing what he loved best—enjoying the world's beauty.

* * *

"We're on again, Jackie. The old biddy might be right. The girl's headed back."

"That's *great* news. I made her so hot at the birding center she was trembling."

"We're being paid to follow her, not screw her, although your thought has merit."

"Give me half a chance."

"That might be harder than you think. You know that trembling you mentioned? There might be another reason."

"I don't like your tone of voice, Mrs. Mansfield."

"Her mother suspects she might be gay."

"Bull. The girl had an orgasm looking at me. Trust me, Edith. The sweet-assed bitch isn't gay, and I'll prove it."

"Whatever. That's not why I called. Her mom wants audio surveillance, and I need to borrow some equipment. I'd also appreciate your help tailing her."

"I'm still booked, but I'll try to work Ms. Sweet Ass in. When do you need the equipment?"

22

Bird Droppings

Jim reclined on the sofa, legs propped on pillows, drifting in and out of sleep.

A petite brunette splashing in the waves blew kisses at him. Aroused, he rushed toward her, but in agonizingly slow motion. She disappeared, leaving him alone and naked. He covered his erection with his hands while inching past people on the beach. If only he could reach the bathhouse.

He awoke sweating, relieved to discover it was a dream. He didn't usually remember them, but this one was vivid. More troubling was why he'd dreamed it.

Although the clock on the wall read 7:45, the RV's interior was dark, fairly usual for late afternoons in April. Sea haze dulled the sun and made the air uncomfortably cool.

His phone rang, and he raised up slowly to keep from causing his legs more pain. "Hello?"

"It's me, lover. I'm entering Fulton. What would you like to eat?"

Lover? "Um ... hi, Liz. As for food, I have tuna and cans of other things Marsha sent with me."

"I don't want tuna. I'll pick up a roasted chicken at Walmart in Aransas Pass, if it isn't too late, and HEB has a nice deli if it is."

"Don't go to any trouble. As soon as we hang up, Maggie will knock on the door. She knows I can't eat before seven."

"I feel like I should get something. Woops, traffic's picking up. Love ya."

Jim also said I love you, but the call had ended. Sobered that he'd told a woman he barely knew he loved her, he vowed never to make the mistake again.

A knock sounded on the door.

"Hold on a minute."

The knocking continued until he opened it. Maggie grinned up at him and held out a grocery sack. "You may be old, but you sure are slow."

Jim took it. "Thanks, Maggie."

"Aren't you going to invite me in?" She fisted her hands on her hips while pretending to peer past him into the RV. "You don't have a woman in here, do you?"

Jim laughed.

Maggie's eyes twinkled. The barest smile graced her flawless face. "That's why I kept knocking ... to give her time to get out the back door."

The fifth-wheel only had one door.

She skipped up the steps, noted the rumpled bed at the end of the RV, and sat in the recliner nearest the door. "I'm going to tell Marsha."

Jim couldn't think of anything. "What?"

"That I haven't seen your bed made yet. Those look like the same sheets that were on it when you arrived here a week ago."

Jim looked sheepish.

"There's a laundry room only fifty steps away."

"It's at least twice that far, Maggie, past several trailers and a motorhome. Besides, I have a bum leg. If you were a true friend, you'd help me out."

Maggie's dark eyes smoked. "If I ever help you out, Jimmy, it won't be as a housemaid."

Jim worried that his new worldly imagination was causing him to hear double-entendres in innocent comments. And creating sexy dreams. He kept his mouth shut.

"How's Marsha?" Maggie asked. "I've called her every day, and she won't talk for more than a few minutes."

"Same here. I'm ready to head home to give her relief."

"Speaking of that, when's Liz due back?"

"She'll be here in an hour or so. She wanted to pick up a chicken at Walmart, but I hope I talked her out of it. I told her you'd bring me something."

"Why would you tell her that?"

Jim held up the sack. "Because of this food."

"Food? That's the trash I was carrying to the dumpster. We're cleaning up, and I wanted to stop by on the way."

Jim flushed. "Uh, I assumed—"

"That Marsha's paying me to be your cook and housekeeper? Personally, I couldn't care less if you starve to death." Maggie glared at his protruding belly. "In a year or two."

She winked. "Jeff and I wanted a quick meal, so that's half a roasted chicken from IGA. Most of a bowl of salad, too, plus a few things I cleaned out of our pantry. Anything else, you and Liz will have to scrounge up."

"Maggie, you almost gave me a heart attack. I thought I'd insulted you."

She rose and gave a pleasantly-voiced command. "Bring Liz over when she gets in and has time to rest. I need to visit with you two."

She smiled her sly smile, pressed her body into his, and kissed him on the cheek. "Come over any time this evening. We always stay up late, even the night before a trip."

Feeling awkward, Jim thanked her again for the food and promised to bring Liz to her motorhome.

"Later," Maggie said as if she hadn't touched him.

When he closed the door, Jim collapsed onto the sofa. Was Maggie going nuts? Or was he? He'd definitely been away from home too long. His prayers were taking up half his thoughts.

With Liz approaching and a meeting scheduled with Maggie and Jeff later that evening, he called Marsha to make sure he didn't forget.

"Everything's great," she said. "We're watching *Cars* and eating popcorn. How's your leg?"

With the leisure of silent and contented grandchildren, they had a long and pleasant conversation. They were talking when the door handle moved.

"Hold on a minute, Marsha, someone's here."

Liz stepped in, emptied a small sack of groceries on the kitchen counter, and made herself at home in a recliner.

"Who is it?" Marsha asked.

"Maggie, inviting us ... me to their motor home," Jim said, wondering why he lied.

Eyes closed, Liz made a shaming motion with her fingers.

"What was I thinking? It's the woman who's helping me with photography."

Marsha ignored his previous statement. "You mean Liz? The one the girls told me about?"

As always, Jim marveled at the efficacy and speed of the female information network. "Yes. She went home to Houston and just returned. Maggie asked her to stay until next Thursday, when Dr. Gutierrez releases me, and she agreed. You know Maggie. I guess she thought I needed someone to help me get around."

Too late, he regretted what he'd said—making it all Maggie's fault.

Liz yawned. "It's Kingwood," she murmured, as sleep overtook her.

Jim felt a wave of relief. Confession *was* good for the soul.

"Maggie says she's a nice young woman," Marsha said. "Patsy isn't so sure. Nadine told me I should put my foot down and make you send her back home. I probably should be telling you that, anyway, but Maggie's so perceptive, and I trust you."

Liz was sleeping soundly when Marsha asked a question about her. Jim thought Liz should sleep but spoke her name.

She groggily lowered the leg support and opened her eyes. "Yes?"

"Marsha wants to know if you're staying at the Condo."

"No, here at Palm Gardens, cabin thirty-three. No reason to drive across town every day."

Jim thanked her and told Marsha.

Ten minutes later Marsha said, "Rest all you can, hon. Take care of yourself."

"You, too. Don't let Anderson and Taylor get you down."

They said they loved each other and ended the call.

When Jim turned to Liz, she appeared deep in thought.

She blinked out of her trance. "I didn't find anything I wanted at the deli, so I picked up some Black Forest Ham, and some nuts and fruit for lunches and snacks this week."

"Maggie dropped off half of a chicken and some salad right after you called. I knew she would."

"You have nice friends. I'm jealous."

Liz's smile faded, and the look on her face made Jim wonder what she was thinking. What she did next worried him. She walked to the sofa and kissed him on his forehead.

On reflection, he decided it was his response that caused his concern.

"I missed you, Mr. Brown Eyes."

Liz set the table, and they ate in relative silence.

"Maggie wants us to visit this evening, no matter how late," Jim finally said.

Liz nodded. "I thought she might."

When they arrived at Jeff and Maggie's motorhome, Liz and Maggie embraced. Jeff paused the DVD he was watching and gave Liz a hug, too.

After being with her only a week and having witnessed the angry side of her personality, Jim wondered if she was affectionate by nature.

The visit began with Liz showing family photos. One was a picture of her mother and father that was taken at a birthday party for one of their grandchildren earlier that year. Another was of the two by themselves. The last was a family photo.

"Jimmy, you told us Helen was a beautiful lady, but you didn't tell the half of it," Maggie said.

Jeff whistled. "She could be in her fifties."

"It's genetic," Liz explained. "Everyone on her side of the family has always looked young for their ages. You wouldn't believe what she eats. She doesn't exercise but looks as slim as she does in her high school pictures. And no, she hasn't had cosmetic surgery. If it weren't for me making her life miserable, she'd probably look forty." Liz said it unapologetically.

Six-feet-four-inch tall Frank towered above Helen. Broad-shouldered, he displayed a flat waist, strong thighs, and head full of silvery hair. His weathered face was distinctive—firm jaw and pleasant smile. As Jim had guessed, Liz's face was a feminine version of Frank's, while her body was a stretch version of her mother's.

"Your father looks like he's in his early sixties," Jim said, thoroughly impressed by the man he knew to be seventy-four. Maggie and Jeff murmured the same thing.

"Dad's strong as an ox. He's always been active hunting, fishing, and playing golf, and he's anxious to get back into the swing of things."

There was no denying Liz's brothers were her father's children, although none matched his height. All had athletic builds. Joshua's wife, Becky, was tall, but David's and Daniel's wives resembled Helen.

"You aren't in any of these pictures, Liz," Maggie observed.

She waved dismissively. "I was busy and arrived late. Since I was in a hurry, I spent the night with Becky and didn't take the time to find a picture with me in it. Besides, y'all know what I look like."

Maggie flicked a glance in Jim's direction while asking Liz, "Did your mother object to your returning?"

"Daddy and everyone else thought it was a good idea for me to come back, so Mother couldn't very well object. Of course, I had to promise to call her three times a day."

Liz smiled at Jim. "They seem to think you're safe, Jim. Mother gave the impression that you're a nice little old man. And I told them that besides helping you convalesce, I'm going to help you buy a decent camera and some picture-editing software.

"For your benefit, Maggie, I plan to take him to some local birding spots in the early mornings and late afternoon. During the day I'll make sure he rests his leg while we work on the basic photo editing procedures I use the most."

Maggie appeared satisfied. "It sounds like you and Jimmy are going to have a fun week chasing birds and taking pictures."

"And convalescing," Jeff added. "Do you charge by the hour or by the day, Liz? The next time I'm down with my back, I'll call you."

Liz winked at Maggie. "I only take care of birders and photographers. If you two want to stay the week, I'm sure Jim wouldn't mind if you accompanied us."

"I'm not a pansy birder."

"You sure know how to hurt a guy," Jim said, pretending to look pained.

He stood. "We're keeping you guys up, and you have a long day ahead of you, tomorrow. Liz has had two tiring days, so she needs rest, too."

"Don't forget, Maggie, I'm in cabin thirty-three," Liz said. "I want to see you off in the morning, so if I don't show up, come get me."

Maggie reflected. Had she not stepped in, Liz would be home with her overbearing mother and Jimmy would have found a way to get his doctor's permission to return to Oklahoma

She smiled. She'd had fun getting even with Marsha for not coming to Port A with Jimmy, then refusing to come when Jimmy hurt himself. Jimmy was so addled by her flirting that he wouldn't consider leaving until his doctor released him. Besides, Jeff flirted. Why shouldn't she?

But it wasn't all about Jimmy. Liz needed to spread her wings without the destructive weight of her manipulative mother. And an escaped canary—or one set free—could fly directly into a cat's mouth. There wasn't anyone she trusted to help and protect Liz more than Jim.

A major concern remained, but she'd run out of time. Helen should have opposed Liz's return. It would be up to Jimmy to find out why.

She gave him an affectionate hug and escorted him to the door. "That infection will heal faster, the stronger you are." She held his hand a little too long before releasing it.

Jeff mulled over his wife's actions. He normally trusted her judgment, but she wasn't infallible. And recently, she'd been acting weird, but it was that time in her life. Other wives had hot flashes, ripped off their clothes, and made their husbands miserable. If Maggie's Cherokee or Cajun herbal remedies made her flirt with other men, so what? Especially since she ripped off both his and her clothes, and their nights left him weak.

She was the most exotically beautiful woman he'd ever seen, although her sister, June Walker, was a close second. They could pass for twins when not side-by-side. Too bad June was disdainful of men. He'd like to take her for a test ride—find out how similar she and Maggie were.

Jeff's thoughts returned Liz. She was a desirable woman—one he fantasized about. She was expending emotional energy and financial resources helping his friend, and someone had to pay. He could handle it, but Jim had a rock-solid marriage. Plus, Jim gave the blessings and devotionals at their meals and RV club business meetings. That type could be blindsided by willing young women.

Jeff gave Liz a final appraisal, imagined her long legs clamped around him. *Too bad it's not me.*

"See you guys in the morning."

23
Kiss Kiddies

After taking his morning meds, Jim recalled the previous evening. His call to Marsha proved that not only Maggie, but all his friends were looking out for him. He was glad to learn they each voiced a different opinion. And during the visit with Jeff and Maggie, Maggie asked all the right questions.

As usual, she had her way and made sure he wouldn't be spending the next four days by himself. He felt weak for not countering her machinations, but to be honest, he wanted Liz around.

Why? And what were Liz's intentions?

Maggie had elicited several things that were as much for his information as hers—like Liz's absence in the family photos. He'd assumed she'd taken the pictures, but Maggie had reservations.

Of more concern to Maggie was that Helen didn't prevent Liz from returning without her. Jim had seen the cogs turning in Maggie's mind without coming up with an answer.

It didn't make sense to him, either. Why would Helen relinquish life-long control over Liz so easily? It had nothing to do with his integrity. He'd met Helen that one time at Paradise Pond, so for all she knew, he could be a mass murderer. A Jack the Ripper.

Jeff was busy unhooking hoses and the electric cable, Maggie beside him with a checklist, when Jim arrived to see them off. "Hey."

"Hey, yourself, Jimmy," Maggie hailed back.

"I came to see how the experts do it. I never remember whether to dump the black-water or the gray-water first."

She rolled her eyes and followed Jeff, who replied with his own, "Hey."

Liz arrived two minutes later, wearing a pretty, white and blue, mid-calf dress that Jim thought too beautiful to cook in.

"Whoa," Jeff flirted. "You didn't tell me you'd be birding in that. I'll be happy to go with you."

"Sugar," he began, glancing at Maggie, "we're changing plans. I've always wanted to be a birder. You run along home without me and drop off Jim on the way."

Liz giggled. "How y'all coming?"

"On schedule," Maggie replied. "And Jeff's right, Liz, you're extra-beautiful this morning."

To her credit, Liz blushed.

"By the way, Liz, I found more food in my pantry for you." Maggie nodded at a grocery bag on the picnic table. "Be sure to try all the teas. They're my special blends."

She and Jeff were ready in five minutes and were among the earliest snowbirds to leave that morning. Everyone hugged, wished each other well, and waved their goodbyes.

When she entered Jim's fifth wheel, Liz was surprised. "You've already set the table. How nice. Thanks for making the coffee, too." She poured a cup and took a tentative sip to make sure it wasn't too hot. Or of gag quality. "Great *coffee*. I'm impressed."

"Thanks. It was some Maggie gave me last night ... with instructions."

Liz took occasional sips while placing Maggie's new leftovers in the pantry. She bore a sweet, innocent smile and hummed off-key all the while she made breakfast.

Jim couldn't conceive that she would connive him in any manner. At the same time, he couldn't envision someone so beautiful helping him in the first place. Odd, but wonderful.

"Jim, what did you think of our visit with Maggie and Jeff, last night?"

He wasn't sure what to admit. "I thought it was nice, but I think Jeff would have preferred to watch John Wayne."

"You know what I mean. Maggie was inspecting us. Interrogating us might be a better term. Well, not you so much, not that I minded." She gave an evil grin. "Come into my parlor, Mr. Fly." She became serious. "I assure you, Jim, I won't harm you in any way. I like your company, and you share my interests."

He was drawn into her earnest gray-blue eyes. "I trust you. And you don't know much about me, either. I promise that I'll treat you like a gentleman."

Liz couldn't resist. She pouted. "Do I look like a gentleman to you?"

He chuckled. "I guess I put that wrong. I'll be the gentleman. You can be the lady. Okay?"

"Sounds good to me."

Jim eagerly told her about the birds he saw the previous day. "On our way back from the dollar movie at Corpus, I saw a pair of oystercatchers at the Packery Channel. There was this strange great egret, too. It chased fish around."

Liz smiled mischievously. "Oystercatchers are beautiful birds. So are splashing egrets. Maybe we can get their pictures for your editing lessons."

When they left Jim's RV to go to church, Liz noticed a car parked near the dumpsters. It seemed familiar, but she didn't mention it.

During the service, Jim started when Liz clasped his hand, but he didn't pull away. He found it comforting.

At the end of the sermon, she squeezed it and smiled a contented smile that induced a similar one on his face.

It was only nine forty-five when she dropped him off at his RV to change into more appropriate clothing. "We have time to kill before Best Buy opens, so we'll stop by Paradise Pond. I'll pick you up in ten minutes."

When she returned, she asked, "Do you have your cellphone?"

Jim smiled and tapped his shirt pocket.

"Is it on?"

"Yes, *mother*." He pulled it out and showed her the screen.

"I'm impressed. I apologize for not believing you."

Jim smirked.

She giggled. "Hey, we match."

Liz wore a baggy, tan-colored sports shirt and cargo pants. The pants were zippered above the knees, so they could be converted to shorts. She could wade while following shore birds without ruining her pants.

Jim smiled. His clothes were the same color, but his outfit wasn't baggy. The XXX-large pants were snug. It made him wonder why he hadn't seen her in form-fitting clothes except for that morning and the evening they played Pegs and Jokers. "You look cool."

"I hope you're referring to the temperature, Jim. I won't wear revealing clothes." Liz said it so matter-of-factly, he decided she meant it.

Not wanting to mislead her about his intentions by asking why not, he didn't pursue the subject. Her statement confirmed that her attire was intentional. It also explained her modest apparel, like her Sunday dress, and her lack of facial cosmetics. He wondered what she'd look like if she tried to be beautiful.

When Jim strapped on Helen's binoculars at Paradise Pond, Liz asked. "Did you get a chance to use them while I was gone?" He nodded. "Still like them?"

"Oh, yes. And Maggie' binoculars were exactly like my old ones, so I let her use them to look at pelicans near Rockport. You should have seen her face."

Liz smiled broadly but didn't say anything. She slung a tripod over one shoulder and her camera on the other.

The day was sweltering. A drop of sweat trickled down the side of Jim's forehead, around the crease of his eye, and down his cheek by the time they reached the Paradise Pond boardwalk. He blushed when Liz reached out and wiped it away. "I hope I don't get any sunscreen in my eyes," he murmured, to hide his discomfort.

"Yeah. I hate it when that happens."

They stopped to peruse the bird list. "The kiskadees were here this morning," Liz said. "Keep your fingers crossed, lover."

The term unsettled him. Again. But she was already peering expectantly down the boardwalk. It must be a remark she used regularly—like waitresses who called all men honey or sweetie.

They didn't see the kiskadees but spotted the grebes across the pond, still too far away for a quality photo.

At the end of the boardwalk, she touched his arm. "Jim, seven o'clock. Any idea what that white bird is?"

Jim thought it too small for a great egret. "Could it be a snowy egret without yellow feet?"

"Study its bill."

He became more puzzled. "That's strange, it's not orange ... more black and gray. Or is that blue?" Stumped, he gave up. "I know it's not a cattle egret or great egret, so what egret is it?"

"Who said it's an egret?"

Jim flipped through his bird guide. "It could be a white reddish egret." He stared at the bird through the binoculars, then back at the book. "But that doesn't look right, either."

Liz stared without speaking.

He flipped back and forth between two pages before his frown changed to a smile. "Is it a juvenile little blue heron?"

She nodded happily. "You have to look at a bird's features and characteristics, rather than at it as a whole."

"Thanks, Liz. You're a good teacher."

She kissed him on the cheek. "I learned those birds the hard way, too. Becky makes me think when I see a bird for the first time. And speaking of time, we have to go."

Jim gripped her arm and pointed. "There's a kiskadee, and it's perched on a limb in the sunlight."

The black band on the stocky flycatcher's head looked like a mask. Its breast and belly were lemon-yellow. Its tail and what he could see of its wings were brown.

Liz's mouth turned down. "It'll fly before we get close enough."

They eased along the boardwalk, trying to keep out of the bird's field of vision. When they reached the second turn, a couple stepped onto the boardwalk.

"Oh no," Liz moaned. "That kills it."

Jim waved at the couple and held up his right hand while pointing at the kiskadee. They nodded and waited.

"We want to take a couple of pictures of the kiskadee," Jim said, when they reached them. "Thanks for waiting."

The couple stared in awe at Liz's camera, long lens, and tripod. "Nice camera. I'll bet it takes good pictures."

While Liz eased forward taking photos, Jim and the couple studied the bird through binoculars. "Beautiful," the lady exclaimed.

"Cool," her companion agreed.

Jim nodded. "Great colors."

Liz shot repeated bursts as the bird shifted on its perch. Satisfied she had enough shots to edit, she gave Jim an admiring look. Eyes wide and round, she blew him a kiss.

He marveled at her beautiful lips.

The man gawked at Jim, then stared perplexedly at Liz. His companion winked.

Jim and Liz were oblivious. They introduced themselves as grandpa and granddaughter and spoke with the couple for a few minutes. Liz thanked them for allowing her to take the first pictures. They thanked her and Jim for alerting them to it and announced it was a lifer—their first kiskadee.

When Liz and Jim exited the boardwalk, the woman nudged her companion. "What won't they think of next? Birding hookers."

"Definitely more than a doting granddaughter, but she looked at him like you look at me."

"I imagine that's what they're paid to do."

Alone behind the thick pepper trees, Liz leaned jubilantly into Jim. She breathed heavily and kissed his cheek. "Wasn't that breath-taking? I'm glad you signaled that couple." She kissed him again, this time lightly on the lips.

At a loss how to respond, Jim stood with his arms at his side—and a stupid smile on his face.

When Liz turned right on Cutoff Road, she didn't notice the car sitting at the Snack Shack—the same one she'd seen at Palm Gardens that morning. Its engine started when they passed the San Juan restaurant. When they reached the curve at the car wash, it followed.

Liz bounced in her seat. "Pinch me to make sure I'm awake, Jim. A great kiskadee. Not twenty feet away. In perfect light." She patted his thigh.

Jim wondered if she might be bipolar. Her exuberance seemed excessive.

Her hand on his leg felt good, though.

24
Return of Birdzilla

When they neared Mustang Island State Park, Jim began peering around. "It was about here I saw the great egret chasing fish."

A smile played on Liz' mouth. "Didn't you tell me that a tiger can't change its stripes? Why would a bird that stalks its prey chuck eons of instinct to chase it instead?"

"Adaptation?"

"This is Mustang Island, not the Galapagos."

"Wrong bird?"

"Good guess. See if you can find it in your guide. But don't worry, we'll see it later, and you can study it then."

Liz slowed when they approached the Packery Channel. The oystercatchers weren't in sight.

"The light's wrong, anyway," she observed. "The only place to park is on the east side of the pool, so we'll need morning sun at our backs."

They stopped at a sub sandwich shop on North Padre Island. ""Leave those alone," she demanded when Jim started to order chips. "You need to lose at least forty pounds."

Jim knew she was being kind. He could blame his weight on Marsha's cooking, but that would be blaming the wrong person. At the same time, he already had a wife to call him down. Like mother, like daughter. Could part of Liz's problem be a conflict of wills, and Helen had the upper hand?

He got over it. Liz was concerned about his health and comfortable enough to scold him about it. But he acted hurt. "Yes, Ma'am."

Liz was unimpressed. And unmoved.

Jim recalled how perturbed Marsha became the few times he'd tried to diet. She complained when he didn't eat the high-fat foods she cooked. When they were out together, they invariably ordered foods loaded with cheese. "Supersized, please." One order demanded a second, and he devoured them in a shark-feeding frenzy.

He couldn't deny he needed to lose weight. A recent calcium scan revealed him to be at high risk for heart disease. His doctor prescribed a cholesterol-reducing drug and warned him—as he had the past ten years—to limit his fat intake. But any meal with less than a hundred grams of fat and not filled with salt tasted too bland.

Now, someone was as concerned about him as his doctor. Plus, he hadn't required Omeprazole since Liz started caring for him. Come to think of it, no Tums, either. But he always felt hungry. He would humor Liz until they parted. A few days without real food. He could do that standing on his head.

At Best Buy, Jim started looking at Nikons.

Liz grabbed his arm. "Nikons are great cameras, but if you look at the paparazzi and at photographers on the sidelines at football games, most have white lenses. Nikon lenses are black. There has to be a reason why people who make their livings with their cameras use Canons."

She waved her arms about while she talked, obviously passionate about her avocation. "We birders don't just ride around in cars, shooting out the windows, although we do that, too. Birding's for everyone, not just those blessed with good health. And let me tell you, hiking above thirteen thousand feet in the Rocky Mountains in search of white-tailed ptarmigans isn't the easiest thing in the world."

Her seriousness and arm antics amused him.

"Hunters go into the woods a few times a year," Liz continued. "They wander about, sit on a stand, kill a deer or turkey, and people call them sportsmen.

"Birders and photographers hike for miles in those same woods. They photograph tiny birds and animals far more difficult to find to share their beauty and research with the world. And photographers let the animals live, so who're the real sportsmen?

"Jim, due to the stigma some have attached to birding, people pass up the opportunity to see a once-in-a-lifetime creature God robed in a splendor Solomon couldn't match."

"I've experienced the same thing," Jim said. "Most of my friends will get in a gas-guzzling diesel and drive a mile to see Boots, but they won't walk a few blocks to Paradise Pond to see a painted bunting or vermillion flycatcher.

"Of course, when they do stumble over that bunting, they act like they're the first people in the world to see one. That's when they find out what goes around comes around. They urge their friends to come see, but their words fall on deaf ears."

Liz nodded. "Birding is a sport, and Texas has a reputation for being one of the best states for it. We do great in bird census competitions, like the Great Backyard Bird Count in February, the International Migratory Bird Day count, and the Big Sit. Mad Island, in Matagorda County, perennially does well in the National Audubon Society's Christmas Bird Count.

"Besides here and the Valley, the Quintana Beach woodlot near Freeport and the High Island bird sanctuaries and rookery are great places to see birds. So are Lafitte's Cove Nature Preserve in Galveston, Sabine Woods near Port Arthur, and Anahuac National Wildlife Refuge.

"For people stuck on gators, Brazos Bend State Park near Houston provides the best of both worlds. You can stand right beside one as large as Boots while you're taking pictures of anhingas and purple gallinules. I wouldn't recommend it, though. There's nothing between you and those gators but grass and gravel."

Her eyes widened. "Texas has bird and nature photography contests with thousands of dollars in prizes. It's great for nature. Photographers share the winnings with the landowners, who use the money to improve their wildlife habitat. Not to mention the prestige the landowners must feel when their properties do well. Sweet, huh?"

Jim nodded. Liz's face radiated when she was excited. He wondered what her full lips would feel like on his—then prayed for forgiveness.

Two aisles away in the movie section, wearing what appeared to be a Bluetooth earpiece, Edith Mansfield wished her quarry would shut up. *How can anyone waste time chasing birds?*

The mutual admiration society ran its course, and Jim and Liz turned their attention back to cameras.

"Sorry about the soapbox, Jim. Nikons are great cameras, but the reason you need to buy a Canon is because the lens I brought for you is a Canon. It doesn't fit a Nikon."

They settled on a new camera on the market. "Be not the one by which the new is tried, nor the last to put the old aside," Jim said, staring reluctantly.

"I love your old saying, Jim. Now, forget it and buy the camera."

At Liz's insistence he purchased a three-year warranty that included accidental damage for his camera.

"Based on what your friends told me, it's mandatory. And if you fall off the jetty, again, you can't blame me."

He winced. The cost would hammer another nail in his coffin when Marsha found out.

Liz selected picture editing software. "Here's a nice beginner's program. It's intuitive, but to become proficient, you'll need to find a tech training center and take lessons. I find real classes the best, but online courses aren't bad. If you decide nature photography is for you, you can buy the full-blown version I use."

Jim frowned. Liz would make a great wife. Her husband wouldn't even have to drive—just turn the steering wheel in the direction she ordered him to.

Liz squeezed his hand in excitement and pushed the cart toward the exit counter. "Since we've been told about the excellent birding at Hazel Bazemore Park, let's go there tomorrow to try out your new camera."

The final cost tally dazed Jim. He gulped and nodded.

How did I let someone talk me into charging this much money?

Edith scratched her head. More than $2,000 to take a picture of a dumb bird? Matthews was right—her daughter was a lunatic. And old men were dodo birds when pretty girls smiled at them. They deserved to become extinct. Or maybe not. This dinosaur had the most intriguing eyes.

Jim and Liz found the heat and humidity stifling when they exited the air-conditioned building. To cool off, they stopped at a convenience store on Padre Island to purchase soft drinks. Liz, gaining confidence and stature with every passing minute away from her mother, refused to let him buy a regular soft drink. "Are you aware how much sugar is in a forty-four-ounce drink?"

"Do you know how much I love them?" Jim said, panic stricken.

"How much do you love your heart and body? As fat as you are, I'm surprised you don't have diabetes."

Liz was overdoing it, but Jim's better nature regained control. They would be together only a few more days. What were a couple of diet drinks?

"We'll limit ourselves to one diet drink a day," she stated. "The jury's out on artificial sweeteners, so we'll pick up some bottled water at IGA on our way back."

Women. Jim took a sip of his diet drink, made a face, and placed the cup in the holder. He opened the box containing his new camera and read the instruction booklet.

At the RV, Liz filled a bowl with almonds, walnuts, and raisins. She filled another with fresh fruit. Hands on her hips, she counseled, "Nuts are high fat, Jim, but they contain Omega fatty acids. Fruits are full of sugar, but they're fine ... if you don't eat too many." She cocked her head. "As in all of them at one time."

After demanding that he drink a large glass of water, she fluffed two pillows and placed one at each end of the sofa. "Lay down. I'm going to install the software program on your laptop while you rest."

When he fell asleep, she examined his right leg. It appeared much better. Not so, the left.

When he awoke, Jim discovered that she had positioned a recliner so that he could edit pictures while sitting on his sofa with his left leg elevated. "You think of everything, don't you?"

She nodded. "Let's edit those pictures we took this morning."

She showed him how to darken and lighten backgrounds, how to improve colors until they looked natural in marginal pictures, and the easiest way to crop slanted pictures to level them.

When he became sufficiently proficient, she edited her own pictures while observing him out of the corner of her eyes. She noticed that he rapidly became uncomfortable in any one position—squirmed, changed position, stood, walked, and sat—all the time favoring his left leg.

* * *

Edith scowled. Tailing Liz and bugging her SUV hadn't revealed anything useful—other than the odd bird was an overbearing snot. First, Liz gushed ad nauseam over some creepy old bird. Then she told Fats what camera to buy and how to use it. Next, she berated him for what he wanted to eat and drink. If it wasn't for her looks and the fact she was spending time with him, he'd split.

But that wasn't going to happen. Edith knew older men. Their moral gyroscopes spun out of control when they were around anything young and beautiful. Friendly women of any age, for that matter. Fats was no different. She saw it in his face, his mannerisms. He was smitten. She felt sorry for him. His gonads would become granite and ache before the girl finished with him.

And that was one of the perplexing mysteries. Why *was* Ms. Liz spending time with him? Based on their conversations, she appeared legitimately interested in his well-being and photography prowess. That didn't make sense. The man was homely, klutzy, and obese.

Edith was inclined to agree with the girl's mother. The girl wasn't all there.

But did she have a lover? She was an anachronism—a beautiful woman who wore unflattering clothes and didn't use makeup. Her hair looked like she styled it with a fan. Probably didn't shave her legs or armpits, either. She sure didn't belong in this day and time. At least not in the U.S. What man or woman would want to have an affair with a whiny, domineering witch who purposely tried to be ugly?

Or could it all be a ruse? Did the girl want people to think that? Was Fats a decoy—the red herring everyone focused on while she had her fun?

They were presently in his RV where she couldn't eavesdrop.

But I can easily remedy that.

25
Jetty Birds

Jim studied Liz while taking his late afternoon antibiotic pill. Editing her rail photos—with her brow furrowed and lips pursed—she reminded him of the song, "Pretty Woman."

She caught him staring and smiled when he looked away. "It's time to take a few more pictures, lover. Get two bottles of water, and we'll head to the jetty. The beach there has terns and skimmers. I'll position the Tahoe, so you can shoot out the window. That'll keep your legs sand and water free."

Jim faked a relieved smile. "I thought you were planning to push me off it."

"Get your things," Liz said, shaking her head." This is your first chance to use your new camera. Have you read the manual?"

He nodded. She was so like Marsha. Or did all women treat men like children?

The skimmers were missing, but terns and gulls comprised a large flock of birds near the shore. Liz eased close and parked with the sun at Jim's back. She reached into the back seat and picked up a beanbag. "Prop this on the window ledge to steady your shots."

Jim lowered his window and adjusted the bag. "Like this?"

"Works for me. Be sure to shoot in various modes and settings. It's laborious, but the camera will keep a picture count and record the settings. You can compare the photos to see which work best under the different lighting conditions ... Oh, a snowy egret."

It wasn't a bird on her must-shoot list, so Jim looked to see what made it special. "Where?"

"Beside the jetty, in the surf."

The small egret perched on the tip of a granite boulder poking above the gentle swells. Its wispy breeding feathers whipped about in the breeze. In movements too fast to follow, it plunged its black bill into the surf and plucked up silvery minnows.

Jim understood Liz's excitement. And why she'd trashed his binoculars. Helen's high-end model quickly achieved a sharp focus and provided brilliant colors.

Liz exited the Tahoe, unzipped and removed her lower pants legs. She pulled a pair of old sneakers from the back floorboard and donned them. "See ya later."

Jim watched her wade into the surf. Her shapely calves and shins were creamy white, not tan, so she must not jog during the middle of the day or in shorts. It took him a moment to realize why her legs glimmered. She didn't shave her legs, and her fine, wet leg hairs glowed radiant gold.

The egret eyed Liz's cautious approach, but it was more intent on satisfying its hunger than worrying about its stalker.

Liz bent and held the camera close to the rolling waves to take photos from a bird's-eye view. Jim's eyes widened as her wet shorts inched up her legs to reveal equally creamy white thighs.

Great binoculars!

Her wet shorts didn't become transparent but clung to her body. *So much for Liz not wanting to wear revealing clothes.*

Tearing his eyes away was like wrenching apart two magnets, but he turned his attention to the flock of birds in front of him. Some birds balanced themselves on others' backs as if trying to get a better bearing on their surroundings. Some birds had pink breasts. Birds sailed in with minnows in their mouths and presented them to others.

In the past, Jim assumed such flocks were comprised solely of the ever present, ever squawking laughing gulls. Relegated to sitting in a car and peering out a window, he was surprised to discover the bulk of the birds were terns.

The large gray and white ones with bright red-orange bills and shaggy black crowns were royal terns. He was all too well aware of the silver-gray sandwich terns that might include the one that contributed to his jetty debacle. Many of those had pink bellies. Red and black-billed Forster's terns were squat, compared to the tall royal terns and sleek sandwich terns.

He searched his bird guide to identify terns with thicker bills and discovered they were gull-billed terns. Small, brown-spotted ones were winter-drab black terns. There were even smaller terns farther away. Too far away for photos, they didn't hold his interest.

There were at least two species of gulls besides laughing gulls. Both were larger, and one was huge. Liz's earmarked bird book made identification easier than his did. The smaller ones were ring-billed gulls. Juveniles were the more colorful—bluish-gray backs, brown tails, and brown speckled heads, flanks, and breasts. Their legs and bills weren't yet yellow like those of adults, and their bills were tipped in black, not ringed. Adults were comely. Their heads, breasts, and bellies were white. Gray backs gave way to white-dotted black wingtips. A black ring encircled their yellow bills.

The other species dwarfed the ringed-bills. Herring gulls were similar-colored, but adults' bills weren't ringed. A large red dot graced their lower bills. Their legs were pink instead of yellow.

Laughing gulls were mostly in summer plumage—black heads, blood-red bills and legs. White split eye rings appeared poised to clamp on their red-ringed pupils. Several had pink breasts. Surprised that he hadn't noticed such beauty before, he looked them up to discover they weren't laughing gulls. They were the similar-sized, nearly identical Franklin's gulls.

At the edge of the surf, behind the flock, ruddy turnstones and a variety of peeps raced and chased in front of oncoming waves. Fun to watch, they were too small and far away for pictures.

He took group photos of the mixed flock, then began selecting individual birds. It became fun, challenging, and he soon had a lifetime of editing material. Realizing it, he looked for Liz.

Frustrated because the bird faced away from the sun, Liz positioned herself between it and the jetty. But no matter how she angled her body and camera, she couldn't get the photos she wanted.

Jim smiled at her contortions and scanned the jetty to see if the fishermen were having luck. They were. Their backs were toward their fishing lines, because the catch was in the surf. Liz's heart-shaped rump and the backs of her flawless legs faced their direction while she bent to take photos. Her surf and sweat-soaked clothing revealed every curve.

Edith adjusted her binoculars. She enjoyed sex any way it was served, and Liz was a beautiful creature. Edith couldn't visualize her obviously confined breasts, but she might learn more about those later, if there was a lover.

The RV listening device was in place, so maybe away from idiotic birds, the couple would engage in the substantive conversation she desired. If so, it was a matter of time until she obtained photographic proof.

She scanned the jetty, in case the girl's lover awaited her there. All men within ogling distance were perfecting their lecherous stares, so it could be any of them. Women watched with interest, too.

She swung the binoculars toward Fats. He was as bad as the rest. Drooling. His intriguing mouth caught her eye—its shape and texture. When he lowered his binoculars, she studied his eyes. She'd known they were unusual, but the shade of brown was spectacular. And he wasn't ugly, just obese. He'd be incredibly sexy if he shed weight.

She refocused on Ms. Liz. As suspected, she didn't shave her legs.

Edith's smile widened. With luck this could be an extremely rewarding case.

Jim ridiculed the gawking fishermen, then frowned. He was no different. It took all his effort to rip his eyes away from Liz even as he thought of the scripture: The spirit is willing, but the flesh is weak. *Please Lord, forgive my—*

A man, accompanied by what must be his two pre-teen sons, laughed delightedly while speeding his pickup through the flock of resting birds. Flapping urgently into the sky, the birds' cries sounded like screaming children. Four didn't escape. Three flopped on the beach and one lay still.

Jim became incensed. The birds had been conserving energy until time to feed. They'd provided a glimpse of the grandeur of God's creation. Now this. Trembling with rage, he was glad he couldn't get his hands on the pickup driver. Either he or the driver would lie flopping on the beach.

The birds that escaped the inconsiderate idiot circled out over the surf, and Jim turned his attention back to Liz. He admired her stunning beauty—until she turned and waved. Her look of thrilled innocence made him pray for staring at her.

She gushed giddily when she returned. "Wasn't that the most incredible sight?"

Jim nodded, but the egret didn't have much to do with it. He was a third-degree Peeping Tom and completely miserable about it.

"I'll have to clean my camera and lens, tonight," she said as she placed them in her camera case. "You'll need to do that, too."

She tried reattaching the lower pants legs. "Guess they're too wet."

She gave Jim a curious stare. "I hope you didn't watch me while I was in shorts."

"No, I was taking pictures of the gulls and terns."

He reflected that he'd only thought he was completely miserable before and hoped Liz would think his blush was due to the heat in the dark SUV. He prayed fervently for forgiveness, the fortitude to stop lying, and changed the subject. "A man drove a pickup through the flock. I think he killed four birds." He pointed at the still forms Liz hadn't noticed.

"My lord, did you get his license number?"

When Jim shook his head, she drove to the University of Texas Marine Science Institute, a half-mile from the jetty, and made Jim report the incident. At least the birds would receive proper disposal and, perhaps, serve as research subjects.

26
For the Birds

As they left the institute, Liz asked if he felt well enough to stop at the IGA.
Jim's left leg ached, but not as much as his conscience. "Sure."

She looked troubled, and he wondered if she was still upset about the dead
birds.

"Jim, I have to tell you something."

When she didn't immediately continue and chewed her bottom lip, he
prodded. "Yes?"

"When I was in the eighth grade, I held hands with a boy named Harold
Parker. It gave me goose bumps. When I asked Mother why, she exploded. Girls
who held hands with boys, or kissed them, were leading them on. Boys wanted one
thing, and girls who let them do it were headed for eternal damnation, maybe
worse." Liz drew in a ragged breath. "If they let the boys touch them in other places
... well ... they were bringing it on themselves. If I became pregnant, she'd die."

Liz's hands trembled against the steering wheel. "After that, when she saw me
look at a boy ... or a boy look at me ... she made my life miserable. I began hating
them, all of them, for bringing her wrath down on me. I wore baggy clothes, except
for what Mother bought me for church. Wrapping my breasts to keep them flat was
my idea."

Jim wondered how a girl, a woman, could allow her mother such control
without rebelling. At least in the short run? But children reacted to parental and
guardian controls in an incredible range of ways. One was reaction-formation,
where they ended up doing exactly what they didn't want to do. One of his cousins
still did that.

Liz was retarded sexually, if she wasn't retarded in fact. Perhaps that was why
Helen kept such close reins. He recalled the 1960s movie *Light in the Piazza* about
a similar circumstance. He wondered if Liz still lived at home, but it was none of
his business and he wouldn't pry. He became aware that she was still telling him
about her aversion to male attention.

"I cringed when my uncles and boy cousins hugged me at family gatherings
because I knew what Mother would do at her first opportunity."

She smiled. "Except for Grandpa Craig. He was Frank's ... I mean dad's ...
father. He hugged me, rocked me on his lap, and told me stories. Grandpa gave me
the only real nickname I ever had before yours. He called me Dawn. He said it was
because I brightened his day.

"We didn't visit him much, as you might imagine. He was rough as a cob and
turned the air blue with cussing." Liz gave a wisp of a smile. "As you can tell, I
remember a few of his words. For that reason and many more, he and Mother
didn't get along. He argued with her and told me I shouldn't do everything she
wanted. He said I should tell her to shove it up her ... behind. I can't even remember
how old I was at the time. Not too old, because he passed when I was eleven.

"Then, when I was eighteen...." Liz' mouth puckered like she bit a lemon.
"Let's just say that I've found comfort and security in what I wear."

They entered the IGA parking lot, and she didn't offer more.

Jim stared sympathetically. He wondered about the rest of her story. Would he be privileged to hear it?

When they returned to the SUV, Liz managed to reattach her lower pants legs.

"You're such a gentleman, Jim," she said, while he admired her beautiful calves. Out of the corners of his eyes.

"Thanks."

Jim reached the height of despair.

* * *

Helen Matthews, that miserable, stinking piece of crap!

Edith fumed. It was the most pitiful story she'd ever heard. Had it on the recorder, too. What screwed-up mother would deprive her daughter of the Balm of Gilead? Sex beat Valium hands down—without all the side effects.

She thought about Jackie. No, there were always side effects.

Although she'd do everything in her power to determine if Liz had a lover, which seemed more doubtful with each passing hour, she vowed that Matthews wouldn't find out. Her daughter needed help.

Mercy sex.

* * *

When Jim called Marsha at eight, she sounded different. Happy.

"Anderson and Taylor had a wonderful day. They didn't fight over the prettiest pancake at breakfast. They enjoyed Sunday school and played together without arguing all day long. Even shared toys. I feel blessed. I can't wait to be with you, Friday," she whispered.

Jim knew at least one grandchild must be within hearing range. Marsha refused to display affection or talk about love publicly. "I'm happy they behaved. And I can't wait to be home, too."

"You'll be home Friday, won't you, Jim? You can make it if you leave after your doctor's appointment on Thursday."

"Sure."

"I miss you so much, darling," she whispered.

"I miss you, too, sweetheart."

During the entire conversation Jim was consumed with guilt. He hadn't actually thought of having sex with Liz while watching her in the surf, but he'd enjoyed seeing her body. Wasn't that yielding to temptation, making it a sin?

Late that evening he climbed into bed hoping sleep would calm his troubled soul.

He tossed, turned, and remembered. He'd violated Liz's trust and his pledge to himself by ogling her in the surf and her legs at the IGA. And the fault was all his. Had he stayed home, the confrontation at Paradise Pond wouldn't have occurred. Neither would the fall on the jetty, and Liz wouldn't be caring for him. Another failure was listening to Maggie. He should've been morally strong enough to resist her meddling.

Jim agonized how to extricate himself from the situation. For the first time in forty years, he forgot to say the Lord's Prayer and didn't make intercessory prayers for his family and friends.

* * *

Spirits buoyed, Liz hummed while she readied for bed. Despite her earlier optimism, her photos of the kiskadee at Paradise Pond weren't gallery quality. Neither were those of the snowy egret, but life was where you found it. Suffice to have witnessed the events.

She recalled the fishermen on the jetty. How on earth could a jerk sit on a jumble of boulders, waiting for a jerk on the other end of the line, when a wonder of God's creation was a few feet away? Kings would pay a ransom to see such a sight, she mused, not realizing those same fishermen hadn't missed seeing a God-created marvel.

Her great day stemmed from turning in the surf and catching Jim peering at her through her mother's binoculars. He'd become so red-faced when he denied doing it that he had to be lying. And though feeling uncomfortable when Mark Thibodeaux did the same thing, and feeling vulnerable with Jack West, she didn't mind Jim doing it. It pleased her. Something stirred inside her—like with Harold and Jack.

This was a new dawning. Three times in the past week she'd appreciated the attention of men. First Thibodeaux, then West, now Jim. And Jim was like touching a live wire. She needed his body contact as well as his company. He gave her goose bumps.

* * *

Steppenwolf's "Magic Carpet Ride."

Edith swayed in time to the music for a few seconds before punching the answer icon on her cellphone. No need to hurry. It was bitch Matthews.

"Hello."

"Do you know Mary Elizabeth's lover yet?"

"She's only been back a day."

"If you were any good, you'd have found out last week."

"Mrs. Matthews, I've kept your daughter under surveillance twenty-four-seven since you hired me. I planted a listening device on her SUV last night, not thirty minutes after she arrived. I followed her all day, even to church. She hasn't called anyone, and no one has called her.

"She spent the entire day with the man you told me she molested at Paradise Pond. All they talked about were cameras and birds. If you'd like to come down here and take over the surveillance, be my guest."

"There's no need to be grouchy, Mansfield. What about that pilot girl ... Addi? Did you check her out? She acted odd. Her brother and husband, too."

"Yes, and they're absolutely clean."

"You couldn't possibly have trailed all three of them and Mary Elizabeth at the same time."

"Do you actually believe your daughter would send you home and then seduce the first people she met?"

"It's possible," Helen said irritably. "The three people at the airport might be sick predators Mary Elizabeth met online. Now, tell me everything that happened, today. I'll probably see something you missed."

Edith counted to ten. It helped picturing Jackie caning Matthew's butt raw. "Where would you like me to start?"

"Didn't you say they went to church this morning?"

"Yes, by themselves. I didn't go in with them, so heaven only knows what they did during the sermon."

"Do you want to be fired, Mansfield?"

The hell with caning, Edith mused. If she ever met Matthews at a coffee shop, she'd find a way to piss in her drink.

"After church, your daughter dropped Smith off at his RV. Fifteen minutes later, they went birding at Paradise Pond. After that, they went to Corpus Christi and bought a camera. Then they spent the entire afternoon in his RV."

"What did they do in the RV?"

"Talked about birds. I planted a listening device in it."

"Where are they now?"

"Sleeping in their own beds, as far as I can tell."

"You don't know?"

Justice would have to be served in a more painful way. *Oleander leaf tea, perhaps?* "I wouldn't know about Smith. I followed your daughter. She went into her cabin ... alone ... and hasn't come out."

"Have you planted a device in her cabin?"

"No. I can watch it from the side street, and her only visitor has been the old man."

"You can't stay awake 24 hours a day. I demand you put a bug thing on it."

"As you wish, Mrs. Matthews."

Helen couldn't bring herself to believe her daughter was a lesbian. "I bet the old man's the predator. Mary Elizabeth has seen thousands of people with poor cameras, and she's never attacked any of them."

"As I said before, Mrs. Matthews, your daughter's an adult. She can do whatever she wants. That said, I think you're barking up the wrong tree. They haven't done or said anything sexual. The only thing he's done is watch her while she took bird pictures at the jetty, but every other man there did the same thing. Hell, your daughter's beautiful. I watched her, myself."

"I don't appreciate your filthy language. And I don't want you staring at my daughter that way. I mean sexually."

Edith's bill skyrocketed into the astronomical range. "I apologize."

"One more thing, Mansfield. Can't you track vehicles using some sort of device?"

"A GPS transponder. I'll put one on her car, if you insist, but it would be much cheaper if you use the one that's already in it."

"I wouldn't have the slightest idea how to do that."

"What about her cellphone? You can use that, too."

"You can?"

"Sure, any smartphone can be tracked ... if one knows how."

"She's using mine, and it's not smart. It may be the Antichrist ... it drops in the middle of every call. So put one of those ponderous things on her car."

"It's your nickel. I'll get my associate started on it right away."

"See that you do."

Edith bit her lip to keep from screaming obscenities. She would rent the most expensive transponder Jackie owned and mark it up a thousand percent on the invoice. "I'll call you the minute something comes up, Mrs. Matthews. Hello? Hello?"

27
Fate of the Blue Crab

Liz was in the middle of a glorious dream. A stocky, sandy-haired man gripped her wrists with one hand while caressing her naked body with the other. He ravaged her breasts with nips and whiskers. Yielding to his aggressiveness, she spread her legs.

She sprang awake. Her fingers! The clock read 11:37 p.m. She'd been asleep less than an hour.

Liz scrubbed her hands, then re-showered. Although still feeling thoroughly unclean, she decided this might not be such a bad part of her new life—eternal damnation in the fiery pits of hell notwithstanding.

Becky tried to draw her into the taboo topic of a health and sex guide before a birding trip, once, while her mother primped her compulsory two hours. She'd changed the subject then. Now, with her subconscious rebelling against a lifetime of suppressed desire for male companionship, Liz wondered if she'd made a mistake.

Returning to bed, she resisted the urge to suppress her memory of the dream. At least not all of it. Why did her subconscious permit her to be seduced by the one man of the four she'd met during her short escape from reality who scared the living hell out of her? Who made her afraid of herself?

Why hadn't her dream lover been Mark? He was masculine and self-confident. But his eyes didn't contain the lust she saw in Jack's. Or was her subconscious being morally correct because Mark was married to a sweet, lovely woman?

She summarily dismissed ER nurse Jim Edwards. He was single, good-looking, and friendly, but too bold for her. He'd suggested meeting at a bar after he got off work. She didn't drink, but if she did, getting drunk with a man couldn't be a good thing.

As for Jim, she loved the way his body warmed her soul when they touched. Though old enough to be her grandpa, they had an indefinable bond. Or was it just her? He was embarrassed by their relationship—called it wrong.

Jim looked at her surreptitiously, maybe wanted to see more, but that was it. And like Mark, he was happily married. Older, too, and probably not experienced. He'd been married to the same woman all his life.

That must be it. Her subconscious recognized a real lover when it met one. Jack exuded virility and radiated the self-confidence of being fully capable of fulfilling a woman's every desire.

But why had Jack been restraining her in the dream? She hadn't offered resistance, had spread her legs—

Oops, too much remembering. Not only was her subconscious rebelling, her body was, too—filling with desire. But she had no experience. Probably not much defense, either. Trembling, she felt like continuing where her dream left off.

Damn my subconscious.

* * *

Disgusted by his lack of discipline and morals at the jetty and sickened by the awareness that he'd broken his marriage vows, Jim struggled with his conscience all night. When he staggered to the kitchen to take his antibiotic at 5:00 a.m., he knew the right thing to do—leave for home that morning.

How could he break the news to Liz? It had to be a lie that sounded plausible. He was getting better at that, like when he assured her at the jetty he hadn't watched her.

The thought of telling the truth didn't occur to him—a man whose word was his bond.

Jim lay back down, but sleep wouldn't come. He hated what must be done, but it would be best for them both in the long run. And, injured leg or not, he had to help Marsha babysit Anderson and Taylor.

Unable to suppress his overactive and troubled brain, he discarded any hopes of sleep. He got up, turned on KLUX for support, and started the coffee. Slumping in his recliner, he turned on his laptop, selected photos, and piddled with his new software.

They reminded him of Liz the day before. As excited by his purchases as he was, she'd pushed the cart to the checkout lane. She'd laughed, clapped her hands, and given him a high-five for a picture of pink-blushed sandwich terns sharing a silvery minnow. Then pressed her chest against his back and kissed his bald spot that she seemed to find so endearing.

"Beautiful. Good work," she'd said.

Instead of a reward, her kiss had been punishment. He'd wanted to kiss her in return. When she stroked his cheeks with her thumbs as he tried to concentrate on the pictures on his computer screen, it was like she was stroking his groin.

I have to leave before it's too late.

It was already too late. He'd become a pervert, sex maniac, and inveterate liar in less than a week. He couldn't afford making an even greater fool of himself by having his face slapped by a horrified young woman who felt violated. Who might sue him for sexual assault. Who would certainly tell Marsha what he'd done.

He turned off the laptop, poured a cup of coffee, and returned to the recliner to perfect his lie.

Liz awakened to the sound of her alarm clock and stretched. 6:30 a. m. She'd fallen back to sleep without realizing it and was shocked that she'd slept so long and well. She couldn't remember further dreams, so she must have gotten the foolishness out of her system.

She smiled at what the day would bring. She and Jim would photograph exotic birds at Hazel Bazemore Park. They might even participate in the spring hawk migration scientific study. She would also teach him more advanced editing techniques. He was a quick study.

After dressing, she examined her reflection in the mirror. Her baggy clothing looked ridiculous. Jim needed to see her as a beautiful bird, not a frumpy old hen. She and Jim would shop at Academy Sports, so she could find nicer clothing to bird in, and she would wear a bra. Do something with her hair, too. After all, they had three more days to share before she returned to prison—should she choose that destination.

She could also call Jack West, if she chose to live dangerously. She hadn't thrown away his card.

The day was perfect—clear, and cool, not a cloud in the sky. The previous day's heat and humidity had been replaced by a light breeze from the north. Eurasian collared-doves and great-tailed grackles filled the air with coos, whistles, chatters, and chirps. The palm trees swayed bright green against a pale blue sky. It was a day to be alive. She sang, "Amazing Grace ... I once was lost, but now am found."

After locking her cabin door, she noticed a flowerpot out of place on her porch—up against the wall instead of near the parking space. A discarded pen lay in its dirt. Probably a child's toy.

She returned the pot to its former position and removed the pen. It wasn't dirty, like she expected, but wouldn't click open. She found that understandable. A parent wouldn't give a good pen to a child. She put it in her pocket.

When she knocked on Jim's door, he didn't answer. A week earlier she would have freaked. Now, she waited patiently—thrilled to see him after a short night. What a difference each day made. No longer facing a bleak future, she praised God for making things right in her world.

Jim flinched. Should he get it over with quickly—or break the news slowly? "The door's not locked."

Liz bounded in. "Good morning. It's a glorious day. You can shut off that air conditioner and save some of that money to help pay for your new cam.... What on earth happened to you?"

Taken aback, both by her joyful entrance and unexpected question, Jim lost the initiative. "What do you mean?"

"You look terrible. Haggard might be a better description, and your left eye has a blood splotch the size of Texas."

She felt his forehead, walked to the medicine cabinet, and found a thermometer. After the beep, she pulled it from his mouth. "You're borderline fever, poor dear. Sit and rest while I make breakfast." She kissed his forehead, moved to the hook beside the refrigerator, and removed the apron.

Damn. I missed my chance.

Jim blushed. He and Liz were changing places. *First lying ... now cursing.*

"I didn't notice my eye," he said. "I had a bad night and couldn't sleep."

Liz studied him. "Do me a favor and roll up your pants leg. I want to look at your shin."

"My leg's fine."

"I'll be the judge of that. Sit by the door where there's more light."

She gently traced the wound on his left shin with an index finger—felt sparks. "Well, the redness hasn't spread, but it isn't any better. I think we should go back to Dr. Gutierrez."

"He said to come back if it became more inflamed or I developed fever," Jim protested. "You said it isn't any worse and that I don't have fever."

"You win this round."

Liz took a bottle of water out of the refrigerator and handed it to him. "Drink it all. It's what the doctor ordered. Then lie back while I make breakfast."

Within two minutes Jim was snoring softly. Liz stared. *Why does he make my heart beat like this?*

With Jim asleep and no need to hurry, she decided to delay breakfast. She remembered his rumpled bed, tip-toed up the stairs. and rummaged through drawers until she found clean sheets. She stripped the dirty linens, put them in the hamper, and remade the bed. She fluffed the decorative pillows she found stuffed between the bed and the wall in front of Marsha's closet and put them at the head of the bed.

Jim moaned and changed position, so she made breakfast.

"Hello sleepyhead. Ready to eat?" she inquired, when his eyes blinked open.

He gazed at Liz's radiant face and felt like throwing up for what he had to do to her—right after they ate.

"Whatever hid in your coffee pot died," Liz said, wrinkling her nose, "so, I made some tea Maggie gave us. It's a breakfast blend, and it's delicious."

She walked over, patted Jim's tummy, and assisted him out of the recliner. "We'll go to Hazel Bazemore Park after breakfast."

The delicious breakfast required compliments, and the park would be a better place to break the news, Jim decided.

Breakfast and the calls of the morning behind them, their day of birding in front of them, Liz drove by way of the dumpsters and handed Jim a sack. "Here's the garbage and a toy pen a child left in my flowerpot."

To her right, moving away, was the car she'd seen near the dumpsters the previous day. She recalled seeing it at Paradise Pond also. The darkened windows prevented her from seeing its driver, and she couldn't remember who she'd seen with it.

Jim took the discarded pen and tried to click it. He considered taking it to lost and found, but in all likelihood, it would be a waste of time.

He noticed Liz watching a car driving down the lane. "Anything wrong?"

"I've seen that car here before, and both times it has left as we approached."

"Maybe it's a coincidence. Most people make a habit of dropping off trash in the morning."

"Have you seen it before?"

Jim reflected. "No, but this is a large park, and I haven't been here long. We can check with the manager, if you like. Did you get its tag number? I didn't, but it was a red Honda Accord."

Liz dismissed the car. Jim was probably right. "Go ahead and chuck the trash, so we can go to Corpus Christi."

As they drove south toward North Padre Island, neither spoke while they searched the bar ditches, pastures, and marshy waterways for birds.

When they reached the Packery Channel, Liz shouted. "The *Oystercatchers*."

She drove across the channel bridge, made a U-turn, and turned right on Zahn road at the end of the long pool. There were several cars in the parking lot, but their occupants were fishing the channel. She grabbed her camera and tripod. "Come on, Mr. Lucky."

"Hey, I didn't salt the pool."

"No, but you spotted them the other day and alerted me. We could've missed them if we hadn't been looking for them."

They eased their way to the pool and found a spot partially shielded by tall weeds. Liz connected her camera to the tripod. "They're headed this way," she breathed excitedly.

It reminded Jim of deer hunting when he was a youth—sitting in a blind, trembling in excitement.

Liz leaned against him, smelling sweetly of bath soap. "Isn't it nice to have a cool day after all that heat? I'm glad I have you to warm me up."

Jim knew heating up. He couldn't help noticing her shirt's top button was undone. Couldn't avoid glancing at her cleavage mounded above her bra. As he forced his bloodshot eyes up and away, she pulled his arms around her belly and wriggled more snugly against him. Revealing even more. His prayers took a new direction—and dimension—with his growing erection pressing against her buttocks.

* * *

"I lost them, Jackie. I need one of your transponders."

"What about yours?" Jack West asked suspiciously.

"Mine's in the shop. My client wants one, and I goofed up."

"You're usually the cautious one. What happened?"

"I became lackadaisical. I thought my birds would go out of the park the short way, and they drove up my rear. Again. I lost my cover and let them get out of radio range. They said they were coming to Hazel Bazemore Park, so I'm here, but they haven't showed. They must've been distracted by something."

"Lackadaisey what?"

"Jackie, did you graduate from first grade? Or did your teacher pass you on your good looks?"

"I've told you before, I'm busy."

"Let me tell you a conversation I overheard, yesterday. It's good news for one of us, maybe both, if everything works out right. Liz Matthews has been deprived like you can't believe. Just thinking about it makes me wet." She told Jack the young woman's story.

"You're right. You need a GPS."

"How 'bout tonight," Edith asked hopefully.

"I'll meet you in the Walmart parking lot in Portland." Jack studied his watch. "It's eleven. Can you be there at twelve? I have to run by the house."

Edith glanced at the hawk study group. "It beats watching bird watchers."

* * *

A willet, flashing its white and black wings, swooped over Liz's and Jim's heads. Landing at the south edge of the pool, a hundred feet away, it walked to the water's edge and, like they, appeared to await the oystercatchers.

Ten minutes later, the oystercatchers separated, and the closer one approached camera range. High cirrus clouds dimmed the sky. Dull reflections made the water light blue, except near Jim and Liz, where the bank's vegetation reflected light green. Wind-blown ripples covered the pool's surface. Not the best backdrop, but acceptable with editing.

"Can you see what the oystercatcher's feeding on?" Jim asked, thankful his prayers had helped.

"Probably mollusks or something. This one's close enough, let's start taking pictures."

Liz reluctantly slid away from him, swiveled the camera toward the oystercatcher, and snapped a burst of pictures.

The bird, the lighter-colored of the two, had a brilliant red-orange bill with a sun-yellow tip. From the side, the bill seemed blunt. Head on, they could see that its wide base tapered to a thin point. A protruding red-orange ring of feathers encircled the black pupils of its eyes. Dark purple feathers covered the bird's head and neck like a hangman's hood. Its back, wings, and tail feathers were dark brown. It was white-bellied and had light pink legs. Snow-white stripes on the edges of its wings curled up and around its shoulder.

Jim fired a burst of pictures.

Liz gasped. "Did you see that?"

"Did the oystercatcher just flip a crab in the air?"

"End-over-end. Fantastic!"

The bird deftly maneuvered the crab to the water's edge, where the crab defiantly raised its claws.

Liz giggled and pointed at the willet moving unobtrusively behind the oystercatcher. "You thief," she scolded.

The oystercatcher chased the willet halfway across the end of the pool, their feet leaving trails of sparkling splashes. Having thoroughly chastised the intruder, the oystercatcher returned to the small crab, flipped it on its back, and enjoyed brunch.

Amazed and excited, the photographers rapidly filled their cameras' memory cards with pictures.

The oystercatcher eventually meandered past their shield of weeds. It noticed them but only peered warily as it sought more food. The last they looked for it, it was pecking a mollusk shell.

Liz rose to her feet. "Wasn't that fascinating?" She took a deep breath. "I've photographed many oystercatchers, but this is a first."

Before Jim could respond, she grabbed his head, pressed her body into his, and kissed him flush on the lip, in full view of the cars passing by on the highway.

Jim's resolve to keep sexuality out of their relationship dissolved. She tasted— sweet. He wanted—more. He traced the texture of her soft, full lips with the tip of his tongue and moved to enter. When he met resistance, he started to withdraw.

Liz's lips and mouth were virgin to anyone's tongue. Slowly, fearfully, she willed her clenched teeth apart. A serpent entered, searched and probed.

My ... lord. Her heart fluttering so loudly Liz thought Jim could surely hear it, she met his tongue, intertwined it with hers. Morals and birds no longer mattered. She drew away, sighed, and kissed him again.

The second time, they mutually drew apart. They had to breathe.

"That was the most heavenly kiss," Liz whispered.

Jim doubted heaven had anything to do with it, but it was the most brain-addling kiss he'd ever experienced. It pierced his heart like the oystercatcher's bill did the little blue crab's. Would Liz eat him for lunch, as Bill jokingly suggested?

He no longer cared.

28

Shore Birds

Liz wanted Jim's opinion of the shorts and blouse she wanted to buy to please him. Being her first time to dress for a man, it took all her courage. Heart palpitating, sucking air, she opened the dressing room door, stepped warily out, and eased to the fitting room clerk's counter where Jim could see her. Her brow creased in worry. "What do you think? Too revealing?"

The clerk glanced up from her Nora Roberts novel, shrugged, and kept reading.

No cleavage. That pleased Jim no end. He found temptation much easier to avoid than resist. "You look great. It's not revealing in the least."

The knee-length, tan shorts weren't as form-fitting as the shirt. Altogether, the outfit was downright demure. Despite that, the realization that she was dressing and posing for him awakened Jim's need. *Please, not now.*

"Not too loud, is it?"

The clerk raised her head and stared like Liz was a freak. The baby blue shirt over light tan shorts complemented the woman's complexion. Certainly nothing special or ostentatious.

"You're beautiful in anything you wear, Liz."

She blew Jim a kiss and returned to her fitting room.

The clerk gaped, before understanding dawned. The girl might be a pretty woman, but her sugar daddy was no Richard Gere.

Her mission accomplished, Liz felt downright decadent, as if she'd stepped naked from the dressing room. Flush with excitement, she found it not unlike her dream with West. Struggling with needs she'd suppressed her entire life, she had an idea. "Jim, it's too late for Hazel Bazemore. How about the National Seashore?"

"That's a wonderful idea." He fit the North Padre Island trip into each March itinerary, usually by himself, since Marsha preferred visiting with friends, and his fishing buddies weren't birding buddies. This time he would have a companion.

Liz spotted Snoopy's Pier seafood restaurant from the JFK Causeway over Laguna Madre Bay. Jim needed his strength. "How about lunch? My treat."

"No, it's your gas. I'll pay."

"You have cash? They don't take credit cards."

Chagrinned, Jim acquiesced.

They enjoyed the restaurant's seafood on its outdoor deck while watching water traffic on Laguna Madre Bay. Fishing boats raced in all directions. Tugs pushed or towed barges along the 3,000-mile-long Intracoastal Waterway not far from them.

Liz remained on her shopping high. "I can't wait to wear my new clothes. I want to be as beautiful for you as the birds we see."

Jim appreciated that Liz wanted to please him, but she was postponing family, friends, and personal needs to help him. There had to be something more.

And what was it with him? He'd broken his wedding vows less than two hours earlier and, come what may, had signed on for the ride. "You already are, Liz. You're the most beautiful woman I've ever seen."

Enraptured, eyes sparkling, she gripped his hand. "What you say won't change my mind about what I'll let you eat."

They burst into giggles. She'd nixed the fried foods he wanted. With one exception, a hush puppy. Only one. "There's never a right time to eat wrong," she admonished, after catching her breath.

"Sadist," Jim said, when he finished laughing.

Liz raised an eyebrow. "Do what I say, and you'll live to be a hundred. It's a promise."

"Impossible. I flunked my heart calcium test."

"Then you're lucky I found you in time."

* * *

"Are you sure you can't install the GPS for me, Jackie? It's been so long since I did it, I've forgotten how. I'll watch to make sure I can do it next time."

Jack shook his head. The woman wouldn't give up. "You went to the same class I did, did it in less time, and I interrupted my busy schedule to bring it to you."

"Yeah, thanks." Edith resisted the urge to put her hand on his thigh. "I'll muddle through, somehow."

On her return to Hazel Bazemore Park, she brooded about her morning. She'd screwed up. Her car had been compromised. And during the time it took to rent a pickup in Aransas Pass, she'd lost her quarry. Then they hadn't shown at the park. But maybe now.

She didn't see the girl's SUV in the small parking area, so Edith joined the hawk watchers on the park's birdwatching platform. From its deck, on a hill high above the rest of the park and the Nueces River, she scanned the park's roads and picnic areas with her binoculars. *Damn.*

She approached a burly hawk watcher who looked like a football player. Or a bouncer. *Why the hell is this stud looking for birds?* "Pardon me, did you see an old man and a young lady during lunch?" she asked.

"Several couples stopped by during that time. What do they look like?" The man extended his hand. "By the way, I'm Jason Meers."

Edith gave him a flirty look. "The lady's in her late twenties, plain, hair all over the place. Her friend is maybe seventy, but looks older, real chunky, a weird old gander. They're an odd couple, if you ever saw one."

"I couldn't have missed those two, so, no, I didn't see them."

"Crap."

"Who are they?"

"Friends. We were supposed to meet here this morning."

"If they're birders, anything could have distracted them. You might as well stick around and count hawks. That's what you intended to do, isn't it?"

"Yeah, guess I'll do that." Edith lifted an index finger. "Be right back."

She returned to the pickup and left. Her birds must have changed their minds.

* * *

Jim gained entry to the National Seashore using his Golden Age Passport. He and Liz wound their way along Park Road 22 to the Malaquite visitor center.

Ponds beside the road teemed with ibis and other shorebirds too distant to photograph. Birds in the brush and trees immediately beside the road disappeared when Liz hit the brake.

She pointed at a pair of ducks in a roadside ditch. "Any idea why they're called mottled ducks?"

Jim hazarded a guess. "Because they're mottle-colored?"

"Aw, somebody told you."

At the visitor center, Jim reached for his camera.

"Put that away. We took enough photos this morning."

She was right. The oystercatchers made the trip. It would take hours to review the hundreds of pictures, discard the poor ones, and edit the good ones.

They meandered through the exhibits and sat to watch videos of how North Padre Island had changed during the past seventy-five years.

They learned that the tall dunes on Mustang and Padre Islands afforded nearly as much protection as sea walls, and that barrier islands reduced mainland damage from hurricanes.

They also found out that critically endangered Kemp's ridley sea turtles laid eggs on the National Seashore's beaches. Its main threats included being drowned in shrimp boat nets and death by plastic—mistaking plastic bags for the cabbage jellyfish they fed on. People couldn't be stopped from littering, but a Turtle Excluder Device helped the small sea turtles escape from nets.

After touring the exhibits, they sat on the observation deck on top of the center to rest Jim's legs and observe the exotic landscape. Padre Island was dotted with ponds, ranches, marshlands, and small copses of scrubby trees. Laguna Madre bay was a barely visible silver streak in the west. To their left, the Gulf was blue-green and calm, thanks to a rare day with little wind.

Of more importance to Liz were the double rows of beach-side dunes separated by a meandering valley, fifty to a hundred feet wide. They extended as far north and south as she could see. Better yet, the beach was devoid of people. Perfect—if her willpower held. She was encountering major reservations.

"Come on, Jim, let's walk on the beach."

He patted her hand tugging on his arm. "As long as we stay away from the water."

My plan, exactly.

They descended a steep walkway to the beach and strolled beside the dunes. She pulled him playfully toward the shoreline.

"Not the water," Jim cried in mock fear.

"As you wish." She drew him against her and gripped him in a strong hug.

He found her size and strength disconcerting, and he was shy around women to begin with. Marsha was five-foot-three, so he'd never held, nor been held, by a woman as tall as he was. He tried to control his wild, sleep-deprived thoughts, but the woman and bucolic setting forced him to stick a hand in his pocket.

Liz hugged and kissed him repeatedly. "I can't get enough of your kisses."

His masculinity against her groin made hers pulsate. Another first.

Jim savored Liz's display of affection on a public beach—even one with few people. Marsha would never do that for fear someone might pop over a dune on an all-terrain vehicle or emerge from the surf in a wet suit.

Marsha even refused his advances in the privacy of their own bedroom if she thought they might be overheard. They once went seven months without making love when her mother stayed with them. Marsha had rejected his request that they spend a night in a motel, stating it would be rude and her mother would know the reason why. His rebuttal that her mother probably suspected they had a sexual relationship because of their daughters went for naught.

Liz encouraged and cajoled him past a trailer park a half-mile from the visitor center. She was thankful that its few occupants on the beach were headed toward the visitor center.

"Whoo, Liz, I've had it. My leg's aching again."

She peered around and pointed. "There's a gap in the dunes. Maybe we can find a dry place where you can lie down and rest."

"What about the poisonous snakes sign we passed on the way in?"

"We're bigger than they are." Liz raised her eyebrows. "You are, anyway."

She led him into the valley, found a wind-scoured basin, and shuffled her feet. "See, no snakes."

The basin was wide and deep enough they could stand upright without being seen from the beach. Their tracks were far from the surf, where most visitors searched for driftwood and shells and shook sargassum seaweed to find treasures like tiny sea horses and crabs.

She pulled Jim down onto the sand and fixed him with a perplexed stare. Her euphoria from dressing for a man had waned, and undressing presented a far more formidable obstacle. Trembling, she wrapped her arms around him and nestled her head into the nook of his shoulder. "Jim, you've been so good to me these past few days ... your understanding and acceptance—" She began crying.

Struggling with his own emotions, Jim enveloped her protectively.

Liz interpreted it as acceptance. His arms promised protection from the world. She felt loved—truly loved. She sobbed and sought his lips. For the first time since her early adolescent years, her heart filled with desire for a man. She would love Jim for the rest of her life.

Jim was drawn into a sensual whirlpool as Liz bathed his face with her tears and smothered his cheeks, mouth, and eyelids with kisses of appreciation. He couldn't remember when, or if, Marsha had showered him with such unfettered adoration. "Oh, Liz."

To repay him for his tenderness, the caresses and kisses that sent her into a hedonistic spiral demanding gratification, she pulled his hands to formerly forbidden parts of her body that demanded his touch.

Amazed that love could make her heart pound so, she extricated herself from his arms.

Jim released her reluctantly when she pushed away. Her kisses and explorations had stoked a fire within him, one he wouldn't experience again.

Liz stood. "Jim, I've never done this for anyone else." She unbuttoned her shirt.

Her obvious fear engendered mixed emotions. He didn't want to hurt her, take advantage of her, but he'd travelled far past the point of no return.

A war raged within Liz's spirit. Each button made her hands tremble more.

Her chest heaved. "This is difficult."

The last button came free, revealing breasts that swelled above her bra. Her formally sleepy eyes were wide, apprehensive, and brimmed with tears. "Turn around. No. I have to do this while you watch."

Jim experienced his own war between flesh and spirit. "Liz, you don't have to do this."

He prayed for the strength to resist, while wanting nothing more than to see her naked. His flesh being weak and spirit not particularly willing, he gave up and gazed at her enchanting body. Until he was jolted by a horrible thought. Her statements, tears—difficulty.

"Liz, are you a virgin?"

She shook her head. "No. It's my heart fighting with my brain. And Mother." She found the courage to remove her bra.

When her breasts fell free, Jim wanted to clench his eyes or look away. Transfixed, he did neither. She'd hidden them well, but they weren't beautiful. They were the only parts of her body that weren't, but with his will shattered, he longed to kiss and fondle them.

Liz shook so hard, he worried she would have a stroke. "Please Liz, put your clothes back on. I'm hurting you," he pleaded softly, without meaning.

"No, you must make love with me." She squeezed the words through her sobs.

Deliberately not looking at him, she removed her shorts and briefs and stood naked.

Jim gazed in astonishment. Her waist appeared small above ample hips and firm, rounded buttocks. Her thighs tapered to long trim legs and ankles. Her exposed ribcage and breasts shook above her taut abdomen. Swelled with lust, eager to satisfy her request, he protested one last time. "Liz, this isn't necessary."

Sobbing, not looking at him, she lay down on her clothes. "Please ... make love with me."

Jim found it as difficult to remove his clothing as it had been for Liz. He was ashamed of his physique, his belly. His face, arms, and legs, bronzed by the sun, provided a hideous contrast to his white body. Worse, his sex had been the recipient of demeaning names since high school gym class, the butt of jokes from fellow Marines when he refused to indulge in prostitutes in Southeast Asia.

He stripped, reclined beside her, and gently pulled her quaking body against his.

Tears leaked through Liz's tightly clenched eyes. Her body wracked with sobs. As Jim lifted her head to kiss her, her willpower fled. She pushed away. "I can't do this," she wailed. "I'm sorry, Jim. I'm sorry."

With a sigh of relief mixed with disappointment, he whispered soothingly, "Don't worry. You'll always be safe with me. I love you." Rocking her back and forth, he wasn't sure how the young woman fit in his life, except that in some deep way he truly loved her and always would. But he loved Marsha, too. Marsha was his soul mate.

He caressed Liz until she calmed, but his body didn't. Her soft breasts, wet with tears, slipped back and forth against his bare chest while she clung to his neck.

Releasing her, he stood self-consciously and tried to dress quickly, before the sight of him repulsed her. Balanced precariously on one leg, he struggled to keep from toppling.

Liz opened her red, swollen eyes, reclined on an elbow, and watched as Jim hopped on one foot, scattering sand on them both. Granules decorated her haphazard haystack of hair. And though now comfortable with her nakedness, she couldn't force herself to consummate their love. Not yet. "We're a mess, aren't we, lover?"

Her heart swelled with love. Jim had treated her with respect, honored her request to stop. And she was in awe of his body. She was a novice when it came to naked men, but he didn't look at all like she expected—nothing like in her dream with Jack.

Before becoming obese, he must have had a well-proportioned physique. He tanned easily, based on his dark arms, legs, and face, so she would insist that he expose more of his body to the sun. Finding his face ruggedly handsome—a Liam Neeson type—infinitely exciting, she pictured him after the weight loss she would demand. His uniquely colored eyes and gorgeous lips—sucking in a deep breath, she exhaled a sigh. *If only life could be different.*

* * *

They talked about birds near the Packery Channel. I'll try there.

Edith sailed along I-37 toward Corpus Christi. She swerved when a black Tahoe cut in front of her and flashed down an exit ramp. "Sun of a fudging beach."

The vehicle's maneuver fit the girl's M.O.—Matthews' alleged M.O.—and contained three people. Hopeful, she squinted. Wrong tag number.

Her phone chimed "Magic Carpet Ride."

Not so far, it hasn't been.

She glanced at caller ID. Maybe things were looking up. "Jackie, they didn't show."

Now, for the item of interest. He seldom called. "What's up?"

"I got lucky. We got lucky."

"You can help, after all?"

"Not that, but this one's right up your alley. You can fire up the Party Wagon."

"Why? There's nothing in the oven."

Jack West chuckled. "It's day-old bread. We get double the money, and you get double the fun."

"You don't mean—"

"I mean. The wife wants revenge, and she's willing to go the whole nine yards. She thinks the wagon's a great idea."

"Good lord, Jackie, what if she changes her mind? A victim can't do much about it, but a client can." Edith shook her head. "No deal. I won't do time."

"She signed on the dotted line, Edith. And there's better news. She wants her cheater to suffer."

"Geez. That *is* a good offer, but Matthews gave me several people to check out. I'll have to pass."

West saved the best for last. "I can do that for you. Who're the lucky people?"

"The folks at the airport. Even the pilot, now that mama thinks Ms. Liz might be gay. Personally, I think they're pure as the sand on Florida's Destin beach."

Her abdomen fluttered. "Can you really work it in?"

"I'll be free Friday."

Edith's hopefulness fizzled. "That's too late. My birds fly the coop Thursday or Friday."

"Sorry, it's the best I can do."

"Jackie, we're talking a bucket load of cash. Lawyer's rates. A bird's nest on the ground, if you'll pardon a birding term. Matthews claims her daughter assaulted the old man, but she's practically his wet nurse. If I thought she'd take care of me like that, I'd goad her into beating the crap out of me so I can retire again. She's supposed to speak Marine, but nary a cuss word. Drive like a demon but hasn't broken the speed limit. Doesn't even tailgate."

"That *is* spooky."

"I'm betting it's mama who's screwy," Edith continued. "I said a couple of four-letter words, and she called me down for it. Even made me apologize. But as long as she pays—"

"If mama's nuts, how can you be sure she'll pay if we don't find anything?"

"I wouldn't take a chance like that. I get advances."

Edith's brow furrowed. "If Ms. Liz has a lover, it's the Phantom of the Opera or Invisible Man. All I've heard is bird-watching, photography, and how Fats needs to take better care of himself. Bird-watching," she spat "it makes me want to puke."

"Are you sure he's clean?"

"Matthews mentioned the same thing, but I haven't seen a hint of impropriety. And the girl would have to be blind and not have hands."

"Yeah, I saw him at the hospital. But, sorry, Friday's it."

"Jackie, what can happen in two and a half days that hasn't happened already? You can make a grand while sitting on your butt."

"I'm bulling you, Edith. You scratch my back ... I'll scratch yours."

"Say no more."

"Hey, that was only a figure of speech."

"Oh." Edith didn't have to feign disappointment. "So, when's the date?"

"How's Thursday sound?"

"Could work. That's the doctor's appointment, but Fats might not leave until Friday. If so, the girl won't, either."

"Then let the games begin."

* * *

Jim and Liz held hands and kissed frequently during their return to the visitor center. She apologized for not making love, each time.

"My desire is your happiness, Liz. Being with you fulfills all my wish—" He stopped in mid-stride. Caught up in the moment earlier, he'd forgotten. "Liz, we couldn't have made love. We didn't have protection."

Her smile faded. "Do you have an STD?"

"No, of course not."

Her sleepy contentment returned. "Then everything's fine. I'm on the pill."

Jim squeezed her hand. "Since we're into confessions, I'm sure I would've stopped. I'm...." The words a happily married man stuck in his throat.

"Then let's stop talking nonsense." Liz closed her eyes and parted her lips. Her heart pounded when Jim's soft, full lips pressed ever so gently on hers.

"I couldn't conceive of kisses like this," she said when it ended.

Jim hadn't kissed such warm, soft lips, either. Marsha's lips were small and firm. She softened them when they kissed, but it wasn't the same. She always maintained his kisses were magical. Now, he understood. Kisses could destroy a brain and melt a heart.

The dunes backlit by the setting sun cast long shadows. Foraging fiddler crabs scurried back into their holes as Jim and Liz wandered past. Low, widely spaced waves made a ringing sound as they fizzled into small, shimmering rafts of rainbow-hued foam that floated gently onto the beach. A reddish egret chased mullet and small fish flashing in the mounded crests.

Brown pelicans fed in the surf, seeming unconcerned about the gulls balancing on their heads. Terns smacked into the water and darted away carrying shimmering minnows. But, lost in thoughts of each other and of themselves, the lovers didn't notice.

A tiny piping plover stepped daintily over a band of tiny bubbles onto the baby-blue sheen left by a receding wave. Sandy-grey and white, a thin black band surrounded its neck. Another one extended from one eye to the other over its forehead. Red legs and a black-tipped, red-orange bill added color. The endangered plover would normally send Liz racing for her camera.

Not this time. Her thoughts were elsewhere.

When they arrived at Palm Gardens, Liz and Jim hugged without speaking and parted at his RV.

In her cabin, covered with sand she hadn't felt, Liz dropped her clothes into the hamper and took a long, hot shower. Her mother and past had won out, but her body had been willing. A glorious first.

What did Jim expect? Could she meet his expectations?

Damn. I should've read that sex manual Becky told me about.

In the bathhouse, Jim reflected while droplets cleansed his body but not his soul. He'd planned to leave that morning and nearly made love that afternoon. He was married, loved Marsha, and would control his emotions in the future.

Somehow, the thought didn't bring relief.

29

Love Hurts

Emotionally drained by the day's events, Jim and Liz edited pictures in silence. She'd nailed the oystercatcher flipping the blue crab—water droplets flying—while eyeing it intently with its red-ringed eyes. Jim missed that action, but caught the defiant little crab, claws up, in its last-ditch attempt to face-off death.

He was enamored by her photo of the ominous oystercatcher hounding the wily willet.

Pleased, the photographers reclined on the sofa bed—Jim's legs propped on a pillow, Liz curled against him, nestled closer, and pulled his arms around her while they listened to KLUX. "Mother won't listen to this beautiful music."

"Why not?"

"It's a Catholic station. We're ... umm—" She didn't finish her statement. "Mother and Daddy played this same music when I was young. I'm going to send in a donation even though the annual fund drive is over."

She described her church without naming it. "It's the one true way."

"Do you believe the rest of us are Christians in name only and we're wasting our time?"

She peered at him. "I've wondered that for a long time."

"Liz, I was brought up in a church with a tradition opposite yours that believes the same thing. My doubts began when I was a teenager. The more I read and studied the Bible, much of what I heard in sermons and Sunday school lessons didn't seem right.

"When I married Marsha, I joined her church. It's inclusive and denominational. Over the years, we've attended many different Christian churches, Catholic to Four Square. They all preach the same message—peace, help the poor, treat others as you'd like to be treated, love your neighbor as yourself—but most find it difficult to put into practice. They proselytize, run down infant baptism, wrap their arms around the Lord's Table like it's theirs, and demean the way other churches baptize."

He remained silent a moment. "I think, if you polled every Christian, you'd find that each has a different idea about Christianity. None of us would agree totally about everything."

Liz nodded thoughtfully.

The exception, Jim failed to add, was that every single one would agree what they'd done that afternoon were sins. Cardinal sins. Mortal ones. Seventh Commandment sin.

"One of my pet peeves are preachers who become so wealthy they buy mansions. Paul refused to accept payment for preaching. The Son of Man didn't have a place to lay His head. There are so many poor, widows, and orphans that I see it as an affront.

"When I was young, the message was hell, fire, and damnation for not being obedient to God. Now religion has become big business by preaching that He's a cosmic bellhop in the sky, anxious to bless us when we become believers. Old-time scared-straight vs. a new carrot-on-a-stick promise of protection, health, and wealth.

"God and Jesus didn't protect the prophets and disciples. Yet, coincidences and human vanity being what they are, some people honestly believe their faith is so strong and their lives so blameless that they're singled out for good fortune. I've heard people claim that the Lord protected them from anything from a fender-bender to a tornado and that God provides," he made air quotes, "because someone gave them a fish on the jetty. They appear oblivious of people killed while on Church mission trips, the homes and lives of fellow Christians lost in tornadoes, the millions of children around the world starving to death."

Scowling, he set his jaw. "People tell me how God told them this or laid that on their hearts, then rant about people on welfare and rail against those with different lifestyles and religions. Where's the love in that? Never mind that they think they have a direct line to God when even the disciples who lived with Jesus often didn't understand him. But mega-church preachers and televangelists can't get rich by preaching that we can't earn blessings any more than we can salvation—lest we boast."

"Witness," Liz interjected.

"Blessings can't be counted on," Jim countered, "yet pastors request donations to keep messages of blessings and providence flowing ... despite the fact good and bad things happen to good and bad people alike."

"What about those pastors earning jewels for their crowns?"

Jim stared. "Earthly crowns of lavish lifestyles? The Bible preaches that we need to help the poor, not take from them with irrational promises."

"They bring many souls to Christ."

"So, you think they should be rewarded ... say a bounty for each new Christian? What about Scripture that states we aren't to store up treasures on earth?"

Liz smiled and tapped Jim's belly. "You sure are cynical and opinionated. And speaking of storing things, you better reread Proverbs ... and Philippians."

Taken aback, Jim made a mental note to do just that and changed the subject. "Why does your mother dress so fashionably when she insists that you wear long, plain dresses? And your mother wears makeup even though you say your church preaches against it."

"In excess," Liz corrected. "Honestly, I haven't thought about it. And, until now, it hasn't mattered."

Her answer caught Jim by surprise. "Do as she says, not as she does? She sure seems to have you under control ... like a Svengali."

"What's that?"

"Not a what ... a who. He's a hypnotist in a novel who makes a young girl his mind slave. She becomes a singer but can only perform when she's in a trance. Svengali benefits from the situation, so the name stands for someone who manipulates another person for evil purposes and their own gain."

"Now that you've explained it, I think I have heard about him." Liz shook her head. "Mother isn't a Svengali. She makes me to do things for my own good. It upsets me, but I know in the long run, she'll always be right."

"Liz, you've watched birds a long time. When the young are fully grown and able to eat on their own, they still flutter their wings, open their mouths, and try to con their parents out of food. At some point, all parents ... with certain exceptions ... must allow their young to fend for themselves. Some make it. Some don't."

"The mortality rate for first year birds is around ninety percent, Jim. Do you think that's acceptable for humans?"

"No, it's not, but human survival isn't simply a matter of life and death. We pay a terrible price, society-wise, for poor parenting practices. I think you would've made it fine without your mother's intervention after you reached maturity. And she should've allowed you test your wings along the way."

Liz shook her head. "But she's always been right."

"Always?"

"Always."

"Sounds like self-fulfilling prophecy, to me. How can you be sure she's always been right? Had you been able to work things out on your own, you might've done them better than how she made you do it."

Liz didn't answer. She unbuttoned her blouse, loosened her bra, and trembled when Jim responded. First ... after first ... after first.

Jim started to say a mental prayer and shrugged. It would be sacrilegious. Grasping Liz's breast, he took full opportunity of her gracious offer.

Just then an instrumental version of Roy Orbison's song, "Love Hurts", began playing on the radio. Jim couldn't remember the words, but it didn't matter. In Liz's case it was motherly love, not Eros love, but she wasn't strong enough, at least not yet, to bear the pain making her agonize. She responded to her mother's nagging with arguments and malicious compliance. He'd seen it happen among close friends and within his own family.

In his case, the pain was the conflict of doing what he knew was wrong and being unable to resist—like now.

Liz leaned her head back and pursed her lips. Jim stroked her long, smooth neck and placed his lips gently on hers. The kiss was long and sweet.

When it ended, he re-cupped her breast and gently fondled. Becoming again coherent, he wondered how she could let her mother manipulate her so thoroughly—though she was sure stepping out on her own now.

Parent-child relationships could sometimes be more difficult than sibling relationships, and everybody knew how spiteful, and long-lasting those could become. Some were caused by jealousy, others by illness, but most probably by money.

His experience was a little different but as life-long. It seemed like the children who received the most help from their parents and friends, for the longest amount of time, were the most irresponsible. And often, the most troubled.

"Liz, would you care to hear a short story?"

She nodded.

"My brother, Casey, has a penchant for making wrong choices, yet my parents have always bailed him out. When I left home, it seemed my parents couldn't wait. I joined the Marine Corps instead of going to college, and mom and dad were furious. But I was always a little lazy and a lot independent, so I needed that discipline.

"Casey stayed home and went to the local university. Whatever he wanted, he received. When he married, they acted like he was the bride. When he divorced, less than a year later, mom and dad moved him back home. When he dropped out of school, it was the professor's fault. When he couldn't find a job ... the market's fault.

"Casey didn't lack for money, though. He eventually met a woman named Sally and shacked up. If I'd done that, I'd have been disinherited. Not Casey. And when he didn't find his dream job and he and Sally fell into hard times, my parents moved them into a section of their home. When I complained, mom became infuriated and screamed that Casey wasn't strong like me.

"Eventually, dad became strong like me, too. He put his foot down and ordered Casey to leave. Mom stomped all over it and assured him that Casey would make it if they helped him a little longer. Dad refused, and pride being what it is, the divorce was messy. My sister, Geneva, sided with dad. I was caught in the middle.

"Sally eventually had enough, and she was followed by two other women who were a bit quicker to become disenchanted with Casey's life of leisure and self-indulgence. Not Mother. She left him her inheritance."

"What does he have to do with my situation?"

Jim looked sheepish. "I'm sorry. I have trouble not getting mad at the way Casey played mom, but that's my problem, not yours ... or his. Everyone has to make their way through life, and that's what he's doing."

"I guess I can see your point about parents backing off." She turned slightly and gave him a long, wistful stare, along with the opportunity for a better grip. Then gasped in excitement.

"You're good for me, Jim. Thanks for the story."

They became distracted. Liz reveled in the amazement of love and the fingers tugging her nipples erect. Jim savored the beauty snuggled against him and the malleable marvel in his hand. They sat comfortably against each other, enjoying the sensation of body on body, until Jim noticed Liz's jerky, involuntary movements. "Let's walk you home."

"Yeah, sorry. I fell asleep."

She rose, refastened her bra, and buttoned her blouse.

* * *

"Mrs. Matthews, good news. There's nothing to report."

"What did you do all day ... lay on the beach?"

Edith mentally added another thousand dollars to the invoice. "I thought you'd be happy. Nothing bad happened. Your daughter and the old codger went around taking pictures. Then they returned to his RV and edited them while talking about religion and his spendthrift, freeloading brother. They didn't meet anyone suspicious, and she didn't put him back in the hospital. Ha. Ha."

"That's a stupid thing to laugh about."

"Yes, I guess it is."

* * *

Jim's evening conversation with Marsha ended quickly. Children cried in the background, she was exasperated, and they gave up.

Exhausted by the exciting day and previous night's lack of sleep, he collapsed into a deep and untroubled sleep. He dreamed but didn't remember them.

Liz fell asleep when her head touched the pillow. Jim was her dream lover and the proportions were correct. She awakened as he prepared to penetrate her. Her fingers clean, she was thoroughly upset she missed the experience. Then again, her subconscious didn't know any more about sex than she did. It was essentially virgin territory. She forced herself back to sleep counting something much better than sheep, but the dream didn't return.

* * *

Midnight. Edith smiled happily. The bug in Fat's RV had worked perfectly. The conversations were the same as all the rest, but if the girl was clean, they always would be.

Some crabby bird at the Packery Channel had changed their plans, and the photos turned out good, based on all the complimentary bunk. They then discussed ultra-boring topics. The crap bored them, too, the girl fell asleep, and the geezer escorted her home at 9:33 p.m. The light in her cabin went off fifteen minutes later, and her phantom lover didn't show.

The GPS had been a snap to attach, exactly like at the installation course, but her request had been for the pleasure of Jackie's company. That was highly unlikely—as in for the rest of her life.

Her only inconvenience had been the locked side gate after planting the transponder in the SUV. Not a biggie. She'd contorted her body through the bars.

It was schooner time.

Things can't go any way but up.

30
When the Pie Was Opened

The long, deep sleep worked wonders, and early felt good. Jim eagerly anticipated the new day. Antibiotic swallowed, lights off, he reclined to savor the treasures of the dawn—the calls and songs of his beloved feathered jewels. Even the muted roars of diesel pickups carrying fishermen to the jetty and pulling boats to the harbor soothed his restless soul. He enjoyed being alive.

When the sun rays reached the overhead vents, he arose to prepare for Liz. He depressed the switch to turn on the propane hot water heater, so he could shave and have hot water to wash the breakfast dishes later. It ignited with a roar, but the sound ended abruptly.

The water must've stayed hot overnight.

Jim moved to the bathroom sink and turned on the hot water to splash his face before shaving. The cold water made him recall Marsha's last reminder. He'd assured her he would refill the propane bottle.

To be certain the bottle was out of propane, he tried lighting one of the stove burners. No luck. He'd blown it again. Fortunately, RVs carried two propane bottles, because the propane station didn't open until nine.

He pulled on shorts and a T-shirt and stepped outside. The crisp morning air smelled sweet. He watched his breath condensation evaporate in the welcomed chill, so unusual for this time of year. He huffed twice more.

He opened the propane compartment and turned off the empty bottle. When he reached to turn on the second bottle, he noticed a spent battery on the compartment floor. It lay on its side, mostly under the door plate lip. It wasn't something he or Marsha placed there, and no one else had any business in the compartment. Curious, he put it in his pocket.

In the RV, he observed it more closely. It resembled his new SLR camera battery. He opened the drawer on the lamp cabinet between the recliners and pulled out his fine-print magnifying glass. *A listening device.* So that was why Helen gave up so easily—she hadn't. But this was in his RV, not Liz's cabin. The implication made him nauseous. Had he and Liz been overheard? Been seen kissing? Worse? *Crap.*

Shaking, he took it outside, unlocked his pickup toolbox, and withdrew a hammer. Then hesitated. Should he smash it into miniscule pieces, or place it back so the PI would think it hadn't been discovered? The troubling decision required Liz's opinion. Her relationship with her mother caused the mess they were in.

No, I'm standing knee deep in my own mess.

Since it was illegal to lock RV propane tank compartments, he checked it thoroughly for a second bug. Then inspected the rest of the RV's exterior compartments to ensure they were locked, even though he did it each evening to protect his supplies, RV tools, and fishing tackle.

Paranoid, he double-checked the compartments. Then kneeled and scrutinized the ground under the trailer. Clean. Same for tops of the tires, axles, I-beams, hitch housing, hollow back bumper. The spare tire. His pickup was similarly pristine.

He started to re-enter his RV and stopped in mid-step. The fake pen. The PI wasn't taking chances.

He shook from anger. Anger at Helen and the PI. But most of all, anger at himself for being weak and possibly destroying his marriage. He wouldn't let it happen again. He wrapped the bug in a towel and placed it in his pickup. He needed to speak with Liz without being overheard.

When she arrived, he immediately enlightened her.

Her eyes widened. "Are you sure?"

He nodded. "There's no doubt."

But instead of becoming alarmed and worried about being photographed or what they'd done together, Liz became livid. "*Mother*. How could she? I'm calling her. Right now."

"We need to think this out, first," Jim said, shaking his head. "We may have been overheard ... or seen."

"Oh." Liz mulled over the implications. "Just as well, I'm not ready for a confrontation. Not yet. Thanks, Jim."

They discussed the previous two days and couldn't recall saying anything sexual or revealing while in the RV or SUV. They'd been physical, held hands and petted, but hadn't been vocal.

"I think it's lucky we found the oystercatchers at the Packery Channel," Jim said. "We were in a blind, and the area is out in the open, so it would've been difficult for anyone to see us without our seeing them. And we said we were going to Hazel Bazemore Park, so I'd bet that's where the PI went."

Liz's eye narrowed. "I hope he wasted his entire day. I'm sure no one followed us to the National Seashore, and I made sure no one could see us in the dunes." She grinned. "But it got pretty wild after that."

Jim recalled their trip back to the visitor center—kissing and holding hands. "Yeah, the PI could have asked for our autographs, and we wouldn't have noticed him."

They decided that silence was good news and the bug might be useful for misinformation.

"May I put it back?" Liz asked. "It's a way of getting back at Mother."

During breakfast Jim became quiet, somber.

"What are you thinking, Jim?"

"They say a good person does right even when no one's watching. We're being watched by a PI. That, alone, should be enough for keeping our relationship from getting out of hand. But I have another reason. I'm married. Do you realize how close I've come to ruining it?" He grimaced. "I love you, Liz, but we can't repeat what we did yesterday. No kissing or hugging, either."

Liz heard three words—I love you—and Jim's concerned look was more than she could stand. She moved to him, grasped the back of his neck, and kissed him softly. Drawing away to catch her breath, she murmured, "Those sweet lips."

So much for resolve. Jim felt like a boy who'd successfully stole a cookie from a cookie jar. Why not steal another? Maybe one more. The more he dwelled on their relationship, the more he decided he shouldn't have become so upset.

They returned the bug to the propane compartment. Back inside the RV, Liz kissed him and grinned. "What do you want for breakfast? Oatmeal or ...?"

Oatmeal it was. After he cleaned his bowl, Jim suggested, "We missed Hazel

Bazemore yesterday due to the oystercatchers, so how about today?"

"Definitely. We need to see why it's so highly recommended. When Mother's along, we can't get away early enough to visit it." She stroked Jim's wrist with her long fingers, propelling blood into his sex. "And I'd hate to frustrate our PI, again," she mouthed, with a wink. "That can be nerve-wracking."

Jim knew nerve-wracking—a full erection, with no chance for relief.

Liz moved their dishes to the sink. "Finish your toast and prop up your leg while I clean up. I want you rested for our trip. Hazel Bazemore's on the other side of Corpus, and it's going to be a long day."

Instead of the recliner, Jim walked to the dish rack, fully intent on drying the dishes for her. Liz couldn't resist. She hugged him with her wet, soapy hands and kissed him into a stupor.

Before they left, they checked the SUV's wheel wells and bumpers, its grill, and found nothing. They strolled the resort looking for the Honda they saw the previous day. They didn't see it or any other suspicious vehicles. Satisfied, they headed toward Corpus Christi.

* * *

The Palm Gardens' office clerk frowned at the security tapes. He reviewed them twice more before notifying the park's owner.

"Sir, I found something unusual in last night's tapes."

"And?"

"We had a breakout."

"A breakout?"

They watched a dark figure appear from the background and squeeze through the north gate.

The clerk pointed. "See? The person's dressed like a thief, but he's not carrying anything."

The owner nodded. "We can't take a chance. Put that camera on a larger sweep to bring in the road outside the fence. I'll have our night watchman check the monitor hourly and call the police if he sees anything suspicious."

31
An Eventful Morning

On the northwestern edge of Corpus Christi, Hazel Bazemore Park could be reached by taking the ferry and going through Aransas Pass, or by driving to North Padre Island and turning right on South Padre Island Drive, SPID.

Liz preferred the ferry, hoping to take photos of bottle-nosed dolphins in the ship channel. She and Jim were rewarded by a surfacing mother and calf puffing mist into the morning air.

When the ferry approached the dock on the far side of the ship channel, Jim gawked and pointed. "Redfish, Liz. Hundreds of them."

A huge school of reddish-colored fish milled about in the docking area, each at least two feet long. She laughed. "Daddy loves to catch them. He could snag them here."

The bay and island shores between Port Aransas and Aransas Pass contained the usual suspects—herons, egrets, and willets. A single osprey rested on a utility pole, and the ever-present sandwich terns dotted the bridge railings.

The same held true for the bay between Portland and Corpus Christi. The lack of exotic birds was assuaged by the sight of the U.S.S Lexington, a veteran aircraft carrier of WWII, the Korean, and Vietnam wars. Jim stared, nostalgically. "I saw it in Southeast Asia but haven't taken the time to visit it in Corpus Christi."

Liz made a mental note.

The trip to the park took an hour, with the new Liz driving. At the entrance they encountered a Y in the road.

"Heads or Tails?" Jim asked.

"Neither. There's a man standing by that restroom. Let's ask him."

He directed them to a pavilion, a quarter mile down the left Y. Birders stood or sat on folding chairs, staring into the sky. Liz and Jim barely topped the last rung on the deck steps before being approached by a trim, smiling lady Jim thought to be about fifty.

"Are you here for the hawk count?" the woman asked. "Jason said we'd get extra help today, and we need it. We've seen broad-winged hawks by the hundreds. More than four thousand flew over yesterday, plus a couple of swallow-tailed kites."

Liz excitedly shook her head. "We heard it was a nice place to bird. What should we look for? And how often do the kites fly over?"

The lady introduced herself "I'm Cindy Smithers. Would you believe my parents named me Cinderella, and I haven't found the nerve to change it legally?"

Liz laughed. "And I thought Mary Elizabeth was bad. Actually, I would've preferred Cinderella. At least you have a nickname."

They bantered names for a minute before Cindy answered Liz's questions. "The railing to your left is the best for local birds. It's a dry year, so a drip birdbath and a food tray have been set out. Those draw doves, green jays, sparrows, and such. Watch for movement in the mesquite and brush.

"As for the kites, they can appear anytime, but the raptors are more regular.

Come with me and look up. We'll point them out for you."

"We're more photographers than birders, so we'll start at the feeder," Liz explained, lifting her camera.

Cindy appeared disappointed but pointed at a small table containing cookies, brownies, and a large urn of coffee. "Well, be sure to sign our guest register." She winked "And eat as many of the goodies as you can. My friends and I don't want to be forced to eat them all."

Liz's frown kept Jim from racing to the table.

Cindy walked halfway back to the hawk group, stopped, and returned. She eyed them thoughtfully. "Were you two supposed to meet a friend here, yesterday?"

Jim and Liz stared at each other before Jim responded. "Why do you ask?"

"Well, a person asked Jason about a couple fitting your description ... an older man and younger lady."

Jim chuckled. "A couple, huh?" He made it sound ridiculous. "We mentioned that we planned to come here yesterday morning, but we spotted oystercatchers at the Packery Channel. Did he tell you his name?

"Not that I know. Jason's the one who spoke with him, and Jason's at a dental appointment today. And by the time he mentioned it, the guy got in his pickup and left."

"What did he look like?"

Cindy's brow furrowed. "I don't think Jason said if it was a man or a woman. He thought maybe the person found them, because he talked on a cellphone and left."

"What did the pickup look like? Maybe we'd know which of our friends it was, that way."

"I didn't pay it any mind."

Cindy called to one of the other hawk counters. "Eddie, what kind of pickup was it yesterday? The one Jason told us about."

Eddie was about Jim's age, but wiry and athletic-looking. "It was a new Dodge Ram Hemi, dark-blue. Hey, is that the couple the guy was looking for?"

"They don't know. Was it a man or a woman?"

Eddie shook his head. "All I saw was the truck."

"I hope that helps," Cindy offered.

"It sure does," Jim replied without elaborating.

He and Liz listened and peered for fifteen minutes while the hawk watchers identified spots in the sky. The specks wouldn't register on their photos, and they didn't mark the birds on their checklists. They thanked Cindy and strolled to the table to sign the register. Jim stared longingly at the cookies but found the will to resist. Liz slapping his hand away helped.

A plastic milk jug, half-filled with water, hung from a mesquite limb about forty feet in front of the railing Cindy directed them to. The jug's steady drip seeped onto a large, circular pan with a limb across it.

A dull brown bird with a speckled breast and long, curved bill sat perched on the limb, preparing to drink. A second bird, perhaps its mate, skulked in the weeds bordering the mesquite trees.

"I know that one," Jim said. "It's a brown thrasher. A pair comes to our backyard each year."

Liz nodded and took pictures.

Cardinals landed in the light-green mesquite branches beyond the pan. Sunlight filtering through the branches and leaves spotlighted the bluish sheen on their red feathers.

"Pretty," Liz muttered. "Use your camera, Jim."

He stood mesmerized, but not by the cardinals. "Behind them. In the mesquite. Green jays. They're beautiful."

Arriving birders spooked the jays and cardinals, so Jim and Liz surveyed the park. The pavilion perched on a bluff overlooking the large park. The Nueces River bordered the far end, and picnic tables sat along the river. To Jim's and Liz's left a weedy pasture extended the river. At the bottom of the hill, unidentified ducks and shorebirds swam and waded in a pond and small marsh.

Jim lowered his binoculars. "I'm impressed."

Liz nodded. "It's nice someone scattered food and provided water for the birds. Otherwise, it would be hard to find them."

Cinderella walked up munching a brownie and holding a cup of coffee. She pointed at the impromptu birdbath. "That's a nice long-billed thrasher. Have you taken a picture of it?"

Jim grinned. "So much for my expertise, I thought it was a brown thrasher."

"They're redder, and their bills aren't as long.... Hey, a golden-fronted woodpecker."

Jim whirled. "Where?"

Liz was already taking pictures.

"Eleven o'clock, in the mesquite to the left of the birdbath," she and Cindy said in unison.

Picturing the tree as a clock, Jim focused where they directed. The bird disappeared into the thicket as he lifted his camera.

"Don't worry," Cindy assured him. "It'll be back."

The green jays returned and hesitated warily in the trees before slipping down to the food and water. The light-green mesquite leaves and budding yellow-orange oak tree leaves complemented their exotic coloring.

Jim blissfully took several pictures before lowering his camera to study them through the binoculars. Their backs were a dark olive green, the feathers on their bellies and under their tails a greenish-yellow. Their blue heads and faces were highlighted by protruding black, feathery eyebrows.

"They look like Groucho Marx."

"Who's that?" Liz asked.

Cindy winked at Jim.

They were distracted before Jim could respond.

"If you like the jays, Jim, look at 2 o'clock, behind them. Your woodpecker's back," Cindy said.

Jim pointed his camera higher and took pictures of the golden-fronted woodpecker before it disappeared. Its black and white laddered back made it look much like a red-bellied woodpecker, but red-bellies had red foreheads, crowns, and napes. Golden-fronted woodpeckers had a splash of red on their crowns, and their napes glowed a burnished gold. Their lores, the area between their eyes and bills, were yellow.

"Liz, I'm in birders' heaven."

But even avid birders and photographers tired of viewing and photographing the same thing, and Liz and Jim followed Cindy to the hawk watchers. They marveled at their expertise. A pair of dots moving ever so slowly near the horizon were identified as Swainson's hawks. The experts proclaimed a dark form barely visible above them as a white-tailed hawk.

"Hazel Bazemore is the premiere hawk birding site in the world," Cindy said proudly. "Sometimes we see thousands of broad-tailed hawks in a single kettle."

"A kettle?" Jim asked.

"We don't boil them, if that's what you're thinking. It's the name of a flock of hawks." Cindy gave a crooked smile. "But a flock of hawks does have a nice ring to it.

"Spring is good," she continued. "We sometimes spot several thousand broad-tailed hawks a day. But fall's best. The last week in September and first week of October, we've counted four hundred thousand birds in a single day. The record's seven-hundred-fifty-thousand in October 1977."

"How on earth can you count that many birds?" Jim asked, the idea seeming incredulous to him.

"It ain't easy," Cindy deadpanned. "We do it by gridding the kettles," she explained. "With practice, we learn to judge how thickly a kettle saturates a block of sky and take it from there. You can look the process up on the Internet, if you wish."

Jim nodded. "I'll do that. Maybe I can come back some October and help."

"Better yet, Jim, join us in late August. That's when the Mississippi and swallow-tailed kites usually pass through."

He'd been on his injured legs too long, and his belly growled that it felt abandoned. "Cindy, we can't thank you enough for your help."

"Thank you, too, Jim. It's nice to have visitors even if they don't eat cookies. And maybe next time the hawks will be a little more accommodating and fly lower. They sometimes roost overnight in the trees on the hill."

As he and Liz started to leave, Cindy called after them. "Since you like to take pictures, you should check out Friedrich Wilderness Park in San Antonio. It's north of the city, off I-10, and it's a great place to see the endangered golden-cheeked warblers."

"Thanks," Liz said courteously. "We probably can't make it this trip, but where would you suggest we search if we do?"

"I've had my best luck near the windmill. The Fern Dell's nice, too. Just pick up a trail map. And if you can't go there, check out Blucher Park in downtown Corpus. The mulberry trees are covered in catbirds, kingbirds, and yellow-breasted chats, right now, and a pair of golden-fronted woodpeckers are nesting in one of the trees. The nature preserve across the street has a bench in front of a water garden. You can rest while you bird there, Jim."

They thanked Cindy again.

During their trip back to Corpus Christi, they looked futilely for dark-blue Dodge pickups.

* * *

Edith glanced at her GPS tracker. It was nice to follow her quarry at a leisurely pace from miles away. They were on their way to eat lunch, if she had to guess.

She guessed well. They passed her location a few minutes later, talking birds and food. She wouldn't always keep them in radio range, just intersect with them from time to time to make sure they were still together.

Satisfied she could keep track of them, she called Jack's client. The sobbing woman had trouble constraining herself. "After I saw the photos, I wanted to kill the bastard. Then I wanted whack off his privates with a butcher knife. I even stood over him while he was sleeping but lost my nerve."

"What did Mr. West tell you?"

"He said you could help me."

"What you want is extreme. It can't be undone."

The silence made her uneasy.

"Yes," came the halting response. "I signed the ... Mr. West's contract. Please help me, Mrs. Mansfield."

A written contract wasn't worth squat for the stunt they were pulling, but Edith made her decision.

"Of course, I'll help, sweetie. Here's what you'll need ... and what you'll need to do."

32
An Uneventful Afternoon

Jim and Liz stopped at a Cracker Barrel for lunch. He'd wondered all morning if she would continue her Gestapo tactics when it came to what she'd let him eat. He was disappointed. She did. But after a long conversation in the cool atmosphere, he left in excellent spirits. With plenty of photos to edit, they decided to return to his fifth-wheel and elevate his leg.

"Jim, it's a short detour to the beach at the state park. I'd like to kick back and look at the birds. We won't even take out our cameras. If we find anything unusual, we'll go back later."

When they arrived and walked to a picnic table, Liz suppressed her urge to hold hands despite not seeing a dark-blue Dodge. Jim was correct. She didn't need to risk destroying his marriage.

"Let's sit here a while," she said. "It's such a cool day that I want to enjoy it. And I'd like to talk more about what to do about Mother. We can't do that in your RV or my cabin. We can't even risk my SUV."

Despite saying she wanted to talk, she became quiet, pensive. Jim didn't press. He trusted her to tell him when the time was right—if it occurred during their remaining day and a half together. "I suggest we act naturally until you decide what you want to do," he said. "Be what we are ... nature lovers."

Bearing a pained expression, Liz nodded.

At the RV, Jim checked the bug in the propane compartment, removed the empty bottle, and refilled it.

"It was a long morning and you need rest," Liz suggested when he returned. "Why don't you take a nap on the sofa while I edit my photos?"

Exhausted, he nodded. "Sounds good."

"Then lie down while I get some pillows for your leg."

She grasped Jim's hand and led him to the bedroom. He lay on his side, she spooned up against him, and they fell asleep.

At 6:00 p.m., the darkened room jolted Jim awake. Liz was snuggled against him, snoring softly. He stroked her shoulder, felt her hair, and savored their musky scent from sunscreen and birding most of the morning. He tiptoed softly to the kitchen area, swallowed one of the last antibiotic pills, and moved to his laptop.

Liz appeared in the doorway while it booted up. "Let's return to the scene of the crime. I'd like another shot at those grebes at Paradise Pond," she said hurriedly, to keep him from misinterpreting her comment.

When they turned left on Cutoff Road, they saw a dark-blue Dodge pickup with darkened windows in a barbeque shop parking lot up the street. Jim cast his eyes in its direction. Liz smiled and nodded back.

"What do you think? Do we try to get a tag number?" she asked as they strolled onto the pond's boardwalk.

"Not yet. He might change vehicles again, and it's better to know when he's around."

The small grebes kept to the opposite side of the pond, so Liz coached Jim while he took photos of a yellow-throated warbler, and a Tennessee warbler with an especially blue head.

When the setting sun chased them back to the RV, the Dodge Pickup was still at the barbeque shop.

In the RV, Liz glanced at her watch. "It's an hour before you can eat, and I need a shower. Why don't you do the same and come over about 7:45? Dinner will be ready, and I'll have KLUX on. Don't forget to bring your laptop for more editing lessons."

Jim was relieved. More editing lessons.

The hot water in the bathhouse soothed his aching body and legs. The soap stung the ugly, inflamed scrape on his left shin, but the longer he showered, the better it felt. He felt certain Dr. Gutierrez would release him from care, the next day, and found the thought sobering.

He didn't see unfamiliar people or vehicles during his stroll to Liz's cabin. Its bare windowsill and clean flowerpots comforted him. No bugs.

Liz wore a long Granny robe and smelled of bath soap when she met him at the door. "Sorry, I just stepped from the shower."

The robe accentuated her generous hips. Her normally wild, stringy hair was wet, slick to her head, and shone like spun gold. "You smell good enough to eat."

"Good, I won't give you any calories."

A succulent aroma emanated from a pot on the stove. Liz patted his belly. "Don't worry, dinner will be ready soon. I need to change into something more appropriate."

She disappeared into the bedroom.

"Ow! *Dang.* Jim, I think I twisted my ankle. Could you help?" Liz pleaded. "I'm decent."

Jim rushed to the door.

Eyes wide and apprehensive, Liz lay naked upon the bed. And she was more than decent. Beautiful, actually. "I've thought about you all day. I promise, this time I'm ready."

He stood frozen. Marsha was incredibly beautiful in her youth. Liz wasn't more beautiful, just beautiful in her own way.

Both shared the wide, well-rounded hips he found so enticing, but the similarities ended there. Marsha was olive-skinned, Liz an almost alabaster white. Marsha stood five-foot-three and had small bones. Liz reached six-feet tall and was medium-boned. Marsha had dark, comely hair. Liz's hair was a rebellious, dirty blond. Young Marsha's perky breasts passed the pencil test well into her forties. Liz's couldn't pass a package of pencils test, but their super-soft, satiny texture engaged him in a moral contest he didn't stand a chance of winning.

When he didn't move, she moved to the edge of the bed, grabbed his belt, and pulled him to her. She stared into his eyes. "Kiss me."

He met her seductive lips, and the resulting vertigo wiped all traces of Marsha from of his brain. He stroked Liz's smooth shoulders, slid his hands down to her breasts. His need pulsated.

As his hand savored her waist, abdomen, satiny thighs and legs, she whispered, "I shaved my underarms and legs for you." It was her first second. She'd shaved them one time before.

She removed his belt, unzipped his pants, and reclined on her elbows to watch him undress. She raised her arms for him when he lowered onto the bed.

Despite her assurance, Liz stiffened and started trembling. Although Jim wanted to take her immediately, he didn't. Though she denied being a virgin, she had to be one, he thought as he caressed her tongue with his, so she had to make the first move even if it meant not making love at all.

At first tentative, Liz became more receptive. When she felt him kiss her nose, eyes, and neck, the pace of her heart quickened, as her body relaxed. She lessened her grip on his arms. She savored the feel of his lips sliding the length of her nearest breast. Gasped and her head fell back when he suckled its nipple rigid. "Jim," she said, her voice low, "this is paradise."

His lips left her breast and returned to her mouth.

Tears leaking from her clamped eyelids wet his face. "How could I have waited so long?" she moaned.

Despite misgivings for taking her virginity, Jim lowered his lips back to her succulent breasts, found her nipples, and chewed.

Electrical impulses ravaged Liz's body. Her voice trailed off to a whisper. "Lord," she groaned. "Harder."

Jim clamped his teeth tightly at the base of a nipple until she struggled in resistance. Continued until her areola became rigid and bumpy, erotic to the tip of his tongue. He rubbed her belly, sliding his hand ever downward.

Struggling for breath, Liz arched her back. "Make love to me."

Jim rolled slowly onto her, taking care to support the bulk of his weight. He wasn't surprised when she didn't guide him. *It's definitely her first time.*

Liz stiffened again, begged for him, but still wasn't ready. Tears rolled down the sides of her face as she fought the urge to call off the lovemaking.

Shaking with need, Jim waited, not wanting her to do something she'd later regret.

He didn't see the irony. The risks of having unprotected sex or the complications that could arise later didn't come to mind.

Liz's breathing became hot. She slowly spread her legs and lifted her hips.

Lowering his full weight upon her, relishing the sensation, Jim eased into her.

How long had it been, he wondered, how long since he'd made love? Was Marsha this warm and wonderful? He couldn't remember. She'd never been this wet, though.

Liz didn't expect Jim to feel like French bread out of an oven as he entered. He seared her, triggering exquisite spasms in her abdomen. A moan of pleasure exploded from deep within her. She'd worried needlessly about not being ready. He penetrated effortlessly, deeply. She quivered with sobs. "I love you," she said, over and over.

Jim was surprised. She'd been truthful. But for a non-virgin she didn't participate and lay unmoving beneath him after her first convulsion and guttural moan.

His qualms returned with his confusion, making lovemaking awkward. He didn't manipulate her body as he would have preferred to. Remaining gentle, it took much longer to reach climax than he imagined when he first saw her on the bed.

When Jim shuddered, gasped, and rested heavily upon her, Liz delighted in the crush. She'd satisfied him. Herself. She hugged him forcefully. "Thank you, Jim, for making this the greatest day of my life."

Jim remained unsatisfied. He'd enjoyed Liz's naked body against his. And savored the overdue release reverberating through his body. But he'd wanted her to fully share the pleasure.

He gulped deep breaths of air into his lungs for a full minute before gently rolling to her side, being careful not to put too much weight on her arms and body. He shook his head when she didn't move out of his way or assist him. *This doesn't make sense.*

"I love you," Liz whispered, shaking with joy. "I love you with all my heart."

"I love you, too," Jim said, wondering exactly how.

He fondled and kissed her breasts, her lips, during the afterglow. He enjoyed the lovemaking, especially the foreplay—caressing her exquisite body, feasting on her face, abdomen, and chest—but his love wasn't entirely sexual. It was deeper than that, an urge. *Yeah, to satisfy my lusts.*

But no, he could have stopped at any time, just as he had the previous day when she'd changed her mind.

He worried that he'd taken advantage of a troubled woman. Liz had hang-ups. But who didn't? Why did anyone do what they did?

Liz reflected. She'd committed adultery. Jim loved Marsha, and she'd tempted him into violating his wife's trust and his marriage vows. She rationalized her action. She had no interest in stealing him. They would be together less than two days, and something inside her burned for him. Had since their bodies first touched at Paradise Pond, so she considered it destiny, fate.

She thrilled at the touch of their naked bodies, loved Jim's exquisitely rough caresses, his devilish teeth and wicked tongue. She didn't entertain the thought that she might not be able to control his desires and actions—that she could very well crush his life.

Later, while they ate the potato soup she had to re-heat, Liz gushed. "That was the most incredible experience of my life. If it hadn't been for all those people at the park, I would have tried to seduce you there."

Jim wondered why she considered the one-sided lovemaking such an incredible experience. She hadn't climaxed. "And you, Liz, are the most intriguing woman."

Exhilarated, she didn't notice his lack of superlatives. She'd defeated inner demons. One was upbringing—doing something her mother would condemn. Of more importance, she had challenged harmful ghosts of the past and won. Jim hadn't forced himself upon her, had waited until she was ready, been gentle. Nothing hurt—too much—despite his size.

The experience was unlike anything she'd ever imagined. Would her heartbeat ever return to normal? She rose from her chair, moved behind him, and held her head against his. "Lord, I feel wonderful." She nuzzled her soft face against his rough, wrinkled one, pulled his head up and planted her lush lips against his.

When she returned to her seat—head swirling—one hand against her breast. the other steadying herself, a thought gave rise to a mischievous smile. "What should we have for desert, lover?"

Jim felt better about their lovemaking. Her expressions indicated she'd thoroughly enjoyed it

At 9:00 p.m. they shared a long, tender kiss, and Jim left for his trailer with a spring in his step. Liz had planned well. The evening still early. He hoped the PI was watching.

After readying for bed Liz tried to edit photos but felt drained. She called home and told her family she was well.

Before turning out the lamp, she recalled something. She pulled open the nightstand drawer and removed Jack West's business card. "I won't need this." She ripped it to confetti and watched the bits cascade into the wastebasket.

She reclined in bed, her few misgivings quashed by the pleasures she and her lover had shared that afternoon and evening. She welcomed sleep.

Jim called Marsha, an hour late, but she didn't mention it. In fact, she sounded strange—not tired or exasperated as she often did when she babysat the grandchildren.

"Hi, Jim, did you have a nice day?"

Her monotone left him perplexed. "Liz and I took a nice trip to Hazel Bazemore Park, and I saw some new birds. You wouldn't believe the colors of a green jay. I'll send you my best photos."

"That's nice, hon, but if you don't mind, I need to get ready for bed. I'll call you, tomorrow."

Marsha didn't seem impressed. Or interested. It popped to mind that she hadn't asked about his leg. Hadn't mentioned the pictures he'd e-mailed her the previous day, either. "Okay, sugar, see you Friday."

"That will be nice, Jim."

Her response sounded perfunctory. The entire call had lasted a couple of minutes.

What's going on? Does Marsha have telepathy? Jim wondered if something in his voice had said, "Guess what? I just made love to a beautiful, twenty-nine-year-old woman."

He switched off the light, plumped his pillow, and fell anxiously to sleep.

This time, he chased the petite dream woman across a church yard. She laughed, ran like the wind, while he could only move in slow motion. Then she was gone, and he stood there naked—surrounded by people entering the church. The pastor frowned at him and closed the door.

Jim tossed and moaned the rest of the night.

* * *

Positioned so she could see the girl's door through her binoculars, Edith sat across the street from Palm Garden's north gate. The broad kicked the old fart out early, so maybe her lover would appear. Then the light blinked out—the same as the previous night.

She would give it until midnight. Maybe one.

At ten-thirty, she called Helen Matthews.

"I attached the tracking device."

"Good. What did they do?"

"They went to Hazel Bazemore this morning."

"Who's Hazel? Is she a suspect?"

"No, it's a park in Corpus Christi where people look at birds."

"Oh."

"Then they went to lunch for most of an hour. They stopped by Mustang Island State Park for a few minutes on their way back to Palm Gardens." Edith summarized the rest of the day. "So, you're lucky. No news is good news."

"You can't possibly be doing a good job. You've missed something."

Does Matthews want her daughter to be having an affair? "I said, your daughter hasn't met ... or spoken with ... anyone other than the old man, and I've monitored them with listening devices twenty-four seven."

That wasn't quite true. She had yet to replace the bug the girl dropped in the dumpster, but she could guess what transpired in the cabin—supper and photo-editing.

"They're bird lovers and only bird lovers, Mrs. Matthews. Your daughter prepared a meal in her cabin, and they did more photo editing. He was there less than two hours, and I'll wait all night to see if someone else shows. No other PI, or a team of PIs, could do more."

A car with flashing red and blue lights pulled up behind Edith's pickup.

Damned RV park security.

"Sorry, Mrs. Matthews, something's come up. I'll have get back with you later."

Edith ended the call, fluffed her hair, and opened the vehicle window.

"Well ... hello, officer," she flirted, holding out her identification.

33
Storm Birds

Liz knocked on Jim's door at 6:45 a.m. and entered wearing her new shorts and a cranberry-colored sports shirt. "Did you take your medicine?"

"Yes, moth—" Stunned, he stopped mid-sentence and gazed at her head to toe. "You're breathtaking."

She pushed her breasts into his chest, groin against his, and kissed his lips numb. Leaning back, she shuddered from the warmth spreading throughout her. "Your morning kiss," she mouthed breathlessly.

Still excited from their lovemaking, she radiated, vaporizing the remnants of his misgivings.

Laughing, she began her breakfast ritual—apron, pantry, items in the fridge. The aroma of steaming Spanish omelets of egg substitute, English peas, and chopped onions filled the RV. One slice of center cut bacon each, wheat toast, a glass of orange juice, and coffee completed the sumptuous repast.

Jim burst Liz's bubble. "Doesn't coffee cause cellulite?"

"Have you seen something I haven't? It's impossible with my conditioning ... and genes."

She cocked her head and smiled. "You just want a free look," she mouthed, hiking her shorts as far up her thighs as she could and turning slowly.

Jim continued to pester without taking his eyes off her incredibly silken thighs. "You look a bit thin to me."

Liz didn't blink. "I'm perfect. I weigh a hundred and fifty-five pounds. It's the middle number in my BMI range."

"What's BMI?"

"Body Mass Index. It's a weight range the National Institute of Health has determined will lower our risk of health issues. One hundred fifty-five pounds is in middle range for my height, so I keep it there. Or within five pounds either way." She moved to the dishes in the sink. "So, I'm perfect."

"You're certainly that," Jim mouthed, earning another kiss.

"How do I find out my BMI?" he asked while drying the dishes.

"You type BMI on the Internet, click on the National Institute of Health, and enter your height and weight in the calculator. You'll find your healthy weight-range isn't much more than mine."

She pinched his rear while he dried a dish—proving plastic bounced on Linoleum.

"We'll go to St. Jo. Island today," she said innocently. "I loved searching for shells there before I was stung by the photography bug. I remember seeing flocks of birds. I'll pack a lunch. We can take a small ice chest, put our cameras in our backpacks, and make a morning of it. We can even watch the sheepshead fishermen on the north jetty, if you like. Besides, it'll be good exercise."

"You're wearing me out with exercise."

Or does she mean exercise? St. Jo was devoid of houses and shops, and being a weekday after spring break, only a handful of non-fishermen would be there. He smiled. Liz seemed to have a thing for beaches—the National Seashore, Mustang Island State Park. He'd probably be a goner on St. Jo. He'd like that.

Jim recalled that the island was a cattle ranch with an endless beach that could only be reached by a shuttle that ran hourly from 7:00 a.m. to 4:00 p.m.

He and Marsha went there once. He didn't recall birds, but fondly remembered a fisherman in the group catching a huge speckled trout and an oversized redfish. "I'm ready when you are."

When they left, they didn't see any blue Dodge pickups in the SUV's rearview window. None at the intersections. Not much moved early in the sleepy town mid-week with spring break over, and they arrived at the shuttle parking lot assured they hadn't been followed. The pickup didn't show during the few minutes between purchasing tickets and boarding the boat.

"Looks like we're good to go," Liz exclaimed exultantly.

The shuttle took twenty minutes to load, cross the channel, and tie up at a small dock near the north jetty. Seven fishermen were on board. Each had a wagon that looked like the Red Flyer Jim owned as a child, except for wooden rails affixed with white PVC rod holders. The wagons held tackle boxes and ice chests—probably containing lunches, drinks, and enough ice to chill the fish the fishermen caught. A variety of fishing rods stood vertically in the rod holders as if at salute, making Jim envious.

Liz noticed his wistful stare. "Don't worry, lover, you'll get your chance to fish today."

A part of his body instantly interpreted the innuendo.

The nearest fisherman choked and stared. *Lover?* He gawked. *Geez, the fat, old son-of-a-bitch is getting a hard-on. What does the gorgeous broad see in the bastard?*

Jim could swear he was looking at Maggie. "Liz, are you practicing Maggie's smile?"

She nodded. "Isn't it sexy and tantalizing? You wonder what she'll do to you next."

Liz was right—on both accounts. "Well, she's sure done it this time. I wonder what she'd do if she knew what she's gotten us into?"

Liz's smile faded as she mulled over Jim's comment. "So true."

The fisherman shook his head.

At St. Jo, Liz and Jim waved the fishermen off the boat first. Instead of following them to the north jetty, they turned left, toward a huge flock of gulls, pelicans, and cormorants resting and preening on the concrete bulkhead that extended to the southwestern edge of the island.

"The sun's right. Let's go for it." Liz smiled seductively. "But first, take off your shirt. You need sun."

Ashamed of his body and white skin, Jim stared. "Are you trying to embarrass me to death?"

Liz refused to budge, and he caved. She stuffed his shirt into his backpack and soothed his rattled nerves by sensually applying sunscreen.

The birds stared warily.

Satisfied after ten minutes of shooting, Liz led the way to the beach. Two tidal pools near the shoreline brimmed with trash and hermit crabs. She recorded the mass of plastic bags, empty jugs and cartons, tangles of fishing lines, and barnacle-encrusted refuse for a gallery exhibit on pollution. She wanted to expose the dangers they posed for wildlife, such as Kemp's ridley sea turtles.

Jim stepped on the jetty to see how the fishermen were doing. They were further out, so he watched some pelicans and a bird he didn't recognize. "Liz," he called, "there's a fairly large diving bird out here. It's pretty bland and has a long bill."

"Probably a loon," she called back. "They're fairly common this time of year."

After finishing her shoot, Liz joined him. She noticed his skin reddening and allowed him to put on his shirt.

"Now, where's your loon?"

Jim pointed. "Way out there."

Liz's eyes widened. "That's no loon. It's a Clarke's or western grebe! Did you take any shots while it was close? They're so accidental for the area they aren't even on the bird list."

"No, it's always been like this ... too far away."

They each took a couple of identification photos, and Liz turned to face him. Nostrils flaring, a curious stare played on her face.

By the time they reached a mile from the jetty, the southeast wind arm-wrestled the northwest wind to a draw, and the morning became sweltering. Even Liz, who didn't sweat profusely, felt droplets of sweat trickle into the valley between her breasts. Instead of being irritating, they raised delicious thoughts and the now familiar, much-desired yearning in her groin.

She studied Jim. A wide sweat-ring darkened the base of his hat. He kept wiping off the sweat above his eyes to keep stinging sunscreen out of them. He'd been a trooper, trying to please her. Hadn't complained once. "Poor baby, it's time for R & R."

A huge tree trunk that had drifted onto the beach lay nearby. Bleached white by the sun and covered in barnacles, it was about thirty feet long and two feet in diameter. The north side provided a modicum of protection from the sun.

Liz spread a ground cover and secured one end with the picnic basket. Jim groaned when he lowered the ice chest on the other end, and she felt guilty that her plan was making him suffer.

With only their heads and hats visible above the log, Liz scanned the beach back toward the jetty. "*Crap.* I'm going to kill Mother."

"What's wrong?"

"There's a person half-way between us and the ship channel, and he's watching us through binoculars. We only have today, and our *friend* followed us."

Jim held his hat above his head with his left hand while wiping moisture from his forehead with his soaked right shirt sleeve. "Impossible, the shuttles run an hour apart, and he didn't follow us to the shuttle dock."

Liz pretended to scan the beach and dunes back to their position and in the opposite direction. "I'm sure a good PI wouldn't have trouble following us. Maybe it's one of the fishermen."

"What does he look like?"

"A member of the French Foreign Legion I saw in an Abbot and Costello movie my dad has. I can't even tell if it's a man or woman."

"Is he towing an ice chest?"

"No." Liz opened theirs. "Well, there's no reason to give him fodder. Let's have a snack."

"A couple of gallons of ice water will do fine," Jim wheezed.

A cooling wisp of a breeze encircled them. Jim unbuttoned his shirt and flapped its sides. "Praise God. I might live."

Liz handed him a baggie bulging with cut veggies and fruit.

"I thought we brought ham sandwiches."

She stuck out her tongue at him and pretended to scan the beach again. Their observer was nowhere in sight. "I guess I was wrong. The guy must've headed back to the dock."

"He couldn't have walked half a mile since the last time you looked."

Jim lifted his binoculars, slowly scanned the beach and dunes to the north, then swept them back toward the jetty. "Uh-oh. There's a hat in the dunes. The guy wants a better view over our driftwood log."

He clucked. "That's our boy for sure. And he can't be too good to allow us to see him ... unless he has an accomplice and is trying to distract us. May I have a diet soda?"

Liz withdrew two, handed one to him, and kept the other. "It's a beautiful day," she said wistfully, "even if we can't make it more beautiful."

Her jaw dropped. She placed her soda on the log, grabbed her camera, pointed it toward the water, and fired a burst of pictures.

"What do you see?"

"Nothing, I'm doing it for the PI's ben—"

She froze. "Oh, damn. Lightning."

A low rumble from the Gulf punctuated her statement.

Jim, his back to the ocean to keep the sun from his face, whirled to see clouds rapidly building.

"Where the *hell* did those come from? Do we make a run for it, or what?"

Liz stared incredulously. Jim? Cursing? "The weatherman forecast a clear day," she said.

Jim voiced his opinion of TV weathermen and stared fearfully at her. "What can we do? We Okies hide in cellars when we see cyclones coming, and I don't see any hidey holes."

Liz was more concerned about his leg getting wet. His long pants should limit the sand swirling about them from entering his wounds. Hopefully, most bacteria, too.

She calculated. She might outrun the storm, but Jim couldn't. "We need to get to the dunes. We don't want to be trapped if the storm drives waves on the beach."

"But isn't lightning more likely to strike the dunes and turn us into beach glass?"

"Ah, yes, fulgurites ... petrified lightning." Liz laughed to put him at ease. "We'd make a couple of great statues. Can you imagine what we'd bring on E-bay?" She tugged him up. "But I vote for a chance lightning strike over drowning."

A high-pitched, far away sound hit their ears.

"That's different. What does it sound like to you, lover?"

"Like someone who's had the *crap* scared out of them."

Suspicions confirmed. The storm had Jim rattled.

Their stalker grew smaller in the distance. "Anyone that frightened of a storm must be an Okie. A member of your family, perhaps?" Liz joked.

A billowing, anvil-shaped cloud blocked out the sun. Jagged lightning flashes were followed by thunderous booms. The nearly non-existent waves gently kissing the shore earlier became roaring giants chomping up mouthfuls of sand.

Wind gusts whipped sheets of foam from their frothy tops. Even the mist blasted from the churning waves smelled ominous. Birds lifted screaming into the sky and disappeared over the sparsely-vegetated dunes in the direction of the bay.

Liz emptied the ice chest. "Help me protect our equipment. Dump your backpack. Hurry."

Backpacks emptied, they stuffed them with their cameras and put them in the ice chest. Liz began dragging the ice chest toward the dunes, and Jim snatched up the other end.

With the storm gaining ground and intensity and the wind howling, Liz pointed toward a depression between two dunes. When Jim hesitated, she growled, "Forget the stupid lightning and snakes."

She made him sit against her like a couple in a love seat, then wrapped the ground cover around and over them. "Hold tight and tuck your head down."

Jim trembled uncontrollably. "If we get hit by lightning, we're going to bake like an apple dumpling."

Liz blew a raspberry directly into his ear, as much to calm herself as him. The tempest horrified her.

They clung to the cover with death-like grips when the wind drove the first giant droplets into them like paint gun balls.

Within seconds they were rocked by blasts of icy air. Rain slammed into them so hard that it stung through their shield and clothing. They struggled to keep their shelter from being ripped away, but the rain worked its way through. The frigid downpour, violent wind, and fear set their teeth chattering.

Brilliant lightning flashes penetrated their cocoon and tightly-closed eyelids. Crackling thunder exploded so loudly nearby, they were momentarily deafened. Each jarring electrical shock left them terrified, fearful they wouldn't survive the next.

34
Love Birds

After what seemed an eternity, the lightning bolts struck less frequently. The rumbles of thunder became lower-pitched as the storm moved toward the bay. The rain lessened from a roar to a patter.

Drenched and freezing, Jim and Liz were surprised to find their cover filled with large rips. They hadn't noticed that some of the battering their bodies endured was done by their own wrap.

Lightning stopped streaking from cloud to ground and sea. It flashed from cloud to cloud, equaling any Fourth of July display. Dark green clouds extended into the Gulf, blending sky and sea.

Liz peered fearfully, eyes wide and nostrils flared. "I was literally scared to death."

At last hopeful of survival, Jim eyed her nervously. Her wet light-brown hair appeared gold. Her shorts, ridden high on her thighs, and soaked shirt emphasize her curves. "Then you're the most breathtakingly beautiful ghost I've ever seen."

Her full lips curled upwards at his comment, swelling him with desire.

Liz noticed his lust. Touched it timidly with a fingertip. The final pickets of her moral fence splintered, and she grasped his full arousal.

Jim covered her mouth with his. Positioned her body on the tattered remains of their cover.

She pushed him away.

Did I cross a line?

Liz unbuttoned her shorts and worked them over her hips and down her long legs. The panties were easier.

She stared intently, when Jim lowered his pants, but didn't assist. He marveled that she could view his aging body with lust, but there was no denying the look in her eyes. He grasped her thighs.

Quaking with excitement, Liz parted her legs, and pulled him down and into her.

Within seconds they no longer shivered. Their bodies radiated waves of heat.

Jim brushed his lips against hers and lowered his weight upon her. She grasped his head and sucked his tongue into her mouth. He reached down and cupped her sandy buttocks.

"I can't believe how beautiful you are, Liz," he whispered. "Your body's so soft, so impossibly exquisite. You're an alabaster goddess. A soft Grecian statue."

Eyes closed, Liz relished his words and savored the lovemaking that, despite their tempestuousness, seemed gentle as a dawn breeze.

Jim rocked her back and forth, wishing she'd respond. His pleasure was giving her pleasure, and he was failing. She occasionally made love sounds, met a few thrusts, but nothing more.

Breathless, heart hammering, Liz enjoyed Jim's sex without the disconcertion of her own movements. She glorified in satisfying his needs.

Despite every effort to delay until she climaxed, Jim's body released in a long series of explosions that paralyzed him in electrifying completion. He proclaimed his love again and again.

Liz's world whirled about her. Nothing could have prepared her for the pleasure she experienced as she felt Jim lift and lower within her. She wanted to have his child.

When he opened his eyes, he saw her wide, satisfied smile, but it should have been a smile of satiation. What could he do to make her climax? His own had been satiating, beyond description, and he continued stroking her hips and thighs until his breathing returned to normal.

When he started to push off, Liz groaned and hugged him tightly. She sighed, between deep breaths. "Sex with you is incredible." With her eyes closed in ecstasy, she didn't see him shake his head.

She became sad, speculative. What would the next day bring? Where would she go? Back to an unbearable existence? She debated following Jim to Oklahoma and becoming his mistress. She desperately needed love, lovemaking, and regretted destroying Jack West's card.

A thought nagged at Jim's subconscious but didn't surface. Was Liz one of those women who couldn't experience an orgasm? Or was it him? He wouldn't find out. It was their last day together.

A smile creased his face, broadened. It didn't really matter. She had bestowed him with love and companionship, things he thought impossible a week earlier.

The thought made him recall their turbulent meeting at Paradise Pond where their—what did they have together—began.

Wondering the same thing, Liz embraced him. They joined in a long kiss.

The picnic basket and its contents couldn't be seen. The giant log had been swept near them by the storm surge. The ice chest lay upside down in another valley between the dunes.

They carried it back to the dock, stopping often to let Jim rest, to hug and kiss, and to thank God they were alive.

Liz hummed most of the way, and Jim was too embarrassed to ask the name of the song. He eventually decided it sounded more like "Brown-Eyed Handsome Man" than anything else.

It was a few minutes after two when they arrived at the boat dock, and they resigned themselves to an uncomfortable, hour-long wait for the shuttle—if it arrived, at all.

Coast Guard helicopters hovered above the water. A Coast Guard ship and Zodiac boat moved and zipped about in the channel. They speculated that fishing boats must have overturned in the strong winds and waves and that fishermen might have been washed off the jetties.

"Jim, the shuttle."

They were amazed to see it heading in their direction.

When it docked, the captain and crew rushed to meet them. He pumped their hands as crewmen wrapped them in silver-colored emergency blankets to conserve their body heat.

"If you hadn't showed up soon, we would've started a search party," the captain said. "Several boats overturned, and fishermen were blown off the jetties. Some are still unaccounted for." He appeared relieved. "I'll tell them to take you two off the list."

At the harbor, paramedics checked their vital signs and pronounced them fit to leave. When they started to return the blankets, the medics waved them on. "Stay warm and get inside as soon as possible."

Liz gave Jim a smile that couldn't have been wider.

Three TV film crews requested interviews, but they refused. Fortunately, the Coast Guard Zodiac boat arrived with injured fishermen, diverting the reporters' interest.

Liz wrapped the emergency blanket tightly about her while they returned to her SUV. "Who would have thought we'd need to turn on the heater in April?"

Jim pointed at a dark-blue Dodge pickup at the end of the lot. "Let's risk it."

She nodded and drove to it. They saw no one inside, but had difficulty seeing through the heavily-darkened windows.

"Hold on." Jim jumped out, cupped his hands, and peered in. "It's empty."

Liz handed him a notepad and pen through her open window. He wrote down the license plate number, and they returned to Palm Gardens.

They showered in her cabin. The tight and exciting fit didn't lead to bed. Jim's leg looked terrible, and after the strenuous day, she restored them both with chicken soup and one of Maggie's hot teas.

Afterwards, they sat wrapped together in a blanket, kissing and fondling, to speed the warming process.

Liz fixed Jim with her penetrating stare. "We need to take your dirty clothes, bedding, and towels to the laundry room. I don't want Marsha to have to clean them. It's like I owe her."

Jim opened his mouth, then closed it. *What an unusual two weeks.*

In the laundry room, he marveled that this woman, with whom he was having an affair, was considerate of his wife. Nothing made sense, and he wanted nothing more than to savor the nonsensical moment.

"Liz, this has been the most incredible time of my life." His heart caught. "I'm going to miss you."

"You, too, Jim. I've awakened from a dream like Snow White." She kissed him and sighed. "I found my prince at Paradise Pond."

"You mean your frog."

"I know a prince when I see one."

Their cameras had survived the storm due to Liz's quick decision to squeeze their waterproof backpacks into the ice chest. But, physically drained from the storm's battering, neither desired to download and edit pictures. They cuddled on her bed, talking about things they would like to do and places they would like to see.

Their daydreams were interrupted only by trips to the laundry room to move the laundry to the dryers, fold dry articles, and put them away.

Hunger settled in. Liz found a can of cranberry sauce in the pantry and dashed to the IGA for turkey breast and sweet potatoes. Jim surprised her by emptying the vegetable keeper and making a salad in her absence. He decorated the edges of the bowl with sliced cucumbers he scored with a fork.

Liz's large eyes widened. "Nice salad, Jim. You can be my chef, any day."

He gave the proposal full consideration.

Later, they curled up on the sofa, and Liz ordered him to look up his BMI on the internet. At six-feet and weighing more than three hundred pounds, it topped forty.

He gave an anxious look. "Not good, huh?"

She nodded soberly and clicked on the BMI scale. "Anything between twenty-five and thirty is overweight. Above that's obese." She poked his stomach with a slender finger. "You've even supersized obese, buster."

His face drooped. "To be between 18.5 and 24.9, I can't weigh more than a hundred eighty-five pounds." He scratched his head. "I'd have to lose almost a hundred and fifty pounds. Can you imagine what I'd look like with all that loose skin?"

"You could take it to a tanner and make a nice leather coat for Marsha. Talk about a unique original."

"There's no way I could do that." When Liz giggled, he explained. "I don't mean the coat. I don't have the willpower to lose the weight."

She frowned. "It's either do that or become diabetic and die young."

"I'm already old."

"Well, you're not going to get any older, if you keep talking stupid."

She strode to the table, grabbed his phone, and handed it to him. "And it's time for your eight o'clock call to Marsha."

Marsha answered immediately. "Hi, darling,"

After his greeting, Marsha controlled the conversation.

"The girls have been a toot. They've only been considerate of each other two days and ran me ragged the rest.

"And I have a bone to pick with Sarah. You wouldn't believe the dirty clothes and bedding. I washed for two whole days, and it took longer to clean the house. There must have been an inch of dust under the beds and in their closets."

She took a breath. "I needed you here to move the sofas, beds, and chests of drawers, hon. The black marks on the floors in the dining room and kitchen require your strength, so we'll remove those the next time we babysit. Oh, and don't even ask about the bathrooms."

Another breath. "By the way, Deena and Buck and Jimmy and Janice have an opportunity to take a trip to Cancun, next week. I told them we'd baby sit Cindy and Bucky. You'll need to leave right after your doctor's appointment, tomorrow. Everything will be ready when you arrive Friday evening. I'll wash your things, so we can leave early Saturday."

"What?"

Jim shook his head. Marsha had just beat her brains out caring for Anderson and Taylor for two weeks, and she wasn't going to rest before tackling an even harder set of grandchildren. He wasn't delusional. Cindy wasn't too bad, but Buck Jr. was in his terrible twos. He felt fortunate he'd had two weeks of mostly rest. He glanced at Liz. If it hadn't been for her....

"Don't fret, Jim," Marsha continued. "It's been two months since we've seen them. Deena says they're much easier to care for now."

Jim couldn't reason with her, so he mentally planned his itinerary for the next three days. "Okay, sweetheart, I can be in Waco tomorrow afternoon and home early enough on Friday to put the RV in storage."

A couple of I-love-yous, and he sat, slumped-shouldered, drained of spirit.

Liz waited for him to say something.

He stared at her, his face aged and weary. "Marsha and I are going to babysit our two great-grandkids next week." He shook his head. "I'll be dead tired when I get to Kansas City, but I couldn't tell her no—not after deserting her the past two weeks."

Liz didn't know what to say, but she knew what to do. She massaged his shoulders and back until she felt him relax. But not so much that he would accept her body for the second time that day. Even the romantic shower didn't raise him to the occasion. Once in the morning must be his limit, she concluded.

I wonder if Jack West is a two-pack-a-day man?

She immediately felt guilty for her wayward thought. Not having sex again that day might be best, since they wouldn't meet again. And Jim needed his rest. It would take him at least twelve hours of driving, over two days, to return home.

She sat in his lap, wrapped her arms about him, and listened to how he met Marsha, how he loved her, and the things they'd done. He described their children, grandchildren, the troubles they'd experienced.

She absorbed it all. Would she ever experience that kind of happiness? Jim mentioned a couple of times that she would make a good wife. Could she?

So that Jim could go to bed early, they listened to the nine o'clock news to check on the weather forecast for his trip home. The surprise storm dominated the newscast.

"Port Aransas, Aransas Pass, and Ingleside were battered by an unusual storm that built up rapidly in the Gulf this morning," the female anchor reported. The screen switched to pictures of storm damage. "Seven boats capsized in the storm, and fifteen fishermen were swept from the jetties by the heavy seas. The Coast Guard rescued all involved. Two fishermen were treated and released from Bayside Hospital. All other victims refused treatment.

"In a related story, a local private investigator, who wishes to remain anonymous, was allegedly attacked by a seven-foot rattlesnake while looking for shells on St. Jo Island this morning prior to the storm. The investigator was removed from the island by the St. Jo shuttle and transferred to Bayside Hospital by a Medevac helicopter. Medical authorities said the bite didn't appear life-threatening and seemed more consistent with a prickly pear scratch."

The newscaster added that the investigator suffered additional injuries from an ill-advised attempt to board the shuttle as it left the dock and would remain hospitalized overnight.

The newscaster turned the report over to a young female roving reporter.

"The shuttle company declined our requests for comments, but we've located an eye-witness to the investigator's unfortunate experience. I have with me Mr. William Robert Robertson, better known as Redfish Rob. Mr. ... uh ... Redfish, can you describe what occurred when the investigator arrived at the shuttle dock?"

The scruffy-bearded Redfish sported a graying ponytail that protruded from the back of a UT ball cap. His grin revealed a missing lower front tooth. He sidled up to the reporter and wrapped his left arm around her waist.

"Friends call me Redfish." He wiggled his eyebrows. "Close friends call me Billy Bob."

The view on the screen constricted to their shoulders and heads. The bemused reporter's nose wrinkled, and Liz and Jim didn't think it was because Billy Bob was crowding her comfort zone.

"It was the durndest thing I ever seen," the grizzled witness said while apparently being shoved backwards, based on the trim, multi-ringed fingers on the base of his neck.

The screen view enlarged to include heads and torsos.

"This *bleep* hauled *bleep* down the jetty hollering like they'd seen a banshee. The shuttle was already leaving, but the *bleep* jumped the *bleep* gate. Right leg must've cleared the rail by at least a foot."

Billy Bob Redfish spat something black and slimy, and the startled reporter clutched her chest with her free hand.

"Left leg didn't, though."

He doubled over in laughter, then explained that the PI missed the shuttle, fell into the channel, and suffered more injuries when helped onto the boat.

Chuckling, Liz said, "I'm surprised the investigator didn't run all the way across the ship channel."

"And that cute little reporter in the opposite direction," Jim added. He gazed at Liz. "So, now we know why we spotted the pickup at the parking lot, but we still don't know whether it's a man or a woman."

She nodded. "It's interesting that the TV station identified the person as an investigator despite the request for anonymity. I'll bet the other PIs in town are making hay with that."

The weatherman explained that the storm formed when warm inland air and cooler, humid Gulf air created what he called a beach low. The same conditions wouldn't exist the following day, so he predicted only a ten percent chance for rain.

"Outdoor activities shouldn't be curtailed. Any showers will be brief and widely scattered."

With their unknown nemesis in the hospital, the lovers spent their last night together in her cabin. Exhausted, they fell asleep before ten—Liz's head cradled in the crook of Jim's arm.

35
Migration

Jim awakened during the night, suffering a severe thigh cramp. While trying to stretch the knot, the muscle in his other leg rigged into spasms. Then both front and back muscles in his first thigh knotted at the same time. Body arched and rigid, he held his breath, hoping the muscles would relax before ripping in two. Liz brought him a banana and juice, but they didn't work, and he suffered more cramps during the night. Each time she helped by massaging the tight muscles and stretching his legs.

Rising with him to take her birth control pill while he took his morning antibiotic, she winced at his pronounced limp. In her haste to exercise some of his weight off during their short time together, she hadn't sufficiently considered his age and forced him past his conditioning. In addition, his left shin remained red and swollen.

Jim awoke again at seven-thirty, feeling like he'd just closed his eyes. He and Liz had rolled apart, and she was still asleep, so he gently pulled her toward him. Three quarters asleep, she snuggled against him, murmured appreciatively, and promptly fell the other one-quarter back to sleep.

The dark room indicated it was cloudy. With his appointment not until ten-thirty, he lay thinking, hating that he and Liz would part that afternoon. He felt a responsibility for her. She'd called him the best thing that ever happened to her, and he worried she wasn't yet strong enough to confront her mother about the investigator. Or any of the other conflicts that must exist in their complex relationship.

Her birth control pills. The nagging thought from the previous day returned. Why was Liz such an apparent novice at sex? She acted like their lovemaking were her first attempts—backing out at the last second at the National Seashore, hesitantly seducing him in her cabin, telling him on St. Jo, her face filled with sincerity, that she didn't know lovemaking could be so incredible.

Perhaps she'd been in an abusive relationship with a man, although he couldn't see how, with Helen hovering over her. But how could overly protective Helen be unaware that Liz was no longer a virgin and on the pill? Had she met someone after Harold Parker? Or had Liz not told the whole story about him?

Jim shrugged. A virgin without a hymen wasn't unusual, and birth control pills were sometimes prescribed for medical reasons. Besides, he was out of time. He could only hope he'd somehow helped her enough that she could better deal with her problems in the future. It was a troublesome world.

At eight, they rose, dressed, and went to the RV, where Liz cleaned out the fridge and most of the pantry to make breakfast. They ate in relative silence, not knowing how to voice their thoughts about parting, now that it was imminent.

Jim brooded, wondering what to say to a woman he'd made love to twice. *It's been nice knowing you?*

And although they'd expressed their love many times, they both knew it wasn't a stay-with-each-other-till-death type love. And as irrational as it seemed,

Jim was as much in love with Marsha as ever. Would be until he died.

Liz reminisced. She'd seduced Jim twice, even though the first attempt wasn't consummated. Their mutual gentle love-sharing on St. Jo was unlike any sensation she ever experienced. She'd been unaware sex or love could be so exquisite.

She saw him look at her quizzically and realized she must have been staring in his direction while recalling their time together. "Sweet thoughts of you, lover," she whispered.

No one had looked at him that way in years. Liz was such a beauty. And she loved him. Jim choked back the lump in his throat. "Thanks."

After breakfast, she helped him prepare the fifth-wheel for his trip home. He turned off the propane tank but wouldn't remove the bug until on the way home. He then limped to the park office to submit the electrical reading and pay his final bill.

When they returned from Dr. Gutierrez's office, all he'd have to do was climb into the pickup, start the engine, and leave this new world. The thought brought a pang to his heart.

Liz fought back tears. In a few short hours, her first and only love would drive out of her life.

The sky churned with dark clouds. It began to sprinkle. Having spare time, they drove to Paradise Pond in hopes of finding a bird fallout, but the sprinkle became a steady rain.

On their way to Corpus Christi, they passed a pair of rain-drenched crested caracaras standing beside the road. Liz shook her head. "They know when we can't stop to take their pictures."

Jim apologized. "It's my fault for hurting my leg and having a doctor's appointment."

"Don't you dare say that! If it weren't for your injured leg, I wouldn't be with you."

Jim found the thought sobering.

A sudden cessation in the rain amplified their silence. It was broken when they spotted a white-tailed hawk on a utility line. Liz slowed. "Jim, grab my camera and shoot out the window. I'll go as slow as I can."

He lowered the window and lifted the camera to it, but the bird flew as he pressed the shutter button. He looked at Liz and shrugged. "Close ... but no cigar."

She blew him a kiss. "Exciting though, wasn't it?"

She slowed again when they approached a scissor-tailed flycatcher sitting on a barbed wire fence. "It'll probably fly the moment we stop, but let's give it a shot."

The beautiful gray bird, with long twin tail feathers and a salmon pink breast, flew as Liz predicted. To their amazement, it caught a large dragonfly and swooped back to the same spot on the fence. Liz risked easing to a stop. Oblivious of them, it beat the dragonfly to bits against the wire and consumed it.

"I can't believe the luck," Jim said, so excited his voice quavered. He looked at Liz. "Do you want to take pictures, too?"

Exhilarated, she shook her head, pleased by his happiness.

He held his trembling hands out for Liz to see. "I'm shaking like I have buck fever. Did you see how that scissortail spread its tail feathers and caught that dragonfly?"

Liz raised her hand for a high-five. "Welcome to the club."

He slapped it. "To the club."

They again became quiet. Their last half-day was presenting their first truly awkward situation since their stormy meeting at Paradise Pond.

It still seemed like a dream to Jim that Liz had shared her body with him. How did you send someone a Thank You card for that?

Liz worried about Marsha. Would Jim have remorse and confess their affair?

They arrived at Dr. Gutierrez's office early. Thirty minutes and two magazines later, a nurse stepped into the room and called Jim's name. Liz accompanied them to the examination room. On their way, the nurse nodded at a scale. "I need your weight, Mr. Smith."

He stepped on the scale, incongruously fearful that his sneakers and wallet added too much weight.

"Two hundred and ninety-three pounds." The nurse's tone of voice hinted strongly at disapproval.

Jim chuckled. "Your scale needs recalibrating. I weigh more than three hundred pounds."

The nurse peered over her glasses. "I'm sorry?"

"Your scales are broken. I haven't weighed less than three hundred pounds in ten years."

Liz smirked.

"Our scales are correct," the nurse assured him, unsmiling. "You weigh two hundred ninety-three pounds. And if I were you, I'd be happy about it."

Liz interrupted. "May I weigh?"

The nurse indulged her as if hosting a couple of crackpots.

The scale read one hundred fifty-eight pounds, and Liz fixed Jim with a look of blame. "I've gained three pounds. You've taken me off my routine."

Chagrined to have been dressed down by both the unpleasant nurse and Liz, Jim reflected on his weight loss. His infection might have something to do with it, but more likely it was due to the strict diet and regimen Liz forced upon him. The more he thought about it, the more pleased he became. If he didn't have on clothes and shoes, he'd weigh even less.

After the nurse took his temperature and blood pressure, he and Liz sat by themselves for ten minutes chatting softly.

"See what a little exercise and giving up soda pops and fats can do?" Liz said. "And all those heaping seconds?"

"You may have made a convert. I like salads. And, as much as I hate to admit it, I'm beginning to tolerate diet drinks, skim milk, and water. The unsweetened tea I already liked."

"You can do it," Liz said encouragingly, pleased with her success.

Dr. Gutierrez entered the room, shook their hands, and smiled at Liz. "You certainly are a dedicated granddaughter. Did you have anything to do with your grandpa's weight loss?" When she nodded, he said, "I thought so."

"Time to look at your leg, Jim." Gutierrez summarily dismissed the scrapes on Jim's right leg with a glance, and poked and probed the edges of the wound on his left shin. "Your leg has been seriously wet recently, because the scab's softened."

"We were caught in yesterday's St. Jo storm."

"You aren't the person who tripped into the channel, are you?"

Jim smiled and shook his head. "No. But we didn't expect it, so we didn't take raincoats."

"No one else did, either. I hope our weathermen enjoy their ill-gotten gains. It's too bad they don't have to pay the malpractice insurance premiums I do," Gutierrez grumbled through a smile. "I definitely went into the wrong profession."

He became serious. "You have a low-grade fever, so I'm keeping you on antibiotics." He wrote out a prescription and held out his hand. "Make an appointment at the checkout desk. I'll see you next week."

Jim peered at Liz, then back at Gutierrez. "It looks better to me."

"You still have a bad infection."

Jim didn't look forward to traveling all the way to Kansas City, but he felt obligated to help Marsha. He also worried that his reluctance to leave was due to his desire to spend more time with Liz, and he'd stolen a part of her life, as it was.

"Would it be okay if I returned home and received treatment there?"

"Remind me again where you live."

"Central Oklahoma."

"How long's the drive ... eight hours?"

"About twelve, but I'll split it into two days." He didn't mention the additional seven hours to Kansas City after he arrived home.

"I guess that's okay," Gutierrez said reluctantly. "Just don't spend much time with your legs down in a cramped position. It would be better if you were up and walking around to stimulate blood flow. Shins are tough places for injuries. And check in with your family doctor immediately."

"Grandpa has to go to Kansas City when he gets home," Liz interjected. "He has to baby sit some of ... his other grandchildren and won't be able to see his family doctor for a week and a half."

Gutierrez frowned. "That's a lot of driving. And a long time until you see a doctor even if you go to a walk-in clinic in Kansas City, Jim. My advice is for you to stay here, unless the grandchildren you're going to baby sit look like..." He smiled and nodded in Liz's direction.

She blushed at the attention and for her faux pas of saying something Jim obviously didn't want revealed. Had he tired of her company? Her advances?

Jim pondered her statement, his conflicting desires, and stared indecisively.

"I can't overemphasize the danger of your infection, Jim," Gutierrez pressed. "It can kill you if not treated in time. Or require a chunk of flesh be removed from your shin. I'd prefer you remain here another week where your records are. That way, if your swelling becomes worse or your wound starts draining, the hospital and I will know what to do."

"Done," Jim said, still experiencing mixed emotions.

"Dr. Gutierrez, how about exercise. Can grandpa start exercising again?"

Gutierrez cocked an eyebrow and peered at Jim. "What do you have in mind?" When Jim flicked his eyes in Liz's direction, Gutierrez stared inquiringly at her.

"How about an exercise bike or a treadmill. Maybe some upper body machines?" she asked.

"Those sound fine as long as he doesn't overdo it."

Exultant, Liz glanced at Jim and back at Gutierrez. "Thank you, doctor."

They returned silently to her SUV, umbrellas able to shield only their upper bodies from the steady, blowing rain. A dark-blue Dodge pickup in the parking lot caught Jim's attention. He didn't point it out, on the outside chance they were being observed.

In her SUV, Liz looked pained. "You're sure in a hurry to go home. You didn't even mention having to go to Kansas City. Are you tired of my—"

Jim lightly shook his head. "It's noon. Let's go to that Whataburger, we saw, and have a marinated chicken sandwich."

Confused, Liz maintained her curiosity until they were inside the restaurant. "What was that all about?"

"I'm probably being paranoid, but I saw a familiar-looking pickup in the lot. I imagine there are lots of them, but if it was our PI's, I'd expect another bug."

"Well, if it *was* him, someone must have brought his pickup to the hospital."

Liz's eyes brimmed with tears. "And you still haven't answered my question. Do you want me to go home?"

Gazing into her anxious face, Jim recalled her first offer to stay with him and his response then. "No. I thought maybe you'd want to get on with your life. You've been away from your family much too long. They'll think I'm a Svengali, using mind control to keep you around."

"Let me be the judge of that. Right now, you *are* my life. And Marsha's going to think the same thing about me, so that should be one interesting phone call you're going to have with her."

Jim winced. He hadn't thought things that far through.

* * *

Edith stared at her companion. "What do you think, Jackie?"

"You're right. Nothing's going on there. How could there be? And I don't think anything's going on anywhere. My facts check with yours. The people at the airport are clean."

"Well, it's all yours. Let me know when our bird heads home."

"You'll be the one having fun. I gassed up the wagon and stocked it for you."

"I still don't like it. We could lose everything."

"It'll be fine. The area's isolated as hell and buried in the forest."

"But the wife."

"Trust me, Edith. She won't change her mind."

"I have a bad feeling about this."

"You've had them before. They don't pan out."

Edith tapped a receiver and changed the subject. "Thank God, you waterproofed the bug. These damned weathermen."

Jack sneered. "I save your butt all the time. And since you don't have to buy a new one, you might want to invest some of your client's money on a field guide on the reptiles of Texas. It wouldn't hurt to be able to recognize the difference between a rattlesnake and a curved stick."

"Look at these marks. Don't they look like fang bites to you?"

"No. But it's nice knowing a TV celebrity."

* * *

"What do we do next?" Liz asked.

Jim pursed his lips. "First things first, I guess. I need to hook up the fifth-wheel and extend my stay. He glanced out the window. "I'm not looking forward to reconnecting the electricity in this rain. After that, it seems like a perfect afternoon for editing pictures."

"I didn't mean that. I meant with the PI." She stared inquisitively. "And about where we go next in our relationship."

Jim mulled over her questions. "To answer your first question, I think we should go about our business and keep alert. As for the second ..." he visualized taking her to the next level and tried to clear the image, "let's allow things to happen as they may. A little more birding would be nice, too."

Thrilled by his answer, Liz smiled broadly. "Then what say we head to San Antonio," she drawled, in her deep voice Jim found so increasingly sexy, "to meet a little fellow with a golden smile?"

36
Bird of Paradise

Chuck Seager's Caddy Escalade hummed down U. S. 59 well above Texas' de facto speed limit. He punched it after passing the Rosenberg exit and was still chuckling when he approached El Campo and the turn toward Palacios.

His wife, Darla, back home in the Woodlands, was so trusting. His excuse was the same as for the past few years—a redfish tournament, this time in Port Aransas. It wasn't a lie. He just wasn't going to fish. He and his fishing partners, Chip Younkens and Bud Montgomery, had each other's backs, and it was his turn to sit out. It let them do what they enjoyed most—fish and screw around. They had the best of both worlds. Three, actually. They always returned to perfect home lives—played with the kids, petted the dogs, and kept their executive wives naked and happy at night. It didn't get any better than that, and he was on his way to make sure it stayed that way.

Palacios. The detour through the bayside town always delighted him. The shoreline drive was second to none—piers, parks, old buildings on the National Historic Registry. Sailboats leaning into the wind. He lowered his window and drew in a deep breath. *Damn, the salt air smells great.*

In a way, he wished he would be skimming skinny water and chasing redfish this weekend. But if the fish didn't bite and he and his friends just eliminated a lot of water, he wouldn't get a paycheck. As it was, he'd already hooked a fish. One that would prove profitable on a grand scale. Maybe fun, too.

Old enough to be his mother, the tiny bird should have been teaching a quilting class, not chasing him, Chuck mused, as he blazed through Tivoli and neared his destination.

He recalled their meeting. Chip and Bud about fell off their bar stools when she sashayed up and gave him what she must've imagined to be a seductive look. It was all he could do to keep from snorting his mouthful of Shiner Bock in her face when she placed her hand on his arm and flashed her eyelashes.

"Why don't you come over to my table, handsome? I'll buy you another drink." When he sat there, she cooed. "It'll be worth your time."

The elf was a looker for her age, so he figured, what the hell? And he played along in case Chip or Bud had put her up to it. It wouldn't have been a first.

But they hadn't. She bounced in her seat while proving her statement wasn't pure hogwash. Had the bar been darker and not so well attended, he wouldn't have been surprised had she scooted under the table right then ... after he'd turned that table and propositioned her.

Hell, he wasn't an ass. She was starved for affection, obviously needed a hardbody fix, and her round little body was plump in all the right places—enough for him to give her a nickname. Sweet Tits. It might've been the beer, but he'd wanted handfuls of that. And she showed enough leg to reveal she was cellulite-free. He hated the lumps. Envisioning the few pre-C indentations on Darla's thighs, he scowled.

Even mature citizens must dwell on their youth. Sweet Tits had sealed the deal with her feet—the bar wasn't all that crowded—and they'd set a rendezvous.

He'd taken a bunch of shit from Chip and Bud over the incident and chastised them for elder abuse. If they didn't have time for a Rubenesque babe, they should be ashamed of themselves.

They'd liked that one. He could still feel their elbows and hear the hooting.

The entrance to Goose Island State Park came up more abruptly than he expected, and he wheeled into a convenience store parking lot. He didn't need anything, wasn't hungry, just needed to think. It was his last chance to back out. He patted his shirt pocket for the package of prophylactics he knew was there. Didn't know why, just did. What if the silly broad's boobs were too wrinkled? She was too fat? Padded her bra? Crap.

The "Aggie War Hymn" chimed in his pocket. Darla. "Hi, babe."

"Hi, sweetheart, I miss you. I wish I could've gone with you this weekend, but I have that meeting in the morning. And Billy's so excited about his soccer tournament tomorrow afternoon."

"Yeah, sugar babe, I hate missing Billy's tournament, too, but Chip, Bud, and me always have each other's back in case one of us gets sick or something comes up at the last minute. And it's my turn to check out the holes." *True enough.* "But I'll make Cindy's birthday on Sunday, and that's what really counts. Billy's team will win, so I can watch him in the finals."

They spoke for ten more minutes and kissed into their phones.

Now, he was late. Sweet Tits hadn't given him an address, just directions, and the sun was lowering in the west. He'd *Binged* and *Googled* the spot but couldn't pin down a house or cabin. There were several that could be hers. A whole bunch of small homes were tucked into Goose Island's live oak jungles.

At the intersection to Goose Island State Park on the right, he turned left and drove slowly, looking for the road the she described. A couple were nothing more than overgrown trails.

What the hell's the bitch up to?

"Shit." Maybe Chip and Bud were having the last laugh, after all. If so, it was the most intricate stunt they'd ever pulled. Talk about a snipe hunt.

But no, there were the dead palm tree and barbed-wire gate. When he opened and closed it, the insects and frogs gave the darkening twilight a festive sound. The mosquito shrills didn't.

The oyster-shell road wound through and under a twisted-limb, live oak woodland that made him claustrophobic. It wasn't like this out on the bay. This was like being lost in one of those forbidden forests he saw in movies.

When the trail narrowed and curled around a cattail-lined pond, he had the fleeting thought it would be a great place to hide a body. It wouldn't last long—not if the object tucked in the edge of the cattails was an alligator. He shuddered. The place was dark. Isolated as hell.

The road had become nothing more than a couple of tracks in the grass when it ended at a small, dark cabin hidden beneath the forest canopy. The only parking space was a tree-covered nook beside an industrial van.

What the hell's this all about? Geez, I'm shaking.

Chuck's discomfort disintegrated in a loud guffaw when the van door opened and Sweet Tits stepped onto the top step—wearing a mask and dressed in a nurses' outfit right out of a Halloween shop. Or one of the porn movies he enjoyed so much.

She beckoned and disappeared into the van.

Hooker mom. Chuck laughed so hard, he fumbled with the car door.

Dusk and the cacophony of night sounds—not the least those of the howling coyotes and persistent mosquitoes—shoved him to the van. No need to tempt fate. Or the West Nile virus.

When he entered and the little bitch locked the door, his laughter stopped, and his jaw dropped. The interior looked like a dungeon. "I've been to two county fairs and a rooster fight, Sweet Tits, and I ain't never seen nothin' like this."

He ogled the Rembrandt painting come to life. She seemed somehow familiar. The great news was that her body was fine … USDA prime, but he couldn't stifle a laugh. She was licking her lips. Hell, she might keep the smile on his face all night, she was so over the top. Or until he pounded her senseless and left. At her age it might not take all that long.

Chuck drank her in, wondering if she had implants. Her breasts mounded over a bra barely able to constrain them. He hoped they didn't hang to her knees when he stripped her. Her lips might be Botox, too. He couldn't be sure.

The large eyes devouring him from behind the mask were a hundred percent real. The whole package was grade A—jaunty nurse's cap above a Little Orphan Annie wig, nurse's dress bordered in pink, white stockings gartered above the knees. He wolf-whistled.

Then jolted. *She could be Darla's mother. That's why the bird seems so familiar.* But Ma Denise wasn't this damned hot.

"Like what you see … Hoss?"

Right out of Grease. Only Chuck wasn't goggle-eyed like Travolta. He snorted, trying to choke back laughter.

The woman's eyes told him she wanted to eat him up, and she might do just that. She sauntered over, unzipped his fly, and pulled out his puppy. But while it panted and bounced for a pat, she turned and walked toward a shelf with a bunch of crap on it. Talk about ass sway. He grabbed.

She slapped his hands away, lifted a leather hood, and nodded toward a red recliner.

"That's where we're going."

"Why tell me that?"

"Cause you're going to wear this. Bend down."

When he reached for her boobs, she bopped his hands with the surprisingly heavy hood. "Be a good boy. You're getting what you have coming. You said you liked strange."

Chuck shrugged. "What the hell? It's your nickel."

He bent forward and let her put the damn thing on his head and cinch it tight. He cheated anyway—copped a feel of her twin mounds and surprisingly firm ass.

He could see out of the eyeholes, so why tell him about the recliner?

Wait. Who turned out the lights?

"Hood flap. I'll use the ball gag, later."

"Ball gag?"

He could still breathe. And drink. He sat on the recliner, sipping beer through a straw. Shiner Bock, he'd recognize it anywhere. How did she know that? *Oh yeah.*

She was stripping him, and she must be over-excited. It felt like she had four hands. "No need to hurry, Sweet Tits, I got all night. All day tomorrow, if you can handle me. My wife thinks I'm checking out fishing holes on Laguna Madre Bay, but I want to hit a few taverns ... maybe pick up another chick—

"*Ow.* That's my nip— *Crap.* You sharpen your teeth?"

"Expect the unexpected, stud muffin. Didn't you read the fine print on the contract?"

"Fine print?"

Hey, who turned on the light?

He was sitting in the recliner, buck naked, on some type of liner, but the woman still had on her costume. "Come on, Sweet Tits, take it off."

She surprised him again. They were in a perfect place for a porno movie—with her dressed like the star—and all she wanted to do was talk. The good news was that she talked sex, and, man, was she good at it. The old biddy was no fool. She was making sure he could get it up when he saw her naked.

Chuck was buzzed, rock-hard horny, before he realized he *was* in a movie. Two cameras were pointed at him, red lights blinking. How had he missed those? Well, the gal would to get her money's worth, a lifetime of pleasure from the videos. After all, he had to earn his keep.

She was tiny, he six-four, and she'd stalled long enough. "Strip, Sweet Tits, let's see what you've got." He started to stand to do it for her.

"No. No. You're the bad boy," she said, wagging a finger. "Memorize the side of the van."

Damned if the buxom little beauty's sexy demand didn't have him drooling— his groin, anyway.

There go the fucking lights, again.

Was the woman a hypnotist? Chuck thought he remembered begging her to place him in his present predicament—constrained against the side of the van, legs spread apart, arms beside his head, elbows bent forward.

Blind as a mole, he tested the cuffs on his wrists and ankles. Nothing gave. Neither did the shackle that positioned his neck and head firmly against the padded wall. The damn hood was getting hot. Sweaty. Kind of stunk.

He heard a swish and flinched in pain.

"What the hell did you do?"

"Since you're a fisherman, it looks ... something like a fishing pole handle with strips of leather dangling from it. Do you like to fish?"

'It's my life. That and screwing wome—

"Aw, damn it, cut that *ow*— Come on, stop. I didn't sign up for torture."

"What kind of fish do you like to catch?"

"Redfish. It's what we catch in our tournaments."

"What kind of women do you like to catch?"

"Redheads— *Piss.* What the hell was that?"

"Wartenberg wheel. Looks something like a little boot spur. Smarts on tender skin, doesn't it? Makes you bleed if you press too hard. Want to feel?"

"No. *Gaah ... Holy* snot. Come on, I mean it. You're *killing* me."

"No, I'm not. Would you like another surprise?"

"Not if it has anything to do with the fucking whee— *agg— unnng.*"

Chuck held his breath. The pain went on and on before ending.

"What the fuck did you do? Cut it off?"

"No. You can barely see the track, and I don't like blood.

"Besides, I'm not hurting you. Are you sure you don't like surprises?"

"The hell you're not."

"I told you. *I'm* not hurting you, you big weenie."

"Lady, if you think this doesn't hurt, let me do it to you."

"I didn't say *that*. Are you ready for the surprise yet?"

"No. *Oh hell ... crap.*"

Surprised he didn't smell burning flesh Chuck squirmed, yanked against his restraints. "Was that a damned cattle prod? Why did you use it *there*?"

"What do you have against hot links? Now, shush."

"*Gaah.* Enough with the cattle prod, lady, I'm getting pissed. If you don't stop, you're going to hate it when I'm off this wall."

"It's not a cattle prod, it's a neon wand, but it does have a kick. If you turn it high enough. And since you didn't like it there, how about ... here?"

Zzzz. Zzzzt.

"Oh, shit. *Uncle!*" Chuck trembled in pain. He wouldn't father more children.

"If you don't like surprises, why did you tell me you liked strange?"

"I don't like this kind of stra— *Geeez ... Hellfire damnation.*"

Chuck panted, pleaded through clenched teeth, threatened, begged again, promised all. Nothing ended the persecution.

Parts of his body he had other plans for when the evening began were being deep fat fried. He bucked, arched, and twisted. Tears streamed down his face. "I'm going to beat the shit out of you when you let me go."

"*Not* the right answer." Her voice sounded strange. Lower-pitched.

Just when he thought the horror wouldn't end—his arms tingling, elbows aching, thighs burning and quivering from exhaustion—the torment stopped.

"What do you have against surprises?"

Broken, Chuck blubbered, "Okay, okay, I *like* surprises."

He could see again but had trouble focusing. Saw double. No, not double—twins. Which one was Sweet Tits?

"See, I told you I wasn't hurting you." She pointed, as the second nurse removed her blindfold.

"Darla? Darla! What the hell are you doing here?"

His wife tapped a bamboo cane against her left palm. "Getting even, you cheating bastard."

"Sugar babe, this isn't what it looks li—"

Crack.

Unable to breathe, Chuck yanked reflexively at his constraints.

Edith Mansfield winced. "Sweetie, that made *me* hurt." She bent, reached out, and examined the damage. "This blood blister on his pecker will last a month."

She handed Darla a flogger. "Use this instead. Wait. All this screaming hurts my ears." She slipped a ball gag into Chuck's mouth while he caught his breath.

Saliva drooled from the gag and dripped onto his chest by the time Darla finished. No part of his body had escaped unscathed. Sobbing, he promised, "No more mistresses. No more one-night stands." The gag garbled his words, made them unintelligible.

He now knew the meaning of fatal attraction. The movie had seemed silly, if enchanting and sexy. Something like that could never happen to him. The hell it couldn't. The woman standing back, watching and smiling, couldn't weigh more than a hundred thirty pounds. Darla weighed maybe a hundred. He weighed two-forty, more than both of them put together, but he was the one strapped to a wall, begging for mercy.

Chuck didn't like the look in Darla's eyes—like she wanted to choke him to death. Then the two women could drag him to the marsh and feed him to Tick Tock. But that wasn't going to happen. Not since Sweet Tits was stripping.

Whoa. They're real after all. Talk about American made.

All the blood that had drained from his body came flooding back. The little bun stood in high heels and only high heels, and damned if she didn't use him for a clothes hanger. Could all women her age stoke the coals like this one did? "Ooh, Sweet Tits, shake it like you mean it."

Darla removed his ball gag. "What are you trying to say, Chuck?"

He couldn't very well hide his excitement. "Uh ... how 'bout a threesome. Didn't you fantasize about that once?"

He would have hopped if he could. They say you don't hear the one that gets you, but the *whack* made his ears ring and his hanger useless.

"You want a threesome? My stars, Chuck, you can't even be true while I'm beating the hell out of you. Look at yourself. You became hard for a woman who could be your mother. You're sick."

Edith lowered the hood flap and pulled Darla aside. "You sure want to do this next part?" she whispered, loudly enough for their victim to hear.

Darla nodded.

"You don't have to. I won't tell."

Darla's eyes hardened. Her lips curled. "No. I want to."

Chuck began shaking in fear.

Edith lifted Chuck's hood flap and turned on music.

Chuck's eyes widened when Darla began a strip tease, assisted by the naked temptress who lured him to his predicament. He couldn't believe it. He and Darla had been married fifteen years. "Darla, what're you doing?"

Incredibly beautiful, petite and shapely, her thighs weren't perfect, but her face still contained the fullness of youth. Her wide eyes and full lips matched those of the woman dancing sensually with her to the music. He wanted his wife like he hadn't in years. Throbbed for them both.

"Enough. He's ready." Edith opened a cabinet door.

Wordlessly, Darla nodded and removed her husband's hood.

"God, sugar babe, thanks. That damn thing was cooking my brain." *And you two are so hot.*

He didn't see the cylindrical object Edith removed from a cabinet until she began placing it over his head.

He twisted, but his fate was sealed. "Wait," he yelped, his voice hollow.

Darla snubbed on a collar, plugged in a cord, and pushed a button.

Sweet Tits tapped his arm with something he couldn't see.

The wind left Chuck's lungs. He struggled to breath, tried to speak, as his life force was sucked from his body. He banged the side of the van—couldn't break free. His torso and abdomen jerked and twisted spasmodically. A numbness spread from his arm, and he fell limp against his restraints.

Darla frowned. "What do we do now, Edith?"
"First things first. Are you going to fish or cut bait?"
Darla grinned.

37
Birds of a Different Feather

The afternoon became sunny west of Corpus Christi. It became even more bright and cheery when Jim and Liz stopped at the rest stop on I-37 near the town of Whitsett, between Corpus Christi and San Antonio.

Jim peered down the highway. "There isn't a blue Dodge pickup in sight."

"Good. Let's hope we've given him the slip, this time."

Fellow travelers relaxed and ate snacks and lunches in the tree-shaded rest area. Jim propped his leg on a picnic table bench, and Liz propped her camera pillow under his knee for comfort.

A fussy mother hen, she continued to deny him man-food, but he wasn't about to mention it after the great results of his lost weight. Plus, he soaked up her attention, and, lord, was she desirable. She would either make a great wife or lead a man to drink. He wasn't sure which.

"Ready to go?" she asked, thirty minutes later. She'd used the time to reserve adjoining rooms in an upscale motel near Friedrich Wilderness Park. They would arrive in San Antonio too late for birding, but it provided the opportunity to purchase more clothing to please Jim. And to fit her changing image of herself.

After checking into the motel and dropping off their bags and birding equipment, they shared a large combo salad and went to Outdoor World. The huge clothing selection made it a daunting task. When Liz saw a rack of clothing that appealed to her, she looked at Jim for confirmation. If he wrinkled his nose at something she liked, she sighed and moved on. If he smiled and nodded, she browsed.

Good birders weren't supposed to wear white—a book by that title containing fifty amusing and invaluable essays by a collection of the world's leading birding authorities said so. But she hadn't heard anything negative about blues, tans, and pinks. She selected cargo shorts to mix and match with new shirts. The blouses were more form fitting than any she possessed, and the shorts, shorter. She would donate her old clothing to the Salvation Army Thrift Store.

The main event was selecting a new bathing suit. She skipped the bikinis—still too daring—and found two one-piece Speedo-types she liked. They weren't flowery and frilly like those her mother chose for her, but they wouldn't be worn in public. Only for Jim.

Eyes pleading, she showed them to him. "What do you think?" His nod matched the one from her heart.

It proved more difficult to leave the dressing room to show him than it had in Corpus Christi. As in impossible. Was her reluctance driven by fear of being seen by passing men, or the throbbing in her groin?

She needn't have worried about the first suit. Too tight—both above her bust and the tops of her legs--causing them to bulge.

Surely, I haven't gained that much weight.

The next suit, marked the same size, was hedonistic love at first touch. Breasts prominent, nipples showing, she felt sexy for the first time in her life. Her normally half-closed eyes grew round, her smile broadened, as she rotated slowly, arms up. Her flat stomach pleased her. Hips, well, maybe they were a tad wide, but nicely accentuated. She peered over her shoulder at her rounded derriere. There was no way she'd ever leave the dressing room wearing this suit. Jim would have to wait.

"No good?" he asked, ready to head back to the bathing suit racks.

"One was okay. The other not so good. And you've been on your feet for hours. Let's go."

Relief flooded his face.

It was dusk when they left the building. The parking lot was mostly empty—except for a Dodge pickup at the opposite end from Liz's SUV. Jim hoped he was being paranoid.

"Let's go out that exit," he pointed. "It's closer to the access road."

Lips clenched tight, Liz nodded.

A quick glance at the tag confirmed their suspicions.

At the motel, Jim made a show of helping Liz with her packages in case the PI somehow followed and was watching. They remained cautious in the hallways, as well.

"I hope the guy's getting paid overtime," he said when they were safely in her room. "And the tail doesn't make sense. Your mother must've told him you were going home, today."

"Speaking of that," Liz said, "it's time to face the music. I'm surprised neither of us has received a phone call yet."

"Marsha probably thinks I'm still on the road." Jim bore a pained expression. "I'm suffering major guilt."

"You're gutless. I told you to call her when we left the doctor's office."

"Look who's talking."

When he exited her room, she stepped into the hallway and gave him a hug. "Thanks for the help with the packages. See ya in a few minutes for the trip to the fitness room. That should give us time to call our families to let them know where we are."

Jim did a double-take. "What fitness room?"

"Knock on my door, and I'll take you there."

Jim called Marsha as soon as he entered his room and sat. He couldn't do it standing up.

"Hello, hon," Marsha said happily. "Did you have a nice drive to Waco?"

What have I done?

"Uh ... I'm in San Antonio."

"Why on earth are you there? Did the truck break down again?"

He toyed with lying and saying yes. "Umm, I still have an infection. When Dr. Gutierrez heard I'd be going directly to Kansas City and wouldn't be under Dr. Michael's care, he demanded I stay here where my records are."

Jim couldn't stand the silence. "I tried reasoning with him, but he was adamant."

"Your doctor's in San *Antonio*?"

"We ... Liz and I ... thought, since I have to stay another week, we could run up here to look for an endangered warbler that's unique to Texas." He made the hundred-seventy miles between Port Aransas and San Antonio sound like a few minutes' drive.

More silence. He'd lost the battle, and Marsha had only said a couple of sentences. The golden-cheeked warbler wasn't the only endangered bird.

"Well I hope you and *Liz* have a *wonderful* time, while I care for our *two ... small ... grandchildren*." Marsha hung up.

Jim felt disgusted with himself. He'd deserted Marsha when she needed him.

That thought was rapidly shoved out by another. This wouldn't be happening if she'd come when he'd injured himself. They'd be relaxing in the RV to the sound of falling rain. She'd be refreshed and reading a book, instead of sounding bone-weary, and he'd be editing barely tolerable pictures taken with his old camera. Who should be mad at whom? She'd even sounded relieved when she learned someone else would help care for him.

Guilt returned when he wondered what he'd be doing this moment, and where, had Liz not informed Dr. Gutierrez about Kansas City. Was his desire for Liz's companionship—her body—the true reason he didn't return to Oklahoma?

In the adjoining room, Liz's suspicions were confirmed by Helen's faux pas.

"Why are you in San ... Why aren't you home, yet, Mary Elizabeth?"

Liz let her mother squirm for a moment, before saying, "Jim's doctor prescribed another week of meds and care. I decided to stay and help him."

"That's nice of you, sweetheart," Helen said cheerily. "Are you going to stay the entire week?"

Why are you so happy, Mother? Do you want me to get into trouble? Well, I have. Or do you think I didn't catch your mistake?

"Yes, Jim's a quick learner. He has a good eye for the unusual. Have you seen his photos I've sent?"

When she spoke with her father, he supported the change in plans. "I've enjoyed your pictures, Mary Elizabeth, and I think your project's doing you a ton of good. I'm so glad you're happy."

She ended the call with what was becoming a familiar statement. "Bye, Daddy, I love you. See y'all soon."

Afterwards, she wondered who was the real Svengali—her mother? Jim? Herself?

Jim wore shorts and a T-shirt when Liz answered his knock.

"Tweedledee, at your service, but it's ten-o'clock. Isn't it kind of late to go exercising?" He preferred staying in his room to untangle his thoughts.

"A good workout always helps when my nerves are frayed, so it'll help you too," Liz said. "And you saw the scales. My three extra pounds are because I haven't jogged or exercised regularly since becoming your nurse. I've got to lose them before they become four. Then six."

Jim was glad he was wearing baggy pants. "You look too thin to me."

Liz glared. "I'm perfect."

Impeccable reasoning. "Let's get this torture over with."

She burst into laughter. Jim looked like a lamb headed for slaughter. "When was the last time you exercised?" she asked. She thought of an old commercial and deepened her already low voice. "Well, that's too long."

In the empty fitness center, Jim stared around. What do you suggest?"

Liz pointed at an exercise bike. "Start slowly."

He pedaled while she laid a towel on a cushion on the floor and did impossible moves he thought might be yoga. *So breathtakingly beautiful. Such perfect thighs.*

When Liz stepped on the treadmill, he placed a courtesy towel on the pad and attempted a few half-hearted sit-ups. His shoulders barely lifted off the floor.

"Wimp."

Jim gazed up.

"Put some muscle into it. No pain. No gain."

He flopped back, gazed at his mountain of a stomach, and wheezed.

Liz giggled.

Twenty minutes later, sweating profusely despite the air-conditioning, her heaving chest took Jim's breath away. Her muscles amazed him. They bulged under weights and pressure but were long and smooth when relaxed.

Instead of going to the elevator when they finished, Liz counseled him to exercise regularly and ordered him to follow her to the pool. "I need a dip."

He groaned. After 11:00 p.m., with designated pool hours 10 a.m. to 10 p.m., he hoped they couldn't get in.

Two families with teens—three boys and two girls—playing in the pool dashed his hopes.

"On a Thursday evening? During a school week?" Liz whispered. "Let's wait until they leave, so I can have more room."

They relaxed on recliners to watch. One mother left the pool and sat with them. The teens were being homeschooled. They'd scored well on their tests and were being rewarded.

"It's nice for families do that with their children," Liz said.

Jim noticed her stare longingly at the teen girls splashing about. "Having second thoughts about not buying a bikini?"

"No. I'm watching the interplay between the girls and the boys. Mother would have killed me for doing that. I caught hell for even thinking about it."

When the parents told their children it was time to leave, Liz removed her T-shirt and shorts.

Jim heard the teen boys gasp. Or maybe it was him. Her physique surpassed anything the teen girls could dream of without frequent and specific exercise. They were naturally trim, their stomachs gently rounded, but flabby. Liz's body had been sculpted by years of conditioning. Like he, the two husbands and three boys ogled her as they were herded toward the door.

As soon as they left, Liz raised her arms and stretched—laughing at Jim with her eyes as she did. She was about to speak, when they heard a click in the card-key lock. The door opened, and a stocky man entered.

Jack West jolted, quickly recomposed himself, and started where he'd left off at the birding center. "What a pleasant surprise, Liz."

She realized the West of her dreams had been just that, a dream, a fantasy. She shuddered under his lustful gaze. Her subconscious had been perceptive when she dreamed of him restraining her. She could swear he was envisioning doing that now.

"How do you do, Mr. West?" she said icily, crossing her arms over her breasts. She wished she'd purchased the flower-shaped nipple minimizers she considered. "This is my friend, Jim Smith."

Jim was surprised she knew the man doing the perfect imitation of a letch—like he'd been doing seconds earlier. He forced a smile. "Hello, Mr. West."

Jack barely glanced in his direction. "Hi.

"Fancy meeting you here, Liz. Why are you in town?"

Liz backed to the pool, dropped her arms to grasp the ladder, and slipped into the water. "We're here to see golden-cheeked warblers at Friedrich Wilderness Park." Too late, she regretted mentioning the site. "And I'm in the pool to finish a workout I started in the exercise room." She scowled. "You could use some time in there yourself."

Momentarily taken aback, Jack wondered whether she meant he needed to work out, or if he should have been in the exercise room. His ego decided it was the latter. He smiled seductively. "Maybe we can work out together, tomorrow."

Liz's eyes narrowed. How had she ever considered him exciting?

Jim caught her drift. "Mr. West." He had to say it twice before getting the man's attention. "What do you do for a living?"

"Call me Jack."

"What do you do for a living, Jack?"

Jim rapidly followed that question with: "Where do you live? ... What are you doing in town?" ... Looking for the warbler, too? ... What's the best time of day? ... What do they look like? ... Where's the best spot to find them?" He thought some of the man's answers seemed vague and bookish.

Jack's dislike for the fat man grew, but he kept his demeanor light and approving—smiling while answering each question.

When that line of questioning ran its course, Jim asked more meaty ones. "Are you married, Jack? ... Have children? ... Grandchildren?" Tutored by Maggie's third degrees, he kept firing questions. As soon as West answered one, he asked another.

Liz took advantage of the diversion to swim laps, making graceful flip turns in the shallow pool.

Annoyed, Jack found it difficult to ignore the smiling, apparently interested idiot. He flashed glances in Liz's direction, but there wasn't much to see.

Liz finished her laps and pointed at a stack of towels on a table. "Jim, would you mind bringing me a towel?"

Jack stared in anticipation. To his disgust, Fats ambled in front of him, blocking his view as Liz stepped from the pool. The man deftly wrapped the towel around her body, but it didn't hide her curves or flawless legs.

"We've had a long day, Mr. West. Jim has an infection, and I've kept him up far too late, but he doesn't believe women should exercise by themselves." She peered down her nose at Jack. "He seems to think there are dangerous characters around."

She put on her gym shoes and picked up her T-shirt and shorts. "Let's go, Jim. I'm getting chilled."

Jack grinned broadly. "Hey, let's bird together, tomorrow. It'll make them easier to find."

Liz gave him an over-my-dead-body glower. "Good night, Mr. West."

Jim stuck out his hand. "It's been a pleasure meeting you, Jack. You sure know your birds. Maybe we'll see each other around sometime."

"Oh, I'm sure we will, Jim. Have a pleasant night, you two."

He held the door open for them.

* * *

Darla peered up sadly. "Why can't I see you again, Edith?"

"It's a rule set up for your protection as well as ours, sweetie. People get caught up in the emotion of the moment. You'll feel differently, tomorrow. You're still distraught from your family situation and swayed by your desire for revenge. Trust me on this one."

"But the things you've done with me. The things you've taught me. You've opened the door to a new world." She held out her arms.

Edith tousled her hair and kissed her cheek. "You're a sweet child. If, after you give yourself plenty of time to think about it and still want this type of life, you can find the right person."

Darla gave a weak smile. "I have a friend who might like ... something like this."

"It's your life ... but think things through carefully. You have children who need you, who look up to you."

Darla became somber. "Do you think we should've left Chuck out there like that?"

"I warned him he'd get what he had coming."

Edith stared inquisitively. "Not having second thoughts, are you?"

Darla lowered her head, shrugged, and steeled herself. "No. You're right. He deserved it."

"Good girl. Then let's get dressed. I have an engagement in San Antonio."

Edith glanced at her watch. "And you need to go home, get some rest, and get ready for that soccer tournament."

"You'll always have a place in my heart, Edith."

"I'll remember you forever, too, Darla."

Edith's eyes glistened. She hand-combed Darla's hair. "Don't forget what I told you. And don't hesitate to call if you need my help."

"Don't worry. I won't."

38
Birds of Prey

Mentally fatigued, energy drained, Jim made his good night sound as final as he could at Liz's door.

Preoccupied since they'd left the pool, she didn't hug him for the first time since their second meeting at Paradise Pond.

He readied for bed, reflecting on his exceptionally long and tiring day. He'd suffered the anguish of believing he and Liz were parting, then experienced the stress of determining the proper course of action when informed his infection was still severe. Those were followed by the misery of making the wrong decision and not going home.

Now he faced the troublesome aspect of Jack West's relationship with Liz. Overshadowed by the fear of being found out by a private investigator.

He thought he heard a knock, decided it was his imagination, and snuggled his head into his pillow.

The second knock was louder. He arose groggily and peered through the peep hole into the hallway. He'd been mistaken.

When thumping vibrated the door adjoining Liz's room, he reluctantly unlocked it.

She stepped through wearing a pink terry-cloth robe and a towel wrapped around her hair. "That took you long enough." Her voice was sultry, lower than usual. "I thought you might not be able to hear my knock above your snores. I was about to give up."

Jim cocked his head. "I don't snore. Do I?"

"You mean Marsha hasn't complained? She must be a saint. I hate to be the one to inform you, but you snore. Not chainsaw decibels, maybe, but not real quiet, either. You also burble."

"Burble?"

Liz made a burbling sound.

"And you don't mind?"

"It's not the first snoring I've ever heard," she said dismissively. "Sorry I brought it up." She grabbed his arm. "Let's go to bed, I'm dead tired."

She unwrapped the towel from her hair, opened her robe, and let it drop to the floor. Naked, she smiled slyly and began tossing the many thick pillows out of the way. "I lied about that last part."

She patted the bed, and Jim obeyed. She leaned above him and found his mouth.

Weariness gone, he grasped her firm hips and pulled her against him.

She moaned, sucked hungrily on his tongue, and moved one of his hands from her hip to her breast.

Jim fondled it, savored its satiny texture. *So deceptively heavy ... yet so fascinatingly soft.* He squeezed and bounced it in his palm. Then felt foolish.

Rolling Liz onto her back, he slid his hand downward, over her rib cage and onto her firm abdomen. Moving lower, he twirled her silken hair in his fingers.

Liz laughed. "That tickles."

His fingers rubbed and probed.

"And that makes me want you." She moaned. "Oh, how that makes me want you."

Jim plumbed his fingers in her wet warmth and targeted her clitoris with his thumb, kissing her all the while.

"Oh. Oh!" Liz gasped.

He relished her excitement. It stimulated his. He lowered his head, kissed her neck, the space between her breasts, and followed the trail blazed by his hand. He nuzzled the V of her rib cage, tongued her belly button, smothered her abdomen with kisses, and reached his destination.

"What are you doing?" Liz growled. "Gracious *lord*, what are you doing?"

Shuddering, she grasped his head and pulled it against her. "Oh ... *my*."

Her sweet odor, wetness, and thrashing pleasure fueled his passion to please her more.

"Unh. I can't believe." Liz lifted her legs over his shoulders and moved rhythmically in time with his head and fingers. Her hips bucked, thrust, writhed from side to side with increasing urgency. Her body stiffened in trembling rigidity. An ecstasy swept through her. "Oh ... dear ... God."

Gradually the pulsating ended. She went limp. "Stop, Jim. Stop. It's too sensitive." She shoved against his head but couldn't stop responding.

Jim twirled and probed until she was shaking once more, jerking at the jolts within her groin. Though she begged for relief, she couldn't restrain her rotating hips.

He was satisfied. Or would soon be. He moved up Liz's hot body. Changed his itinerary to suck and then nip a nipple.

Fire spread throughout Liz's belly and chest. When Jim's lips left her breast, she rotated, placed the second in his path. He suckled and started to lift his head.

"No. Bite it. Like the other one." She gasped, squirmed, and panted.

She'd been fulfilled, but Jim hadn't. Eager to please him, when their bodies joined, she thrust back and forth to stroke him as he stroked her. She couldn't believe it when another fire began in her belly.

This can't be. Not twice.

An insistent craving demanded satisfaction. Short of breath, heart pounding, she thrust her hips forcefully to meet each of Jim's plunges. She didn't mind the twinges of pain. They kindled her passion, drove her to more intimacy. She whimpered, squealed, quaked with an intensity that dwarfed the first orgasm of her life.

"Jim, where have you been all my life?" She pulled his head to hers, kissed his eyes, his neck, feasted hungrily on his lips. Then bit. Hard.

When her brain was again functional, it stunned her to find he hadn't finished. He was caressing her, sliding back and forth within her.

So much for Jim not being experienced.

His movement changed, stimulating a part of her body she knew was there but hadn't known why. Until now. He slowly withdrew and reentered, electrifying every nerve ending. So sensitive. So deliberate.

She marveled at his stamina. Exhausted, she wanted nothing more than to lay back and enjoy the fire, but she couldn't. She must capture him—become a part of him.

She again matched his movements, bucked with weary anticipation, helped bury him to the hilt, gasped as he plumbed the depth. She trembled as his tip stroked hers, uttered a loud moan when she felt him swell, his body stiffen and shudder.

His heartbeat thudded against her chest as he rose and fell within her, and they cried out in a mutual climax. The orgasm engulfed her entire being—body and spirit. She wanted it to last forever.

Liz's growl propelled Jim into rapture. They might forever be enjoined. Each time he tried to push up, she grasped him more tightly, laughing and sobbing at the same time. He surrendered, rested heavily upon her, and accepted her insistent mouth.

Liz moved her hips in tight circles, rubbing, tugging God's gift of joy within her.

"Jim, Jim," she heard someone say. It couldn't be her. She was in another world, one where time stood still, and love reigned.

Relishing Jim's body upon her, she heaved to breathe under his full weight. She sucked hungrily on his mouth in gratitude and admiration.

Jim thrilled at the hot, living cushion beneath him. He would die a happy man.

It took Liz a long time to speak after she liberated her lover to lie beside her. She searched for words that wouldn't come.

"That was ... I've heard of orgasms ... Becky ... the pain from ... fire in my belly ... Darn, I can't—"

Jim brushed her mouth gently with a fingertip. "You don't have to say anything." He brushed her mouth again, this time with his own. One more brush, and their lips satisfied each other with gentle wonder.

When they came up for air, Liz sputtered. "But you don't understand. If it weren't for you, I would never have known such joy."

Hugging her tightly, Jim pondered her mention of pain. Was it him? Too aggressive? Or something in her past? A piece of her puzzle?

He glanced at the clock and groaned.

Liz jolted. She'd put a severely-infected, worn-out, obese, nearly sixty-eight-year-old great-grandpa through heart-pounding paces. "What's wrong?"

"I think I'm too beat to get up early to go looking for that warbler."

Her belly shook with laughter. "Don't worry. Ya see one bird, yuh've seen 'em all."

When she sauntered to the bathroom, Jim watched in awe—for several reasons. First, he easily recognized the song she was humming. "How Great Thou Art." *A church song?*

Second, if Liz could somehow be considered to have a flaw in her physique, it would have to be her breasts—which, he was rapidly discovering, were an acquired taste. Above all were her hourglass curves, broad, round derriere, and enchanting hip sway.

How can women be so beautiful? He wished he could box her looks, so when they parted he could take them out and fondle and admire them whenever he desired. He sighed. Next Thursday would be difficult to take. After that, only memories of their love would remain. But those would have to serve.

How did I allow this to happen? He'd always been a faithful husband, avoided temptation. Yes, he'd admired some of his acquaintances, and women in general, but those were glances that marveled at their beauty—both their physical and loving natures. Perhaps a bit more, but he'd stopped short of envisioning what they'd be like sexually.

Marsha had always satisfied those needs, however infrequently that might be. The intervals might make him a bit cranky or impatient, but on those few times when he became caustic, she would raise her eyebrows.

"You're too moody and stressed out," she'd say. "I know what you need." That night she would show her willingness to accept his lovemaking by coming to bed nude, or on truly rare occasions, by accidentally brushing against him.

He felt much calmer after sex and eagerly awaited the next night. But Marsha would act like lovemaking was the furthest thing from her mind. She wasn't subtle about putting him in his place and often wouldn't engage in sex for weeks. Or months. Faking moodiness didn't work, but the great times were worth the wait. Maybe the wait even enhanced them.

With Liz, things were different. When she attacked him at Paradise Pond, he felt a sensation warm his body—head to toe. It was something new from a woman's touch. Now, she fueled his imagination.

He'd read somewhere that people suffered something called refeeding syndrome after a prolonged fast. If they ate too much, it threw their metabolism out of whack, and they risked death from cardiac arrhythmias and heart failure.

There might not be such a thing as too much sex, after a prolonged abstinence, but at his age and in his condition, cardiac arrest while making love with Liz was a distinct possibility.

When she returned to bed, Liz watched Jim amble to the bathroom. So patient, so caring and loving—why couldn't every man be like him? He made her vibrantly alive, awakened sensations within her she hadn't thought possible.

Becky had tried to tell her, but feeling guilty for even listening, she'd changed the subject.

She once began reading a magazine article Becky gave her, but guilt stopped her then, too. Such stories were intended to force women to have babies, a duty they must bear. Sex had always been painful, physically and mentally.

Yet Jim had just proved—gloriously and electrifyingly—that Becky and those articles weren't lies. Despite his bulk, he was as gentle as a lamb. And though gentle, he knocked her senseless. Like when they touched at Paradise Pond.

Perhaps this was like being slain in the spirit. She'd witnessed that hundreds of times—been touched by healers who sent true believers reeling to the floor. She'd felt nothing. A few healers touched her a second time before moving on—to those without demons.

She reminisced. Was her relationship with Jim ordained? What had infuriated her at Paradise Pond? She smiled. Paradise—that's where she was now.

As they spooned together in the blackness of the room and sleepiness eroded the excitement of moments past, Liz decided she owed Jim an explanation. "I met Jack West the day I went to pick you up at the hospital. I told you I stopped at the birding center on the way. He was on the boardwalk. It was the day I took the pictures of the king rail. We talked about the rail, Jack's photo equipment. Things like that."

When Jim made a sound that indicated he was listening, she continued. "He's super good-looking, and I found his attention ... especially looking at me all over ... exciting. He invited me to go birding with him, and to be honest, I considered it. Now, I'm glad I didn't. He seems the type who might take advantage of a woman. Perhaps, even by force."

Jim listened quietly. He wasn't that different from Jack. He'd taken advantage of Liz, had stared when she walked into the bathroom, moments earlier. Couldn't that be considered leering? When she implored him to stop after her first orgasm, he'd refused. Wasn't that forcing his will upon her?

She'd now seduced him several times. Even though he'd been a willing victim, she knew he was married. Could any man resist a woman so beautiful if she set her mind on seduction? Wasn't that forcing someone to have sex?

What made the difference in such matters? Who was the hunter? Who was the prey? What made an action by one person acceptable, and an identical one by someone else unacceptable?

Am I an idiot for even considering such things?

It was his last thought before he was again in his dream-world, chasing the petite, laughing, uncatchable brunette—who stopped in mid-stride, glowered at him, and disappeared.

39
Good Birders Don't Wear Black

Liz lay draped over Jim like a rag doll when he awoke. When she didn't awaken, he slowly lifted her arm and leg and tried to slide away without waking her.

She grabbed him and pulled him back.

"I have to take my medicine, Liz."

"If ya dance, ya have pay the fiddler."

Eyes closed, she found his mouth with hers, wriggled her head back into her pillow, and smiled happily back to sleep.

Jim staggered to the bathroom to take his pills. His muscles were sore from the night's exercises. All of them. It was such a pleasurable pain he chided himself for not maintaining an exercise routine. Nothing matched being in shape, and he didn't have an excuse. He'd been point guard on his basketball team and weighed one hundred eighty pounds when he graduated from high school. He studied his reflection in the mirror. *How did this happen?*

He stood gazing at Liz before he crawled back into bed. Well, not everything hurt. Some things felt pretty good.

As soon as he stretched out, she scooted against him. "Umm," she murmured.

Her wide smile made Jim wonder what she was dreaming as he closed his eyes and joined her.

When they awakened, she showered first.

"This is the second best feeling in the world," she called over the spray.

He didn't have to ask what the best one was.

When it was his turn, he relished the hot jets massaging his skin. He could spend the whole day there, just like that, feeling the weariness and pain leave his body.

Before he finished drying, Liz started for her room, walking stiff-legged. She smiled when he raised an inquiring eyebrow. "No pain, no gain. Give me fifteen minutes, and I'll be ready for breakfast. Be sure to knock four times. I'd hate to open the door to the wrong person."

Fourteen minutes later, he rapped four times and was taken aback when the door opened. Liz wore a red hibiscus in her hair and had applied a touch of makeup.

He found the effect startling. For someone not accustomed to wearing makeup, she'd accentuated all the right places—eyebrows, cheeks, a blush of lipstick on her superb pink lips—removing traces of plainness and masculinity. "You're a knockout."

"Be careful. Your great big teeth are showing."

Face impish, she wriggled her eyebrows. "The better to eat me with, right?"

Did she know what she just said, Jim wondered. He stepped back and looked at the door. "Is this the right room?"

She punched his arm. "Seriously, I did this only for you. I wasn't kidding when I promised to be the most beautiful bird you'll ever see."

Beauty was in the eye of the beholder, he'd heard tell. The world might be full of women as beautiful as Liz—feminine beauty came in all colors, shades, sizes, and shapes—but none more spectacular.

"You have nothing to worry about."

Tears welled in her eyes.

Both had the same thought and peered around. They saw no one. Nor anything that looked like a listening device.

In the restaurant, Liz didn't object when Jim stacked four biscuits on his plate, drowned them under dripping ladles of gravy, and topped them with a pile of half-cooked bacon. He forked a piece of biscuit into his mouth, let it tickle his taste buds, and chewed slowly. "This is *so* good."

Looking melancholy, he stared at his plate, carried it to a large trash bin, and dumped it. The kitchen attendant's glare might have put him back in the hospital had Jim seen it, but he was gazing at Liz. "Where's the skim milk?"

She smiled proudly, then became thoughtful and stared into space.

"A penny for your thoughts," Jim offered.

She'd crashed through the razor-wire-topped fence of lifetime conditioning erected around her libido. Having feasted on the tree of knowledge of good and evil, savored its sweet, succulent fruit, she wondered if she could ever be satiated. She'd exploded not once, but twice, during Jim's foreplay. And when she thought herself too spent to do anything but lie in a stupor, he'd rekindled another blaze within her and escorted her to ecstasy.

She leaned forward and spoke in a hushed tone, for his ears only, "If ever there was a great moment in the history of the world, last night dwarfed it.

"I'm looking forward to seeing a golden-cheeked warbler," she said loudly, in case anyone was listening. "Did you know that our President may have become Governor of Texas by disdaining a federal fish and wildlife program intended to protect our endangered summer Texan? It only breeds in parts of Texas and nowhere else in the United States. It's reported he accused his opponent of putting birds above families and jobs."

"I didn't know that."

"Their habitat keeps getting smaller, so I hope they make it. The good news is that a couple of years ago the Federal Government established a credit for protecting endangered species habitats."

"We may all be endangered, Liz. Depending on who you listen to, we're at the crossroads of a rapidly changing planet. As a youth, my father could drink water directly from the Washita River in Oklahoma when he was thirsty. Today people wouldn't think of drinking river water, due to the farm chemicals, ranch waste, and bacteria that wash into the river. The resurgence of wildlife populations, like deer, geese and beaver, due to human-caused habitat changes and predator eradication, add more bacterial and viral contamination.

"Dad's family subsisted on the fish and game he and his brothers caught and hunted. Now, many lakes are posted with warning signs that the fish contain dangerous levels of mercury, some naturally occurring, but much from coal-fired electrical generating plants, if I understand correctly.

"When I was a child in Oklahoma, we lived on a major north-south highway, US 77, the one that runs through Corpus Christi. We had a vegetable and watermelon stand. Sometimes it would be ten or fifteen minutes before a car drove past. Today, it's hundreds of cars a minute. Back then, on trips to the Gulf, lakes, or mountains, I could see forever. When I return to those same places today, the haze prevents me from seeing half the distance."

He shrugged. "But nuclear energy has its own dangers and long-term risks. Environmentalists document that solar and wind-powered energy harm the wildlife and birds we love."

Staring lovingly, Liz nodded and patted his arm.

"Well. Well. What do we have here? Bird lovers? Or love birds?"

Fashionably dressed in a short-sleeved black shirt, black designer jeans, and a broad, silver-studded belt with a large silver and turquoise buckle, Jack West looked on inquisitively. Black gator-hide boots added two inches to his height. He thumped down the chair he'd brought to their small table and sat.

Liz froze. Jim first thought she looked frightened but decided she was furious. He worried that she might explode like she had at Paradise Pond.

"Mr. West, how sweet of you to annoy us."

"We're commiserating about our environment, Jack," Jim explained.

"What's wrong with our environmental policies? Wacko tree-huggers are trying to kill our economy. If they think an oil reserve will make a dumb minnow go extinct, they go berserk. They sabotage people trying to do an honest day's work. How do they think we can get around without oil? Hell, look at all the jobs it's cost us here in Texas, alone. And the damned environmentalists," Jack spat the term, "won't let us touch oil and gas reserves in New Mexico, Colorado, and Wyoming ... not to mention off-shore drilling."

Jim stared amiably. "I thought there was a run on leases for those fields. They're drilling thousands of wells in west Texas and New Mexico."

"You're badly misinformed, Jim. Thousands of e-mails state just the opposite."

"You're probably right. It takes balance."

Liz glowered. "Well, you two idiots can let politicians and politically-motivated television and radio newscasters brainwash you into believing what they tell you, but we're the doomsday species. Case closed."

"Oh, so you're one of those." Jack stared deeply into her eyes and crooked a smile. "You're beautiful when you're angry."

"Go jump in the Gulf, Mr. West. Now, if you two planet plunderers will pardon me, I need another glass of juice. Maybe it will make this conversation more palatable. If not, I can always pour it on your heads and have a good laugh."

Jack nudged Jim as she stomped to the juice dispensers. "Man, she's something. Who wouldn't like to play that fiddle?"

"I thought you were a happily married man, Jack," Jim said, praying for forgiveness. He'd tuned the fiddle early that morning.

"Nobody's that happily married."

Jim managed moral indignation. "Men shouldn't have affairs." *Go straight to hell. Forget salvation.*

Returning, Liz tried ignoring them.

"Our beautiful, little...." Jack laughed. "Make that, Amazon wacko, returneth."

Liz pretended to laugh. "Yeah, I guess I am. Are you two nincompoops praising our President or drilling an oil well? You should see the stupid looks on your faces."

Jack winked. "Actually, I was telling Jim how much I'd like to pump your sexy ass."

Liz stared stonily. "I can assure you, Mr. West. That will *never* happen."

"Don't be too sure, pussy cat."

Jim studied Jack. Was the man as confident as his direct approach made it appear? If so, why? He was undeniably alpha male and incredibly handsome, but Jim was more inclined to agree with Liz's assessment. It seemed more likely Jack pressured women into sex. In either case, Jack's confidence worried him—for Liz, and any other woman he set his sights on.

He diverted the conversation. "What did you say the golden-cheeked warbler looks like, Jack? I've forgotten what you told me last night."

"Huh?"

"Warbler. Bird. The reason we're here," Liz said petulantly.

Jack smiled broadly at her and turned to Jim. "What do you want to know?"

"What it looks like."

"It has golden cheeks, obviously. Its head and neck are black, and its back more charcoal. In profile, it looks something like a black and white warbler."

"Sounds interesting. How large is it?"

Jack looked thoughtful, then spread out his thumb and index finger. "Small, about five inches long, as I recall. I haven't searched for them in years."

"Are the males and females identical?"

Both Jim and Liz thought he looked perplexed. Or was he exasperated with the endless barrage of questions?

Jack shook his head. "No, but close enough you won't see the difference at first glance."

Jim maintained his look of innocent curiosity. "What's the main difference?"

Liz could swear she saw a halo over his head, then reconsidered. He was pretty inquisitive. And he'd screwed up his identification of the long-billed thrasher at Hazel Bazemore. Maybe he didn't want to make another mistake.

Jack masked his annoyance with the idiotic bastard. "The females are lighter colored. Not much, though." He looked at Liz, intending to change the subject.

"Are there any warblers I might confuse it with?" Jim pressed.

Doesn't this doofus ever shut up? How could sweet ass stand the moron, Jack mused. The tub of lard didn't even take a breath between questions. "Nope. It's the only one like it in this part of Texas."

"What about the Townsend's warbler? Or the black-throated green?" Liz asked.

Jack shrugged.

When he didn't respond, she said, "I did some browsing in my bird book last night, so I wouldn't be confused by look-alikes."

Jim stared. When did she have time to study a bird book in the few minutes after he dropped her off at her door and the time she knocked on his?

"I don't think it looks much like either," Jack said, nonplussed. "They're pretty much different."

"How so?" Jim asked.

Resisting the urge to strangle the dumb bunny, Jack gazed at Liz, expecting her to contradict him and explain the differences.

She sat staring, like her ugly companion.

"I'm out of coffee," Jack said. He stood and left the table.

"You're good, Jim," Liz whispered when Jack left. "And quick."

Jim smiled. "I really wanted to know."

Jack returned. "They're out of fresh-brewed, so let's head to the park. Liz, you can ride with me."

He gazed at Jim. "And you can spend the day studying your bird book, so you'll recognize the bird tomorrow."

Jim decided Jack wasn't what he seemed to be, bird-wise. On the other hand, he was exactly what he seemed letch-wise. He didn't like him and didn't want anything more to do with him. "Liz and I have some shopping to do, Jack. Thanks for helping me with the warbler."

"I'm not on a set schedule. I can go when you can." Jack looked on expectantly.

"You've come a long way from Corpus Christi, Mr. West," Liz said. "As Jim so plainly put it, we have things we must do, and we'd hate to deprive you of the best lighting of the day."

She turned her back when Jack extended his hand toward her.

All smiles, Jim reached out and pumped it. "It was sure good meeting you again, Jack. Thanks for the information."

Jack braced himself to keep the turd from yanking his arm off.

40
Lady Bird, Lady Bird

Jim and Liz returned to their rooms for their luggage, equipment, and last-minute necessities. Twenty minutes later, encumbered by their overnight bags and camera equipment, they arrived at her SUV. They kept their conversation light. Just in case.

"We'll take another look at those binoculars you looked at yesterday at Bass Pro Shop, but you need high-quality ones for your camera work, Jim."

They appeared to be what they were, expectant birders looking forward to a great day of birding. They talked about the nice day, speculated what the wilderness park looked like and if a bird list would be available.

The Dodge sat in a different spot in the Outdoor World parking lot.

Once inside the building, in the women's clothing section, Liz asked. "How did the investigator find out we were coming here? Do you think our car's bugged?"

Jim nodded. "I think you've answered your own question. What do you think of Jack's answers to my questions?"

"They fit about any warbler, but I hate him so much I'm probably being overly critical. He was pretty much right on about our warbler, although wrong when he said it didn't look anything like the black-throated green. The females, at least."

"Yeah, when we pinned him down and he left for coffee, I decided to let him get away with it. He was wasting our time."

Liz squeezed his hand. "He probably thinks you're the world's biggest dork and is giving evasive answers to confuse you. There's no need to change his mind."

Jim smiled innocently.

She bit her lip. "Are you thinking what I am ... that he's our PI?"

"It's a pretty good bet. What are the chances he'd be in San Antonio and staying in the same hotel? But how did he make a reservation so quickly? We didn't make up our minds to come until after my doctor's appointment."

"We must have been bugged the entire time. That means he's heard everything we've said since yesterday. But how did he follow us with you staring over your shoulder all the time?"

"He's probably put a GPS tracking unit on your car. That would explain how he tracked us to St. Jo, too. At least that's my hunch, so we need to keep on being careful what we say."

Liz grinned mischievously. "On the other hand, we could give my mother what she's paying for. A heart attack would serve her right. And it would save me the trouble of poisoning her." She clenched her jaw. "That's what I was planning when you asked what I was thinking about this morning at breakfast.

"Mother has spent her whole life keeping me from the joy we shared last night. When I told you how great sex was after the first two times, you must have thought I was out of my mind. My lord, sweetheart, I had no *idea*."

Jim smiled. "At least it gave me a challenge."

She sighed, gave him a dreamy look. "This has been the most incredible week of my life. I can hardly wait to do it again."

"By the way, Liz, you can't poison your mother."

She shrugged in resignation. "You're right. It wouldn't be painful enough."

"What about your church and preacher? Shouldn't they share some of the blame for your fear of sex?"

Liz gawked, opened her mouth to speak, but changed her mind. Her frown changed slowly into a smile. "Only you would think of something like that."

She peered around. No Jack, so she stroked Jim's arm with her long fingers. "I took my own advice about not letting others control our thinking, so I did a little online research."

"Besides the golden-cheeked warbler? How did you find time for that in the thirty seconds we were apart?"

Jim's questions left him totally unprepared for her comment.

"Do you know that the female clitoris has eight thousand nerve endings and only one known purpose?"

He aspirated.

"It's for the enhancement of sexual pleasure. It sure gives a new meaning to being created in the image of God, doesn't it?"

She smiled broadly, linked her arm in his, and pulled it firmly against her breast. "Thanks for showing me where mine is and what it's used for. By the way, the male glans—"

"Stop," Jim sputtered, his face glowing as brightly as a vermillion flycatcher's. "I think I know this part."

A clothes rack and hangers clattered to the floor behind them. A woman, her face as red as Jim's, grabbed frantically to prevent more clothes and hangars from cascading into the aisle.

An eavesdropping salesclerk ignored the flustered woman and stared at Jim in disbelief. *It must be his hidden features.* She pictured a wallet out of this world.

Liz decided the binoculars weren't adequate and led the way from the building.

They drove to the I-10 access road and headed north. They were passing the entrance to a park when she screamed, "*Jim!* There's a toddler beside the road!"

The crying child appeared poised to step into the street, but several cars rushed past without slowing.

Liz tromped her brakes and slid the SUV to a stop off the shoulder. Careful of passing cars, she leapt out. "Jim, take the car and call 911." She pointed. "I'm taking the girl to that pavilion in the park."

She raced to the child, scooped it up, and rushed away.

A second car turned into the park entrance, and a lady stepped out. "Thank God! We were sure the child would walk into the street. Do you need help?"

Liz cuddled the toddler and shook her head. "My friend's calling 911. I'm going to that pavilion." She nodded at one visible through the trees.

"We'll take you."

Jim wondered how Liz knew the tiny, dirt-encrusted ragamuffin was a girl. He turned on the hazard warning lights and called 911.

"The child's a toddler between one or two," he explained.

"Are you sure no one's watching it?"

"It had one foot on the I-10 access road, and no one came to help when my friend reached her. Another car stopped, and they're at the park pavilion."

"What's the park, and where's your location?"

Jim didn't know and didn't want to walk back to the park entrance sign. "Hold on." He moved to the driver's seat and cautiously backed to the entrance. "It's Raymond Russell Park. Look for a black Tahoe."

The technician directed him to stay on the phone until the police arrived.

Jim pulled the binoculars from the back seat and peered at Liz, the child, and the couple in the pavilion that was posted RESERVATIONS ONLY.

The toddler had on a filthy T-shirt and a dirty, puffed-up disposable diaper. Her sun-reddened face, arms, legs, and bare feet were covered with dust. Tears streaked her face, and tiny mud balls dotted her cheeks.

Liz appeared to care less. She held the child's face against hers and swayed her gently. She soon had her laughing. Then began teaching her patty-cake.

Jim thought how comfortable and competent Liz seemed. She was experienced with children—probably nieces and nephews. The couple watched, smiling broadly. He smiled, too, now that the situation seemed well in hand.

The police arrived within minutes, and he followed them to the pavilion. After Liz answered questions, he and she provided their names, addresses, and phone numbers, and asked to remain anonymous to the press.

The other couple, Damon and Edna Mason, were anxious to speak with the media. Although released to go, neither they nor the Masons would leave until receiving some word of the child's parents. They visited while the police searched.

The officers found a young woman in a tiny, wooden one-room house on a nature trail on the other side of the park. The toddler must have traversed a winding road that crossed a wide creek with a large waterhole adjacent the bridge.

Studs, pin-cushion jewelry, and obscene tattoos covered the woman's body, much of which was visible. Her companion was a male mirror-image except for the month of stubble on his face. The child, bawling now that she was being carried around by someone other than Liz, indicated the woman was her mother by reaching for her.

The unsteady woman snatched the child away. "Ashton, I've been looking everywhere for you," she slurred.

"She was just there, over by the playground," she swore to the policewoman. "She couldn't have been out of my sight for more than two seconds."

"We've been searching for you for ten minutes," the policewoman replied. "Some folks rescued her from the I-10 access road."

The woman screamed obscenities at the officer. "Bullshit, they kidnapped her. Where are the fucking bastards?"

She spotted Jim, Liz, the Masons, and those attracted by the commotion. "I'll sue their asses. Arrest them, they stole my baby."

She hugged and kissed her child. "Thank God, you're safe, Ashton." She scowled at her child's saviors. "Don't worry, mommy will put those fuckers where they belong."

She glowered at the Masons, flashed them a finger. "Assholes."

The crowd stared in stunned disbelief.

The ensuing ten minutes featured a tirade of obscenities by the woman to each question and comment by the attending officers.

Until one noticed her companion rising from behind a car in the parking lot. "Hey, what's going on back there?"

"Screw it, cop. I told you I needed to piss when you dragged us here." He zipped his trousers.

The officer pointed at the restroom, a few yards away, and started his way.

The man stared past him. "Go ahead, hit me, asshole. Here come the TV guys."

The officer backed away as a news crew bore down on the scene.

Since there was nothing more they could do and not wanting publicity, Jim and Liz told the Masons goodbye and left.

Liz trembled. "We saved her beautiful daughter from possibly being run over, and that ... that ... druggie accused me of..."

She raised her eyes heavenward. "Lord, please forgive me."

She stared at Jim. "I'm glad we're not still back there with the reporters. I might get sued."

Jim agreed mentally that it might have been an ugly scene. He felt the same, and he tended to be reserved. "I'm glad Damon and Edna corroborated our story."

Liz eyes glistened over. "How can anyone have a child and mistreat them or let them wander off? Mother birds do a better job, and we call them bird-brained.

"Jim, did you see how pretty the child was? If I ever have children, I'll protect them whatever the cost."

She wasn't concentrating on her driving.

"You need to get in the left lane, so we can cross under I-10, Liz."

Jim didn't want to broach the subject but felt compelled. "You know, your mother must've always felt the same way about you."

Liz blinked, realized she'd steered right, and corrected back into the left lane. She didn't respond.

Jim mulled over how to express his thoughts, since they were probably being overheard. "Your mother would never have let you wander off while she smoked marijuana, took cocaine, meth ... whatever that girl in the park was using ... but she looked after your well-being as she understood it.

"I think she's always thirsted for you to be with her, be her little girl, or her ideal of one. She wanted you to be soft, feminine, and obedient. Maybe she wanted to live vicariously, have you do the things she always wanted to do but couldn't."

Liz nodded. "She infuriates me, and I've been getting closer and closer to the edge. I was at my wits' end when we came on this trip. It's probably why I lost it when I heard you whining about your crappy camera and binoculars at Paradise Pond. I'm sorry I made you my punching bag by proxy."

"I'm happy you did. And your situation reminds me of a card I saw about teenagers. It said the more parents correct their teenagers the more teens tune them out. That upsets the parents, so they talk louder. The teens tune them out even more, creating a vicious cycle. I imagine each time you resisted, your mother became more fixated on obtaining your obedience."

"Has anyone ever told you that you think too much," Liz asked. She blew him a kiss. "It's something I find endearing. But you're probably right about Mother. Right about everything."

She thought of a verse and added her own ending. "Lady bird, lady bird, fly away home. Your house is on fire, and your children all gone. Too little care. Too much care. Women have children, only if you dare."

In a vehicle near the Wilderness Park parking lot, a voice said, "Sheesh. What a load of crap."

41
Fern Del

"Magic Carpet Ride."

Yes, this time it had been a hell of a ride. Her premonition had proved false, and a person didn't stop chewing while the flavor lasted. Darla's desires met hers in intensity—all through the night until dawn. Too bad it was a one-night stand, but it was still a great day to be alive.

"Hey, Jackie."

"Where in hell are you, Edith?"

So much for it being a good day. "About an hour out."

"Well, get your fat ass here, pronto."

"I miss you, too."

"Cut the crap. What's taking you so long?"

"I detailed the wagon all by myself. And I needed beauty sleep. By the way, thanks for switching vehicles. Yours is much better in this traffic.

"So, how did it go?"

"You were right—the girl didn't give me any problems."

"What about Seager?"

"Dragged him into the marsh. Listen, do you want me to stop at the next exit to talk, or do you want me there as quickly as possible?"

"All you did was leave him there?"

"Sure. There probably wasn't a trace of him this morning."

"Sounds risky. Did Darla have second thoughts?"

"She said not, but I imagine she will. It's an emotional roller coaster to find out your man's cheating on you. That's why Tuck and I went swinging. He could play with any woman who'd have him, and I didn't feel threatened."

"I imagine he watched more than you did."

"We were a good team."

Edith swore when a car cut in front of her. "Jackie, I can't talk and fight this traffic at the same time."

"One more question. What did she do, afterwards? Cry a lot?"

"Not a tear."

"That's it?"

"Yep. I jabbed him in the arm. She flipped the switch, helped me drag the SOB into the marsh, and cut out. She had to get back to her kids." Edith's lips widened into a broad smile. "Said, thanks, though."

"Well, you might get more than a thank you, if you get here soon enough."

Jack provided incentive. "I need you to detour Fats, so I can screw candy bottom. She came on to me at the pool, last night, and again this morning at breakfast. And the poor thing needs relief. Fats talks even when he's inhaling."

"What do you want me to do?"

"What you do best. Seduce the bum. Get him out of my way."

Edith remembered the lips and eyes. But the body. "I don't know."

"Hey, I'll make your day. I'll set up another meeting in the wagon."

"And?"

"Depends on whether her mother was right about those sleepovers. Regardless, get your butt up here."

* * *

Liz parked in the wilderness park's cinder block parking lot. They saw two other cars, but the PI's pickup wasn't one of them.

"It looks like we'll have peaceful birding, Jim. We have the park to ourselves. Now, strip to the waist. I want you tan."

Jim groaned. "At least it looks like we won't meet many people."

They took the only trail out of the parking lot. Several bends later they came upon a shelter containing a wall map with a trail overview, park information, and a notebook where visitors wrote where they were from and what they'd seen: Three golden-cheeked warblers!!! The entry was dated three days prior. A few black-crested titmice and not much else, read an entry from the previous day.

Liz studied the map. "I can't remember which one Cindy said was best, the windmill or Fern Del, and one's left and one right."

Jim pretended to toss a coin and pin it to his wrist. He tipped his hand slightly, as if to prevent her from seeing. "Right it is. One's probably as good as the other."

Ten minutes later, he wondered if he'd made a mistake. The trail wound through a forest of oak, ash, and juniper trees, with small open patches of weeds and yellow-flowering prickly pears. It inclined upward at each turn, and his muscles screamed in protest. His lungs burned.

"I have to sit down," he gasped, at the first bench they encountered.

While he caught his breath, a young couple walked by. Humiliated to be seen without a shirt, Jim blushed vividly. His mortification lessened when the couple didn't seem to notice.

They judged the man to be military, based on his fit body and buzz haircut. His beautiful lady friend didn't wear a wedding ring and had mischief in her eyes. After exchanging greetings, the couple proceeded up the trail.

Jim groaned and struggled to his feet. "I thought I'd have a heart attack when those kids arrived, Liz. You've got to let me start wearing clothes in public."

"They could've cared less. Besides, you need the vitamin D. It's good for you. Supposedly, for your memory, too." She reached out and stroked his chest. "And you're looking much better."

He obviously wouldn't get sympathy from that quarter. "If my body stiffens, you'll have to carry me back down."

"Why? When I just can roll you."

Liz brightened. "Or did I misunderstand?"

The trail hairpin-curved up the steep hillside, and they saw the couple locked in an embrace on the section above them.

"So, lover, how about some TLC?" Liz puckered her lips.

"I hoped you'd ask."

Liz thought the quality of their kiss far exceeded that of the other couple.

In the first twenty minutes, the only flying objects they saw were insects— dragonflies, butterflies, bees, and wasps. Then a titmouse flit into the brush.

The view was so fleeting, they couldn't tell whether it was a black-crested, or a tufted titmouse like the ones that fed at Jim's feeders in Oklahoma. Both had cardinal-like crests, gray backs, and wings with a bluish cast, pale bellies, and orange flanks, but a tufted titmouse's tuft was gray, not black, and it had a black patch between its eyes. The black-crested didn't. Despite the color difference, both were supposedly the same species.

Liz shook her head. "My brothers and Daddy complain how hard it is to shoot a deer. Imagine what they'd say if the deer were five inches long, didn't sit still for more than two seconds, and flew through a thick mass of tree branches? And their rifle scopes blurred, and the bullets disintegrated within thirty feet? Sportsmen, hah!"

Jim panted, hands on his thighs. "I won't doubt that birders are sportsmen ever again. How much farther is it to the top of this mountain?"

Liz rolled her eyes. "It's hill country, Jim. I doubt we've gone a half mile."

"*Impossible*. It's been at least five miles."

"Only if we're world class marathoners."

Since he was tanning nicely, she allowed him to don his shirt while he regained his breath. His ruddy facial color, however, would remain until they were back in the air-conditioned Tahoe.

More than an hour and a half after they started, they reached a Y at the crest of the hill. A YOU ARE HERE sign revealed it was about the same distance to the parking lot going forward as it was the way they came. Another sign identified the right fork of the Y as the Fern Del Trail. Gulping air, Jim didn't notice it.

Liz felt a twinge of sympathy but wouldn't let him quit. "Come on. It's down this way."

Jim nodded and followed without lifting his head.

He soon felt like he was free-climbing down El Capitan in Yosemite National Park. "It's a good thing there's a foot and hand hold every ten yards," he mumbled sarcastically, wishing he'd looked before starting down. "This takes the dexterity of a mountain goat."

"Oh, for goodness sakes," Liz called over her shoulder. "Hey, a painted bunting ... and a gorgeous finch."

Jim suspected she was just calling out names to encourage him on. He jolted. "Do I have to climb back up this cliff?"

"Beats me, but this trail ties into the Vista Loop ... if we go straight ahead an extra mile or so." She skipped down to an intersecting trail, where the trail flattened, and waited.

"Have you seen any ferns, yet?" she asked, when Jim eased his pain-racked body beside her.

"All I've seen are my fat feet. And the rocks and trees I grabbed to keep from plunging into this gorge." His thigh and calf muscles quivered. "You're going to have to send for the mule train to get me out of here. I'm dead on my feet."

"What mule train?"

"One like they have in the Grand Canyon."

Liz peered up. It wasn't much more than a hundred yards to the top, but Jim couldn't last long in the warm conditions, not to mention having to climb back up the steep trail. She would give him the rest of their water, and he needed to rest.

The trail to their left appeared shaded, secluded, and flat. They hadn't seen anyone recently, and she heard no one. "Let's take this trail. It looks easy, and I think I hear chirping."

It curved left, then gently back right. The spot seemed perfect. All was quiet. "This looks good."

Jim plopped on a large, flat rock. "Does this look like an altar to you, Liz?"

"Sort of."

"Then go ahead, Priestess, cut my heart out and get it over with. You couldn't drag me back up that cliff."

Liz blurted out a laugh. The only other sounds were made by leaves rustling in the light breeze. She peered around. They were alone. Unbuttoning her blouse, she quickly pulled it off and hung it on a low limb. She removed her bra and draped it over her shirt. Pinching her nipples erect, she lifted Jim's head.

Peering directly at a large, pink areola with an alert nipple, he did what any man would under the circumstances—sucked it and reached for the other one.

Liz shuddered. "Works every time."

Jim raised a perplexed eyebrow. "What if somebody sees us?" He stood.

"We're alone." Liz covered his lips with hers.

He knew the routine. His tongue caressed her uplifted tongue while his hands kneaded her breasts and fingers rubbed her nipples. He looked around. Nothing could be heard.

"Take off the rest of your clothes."

Liz removed her shorts and briefs while looking for a place to lie down.

"Turn around and brace yourself against the rock."

"What?" Seeing Jim preparing himself, she said reluctantly, "O ... kay."

Jim smiled. "Not there. And trust me." He tapped the insides of her thighs.

Liz spread her legs and stared over her shoulder, looking unconvinced.

He reached between her legs and stroked her sex.

Her breath caught, frown relaxed. She closed her eyes and trembled when Jim's fingers slid sensually against her clitoris. Her hips came alive, moved in circles. "Yes, oh *yes*."

Jim's breathing quickened. Liz's love juice covered his fingers, dripped down her legs. *So unlike Marsha. Ever.*

He grasped Liz's trim waist and pulled her against him. "Guide me."

Shaking uncontrollably, unable to speak, Liz whimpered in pleasure.

Jim gently filled her. The pleasure swelled him, and he expelled a quavering breath. "Damn, Liz, you're so tight."

He hadn't intended to blurt that out. Awed, he caressed her marvelous hips. So unbelievably smooth.

"Now, hold your legs together."

Liz couldn't wait. She shoved aggressively against the rock, causing Jim to penetrate past her threshold. The mixture of pain and pleasure was intense. And incredible. Finding it impossible to keep the noise down, she moaned loudly while attacking his thrusts.

Jim struggled for control. She must be sore after last night. He didn't want to make it worse, but his own need demanded fulfillment. He couldn't restrain himself as he'd intended.

The slapping sound of their bodies drove Liz over the top. She whimpered in pleasure as pulsations swarmed her abdomen, then shuddered, trembled, and went limp.

When her knees buckled, Jim grasped her hips to keep her on her feet.

"Oh, how I love you," Liz whispered breathlessly.

She wanted to turn and kiss him, but a more immediate need controlled her. "Hold my breasts, squeeze them. Pinch my nipples. *Ow*. Do it again. Harder." She hammered against him. Couldn't get her fill.

She compelled Jim to do her bidding, but he did it more gently than she preferred. Panting with effort, Liz grunted, "Harder! *Yes*." She shuddered in spasms as she reached a second orgasm.

Her throaty squeals drove Jim to climax more powerfully than the night before. He lost control, succumbed to his own needs. Gripping her waist, he yanked her against him as he plunged into her. Three unbridled thrusts, and his groin released in waves of pleasure.

Liz felt herself being filled and couldn't believe her response. *So unlike before.* She craved it.

Trembling, they stood locked together, catching their breaths, for more than a minute after their mutual gratification.

When Jim pulled back, she didn't prevent him. She quaked even after he lifted her exhausted body upright and turned her around. She grasped him. Kissed him. "Thank you, Jim. Thank you."

"Lord, Liz, I should be thanking you."

They joined in one of the slow kisses that drew their minds into a whirlpool of indescribable feelings of love. Their brains relished the senses, and they knew—without a doubt—they loved and were loved.

"I'll love you, forever," Liz promised.

Jim vowed the same.

Amazed by the turn in his life, he caressed her naked body. They'd just made love, in the open, in danger of being overheard and discovered. Marsha would have been mortified. Rather, would have refused to do it.

Liz dressed slowly, taking her time to smile often at him.

Between her loud lovemaking and satisfying their burning needs, neither heard the slow, buzzing song of the tiny, golden-faced warbler feeding in the juniper above their heads. The lighting was good, and the warbler fed unhurriedly—a perfect photo op. But it had other places to visit and insects to eat, so it flew as their pleasure reached fulfillment.

Re-invigorated, Jim tackled the climb back to the main trail. They rested at the top while he caught his breath.

"We'll go back the way we came because we know it's all downhill," Liz said.

At the second turn, a small woman lay on a rock, looking much like Jim had on his way up—ruddy-faced, with sweat-soaked clothing, gasping for air.

"Need any help?" Jim asked, fearing for her safety.

Bolting upright, she grabbed her chest, and looked away. "No. I'm ... fine," she puffed.

Jim smiled good-naturedly. "My sentiments, exactly. Have a good day."

Liz hummed something that sounded remotely like "Ebb Tide" as they strolled down the trail, and Jim's love grew stronger. Revitalized by her TLC and the descent, he recalled the lady they met. "Some people just don't get in shape for this sporrr—"

Liz elbowed him sharply in the ribs. "Look who's talking, Mister Bird-watching Athlete."

"What? What?" Jim rubbed his chest.

He received a raspberry.

The walk down the hill took half the time it took to hike up. At the parking lot, they stared at each other—and at the dark-blue Dodge pickup.

Jack hailed them. "Great minds think alike."

Neither smiled.

Then Jim faked his friendly manner and stuck out a thick paw. "Well, hi, Jack. Just arriving? Or back for a second try?"

Jack promptly engaged in his favorite pastime. Liz-ogling. The air felt cool, but she and the geezer were drenched in sweat. Maybe the temperature was deceiving. *Or something else?*

"My second. I got several shots of the warbler this morning."

He glanced at his watch. "You two must have spent a lot of time out there. You're soaked to the skin." He bumped his eyebrows up and down and winked.

Ignoring the insinuation, Jim smiled broadly, "Well, we had a little excitement getting here. Liz spotted a toddler about to cross the I-10 access road, and we stayed with her until the police showed up and found her mother."

Jack acted surprised. "So, you're the ones I heard about on the radio. The anonymous ones." He smiled. "Well, I'll be darned. I'm in the midst of shy celebs."

Liz hated every word he uttered. "Yeah, little old us." She visualized wringing his neck. "Of course, now we have to kill you."

Encouraged by her wordplay, Jack bantered back. "The dying man gets his final wish. Care to guess what mine is?"

"A lethal injection?" Liz stalked into the restroom.

Jack nudged Jim with an elbow. "Man, what I wouldn't give to bend her against a tree and bang her until her legs give out."

Jim hoped he kept his surprise off his face. "You don't mean that, do you, Jack?"

"Wouldn't you ... if you had the chance?"

Chagrined and now worried, Jim changed the subject. "Where did you see the warbler? All we saw was the north end of a southbound titmouse."

"At the windmill. It's not far from here."

"You, lucky dog," Jim said, elbowing him in the side as hard as he dared without arousing suspicion. He stared expectantly at the camera on Jack's tripod. "Can I see it? It would help justify my pain from climbing the mountain."

Jack rubbed his sore ribs. "Sorry Jim, I already downloaded them to my laptop and it's back at the motel. Maybe next time."

"How about your business card? I can see them on your website."

Jack perfunctorily patted his pockets. "Sorry, flat out of cards. And it'll be a while before I edit the photos. I have a big backlog. I guess your girlfriend told you about the rail we saw."

"She did," Jim said, pretending excitement. He shrugged off the disconcerting girlfriend comment. "You have all the luck, Jack. Where did you say that rail was, again?"

Jack started to say something and then glanced at his watch, "Your sexy girlfriend sure likes to use the restroom."

"Well, if you'd climbed that mountain, you'd be cooling off, too. The trail's at least four miles, straight up."

Jack treated Jim like an overenthusiastic child. "It's only two miles to the top, and a four-hundred-foot elevation gain."

Jim feigned admiration. "You must be in great shape. You're not sweating.

"By the way, we met a woman near the Fern Del Trail. We thought she might be having a heart attack, but she waved us off. If you're heading that way, you might want to check on her."

Jack glowered.

Jim peered at the parking lot. "There are only two cars here, besides ours. Since she's not with you, one's got to be hers. Which one is it? We'll notify the police to check on her if it's still here when the park closes."

"That won't be necessary. I have till sundown and want more pictures."

"Then which car is yours? You might want to leave a note on the windshield, so it won't get towed if you don't make it back in time."

Exasperated, Jack spit out, "It's the Toyota near yours."

Jim pretended to miss his blunder. "If you need paper and a pen to write the note, I have some in my backpack."

Jack shook his head.

Jim became concerned by Liz's prolonged stay in the ladies' room, but the men's room beckoned. "Excuse me. I have to freshen up." He glanced apologetically and hurried into the restroom.

"You need any help in there?" Jack called to Liz, after giving Fats time to become indisposed.

"Not from you."

"Ready or not—"

Jim bolted out the door and smacked into Jack in the small opening between restrooms. "What are you doing?" he asked, wide-eyed, while zipping up.

"Just teasing Sleeping Beauty." The smirk on Jack's face belied his statement.

"That's a strange kind of teasing. If a woman called out what you did into the men's room, I'd wet my pants."

"I bet you would."

Liz stepped from the restroom. "Mr. West, I suggest that you tease someone else. I'm not defenseless, and I don't take a joke well."

She grabbed Jim's arm and dragged him away.

Jim glanced back over his shoulder. "Nice meeting you again, Jack. Please check on that woman up the hill."

"I'll do that."

When Liz's SUV exited the parking lot, Jack pulled out his cellphone and forcefully punched a number. "Where in the hell are you?"

"Shut up and get your rear up here."

"I can't find you, if I don't know where you are."

"At the Fern Del trailhead. And hurry, I think I'm dying."

"Well, it's about time. Good riddance."

When he arrived, Edith glared. "If anyone ever asks me to do surveillance on a birder again, I'm going to shoot them directly between the eyes … even if it's my own saintly father."

"He's dead."

"Then I guess they couldn't find me guilty of murder, could they?"

42
A Little Bird Told Me

"Where to?" Liz asked, when they left the parking lot.

Lost in thought, Jim replied, "Home, I suppose."

When she giggled, he realized what he'd said. Had he become that comfortable with the young lady?

"I meant the Hometown Buffet."

"What's this about a buffet? Your dietician wouldn't approve of that. I know her personally.

"But first, you're soaked as much as you were on St. Jo. You've got to change. Then we'll see if rooms are still available at the inn. If not, it's back to Palm Gardens."

A large lot beside the access road caught her attention. Bordered on two sides by a forest of brush and trees, it contained an industrial dumpster and road-working equipment but was otherwise deserted. She drove to the far corner of the lot and angled the Tahoe close to the brush. Jim stared at her.

"Get out and change your clothes. I don't want you catching pneumonia."

He started to argue, but she was right. His teeth were chattering, and the SUV's open passenger doors, combined with the thick vegetation, created a changing room.

Liz unnerved him by scooting across the seat and watching while he opened his overnight bag.

Embarrassed, Jim said, "I don't need help, Mother."

She removed her top and bra. "I'm putting on a dry bra and clean underwear. I threw away my panties back at..."

Jim's eyes widened. Liz's eyes narrowed. Both peered around. She stretched out on the back seat, grasped the door arm behind her head and extended her legs.

Jim removed her shorts, gripped her satiny thighs, and moved between them. "You're incredibly beautiful, Liz."

"You, too," she murmured huskily.

Using the door arm for leverage, she leisurely wrapped her legs around him. As before, she didn't need foreplay.

Securing his grip, he plunged into her thermal heat. They gasped simultaneously at the staggering sensation.

"Oh, Jim, lover, you're ... Oh *yes*."

"Liz, you feel so *damn* good."

Enchanted by the sight of her breasts swaying up and back on her chest with each of his thrusts, lust propelled him to ruthless abandon.

Excitement surging, Liz shoved forcefully against the door while pulling with her legs to capture each collision, savor the sensations as he speared her. She strained for more, then climaxed as Jim released.

His knees went as weak as hers did at the park, and she gripped him tightly between her legs. Using leverage, she curled upward and mashed her chest against his. She grasped his head and crushed his lips until the electrical impulses ravaging her abdomen subsided.

"You've been promoted," she whispered in his ear as she caught her breath.

"Promoted?"

"You're no longer my knight in shining armor. You're my king."

Jim was oblivious that police might become curious about an SUV parked near equipment beside an Interstate access road. Encircled by silken legs, he held in his bare hands the downy-smooth cheeks of a flawless derriere. Naked breasts mashed against his bare chest. Perfect lips and teeth nibbled his ear lobes. Exquisite tremors wracked his body. And he had—in less than.... His grin wrapped around his head. *Goodbye, Kansas. Hello, Oddz.*

That was *so* hot," Liz gushed, watching Jim as they quickly dressed.

His reddened face grew perplexed. "Aren't you going to look away?"

Her eyes danced. "Not a chance."

How could she enjoy gazing at a body as obscenely ugly as his was?

What the heck. Jim pulled on clean underwear and the clothes he wore the previous day. He still smelled sweaty but, then again, *what the heck.*

When Liz drove past the motel, Jim stared quizzically. "I thought we were going to check in."

"The steering's pulling to the right, and the low tire warning light is on. There's a Walmart nearby. Maybe their tire shop is still open."

After explaining the symptoms to the shop manager, she handed him the key.

"Your right rear tire's half flat," he commented.

When they entered the main store, Jim apologized. "I'm sorry for back at the lot."

"Why?"

"Uh ... for losing it like I did back at the park."

"Oh, that?" Liz laughed. "I thought it was me."

He asked a nagging question. "We've been pretty active. Aren't you ... uncomfortable?"

She tucked her arm in his and pulled him tightly against her. "I can barely walk. Lord, like I've said, this is the greatest day of my life."

She led him down the main aisle. "Let's hit the restrooms to clean up a little, then head to the food section. We'll pick up some snacks for the trip back to Port A. I bet you're starving."

He hadn't thought about food even when he mentioned the buffet. There were other things on his mind—worrisome things—but her comment broke his concentration. He'd exercised more the past week than in years. "Believe it or not, I'm not that hungry, even with all the ... exercise. And right this minute, my muscles aren't all that sore. You're a miracle worker."

"Don't hold your breath, Jim. When your endorphins stop raging, the lactic acid will stiffen you like a board. As for food, I need to keep your energy level up. I have plans for you." She glanced down. "Whoa."

Jim couldn't believe it. *Already? No way.*

They drank tea in the store's McDonald's to refresh. "Not nearly as good as Maggie's," Jim said. "By the way, why were you in the park restroom so long? I was getting worried."

Liz's smiled playfully. "First, you're quite a lover. Hygiene," she explained, when he didn't get it.

"And I thought about my mother, what she's gotten me into. Or maybe what I did when I didn't stand up to her. I gave that a ton of thought.

"And, of course, there's you. You've made such an impact on my life ... the biggest ever ... and that's saying something. I'm still trying to decide what to do about that."

"Would you like some help?" Jim realized he was being presumptuous.

Liz continued to stare until he glanced away. "Maybe, but not yet. Some things a girl has got to do herself ... if she can.

"And there's your friend. Or should I say, fiend?"

When Jim started to object, she cut him off with a wave. "Just kidding. I was waiting for him to leave. He sure doesn't take a hint, does he?"

"Maybe he thought he'd impressed you so much that you were waiting for him."

Jim debated voicing his concerns about Jack's insinuations and decided not to.

Liz wrapped her arms under her breasts and shuddered. "West's so obscene. I wonder if all PI's are like him."

"He may not be the PI, just the local neighborhood pervert. He was driving a Toyota SUV. That is, unless he lied to me."

Light dawned. "No. I remember. Jack drove a RAV4 at the birding center."

The realization stunned her. "My lord, the lady on the trail. I remember meeting her at the birding center. She was talkative, and I tried to tune her out and escape, so I don't recall her name.

"But I still think Jack's in on it. I thought it was strange that he left the birding center right after I did when I went to pick you up at the hospital. Then he showed up the hospital."

Jim again considered mentioning his conversation with Jack—its implications—and again decided against it because of its vulgar nature.

"So, he isn't the PI." Liz shook her head. "I'd better take karate lessons."

She put on her perfected Maggie smile and lifted her eyebrows. "Wanna teach me some moves, big boy? You know all the good ones."

She could turn him on at the flip of a switch, Jim realized. Maybe that was her secret. She'd hypnotized him and was using key words to control him.

He resisted embarrassing himself by dwelling on her comment. "I agree. He was at our hotel, and both showed up at the park. That's too coincidental."

Liz nodded thoughtfully.

"We need to search your SUV for a bug so we can say what we want," Jim continued. "Then there's the GPS tracker. We need to go online to see what they look like."

Liz jerked her hand to her mouth. "Oh, *shit.* Sorry. What about when we changed clothes?"

Jim jolted. Had they blown their cover? "Maybe we were out of range," he said hopefully.

At the deli Liz ordered a sub sandwich to share. She picked up a case of water and a couple of cartons of yogurt—Activia—for Jim. "This should do it."

"A real meal," he snorted. "And why the probiotic yogurt? You don't let me eat enough to need it."

They heard Liz's name paged.

"Talk about timing. The car's ready."

Instead of a waiting bill, they found a waiting manager. "We found a small leak in your tire, but we found a couple of other things, too."

Jim frowned. *Here it comes. Show me the money.*

The manager held up what looked like a small, rectangular box, about three inches by four inches and one inch deep. "We found this attached to your car. Charlie barely noticed it when he put the car on the rack."

"What is it?" Liz asked.

"A GPS device ... the first one we've ever seen. At first, we thought it was a spare key holder, but it was too large and looked electronic." He pointed at a name. "It's a Flash Bolt GPS."

"My mother's having me followed," Liz said matter-of-factly, "and she's spending thousands of dollars doing it. She thinks I'm having an affair with some young stud and that grandpa's covering for me, but we're only chasing birds to take their pictures."

Jim's mouth fell open. *Stud?*

The shop manager wrinkled his nose.

His opinion of bird-watching must rank right up there with taking his wife to the mall, Jim thought.

"In fact," Liz explained, "that's why we smell a little rank. We climbed a hill in Friedrich Wilderness Park searching for golden-cheeked warblers."

Liz's pheromones were alive and well. The manager's face changed to a smile. Most repairmen in the service department were drawn within optimum ogling distance. She softened her eyes and asked, in a lilting voice Jim didn't recognize, "Would you do me a favor?"

The shop manager beamed. "Sure."

Jim shook his head. Two weeks earlier, she'd have been mortified to use her feminine wiles. Now, she could make a man agree to a request before he heard it. The new Liz could be—was—dangerous.

"Would you give this to your mechanic who lives the farthest away? Or someone going on vacation? I want the investigator to run up a huge bill, so Daddy will hit the ceiling when he finds out. I'll pay for leading the investigator on a wild goose chase."

The manager chuckled conspiratorially. "Pete's going to the Texas Motor Speedway in Fort Worth, this weekend, and he's leaving in about twenty minutes."

Liz placed a fifty-dollar bill in his hand and curled his fingers around it. "Here's a little something for Pete's trouble."

The manager held up a familiar battery-shaped device. "And what do you want me to do with this? We noticed that your windshield wipers need replacing, and it was tucked in the drain well."

Liz frowned. "Another bug. Fix the tire, replace the wipers, and give me that."

He handed it to her. "I'd say that the Man upstairs is looking out for you, but we think somebody has it in for you."

"What do you mean?" Liz asked, her gaze genuinely curious.

"We think someone stuck an ice pick in your tire."

Liz and Jim reached the same conclusion. *The girl's boyfriend at the park.* They wondered about the Masons' car and police vehicles.

"It's one of those no good-deed goes unpunished things," Liz said. "We helped someone out, and it must have ticked off her boyfriend."

"In that case, I'll have Charlie check under the car while it's on the rack to make sure there's no other damage ... or another bug."

"Thank you *so* much." Liz's eyelashes fluttered in gratitude as she handed the manager another fifty. "This is for you and your technicians. The nachos and beer are on me."

Five minutes later the listening device died a gruesome death, and Liz buried it in a shallow, unmarked grave under the pebbles in one of the tree islands in the parking lot. The funeral service was well attended by gulls and grackles hoping for a handout.

Liz and Jim returned to the McDonald's to await the page from the service department. She remained silent, trying to remember the woman's name, but finally gave up. "I wonder where Jack and the lady PI are now. I'd bet he didn't even go to see if he could help her."

"He sure doesn't seem the type to help anyone but damsels in distress ... and help himself to those. What confuses me is why they're in separate cars."

Jim's gnawing concerns won out. "Liz, we may have been compromised even before we changed clothes."

"What do you mean?"

"Jack said a couple of things that worry me. They may have been coincidental, but—"

"What?"

Jim glanced around to make sure they were outside the hearing distance of other customers before whispering Jack's comments. "And he called you my girlfriend."

Liz blanched. Her heart rate quickened. She chewed her bottom lip. "The lady PI may have seen us ... heard me, anyway ... taken a picture with her cellphone and sent it to him. What should we do about it, Jim?"

"Nothing. What can we do? And it might be just my overactive imagination."

"I promise you, Jim, if the PIs find out we're having an affair, I won't let your marriage be ruined. Mother isn't the only one with money."

"Only if they're unethical. If they're legit, we won't be able to do anything about it."

"Whatever it takes." Liz said darkly.

Her countenance heightened Jim's concerns.

Twenty minutes later, the GPS was on its way to the Texas Motor Speedway, two hundred eighty miles away, and Jim and Liz were headed southeast on I-37.

"Well, today was a bust," he said, thinking of the warbler.

"A bust? I give you the best sex of your life, and you consider it a *bust*? Don't you *dare* speak to me again."

Liz trembled. "Men, all you think about is sex. And when you get it, you drop a girl like a rotten potato. I hate you!"

Jim crawfished. "I meant ... uh, your bust. It's so beautiful."

"You can't weasel out of it *this* time, buster. The minute we get back to Palm Gardens, I'm splitting."

"No. I meant not seeing the—" His breath caught as a hand unzipped his pants, extracted his monument to manhood, and fondled it erect.

"Well, well, what do I have here?" Liz said. "Umm, feels so good … doesn't it?"

Jim tried to recall his honeymoon. Had Marsha acted like this? No. Was it the times back then, or Marsha? He didn't know. Before Liz, there had never been another woman.

He quivered when she raked a nail over his tip. The car swerved.

"Sorry about that," Liz said unapologetically. She stroked his smooth hardness, traced the ridge around his wondrous marshmallow tip with a fingertip, and squeezed it like a bulb. She admired his length, relished the throbbing between her fingers. "You're so firm, so beautiful."

She tilted her head. "I wonder why it curves a little to the left."

The tires roared as they crossed the rumble strips.

She tried to stuff him back in his pants and gave up. "Don't worry. I'll make it all better later. I don't want to wreck us."

Jim exhaled a quavering breath. From his perspective a wreck was inevitable. Just a matter of time.

43
Flight of the Falcon

Jack and Edith were drenched in sweat. Their clothing chafed their bodies in the most awkward places. Their tempers exceeded the temperature when they hobbled down the hill.

"Why didn't you come the first time I called?" she demanded.

"The girl was eating out of my hand, Edith. She reeked sex. And what idiot would try to find a couple in a square-mile park with dumbass around? The imbecile talks your head off." He shot Edith a sharp glance. "Not unlike someone else I know."

She ignored the insult. "You can't tell. Maybe she arranged a rendezvous, and the old man was their cover." But even she didn't think it possible. *What possessed me to go traipsing up that god-forsaken mountain?*

"Impossible. She wouldn't make love out in the woods, where it's hotter than hell and some nincompoop might stumble across them." Jack stared pointedly. "Besides, we were the only other people in the park."

"What about the Army stud and his horny good-luck charm, I ran into?"

"Case in point." Her irate companion sneered. "And the girl was waiting for me in the bathroom. At the very least, I could have arranged a meeting."

Jack pulled his shirt away from his body and flapped it for air. "Then Fats races out of the bathroom, zipping his fly."

Edith acquiesced. "Maybe I miscalculated. The girl's mother is positive she has a lover, and she's threatening to fire me if I don't give her what she wants." She didn't share Jackie's confidence, but he was super handsome and incredibly sexy.

"As horny as she was this afternoon, it shouldn't take long. But we have to coordinate."

Edith nodded humbly.

Jack gave her a scathing look to make her suffer for forcing him to climb the mini-mountain in sweltering heat. "For all I know, she was ready to bang me in the john. And, where were you? Two miles away … sacked out on a rock."

He tapped his spy camera. "I could have taken photos if fart face had been out of the way. That's why I'm so exasperated, Edith. I ask you to get your ass here to help, and you decide to take a hike."

"You're right, Jackie, I screwed up. It won't happen again. From now on, I'll do things exactly your way."

Her submission heightened his optimism. "We'll divide and conquer. You button-hole Fats while I use the Party Wagon. I'll have Ms. Liz doing things that would fry her mama's eyeballs … either willingly or from fear of being exposed. The girl has a lover. Her mother has to have a reason for suspecting an affair."

"What if we don't catch them in the act?"

"I can bluff with the best of them."

Jack's confidence rubbed off on her. And Jim Smith's face looked a bit thinner, sexier. "Fine, I'll do Fats. And I want a copy of the video." She chuckled. "Wonder what witch Mathews will do when she sees her proof?"

"That won't happen if the girl plays ball. Besides, you always say you don't do this for the money. We'll have our fun and let mama insult you. Case closed."

Edith's smile broke, "Let's hope. I think the case is cursed."

Jack didn't mention his faux pas of letting it slip that he knew which vehicle belonged to the girl at the wilderness park. "It's only a run of bad luck." He chuckled. "Unexpected storms. Stick snakes."

In the parking lot, while waiting for Edith's laptop to power up, they checked the listening device and heard only muffled noises and the conversations he taped while following their quarry.

"Crap, out of range."

Edith grew impatient with the computer's start-up time. When it booted, she punched in her code and studied the GPS track.

Jack exulted. "I knew it. They stayed at that lot by the access road, where I did for fifteen minutes. That's where they swapped cars."

"That's one scenario," Edith said doubtfully. But it was now Jackie's show.

"We're on a roll, Edith. From there to the intersection of ... hey ... Walmart ... for more than an hour." He scratched his head. "The SUV's headed north on I-35." His smile broadened. "Know what this means?"

"A long weekend and lots of overtime?"

"That, too. No, the old bastard wouldn't go anywhere but back to his RV. It means sweet Liz is with her boyfriend." Jack gave a warped, evil-eyed smile. "I'm only a few steps from heaven."

Edith's mouth pursed. Why would the girl use her car? And why would her boyfriend let Fats take his? It should be the other way around. *Oh well, Jackie's boss.* "I have an idea. You can bang me to practice up for your angel wings."

"I have a better one. Let's go to Walmart and drop off your truck. I'll drive from there."

"You said we should split up. I could check on Fats and establish a connection." Edith looked impish. "Or better yet, take a cool bath and drink a case of Tecate to rehydrate."

"What, and miss all the fun? Old Betsy's in the car." Jack's camera was his bread and butter. "You can watch while I get our proof."

Despite being bone-tired, sweaty, and reeking, Edith reluctantly agreed. Then smiled. "It'll be late when we get through. Maybe we can find a nice motel and shower together. I could get you drunk and ease your frustrations of seeing the girl making out with someone else."

"I thought you learned better about that kind of thinking."

His glare frightened her. *The carpet burns. Monique, the dominatrix.* Edith nodded and shut up.

* * *

The light traffic on I-37 allowed Jim to reflect on Jack's comments. Recalling his exact words and expressions, he believed they were coincidental. If the PI knew of their affair, she would have already informed Helen. "Liz—"

Peering out the window, she gasped and grabbed her binoculars. "Slow down. I think I saw something special. A falcon. It might be an aplomado."

She looked down the road—not an overpass in sight—and glanced back. The bird was still cruising, searching for prey. "Park on the shoulder and turn on the hazard lights. I want a closer look."

Jim did so and reached in the back seat for his binoculars.

Traffic initially slowed when they noticed the SUV's emergency blinkers, but Liz held up her camera, smiled, and waved them on.

She studied the falcon as it flapped and glided in their direction. "It doesn't have the right coloring for an aplomado, but any falcon is a good find ... other than kestrels. My guess is a peregrine. I've only seen a few in my life, mostly on Bolivar Peninsula. What I recall most are their speckled undersides and heavy mustaches."

She took two long-range ID photos in case it disappeared.

The falcon climbed, swooped away from them into the distance, and dove. They couldn't tell if it caught anything.

Liz's face beamed. "Did you see that dive? I've heard peregrines can reach two hundred miles per hour."

She embraced Jim in a long hug and kiss. "Wasn't that spectacular?" she gushed when they stepped apart. "You never know what you're going to find ... even when driving along."

Happy that Liz was happy, Jim nodded. He didn't have the best view of the bird in the dimming light. On his own, he would've thought it a small hawk.

Jim drove while Liz called home. With one exception, it was a standard phone call.

"Love you. ... Didn't see the bird we came to see. ... We're on our way back to the resort. ... I promise to call Don. ... Love you. See you Thursday."

Who's Don? Why is Helen so insistent Liz call him? Liz had said he was one of her mother's impositions—or was that manipulations? What did that mean? Jim trusted her to tell him when the time came.

He tried unsuccessfully to find a comfortable position. As Liz predicted, his muscles were rigging up.

When his driving became more erratic, Liz knew it was time for rest, not stimulation. "My turn, lover. I'm too excited to sleep."

When she took over at the rest stop, Jim called Marsha. The call went worse than the one before. "Hi, sweetheart, we're headed back to Palm Gar—"

"You must not love me anymore, Jim, leaving me helpless like this."

"I was inconsiderate, I'm sorry."

"You must hate your grandchildren, too, if you prefer chasing birds to being with them." She didn't ask about his injury or how his day went.

"Marsha, that's not true ... Marsha?" He pushed the off icon.

Liz winced. "I'm sorry you're catching hell, Jim. We shouldn't have come to San Antonio. If we'd stayed in Port Aransas, Marsha wouldn't be so mad."

"I'm not so sure about that."

He didn't fret long before succumbing to the day's activities.

Liz awakened him when she parked in front of her cabin. He accompanied her inside to be sure all was well. They kissed, and he limped to his RV.

Liz showered an extra-long time. The hot, cascading water cleansed her pores while she recalled the day's events. She was torturing Jim and might be destroying his marriage. Jack West was dangerous, and they had one day before he returned to the Port Aransas area—if he took the bait and followed the GPS to Fort Worth. And what about her fractured life?

She drifted to sleep contemplating how to make her mother call off the wolf. Or wolves.

"Ready or not, here I come."

Liz found herself in the rest room at the Friedrich Wilderness Center. Jack West stood in the doorway, holding out his hand.

She took it.

They were in Fern Del, at the boulder.

"Know what to do?"

Nodding, she stripped, turned, and braced herself against it.

Jack grasped her arms and wrenched them behind her. Bent her forward.

She heard clicking. Something cold and metallic clamped her wrists. She couldn't free them.

He gripped her hips and yanked her back. Speared her.

Her struggles to steady herself only served to tighten her vaginal walls, providing him more pleasure. She gasped at the sensation, then matched his rhythm.

Suddenly, her wrists were free. She grabbed the rock. Became the aggressor. Feeling his engorgement, her abdomen swarmed in spasms as intensely gratifying as those she'd enjoyed earlier that day.

She turned defiantly. "You can't control me, Jack."

He bellowed in laughter. "I just did what you assured me at breakfast couldn't happen."

Naked, feeling vulnerable, she lowered her eyes and covered herself with her hands and arms.

"No! Hold them out. Look at me.

"Now, clasp your hands behind your head.

"Turn around."

Jack gripped the small of her waist, pulled her derriere against him, and rocked her from side to side. His hands moved to her breasts, hefted and kneaded and tugged.

He turned her, cupped her buttocks, and drew her abdomen firmly against his erection.

Stepping back, he grinned and dangled handcuffs. "Ready for more?"

She unclasped her hands from behind her head and held them out.

44
Je Te Plumerai la Tête

"They took this intersection, Jackie."

Jack nodded. "I see an RV park, Edith. That has to be their destination." He gave a frightening grin. "Our quest is over."

"That's where the transponder is," Edith said skeptically. There were hundreds of motels in the Dallas-Ft. Worth area.

The vehicle they sought backed up to a small Airstream travel trailer. When she expressed her doubts about fancy Liz camping in a tiny trailer, Jack glowered. "It's the Texas Motor Speedway, for Pete's sakes. They like racing and are spending the weekend. That's why Fats drove his vehicle. They needed something to tow the trailer."

Edith didn't point out the obvious. The trailer wasn't a rental.

He snapped pictures of the vehicle and trailer. "Now, we need boudoir pics."

Edith flirted, extra wide-eyed. "I vote we find a nice motel and do that tomorrow morning. We can shower. I'll soap and massage wherever you—"

She became practical under Jack's scowl. "We're both exhausted, Jackie. We'll get our own rooms and charge the R and R to the expense account. We can get up early and take their pictures when they leave the trailer."

"You don't give up, do you? I want proof positive. And we won't give it to mama. Since the girl's hiding a sexual relationship, she can't risk exposure. She'll give me a night of whatever sex I want."

"What about me? Can I get in on it?"

"Yeah. I'll gift-wrap the DVD."

"So, what do you suggest?"

"It'll be slick. I'll knock on the door, say there's an emergency, and shoot when they open it."

"Why don't I knock on the door? It'll reduce their suspicions, and you can use the car to steady your camera."

"This is *my* show, Edith. You can back me up with *your* camera."

"The trailer's small. You can stand over there and take pictures of everything in it."

"My show," Jack repeated.

The short, dark-skinned man who opened the door was buff and wiry. It should have raised suspicions, but Jack was in a fervor. Instead of taking pictures from where he stood, he elbowed the man aside and leaped into the cave-like room.

He didn't lift the camera before the man caught him flush in the face with two lightning-quick jabs. The blows hurled Jack back through the door and over the steps. He slammed to the ground and slid on his back on the gravel. His camera bounced and flipped ten feet away.

Edith watched the man leap from the trailer and kick Jack in the ribs. A foot in the face brought blood gushing from Jack's nose. It was like watching one of the hawks in her back yard that picked off birds that came to her feeders during the winter. Jack was hapless prey.

A burley, black-haired woman—naked except for the towel around her ample bosom—leaned out the doorway. "Kick him in the *nuts*, Eduardo. Kick the asshole pervert in the *nuts*."

Side and door lights on the adjacent RVs flashed on. Doors opened. Window shades rose. People stared.

Curled in the fetal position, Jack tried to protect his head and face from further damage.

The small man stomped his back and spat on him. "Get the hell out of here, shithead, or I'll shove my jack handle up your ass."

A couple in the RV across the lane urged the little guy on. The wife, aware of the ruse, agreed with Eduardo's female companion. "I hope that guy stomps the bastard's balls."

Uncertain his life wasn't still in danger, Jack pushed himself up painfully and backed warily away. A trail of blood marked his path.

Eduardo stared menacingly but didn't follow.

"Did you get my camera, Edith?" Jack asked. She shook her head. "Then *get* it."

He sent a spray of gravel flying when he gunned past the 10 MPH sign on the way out of the park, then slammed the steering wheel. "Damn all RV parks. Damn the *curse*."

Neither heard the cheering neighbors—or the one who smiled and said, "Serves the asshole right. Trailing that nice young babe and her grandpa like that."

* * *

After her paramour had beaten the intruder to a pulp, the woman in the Airstream panicked that the man was a private investigator hired by her husband. It seemed the only explanation. She was supposed to be staying with her sister in Abilene.

"What can we do, cariño? Paco will kill me."

"No, he won't, querida," Eduardo said soothingly. "I have pictures of him with Alice.

The woman blanched. "Your Alice? With my Paco?"

Eduardo nodded.

"I'll *kill* him!"

* * *

Something hit the side of the fifth-wheel beneath the bedroom window. Groaning, Jim lifted the window shade and peered down. He bolted upright. "Liz?"

She stared up, a horrified look on her face. "Let me in," she mouthed.

"What happened?" he asked, when she bounded up the steps.

Shaking uncontrollably, she held out the listening device from the propane compartment. "Kill this thing, first."

He mashed it with pliers from the utility drawer, drowned it in a bowl of water, and took Liz in his arms. "What happened?" he repeated.

"West raped me." When Jim staggered, she said, "In a nightmare." Her words were only partly true. Her dream-self enjoyed it. Waking was a different matter.

Why was her subconscious so hell-bent on making Jack her lover? The thought scared her senseless.

Jim felt her trembling. "Do you want me to make coffee or tea to warm you up?"

Liz shook her head. "No. I want you to make love with me."

"What?"

She grasped his hand and led him up the steps to his bedroom. Removing her robe, she crawled naked into bed.

Jim stripped and joined her.

Desiring to wipe the remnants of the dream from her memory, Liz stroked him erect while he kissed her.

"Jim, would you do what you did in the hotel ... with your fingers and ..." it was difficult to say, but she was growing in confidence, "your mouth?"

He kissed his way down her belly. "Like this?"

"Oh ... *yes*."

* * *

Edith magnified the photo on the camera display. The SUV was a slightly different color—they couldn't see that in the dark. And Jack had been so sure it was the girl's SUV that they hadn't paid attention to the tag number.

"Ha-ha, Jackie, you aren't going to believe this. It's *hilarious*. It's not the girl's license number. She must have found the tracker and put it on another vehicle. How'd you miss that?"

His eyes frightened her. They were made more ominous by his blood-encrusted nose, face, shirt, and pants.

"Now, don't get your bowels in an uproar. I promise ... next time I'll take care of Fats."

She became relieved and titillated to discover the girl would be the focus of Jack's deviant rage—if he didn't change his mind when he cooled down.

Her eyes brightened when she recalled the man on the mountain. He wasn't that bad—great eyes, sexy lips, brilliant smile. "We'll both get a piece of ass, Jackie. After running around with that maiden, he needs relief."

She gazed longingly at her partner. "And so do I." She licked her lips. "Maybe we can split the fun. Have a group grope in the Party Wagon."

Despite his pain and not wanting to give Edith the pleasure, Jack couldn't help smiling. "You're a horny bitch."

His smile faded. "Damn, Edith. We'd be sleeping like babies, right now, if you hadn't screwed things up back at the park." He glanced at her, "But you have sent a lot of fun work my way. Hell, a couple of the broads still ask me out, from time to time."

She stared at the object of her affection. His vulnerable appearance gave her groin conniptions. "Sometimes you can be a bit rough."

"They can only blame themselves. No one screws me around."

She knew that from experience. Her breath quickened, nostrils flared. "You're the best, Jackie. Mama's going to get her money's worth."

It was 4:00 a.m. Jack was tired. His muscles ached from his mountain climb, but mainly he concentrated on his nose. Still leaking blood, it throbbed. He tried touching it to see if it was broken, but it hurt too much.

"I can't believe you didn't help me."

"At least most of the bleeding has stopped." Edith made a sympathetic face and clucked sweetly. "I can kiss it and make it all better."

"Touch me, and I'll break every bone in your body. Some twice."

She couldn't be deterred. "Well, look at the bright side. You still have the girl's ass to look forward to."

Jack's face contorted in rage and pain. "Yeah, and she won't like it so much when I get my hands on it. We were bamboozled. No one gets away with that."

45
Fire Birds

Edith talked Jack into stopping at a truck stop to shower and change clothes. His bruises and bloody clothing drew a few suspect glances, nothing more. The shower invigorated him—as in envisioning making the girl pay for toying with him. He shackled her in the Party Wagon. The agonizing event would last for hours.

Smith would pay, too, but he left that to Edith's imagination. With the restraints in the Party Wagon, she might get the fulfillment she pressured him for. Maybe. Dumb bunny didn't seem the type who could give women pleasure. She probably couldn't find his dinky pecker in his rolls of fat.

Edith pestering him for sex was the opposite of home. She claimed to be five-feet-two. Right—in four-inch high heels. Her face was lightly wrinkled and pixie-like, her short, curly hair dyed a streaky blond.

He once told her he'd have to put a bag over her head to make love to her, but she was beautiful, remarkably shapely. She weighed maybe a hundred thirty pounds, plump in all the right places.

He should know. He'd seen her naked in the Party Wagon often enough. In fact, he found her difficult to resist. Her breasts were disproportionately large for her body. Downright mind-blowing. Hard to keep his hands off. Plus, she didn't mind them being nipped.

Or, he discovered the time with Monique, nipple clamped. She'd yelped but hadn't begged for their removal. Then twirled them like a burlesque queen. Her round rump could take swats, too. She appeared to enjoy it from the men he'd watched her with.

Though Monique the dominatrix had been intended as punishment for breaking his rule, Edith stunned him afterward. The memory filled him with pulsating need. If he stopped the car, Edith would provide relief, but he needed to keep their association professional. And she might capture too much of him, if he ever gave in.

His wife, Amanda, had been passionate when they were newlyweds, but she always kept their lovemaking traditional. It remained that way until their first child was born. Then her passion waned. Their infrequent sex life had still been satisfactory while their children lived at home.

His problems began when their last child left for college—just the opposite of what he'd long anticipated from an empty nest. Always active in church, Amanda joined every committee. Discontent with her spare time, she added civic duties.

He'd been a member of a few of those organizations for business purposes, but she talked him into joining more. They soon met each other coming and going, and their sexual activity slowed to a trickle—once every other month at best.

When those dates, as she called them, occurred, she wanted them over with as quickly as possible. Why couldn't she terminate some of her other duties to make time for him, instead of the other way around?

Several women in church committees and Bible study groups seemed to require his expertise. They invited him over to check their doors, windows, the gopher mounds in their back yards. A few were married. So much for religious women. Despite longing to whet his appetite, he didn't yield to the temptations of those all-you-could-eat buffets and curtailed most church functions.

His business eventually made more money than he and Amanda needed. It even supported their sons and their families. Expecting retirement to do the trick, he bought a motorhome to tour the country.

Then the grandchildren arrived. Amanda found the time to babysit them by tossing his sex needs into the street—literally—although she wasn't aware of it.

Essentially becoming a latchkey house-husband, he needed a pastime, something that allowed travel without Amanda. She only attended committee functions, religious retreats, or babysat.

Abstinence for a mature married man wasn't healthy. Travel helped. Amanda not only didn't complain, she encouraged it, so he visited places like Balmorhea State Park, where the cold spring water could chill his frustrations out of him.

The diversion allowed him freedom to release his sexual passions without the danger of being caught—as Amanda once did him while he was in the shower. Instead of realizing she was starving him, the act made her nauseous. She barraged him with scriptural references about it being a terrible sin. He hated it, too, but at least he was being faithful at the time.

A flyer about a seminar on investigative work at a local college caught his interest. At the first break he ran into Edith. Rather, she approached him. Excellent at ferreting things out, she quickly wrangled his sex life out of him—as in a few times a year—then told him she was a widow with a healthy sexual appetite.

He refused her advances, so she suggested a partnership. He nixed that, too, and they started separate companies. Both successful.

To pay for the cost of his services, a couple of his customers bartered properties they owned. Visualizing himself secreting Amanda away from friends and family to exotic locales, he planned to surprise her with them as a Christmas present. That fell through when he discovered she had surprises of her own.

He recalled the day he received the call from Edith that changed his life.

"I need backup on a case, Jackie."

"You can't get me in the sack, Edith."

"It's not that at all." She gave him the address where to meet her.

He'd just completed a bewildering pro-bono case—one that left him mentally fatigued—or he probably wouldn't have been sucked into her web of sin.

"What the devil is this?"

"I received it in trade from one of my customers. What do you think?"

"That it's a moving van ... converted into a bordello-dungeon?"

"Like it?"

It contained a sound system, satellite computer, and TV cameras to record who knew what. Too embarrassed, he didn't ask. "Not really."

"Do you think there are enough restraints?"

"What on earth are they for?"

"Fun."

"Ugh."

She showed him the hidden room with the one-way window intended to fool participants into thinking it was for enhancing their pleasure. "This is for my protection."

"Um ... Edith, what do you plan to do with this thing?"

"I need sex ... and you know why. I videoed a couple doing kink, and it knocked my socks off. I offered them a way to remain together, they accepted, and I'm afraid it might not be what I imagined. Or dangerous. I need you to watch my back."

"No way."

"Just this once, Jackie. I promise."

"You're not going through with this idiotic plan, are you?"

"With or without you."

Edith being so small and fragile, he couldn't risk that she was lying. So, as much as he hated himself for doing it, did as she asked. He still wondered if the opportunity to see her naked prompted his decision. And once he had....

She embraced fetishism. Her excitement and wanton enjoyment stimulated him, swelled him. The hidden room provided perverse gratification. Afterwards, she successfully argued that he could experience the same pleasure—if they worked together on her Party Wagon project.

He caved. It took all his willpower to keep his hands off her, so he restricted her from touching him. She violated his rule that one time.

Now, she knew better.

"Jackie, what took you so long in the shower?" Edith winked. "I could have done it for you. Man doesn't have to live by hand, alone."

"You know me better than that."

"Well, you look a hundred percent better, so—"

"Come on, we need to get back to San Antonio."

"Let me drive. I don't want you falling asleep."

"Fat chance, in my condition." Jack yawned. "But go ahead."

He reclined the passenger seat, laid his head on a soft pillow, and immediately dreamed of the girl chained in the Party Wagon, begging for mercy.

Edith was intrigued. It wasn't Jackie's nature to be mean and hateful, although the beating he received played a part. Yes, he could become aggressive when he lost control, but that was lust. Since she'd tricked him into debauchery, he was yielding to it more and more enthusiastically. As if entitled.

This case was an anomaly. Ms. Liz appeared clean. For that matter, she didn't appear to pose a risk to anyone despite her mother's determined effort to prove otherwise. She seemed sweet, mothered Fats like a hen with a baby chick—except for the ridiculous exercise.

Exercise. What a horrid case! The beach and rattlesnake, no matter what anyone believed. The mountain in the wildlife park.

Recalling Fats on the mountain trail, she wished she'd been able to speak with him. He seemed like a grand teddy bear—one she'd like to take for a trial hug to see if she could kindle a fire in his huge heart. She was confident she could. And Teddy's groin didn't look all that bad, either. Maybe that was what turned her on. That, and his unusual brown eyes and incredible lips.

She licked hers. The night in the party wagon with Jack and the dominatrix proved beneficial, helped her become much more adept in applying her tools on all the projections, nooks, and crannies that made her partners quiver and plead for more. Plead, anyway.

The night with Jack, in his surly mood, may have been beneficial for Monique, too. She had removed her online ad. Edith found that satisfying. Monique's night job could be dangerous, and she had three young children at home who didn't need to become motherless.

It would be fun to broaden Teddy's horizons, Edith thought. He probably didn't get much sex at home—older men and women seldom did—and they rarely indulged in the taboo.

Kink became vogue, found its niche, after their time. It was in mainline novels these days. Adult boutiques were available to provide couples anything their hearts and bodies desired—handcuffs, crops, delights of all kinds.

Most senior wives shunned such shops, so Teddy might enjoy a trip to fairyland. She could be his nymph, his muse. A pinch here, a swat there, a prickly wheel across.... Her mind ran free.

I need a man, damn it!

She wanted to awaken Jackie but, after Monique, she didn't dare. If he punished her that severely for one violation, what would he do for two?

She thought of Darla. On the other hand, Monique had opened the door to the softer side of sensuality.

Edith sighed. If she hadn't screwed up, she could share Liz's incredible body. She'd desired it from the moment she saw her taking pictures of the bird in the surf. How could she persuade Jackie to share, if he was successful? She disdained the thought of the girl being tortured. Pleasured, yes.

Another reason was Jackie. The girl would be petrified by her first view of him in the buff, and she could be the calming influence. She had been before.

Edith reflected on her life after her husband, Tuck, passed on. He left her well to do—a large insurance policy, paid-for home, condo near the beach—so she took early retirement. Tuck also left her with a voracious sexual appetite. They'd become swingers late in life, and though she was still a desirable commodity, she'd evolved away from that scene.

Men in her church's singles-group only wanted one thing, and they wanted it quickly, damned the old dogs. She'd scared the fool hell out of a couple of the pantywaists.

Singles bars proved even worse. Drunks didn't provide pleasure, only danger.

What was a granny to do? Her children and adolescent grandchildren seldom came to visit, and when they invited her usually wanted a free housemaid and babysitter.

She'd listened to the women in her Sunday school class who sang praises of quilting. Bull hockey. She didn't have the patience for it, nor the inclination to listen to their inane babbling. While they cut and stitched, she cut and ran.

Thirty-plus years teaching in elementary schools honed her ability to spot the guilty, even when they were behind her back. Her natural curiosity—snoopiness, Jackie called it—allowed her to transition easily into investigative work. Running into him in a seminar offered the salvation she was searching for.

Her desires weren't immediately fulfilled, but his background as a family man, deacon, community leader, and impeccable businessman opened doors. The idea for the Party Wagon came from one of his friends, a well-known attorney, who hired her to assist in a divorce case.

She caught an innuendo during one of their conferences, and the remark allowed her to wheedle the rest of the information out of him. He said some women seeking divorces were easy prey for him. Either they or their husbands had been caught in affairs, and couples seldom parted without that incentive, no matter how difficult or tedious their marriages.

If the wives were guilty, their libidos were already increased. If not, they sometimes sought revenge, and sex was the best weapon at hand—under the tutoring of an experienced counsel, of course. It didn't matter that their husbands never found out.

The attorney suggested that men might entertain the same opportunities, and as her mentor, he helped design and break-in the Party Wagon. His speculation proved correct.

Unfortunately, the codger was only in his early seventies when he suffered his fatal heart attack. The babe who met the EMTs at the door of the house he owned on the sly was dressed in a black satin G-string and a spiked dog collar.

Pity. Edith missed him dearly. Had she known his heart was that fragile, she wouldn't have stressed it quite so frequently.

Needing a replacement—special thanks to Amanda—she lured Jackie into watching a tryst in the Party Wagon. It was a setup, and she hooked him as easily as a perch on a worm-baited hook. He even allowed her to romp naked with him and his playthings, from time to time—until she reached out and touched.

Candidates were evaluated for looks, acts, and apparent safety. The selected few were shown proof they'd been caught in adultery, but nothing was suggested. Some raised their eyebrows and left. The customers received their proof. She or Jack the money. Case closed.

Others offered to do anything for silence. Anything.

Easy pickings. Sexual misadventures were what they were about in the first place, and Jack was, after all, a handsome man.

Once in the Party Wagon, only those women who panicked at the sight of Jack's size received his form of mistreatment. When his engine started, he found it difficult to turn it off, and that didn't always equate to pleasure. If not for her damage control, their fun and games might have come to a screeching halt.

Edith wasn't sure she could always be so successful. One lady, in particular—Mrs. Sandra Perot—threatened to go to the police but evidently changed her mind. Edith recalled voting against the prissy predator bitch and refusing to back Jackie up that night on the beach near Port Aransas, but he'd been smitten. And to think, before the Party Wagon he'd been the epitome of religiosity.

Neither he nor she considered financial blackmail. Their word that a single sexual interlude secured their silence was their bond. And despite assuring their victims money wouldn't be accepted, some offered copious amounts for repeat performances. Or for videos of the encounter. Too bad, their memories had to serve.

As for the videos, she and Jackie made sure their own bodies weren't identifiable—no moles or unique physical characteristics displayed, nothing to indicate they were ever there.

If necessary, it would be word against word, and the only clearly identifiable people were the philanderers, with audios that established their willing participation.

She glanced at Jack. He was sleeping like a baby, and she saw the reason for the smile on his face. Could she handle him as well as those women who truly could? He'd said some had invited him back into their boudoirs, but he wasn't about to be lured into a trap. Besides, one encounter seemed to satisfy his curiosity.

Not with her. She'd be intoxicating, addictive—if she could entice him into bed.

She reflected on the girl who'd just made a fool out of him. If Ms. Liz was innocent and he harmed her, it could destroy everything. But if he was right, she would enjoy watching him exact his revenge.

Her gut feel, though, was that things would be best if the accursed case ended.

46
The Rookery

Jim hurt so much when he rose at 5:00 a.m. for his antibiotic pill that he gave serious consideration to not getting back up before noon, when returned to bed. He smiled. He'd shared more lovemaking in a week than in the past year. Maybe longer.

An urgent knocking awakened him seconds later. Groggy, like when antihistamine tablets affected him twenty years earlier, he struggled to focus his eyes. Who would be knocking at this time of day?

He felt the other side of the bed for Liz and jerked instantly awake. After bouncing the fifth-wheel to within inches of knocking it off its stabilizing jacks earlier that morning, he'd escorted her back to her cabin. Had Jack forced his way in? Heart pounding, he didn't notice his pain as he rolled out of bed and rushed to the door.

Liz peered up with a mixture of concern and relief. "I was ready to call the police. I thought you'd had a heart attack. Or a seizure. I was scared to death."

"Why are you here so early?"

"Early? Look around, it's broad daylight. I knew you'd be tired, so I let you sleep. I went jogging and swam in the pool. Then I was petrified when you didn't open the door after I knocked for five minutes."

The sun was high. People were taking their daily strolls, walking their dogs, leaving for work—and he could easily be seen in his jammies. He stepped aside to let her to enter.

Liz slammed the door shut and leapt into his arms. "Oh, darling, I was so worried, I cursed myself for making you hike in the park and for waking you up last night." She wiped tears from her eyes. "I was afraid I'd killed you."

"I thought you said if I did and ate what you told me to, I'd live to be a hundred."

Liz laughed and hugged him more tightly. "Oh yeah, I forgot."

"Well, I'd better get dressed."

When he headed toward his bedroom, the pain surged. A groan escaped his lips.

Liz frowned and shook her head.

When he returned, he stared open-mouthed. She wore a blush of makeup on her face and a red hibiscus in her hair. Her sky-blue, satiny shirt and tan shorts emphasized her figure. Was this the same woman he met two weeks ago? "You look marvelous, absolutely stunning."

"You don't look so bad, yourself."

Liz smiled. "I made a larger breakfast than usual, but don't expect it to become a habit."

He shot her an inquisitive look.

"That was quite a hike, yesterday, Jim, and I have something fun planned for today. I need to keep your strength up."

During breakfast, she sat quietly, gazing at him frequently. Finally, she spoke. "Jim, I worry about you and Marsha. A lot. I don't want you in trouble with her.

Your conversations haven't gone well, so I'm sorry I hauled you to San Antonio. We didn't even see the little rascal we went looking for.

"And I'm borrowing you from her, sexually, like she was my best friend and you were a cup of sugar." Her special smile flickered. "Which you are."

She sat silently for another minute, sipping orange juice. "While I was jogging, I thought about going home and getting out of your life." Her eyes glistened. "We'll have to leave Shangri La, Thursday, but I can't give you up before then. I ache for you, Jim. The smell, taste, and touch of you. Making love with you."

He didn't know what to say. He'd somehow divorced Marsha in his mind and was married to Liz while they were together.

No, that wasn't right. He loved two women at the same time. Since he wasn't sure how to express that, he smiled wistfully and took her hand. When he raised it to his lips, one of his dumb thoughts popped to mind. "You're lucky."

Liz cocked her head. "What do you mean? And your eyes are laughing. What are you thinking?" The set of her jaw said it better be good.

"That you don't have to wait till I leave Shangri La for me to turn old." When she stared quizzically, he added, "You'll have to read the book. Or see the movie."

"I don't understand."

"In the movie, people who are young and beautiful in Shangri La grow old as soon as they leave the place."

She surprised him with a sultry smile. "No need to worry there, Jimmy boy, I'm doing my online homework. Sex promotes the human growth hormone and makes men and women look and feel younger. It boosts immune systems, burns calories, and reduces weight. It also reduces stress and promotes sleep."

She planted a long, wet kiss on his mouth that raised both their heart rates into the anaerobic stratosphere.

"I'm your damned fountain of youth."

"You are that," Jim breathlessly agreed.

Cleanup and a plethora of kisses later, they were on their way to Goose Island State Park on Copano Bay north of Fulton. Unlike the previous two days in the area, it wasn't raining, and the wind wasn't overturning boats in the ship channel. Fluffy clouds floated lazily across the sky.

Liz pointed at one. "Look, there's a poodle."

It was Jim's turn. "That looks like Boots about to swallow a mouse."

"Doesn't that look like the profile of a great blue heron?" she asked.

He nodded.

Liz kept patting his leg and sliding her hand up it. He kept pushing it away—laughing—while wanting to let it find its target.

At Rockport, she turned toward the bay. "This isn't Goose Island, but I have a treat for you."

She paid the five-dollar daily fee and entered Rockport Beach Park. They passed picnic shelters and lazy palm trees that paralleled the ground for five to ten feet before curving gently toward the sky.

A large pavilion fronted the well-maintained beach on the aqua-blue bay. On their left, a dock and ramp provided boat access to Little Bay. Not far past the ramp, a cabled-off area protected a gull, heron, and tern-filled area. Signs declared it a bird sanctuary.

Liz parked next to a pavilion fronting a salt-water swimming pool. "Get behind me in the back seat. That way we can both take pictures."

She turned right leaving the parking lot, right again at a T in the road, and entered a black skimmer nesting area.

"This is incredible, Liz."

She eased to a stop beside a picket fence, rolled down the windows, and turned off the engine. "As long as we don't get out, they'll ignore us. What's funny is that someone doesn't want these cuties at this location. They're trying to lure them inside the cabled-off area with the other birds. The last time I was here, I saw skimmer decoys over there and heard recordings of their calls. I'm not sure why, because the gulls snatch their unprotected eggs and chicks."

She noticed Jim's hopeful look. "Sorry, you won't see chicks. They don't hatch until mid-June or later."

They snapped photos of the birds sitting and standing. Some lay still, their bodies, heads, and long red and black bills flat against the ground.

"Are those dead?" Jim asked.

"No, they're fine."

"You sure?"

Liz laughed. "If you had lips like theirs, you'd be plastered to the ground, too."

As if to soothe his fears, a perceived dead bird stood and flew away.

Liz drove to an observation deck overlooking two islands in the bay that contained man-made rookeries. Great egrets, reddish egrets, and spoonbills appeared to make up the bulk of the nesters, but the islands were too far away for Jim and Liz to be sure or take crisp photos.

On their side of the bay, nesting tri-colored herons ruled the area nearest the shoreline. Laughing gulls were interspersed among them in the tall grass.

Liz pointed to a large open area away from the water. "There are the skimmer decoys, and not a skimmer around."

"They're pretty good imitations," Jim observed. "A little shiny, though." He took a photo to email home.

"One more stop, lover. The salt-water pool pavilion has bathrooms."

The pool impressed him. It bordered a channel between Little Bay and Aransas Bay. He jumped when a huge swirl churned the water next to the bulkhead below his feet, where a bottlenose dolphin chased a mullet.

"There's another one," Liz yelled. "I'll get our cameras."

She raced to the SUV and back and snapped a photo of a mullet leaping in front of a dolphin's bow wave. She checked the display and smiled wistfully. "At least I tried."

The feeding dolphins sent huge swells surging across the wide pool until they moved into the channel and disappeared.

Jim's heart palpitated. "Can you imagine what would have happened if there were swimmers in the pool?"

Liz nodded. "If dolphins can enter, sharks can, too. I wonder how they keep those out? Do you suppose they put up a screen or something during the swimming season?"

"It's warm enough to swim now, and there's nothing to keep sharks from biting swimmers out on the beach, so I guess it's something that doesn't happen. But I'll bet blue crabs nibble people's toes."

Liz shuddered. "That why I prefer backyard swimming pools."

As they left the park, she directed Jim's attention to the Bay Education Center on their left. "That's the most incredible place. They have a six-foot globe they call the Blue Marble. Projectors make it appear to spin, and they have exceptional presentations about hurricanes, the oceans, land, and space. You and Marsha need to check on the show times and visit it the next time you're here."

"We will." He pointed. "That giant blue crab statue by the bay is quite a treat, too."

47

The Big Tree

When Liz used her Texas Park Pass to enter Goose Island State Park, she asked the attendant if the bird lady was still giving tours.

"Yes, but the morning tour was at 9:00 a.m. You've missed it by two hours."

Liz thanked her, glanced at Jim, and parked in the visitor center parking lot. "Here's a chance to get on Marsha's good side ... and your grandchildren's and my nieces' and nephews'."

More than two hundred dollars' worth of T-shirts and keepsakes later, they laughed their way back to the car.

Their fun on the beautiful day made him agree with Liz's morning assessment. He'd never shared such love and affection with someone who shared his interests. She waded into places that would have sent Marsha shrieking into hysterics just watching him do it. They were in Shangri La.

But even paradise had its curses and dark sides. No two lives ever linked perfectly. Like Liz said, they could live and love until Thursday. Then it would be time to part.

Overcome by a nauseating stench, Jim scowled. "What on earth is that? It would puke a buzzard off a gut wagon."

Liz giggled. "It's Stinky Beach." She pretended to take a deep breath. "Ah, doesn't it smell great? Look at all those shore birds. They love it."

Seaweed ranging in color from pink to black covered the small beach. Scampering about, plucking insects, sea life, and other tidbits from the rotting vegetation, peeps and short-billed dowitchers seemed oblivious to the smell.

"Can't we shoot the birds from upwind?" Jim pleaded. "Better, yet, let's forget these birds and go someplace else?"

"Well, I'll shoot from upwind, but you can't. A person has to wade in the water to get the best pictures." She gave a dark stare. "You're sure a wimp at times."

"You don't have a problem with the smell?"

When past the beach, Liz rolled down the windows, took a deep breath, and burst out laughing. "Wasn't that horrible? Seaweed collects and rots in that little cove." She pointed. "And it's really named Stinky Beach ... look at the sign. It's a great place for shorebirds, though. It's full of things they love to eat. I'll park, and we'll walk back."

"You have your priorities backwards, Liz. You pushed me around in a wheelchair when we first met. Now that you've destroyed my body, you force me to walk for miles on beaches and up mountains. Why can't I sit on the hood?"

"I don't want to take my car to a body shop, buster, so quit belly-aching." She shoved. "*Out*."

She clutched his arm when he grasped the door handle. "But first, off with the shirt."

Jim stared in disbelief. "There are people all around us."

Liz granted no mercy.

He determined to disobey her, then changed his mind. His fear was irrational—like Marsha's refusal to be affectionate in public. What he looked like was nobody's business but his own, and he was working on that. Still, he blushed when he took off his shirt and draped it on the seatback between them. "Will you rub sunscreen my back?"

Liz blew him a kiss.

He groaned as his muscles threw tantrums worse than any of his grandchildren when he gripped his camera and started toward the peeps. "Slave driver," he called after her.

"If you think this is bad, wait till later."

"Why? What devious torture are you planning?"

Liz grinned and waded into the water.

The excruciating pain in Jim's legs and arms lessened as he approached the sandpipers. The tiny birds were framed by a band of pink seaweed. He knew they were least sandpipers, the smallest peeps, because of their size and dull gray-green legs. Beyond that, olive-green seaweed bordered the milky-blue bay. Walking obliquely, he pretended to pass them by.

He lifted his camera slowly, but not slowly enough. All but one flew fifty yards further down the beach. The one that remained ignored him and provided as many pictures as he wished to take. In his excitement, even the smell and his muscle pain were masked.

Absorbed, he was surprised to not see Liz in front of him or in the water when he looked up.

She stood behind him. "It's easy to waste time chasing birds, isn't it?" A smile played at the corners of her mouth. "We could be doing something much more creative."

"Oh? What?" Her finger in his gut hurt.

"It's time to see the Big Tree."

Jim rubbed his tummy. "Big tree?"

"It's a live oak tree near here. It's supposed to be the second or third largest in Texas and one of the largest in the U.S."

Outside the park's main boundary, the parking lot at the Big Tree was empty when they arrived. The sight of the monstrous tree took Jim's breath away. "It's magnificent."

The tree's long limbs, some supported by timbers, curved and dipped like Medusa's coiffure. The majestic oak obviously received TLC—dead limbs pruned, gashes doctored, the grounds beneath it immaculate. It was also protected by a security fence.

A sign told visitors that the tree was more than a thousand years old. It had an eighty-nine-foot canopy. Its trunk was eleven feet in diameter and more than thirty-five feet in circumference.

Jim whistled. "It would take at least seven of us to hold hands around it."

Liz took photos of poems by John E. Williams and Mary Hoekstra posted at the fence. They read as if written by the tree itself.

Williams' poem wasn't at first complimentary of humans. It referred to them as being callous, thoughtless, and destructive. But the tree eventually gave grudging appreciation to those who healed it, pruned it, and treated it for insects.

Hoekstra's poem was thought-provoking and heart-wrenching. It described what the tree had witnessed and experienced during its long life—swayed but remained unbroken through ice storms, sandstorms, wind, and gales. Her children and children's children surrounded her.

One thing it couldn't do, however, was grow leaves of silver and gold. It asked for support, so that it and humans could grow old together.

Tears welled in Liz's eyes.

Jim's, too. Marsha was much like that old tree. Their family had survived storms. Thoughts of Marsha, their children, and children's children, raised a lump in his throat. She was with two of them now. He choked back a sob. *What on Earth possessed me?*

What possessed him grasped his hand and led him around to the far side of the tree. Liz's glistening eyes turned mischievous. She used the tree as a shield and opened her blouse.

Jim was surprised. She wasn't wearing a bra, after all. It was a lacy, transparent aqua top that took his breath away faster than his first sight of the Big Tree.

She tugged the top over her shoulders, through a sleeve, and put it in her fanny pack.

"Kiss them," she ordered.

He grasped her soft breasts in his hands and sucked their nipples erect.

Liz let her head loll backwards and moaned softly. Enjoying the freedom, the delicious ripples of sensation in her abdomen, she encouraged him to do it harder.

Why, she wondered. The sharp pangs and electrifying nerve impulses weren't gentle.

It must be my demon of perversion. She was glad it hadn't been prayed from her body.

Jim found her mouth.

In the middle of one of their feverish kisses, they heard a car pull into the parking area. Jim jolted, when the door slammed, and attempted to pull away.

Wrapping her arms tighter around him, Liz her lips to his as he squirmed. She found it thrilling to hold him until the sound of approaching footsteps before releasing him and buttoning her shirt. "What's the matter, lover? Isn't this exciting?"

Jim remembered her first failed attempted to make love with him. How could she lose all inhibitions so rapidly? She no longer slouched, carried her bustline high. He hoped he wasn't creating a monster. "Yes, incredibly exciting, but I'm worried about you."

Liz smiled demurely. "I'm doing this for you, Jim. Only for you. Don't you want me to turn you on?"

He smiled back weakly. "I've had almost forty more years of mental conditioning than you, and it's harder for us old dogs to learn new tricks."

Liz stuck out her tongue at him.

"And much easier to die of heart attacks when we're caught with a naked woman."

Liz fixed him with a quizzical look and cocked her head. "Who told you I was naked? ... Genesis," she murmured, when Jim reflected her questioning look back at her.

Her mouth widened into a grin. "Okay, let's test your theory." She undid four buttons to expose braless cleavage and kissed him in a long embrace. When they parted and opened their eyes, a young couple stood nearby, staring in disbelief.

Beet-red, Jim imagined the couple was stunned to find a fat old man kissing a half-dressed goddess. Or was it a demoness? The bulge in his pants didn't help matters.

Liz waved to provide the couple a better look at her unfettered breasts swaying behind her blouse. She then linked her arm with Jim's and led him toward the Tahoe. "You were wrong, lover. You didn't die. And ... might I add how great you look in those tight-fitting jeans."

He was wearing baggy pants. Had been.

She reached down and squeezed.

"Whoa! Wait till we get to the car, you minx."

Grinning, Liz squeezed again. "I'm making them jealous."

* * *

The woman glared. "Jared, did you see what she did? That's gross."

"Some women will do anything for money," he snorted, wondering if the beauty advertised online.

I'll never forget that face. Or body.

48
A Whooping Good Time

Instead of back-tracking the way they came, Liz turned toward the bay on their left.

"Jim, the Big Tree reminds me of you."

"Because I'm old and gnarly?"

"Not even close." She gave a quirky smile. "Well, maybe a little."

The road curved right at the bay, and Jim spotted something large and white in a pasture on his right. He grabbed his binoculars.

"Whooping cranes ... *here*."

Liz steered onto a pullout and peered through her binoculars. "This is the first time I've seen them this far from the Aransas National Wildlife Refuge. There's another road where we can get closer, but let's take some shots in case they fly."

From the spot on the intersecting road, they could see that the cranes were a family of four, two adults and two chicks. Their humped tails made them appear to be wearing bustles. The adults were taller than the chicks—Jim guessed them to be about five feet tall—their bodies completely white. Their foreheads and cheeks were red to dark red. Their bills were mostly gray, with red-orange near the lores in front of their eyes. Their legs were black, as were their wingtips when they flicked them. The chicks looked similar in shape and stature, but their necks were tan, and their foreheads looked black.

Despite the distance, Liz was ecstatic. She snapped photos of the birds in different positions—standing tall, necks and heads down while eating, ambling single file.

After she and Jim put away their equipment, she flung herself into his arms with such force he thought he might topple backwards. "You sure get sexy when you get excited."

"Don't you and Marsha feel the same way? I get so excited, I tingle." Her face beamed "And want to tangle."

"Marsha seldom goes birding with me, so I couldn't hazard a guess how she might feel. But, after today, I might drag her along to see if it helps."

"Helps what?"

Jim didn't go there, and Liz didn't press the issue. Instead she pressed his lips with hers and rotated her groin against his. She could care less that the area was in full view of several houses and cars driving past.

The sun, the drive, birding and sightseeing had taken their toll. Tired and hungry, they drove to a Rockport Mexican restaurant where they shared a taco salad and drank a gallon of water.

Feeling sexy, Liz made a display of licking salsa off a nacho. "I'm ready for you, Jim. Any new tricks you want to teach me?" His old ones were exquisite, and she desperately craved more.

Jim couldn't think—period—other than envisioning having sex with her. "Um ... what?"

"New tricks, old dog. They may be old for you, but they're new for me."

She dragged him out of the restaurant. When the speedometer needle passed the speed limit, Jim cast a disapproving look. She pouted. "Not even for that?"

"I want to make sure that we stay alive to be able to do that, whatever *that* is."

She glanced at his lap. "Don't those commercials warn about erections lasting longer than four hours? I'm trying to keep you out of the ER."

They showered in her cabin, and Jim thrilled her by using more imagination and intensity than he had that morning. "Turn around, love."

She eagerly obeyed.

He massaged her shoulders, neck, each vertebra, every muscle.

She moaned in pleasure. The scalp massage left her murmuring love words.

Afterwards, his lips and teeth gently nibbled her neck and ears while his hands reached around, caressed her slick breasts. The foreplay under the cascading water made her fantasize making love under a waterfall on an exotic, deserted island.

She braced against the shower wall and rubbed her broad derriere against his erection while savoring his finger and lip play. She widened her legs. When his sex slipped between them, she clamped them back together. It felt like sitting on a hot, thick rail. "Incredible doesn't even begin to describe this."

When Jim carried her to bed, the squeaking at first bothered him, but Liz seemed not to hear. He reached down, pulled her left leg over his right one. Then her right leg over his left. "Put your hands against my chest and lock your elbows."

"I love everything you do," she murmured.

Bracing his torso above her, he whispered. "Push against my chest and move."

Already experimenting, Liz thrust her pelvis upward, filled herself with him. Drew back and thrust again. And again. The sensation became a burning need. She rushed past her threshold into the realm where previously pain and pleasure melded into volcanic fury. But pain was minimal as her body adjusted with the frequency of their lovemaking.

The knowledge that she could control her orgasmic destiny sent her into a state of delirium, her body into frenetic motion. She reached the peak of emotion and sailed gloriously into a cloudless sky of pleasure.

Jim couldn't believe the strength and swiftness of her movements. He struggled to maintain balance. It thrilled him when she growled her deep, animalistic grunt, started trembling, and pulled him down upon her until the convulsions stopped.

"That was beyond belief, lover."

He didn't let her rest before he began the slow, deliberate motion he enjoyed most—probing the depth of her, withdrawing, and stimulating their thousands of God-created nerve endings as he reentered. The sensitivity made both moan.

"I love that," Liz panted. "Keep doing it."

Within seconds, her throbbing, shaking body raced up the cliff of near endless ecstasy. She found herself floating, out-of-body.

She yielded her body willingly when he repositioned her after each orgasm to expand her knowledge and enhance her pleasure.

Jim marveled at his ability to withhold his own final pleasure. Perhaps it was the frequency of their lovemaking. Two and three times a day was different from once every other month or so. He found his ability to give and receive prolonged gratification exhilarating.

Between each delirious orgasm, Liz marveled briefly at their effect on her. She now loved life. It was so different from the suffering lie she'd been living. She knew what to do about her mother and contemplated whether, after Thursday, to make a complete break with her past.

The beginning of a new storm surged when she sensed Jim's engorgement. She matched his passionate movements, exceeded them. Forcing his bulk up, she cherished the moments when he slammed, full-force, back down upon her—forcing the air from her lungs and mashing her breasts against her chest. Could she pass out from intimacy?

Experiencing the lovemaking of his life, Jim finally shuddered at the same time Liz gasped.

When the sensations ended, she clutched him on top of her as forcefully as she had after her first orgasm. Empowered, she wouldn't let him go, restrained his sex within her own.

"Liz," Jim grunted ten minutes later, "if I starve to death in the next few days, just roll me off the bed and have someone haul my body to the fish dumpster."

Her bouncing abdomen rolled him to one side.

When her laughing calmed, she reached below his sex and grasped the objects of her curiosity—assessed their size and texture. "You know what amazes me? Starts me panting?"

Jim suppressed a yelp. "Careful, not too hard."

"Sorry." Liz softened her grip and grinned sheepishly. "It's these two puppies tapping my bottom."

Jim shook his head. If he tried to initiate a similar conversation with Marsha, she'd lock him out of the house.

* * *

Edith glanced at the phone and then at the clock. She was in bed, reading a Sandra Brown novel after taking a soothing bubble bath, but this call she would answer. "Hey, Jackie, I thought you were going to crash."

"Can't sleep. All I do is think about the bitch."

"Take two sheep with a glass of water and call me in the morning."

"No, Edith, wait. I've figured out what to do."

"And it can't wait till *tomorrow*?"

Jack ignored her. "I have a sound dish. It's more effective than your bugs."

"And you called me to tell me that? Get some sleep before you have a nervous breakdown."

"What I'm trying to say is, I'll go on stakeout with you."

"You're fixated, my friend, and that ain't good." She hung up.

* * *

"Where did you learn this amazing lovemaking?" Liz asked, as she and Jim busied their afterglow with searching hands and tender kisses. "Did you learn it all by yourself, or did your friends tell you how to do it?"

"Mostly trial and error, but I learned a little from books and novels. I didn't learn anything from our friends. We don't talk about sex or positions."

"Speaking about sex and positions, I did more online research."

The young woman was a constant source of wonder, Jim mused. He couldn't anticipate what she might do or say next.

The thought didn't begin to prepare him.

"Did you know that an uncircumcised penis might have more sensation than a circumcised one?"

This was a topic better avoided, but Liz was giving him the stare.

"Uh, no."

"Yes. There are thousands of erogenous nerves in the foreskin that are removed during circumcision."

"Do we really need to talk about—"

"It makes you wonder ... since God created us in his image and ultimately sexual ... why He would design man for intense pleasure during lovemaking and then order him to cut some of it off."

"Weren't you the one who told me to stop thinking so much?"

Liz didn't appear to hear him. "It's so beautiful."

She ringed his glans with a fingertip and sighed. "Marsha's so lucky. She gets to make love to you every day. I sure wish I was her."

Breathing heavily, Jim wished it were so.

49

Broken Nest

Sunday dawned dark and muggy with an eighty percent chance of storms, some severe. As the morning progressed, however, the clouds became light and fluffy, surrounded by light blue sky. Only in the southwest did the sky appear dark, but not threatening—no lightning or distant thunder.

The night before, Liz had ordered Jim to accompany her while she jogged this morning. She granted him a reprieve due to the possibility of a downpour. That didn't prevent her from dragging him to the Palm Gardens fitness center. "Jim, this is state of the art. Why didn't you tell me about it?"

"This is my first time here."

"You've got to be kidding." She peered down her nose at him and patted his tummy. "No, you're telling the truth. But that's going to end, buster, starting right here and now."

The pain in Jim's muscles gradually subsided as he followed her around and exercised on each station as she instructed. "You're right, Liz, no pain, no gain, but the pain lessens the more you gain. I'll make this a routine, from now on."

They went to the late service at the Presbyterian Church. The prelude music put them in an especially good mood, so good that they were totally unprepared when the message on trust hit them like a steel wrecking ball smashing a cinder block affair. Their clothing and faces changed to swirling, flashing beacons of florescent scarlet. The capital letter A imprinted itself on their foreheads. Liz let go Jim's hand and scooted away.

Still in shock, they absently shook the minister's hand on their way out of the chapel. Jim robotically told him what a great sermon it was.

They skulked to her SUV without touching or speaking. Liz stopped at the IGA to pick up items for their meals. Following dutifully, Jim refused to look at her—lest he sin.

Liz thought of her family, how she'd let them down. Her heart ached for Jim. Her seductions had damaged his marriage, hurt Marsha, although Marsha wasn't aware of it.

Jim thought of Marsha. His sin could still destroy their marriage. Might already have. They hadn't seen the PI's truck for more than a day.

Both trembled. Felt nauseated.

When Liz dropped Jim off at his RV, she said she would change and be back in a few minutes to make lunch. Unsmiling, her voice didn't even sound like hers. It was high-pitched. Pinched.

When she returned, more than thirty minutes later, she was sniffling, her eyes and nose red from crying. Her demeanor didn't change while she donned the apron and busied herself preparing the noon meal she salted with her tears.

Jim hurt for her as much as he did for Marsha, at such times. He wanted to hold her but couldn't bring himself to do it. Tears welled in his eyes. His throat constricted.

The meal didn't go well. Neither looked at each other as they picked at their food.

Giving up, Liz put their uneaten meals in the refrigerator while Jim washed the dishes. After they finished their tasks and sat in the recliners, he found the courage to speak. "That sermon really put things in perspective, didn't it?"

Liz gulped and nodded. Rising, tears flowing down her face, she went to the bathroom.

Jim wondered if she was going to throw up. He felt like he might.

She returned naked. Kneeling subserviently at his feet, she leaned her head in his lap.

Stunned, Jim didn't know what to say. Or do. Or expect. Her sweet smell added to his addled emotions. Tears trickling down his cheeks, he reached out and caressed her head and satiny shoulders.

The wind picked up. The fifth-wheel reverberated from the sound of rolling thunder.

"Jim?"

Although it sounded like a question, he didn't speak during Liz's long pause. Couldn't, with the hitch in his throat.

"I need to be truthful with you. I should have been from the start, but I fell in love with you. I wanted to have you, if only for the week, and was afraid you wouldn't let me if you knew the truth.

"The minute we touched, heat surged through me. I felt dizzy, thought I might faint. I've wondered, since, if it was like being slain in the spirit. Then we met, again, and it was like fate, like God, put you in my life. You were hurt and needed someone. When Marsha didn't come to help you, I felt ordained."

Jim nodded even though Liz couldn't see it.

"And once alone with you, it was as if you reached in and grabbed my heart," she whispered.

He wondered if his desire to avoid her after their first encounter at Paradise Pond wasn't so much the fear of her violent nature as it was the shock of their touch. "I've fallen in love with you, too."

"I know. And the more I knew you, touched you, and kissed you, I couldn't help myself. I wanted you and wasn't going to let anything stop me ... not even Marsha." Chest heaving, Liz sobbed, "I would've come back from Kingwood even if Maggie hadn't told me to."

Her trembling increased. "I hate what I've done to your marriage, but I'm not sorry ... not even with the sermon. Your understanding, companionship, and great sex have given me a will to live that I couldn't imagine when Mother and I arrived here."

Her tears rained down Jim's legs. He kept caressing her head and shoulders.

"I was at wit's end. Oh, I wasn't suicidal, just confused. My home life was a wreck. I lived in a make-believe world of niceness and felt so hopeless that I lashed out at everyone. I didn't think anyone could help me, not even the psychiatrist Mother demanded I see."

A gust of raging wind rocked the RV, lightning illuminated it, and peals of thunder rattled the door, vents, and screen. Jim moved Liz, made sure the door was secure, and closed the open windows. He retrieved a box of tissues and returned to the sofa.

Liz extracted one, wiped her eyes, blew her nose, and re-settled on his lap—head bowed, eyes downcast.

"It's time for the truth, Jim. I hope you won't hate me, hope you won't make me go away. I promise, come Thursday, I'll leave. I won't like it, but I know it's the right thing to do. And I'll do anything for you. *Anything*."

She bobbed her head, let out a trembling breath. "Sweetheart," her body shook as severely as it had the afternoon at the National Seashore, "I'm married."

He'd known she was withholding something, but her revelation stunned him. He jerked involuntarily, tossing her head into the air.

Liz glanced up and burst into uncontrollable sobbing.

"Lord, Liz," Jim whispered, "I never suspected that. But I love you, so nothing can be done about it now." He should have read the signs—a non-virgin, on the pill, her statement that her mother wasn't the only one with money. But her lack of experience?

It was several minutes before either spoke.

"When I was a senior in high school, Mother told me that she'd found the perfect man for me. He was older, eleven years older, and established. I wouldn't know want ... wouldn't have to work a day in my life."

Liz paused to catch her breath.

"I couldn't resist her. Why I've let her control my life all these years is a mystery."

Liz quaked and cried for more than a minute.

Jim's tears ran dry. He sat caressing her, sharing her pain.

His soothing manner calmed Liz enough to continue. She blew her nose.

"He was ... is ... a pastor."

Jim jolted. His head spun as she told her tale.

"My girlfriends all thought Don was terrific and that I was lucky. It was one of the largest weddings ever in the area. The congregation collected a love offering to send us to Barbados for our honeymoon."

Liz sucked in a large breath. Her eyes brimmed bright with tears, but droplets no longer ran down her cheeks. Her trembling lessened.

Jim lifted her chin and kissed her.

A detonation of thunder accompanied a blinding flash. The RV jolted as if slammed by a giant fist and continued rocking in the howling wind. Huge raindrops drummed a staccato beat on the roof. Heavy clouds darkened the interior, but Jim didn't move to turn on a light.

"I was apprehensive, but I enjoyed the atmosphere. As our wedding day approached, I looked forward to it more and more. Don was the only man Mother let me go out with by myself.

"We went to revival meetings, and he treated me like the perfect lady—rarely held my hand, didn't hug me. He only kissed me goodnight a few times, and they were pecks on the cheeks. He made me comfortable. Things were fine. Godly."

Liz gave a sarcastic laugh. "Like Daddy says about sports figures that don't live up to their billings, I got caught up in the hype.

"But thinking about my wedding night frightened me to death. None of my close girlfriends were married. We'd taken vows of celibacy, and we were. We didn't watch dirty TV shows or movies. We turned off suggestive, sexual, and obscene commercials. We stayed away from the bad girls, which by Mother's standards were the rest of the girls in school. Talking about sex was taboo ... until one of my friends told a horror story. Her bedroom was next to her parents' and she said her mother occasionally screamed. She feared her daddy was hurting her mother even though she never saw bruises or a black eye. We recited our vows of celibacy over again, right then and there."

Liz gave a dark chuckle. "Good old Mother. The night before our wedding, she came to the rescue. She told me to let my husband do whatever he wanted to with me in bed. It was my wifely duty and wouldn't last long. When she mentioned that I would bleed a little, I panicked. I wanted to run away but didn't have a place to go. I cried most of the night, then convinced myself that Don was such a gentleman he would surely respect me.

"The flights to Barbados were tiring, and I didn't want to do anything but rest. Boy, was I in for a surprise. Don became aggressive. He kept placing his hand on my leg and gripped me hard when I tried to pull away. I noticed something was wrong in his lap, but I was more naïve than you can believe ... more than I can believe even now. But I'd been excused from anything remotely related to sex education due to my religion.

"He dragged me through the airport. In the hotel room, he became a beast—groping and pawing me ... screaming for me to take off my clothes.

"I'd never undressed in front of another girl, not to mention a man. At home, during sleepovers with my girlfriends, I changed in the bathroom. In high school I wore gym clothes under my long dresses so I wouldn't have to shower in front of anyone.

"I smelled pretty good back then, and with my attitude and looks, boys left me alone. I weighed more than two hundred pounds, so I didn't have to worry about boys speaking with me. And their talking behind my back, making fun of me, didn't matter."

Jim found Liz's confession difficult to believe. He tried to imagine what she'd looked like and gave up.

Liz had expected his reaction to be worse, so his quiet empathy calmed her. *I should have known he'd be supportive.*

She longed to kiss him and pull him into the bedroom, but first she must finish her story.

"I screamed and jerked away. Don demanded that I do my Biblical duty and chased me around the room and into the bathroom. I tried locking the door, but being so flabby and overweight, there was no way I could have kept away from him for long. He was past the point of no return. I wasn't going to escape. He dragged me to the bed.

"While I was struggling and crying ... screaming for help at the top of my lungs ... he was binding Satan in the name of Jesus and commanding him out of me.

"Looking back, I can only imagine what people in the adjoining rooms and hallway must have thought. Someone could've been being raped in that room, but no one checked." Liz swallowed. "Someone *was* being raped, but no one cared."

Another brilliant flash and explosion rocked the RV and rattled the food cans in the pantry. Jim strained to hear over the roar of driving rain mixed with small hail.

"I kicked and screamed. I bit. Don lost his breath while trying to hold me and run off Satan at the same time, so he slapped me until I stopped resisting."

Jim gasped. "He what?"

"Beat me," Liz whispered, so softly that she had to repeat it. "He thought I was possessed." She chewed her lip. "He may have been right."

Jim moved Liz off him. She sat back on the floor, startled, ready to cry—until he stood and lifted her to her feet, kissed her and hugged her tightly to him. "Let's sit on the sofa. You'll be more comfortable."

Liz whimpered with joy. Once seated, she snuggled against him and continued her story. "I hurt horribly but realized no one would come to my rescue. Mother had told me it wouldn't last long, so I closed my eyes and held my breath.

"Don didn't remove my clothes. He pulled up my skirt and ripped off my panties. In the end, I was a pile of bruised and bleeding blubber on the bed. He didn't seem to mind seeing me like that, just like I've enjoyed looking at your body."

She noted Jim's expression and clarified. "I'm sorry. I had every girl's dream that I was beautiful, and when I look at you, that's what I see."

Jim had wondered why.

"I'd given up on salvation, so I prayed for strength and that it wouldn't hurt any more than it already had." Reliving the event, she shuddered. "It hurt and took forever ... at least it seemed to. It was the most painful experience of my life. Don tried to force himself in and couldn't. I couldn't help screaming, so he hit me one last time."

Jim shook his head and clutched her close.

"He never fully penetrated me, but I was burning. On fire. Blood flowed out of me.

"And then he did something that sent me into hysterics. He covered my stomach, chest, and face with semen. I would've screamed all night, but he grabbed my shoulders and shook me until I thought my neck would snap, yelling at me to shut up, telling me I was embarrassing him."

"Oh, Liz, I'm so sorry."

"I found out later, after we returned home and he couldn't pray the demons out of me, that he was sure I was the devil's child. Although it's against our religion, he bought condoms because he wasn't going to give the devil another one.

"The birth control pills were something I did behind his back. When mother discovered me taking them, she demanded that I stop because it was anti-God, so I pretended that I did. That's one of the many reasons for our problems. She's upset that I'm childless. Besides the psychiatrist, she wants to drag me to a fertility clinic."

The lightning drifted away, but a final bolt struck near the park, followed instantaneously by a thunderous roar. The hail ended, but the rain and wind remained heavy and fierce.

"Once I settled down to just crying, Don was okay with it." Liz stared. "You won't believe this, but after cleaning up, he thanked me. He thanked Satan's spawn.

"I stumbled to the bathtub, ran hot water, and sat in it for hours.

"We were in Barbados for two weeks, and other than the trips to and from the airport, I don't know what it looks like. Don didn't touch me again during our honeymoon. He wouldn't let me leave the room or call Mother. He didn't use Room Service, probably because my face was so swollen that you wouldn't have recognized me.

"After our week was up, he called the congregation, told them that we were extending the honeymoon because I was having difficulty adjusting to married life, and asked for their prayers.

At the end of the second week I didn't look so bad, so we went home. Mother ignored the yellow-green splotches on my face. I guess, based on Don's prayer request, she thought I'd been sinful and deserved punishment."

Liz's brow furrowed. "You know, Jim, to my knowledge, Daddy's never mistreated her. You'd think, after her protection all those years, she would've been all over Don.

"The first week, Don held a healing service and asked people to lay hands on me. Well, my demons didn't leave, but fat entered. I ballooned to more than two hundred thirty pounds before I started gaining self-respect.

"A couple of my girlfriends still haven't married. I guess my appearance and the healing service convinced them a lifetime of celibacy was the way to go. I didn't ask them to change their minds, either." Liz smiled weakly. "Maybe I'll do that now, and if I do, they'll get earfuls of advice."

Jim did what he would have thought unthinkable after the church service, fondled her breasts, kissed the back of her neck. "Has he ever abused you again?"

"No. Never."

Jim found that slightly comforting. "What about domestic abuse counseling?"

Liz shook her head. "I exercised myself into shape in case I needed to defend myself against him again, but like I said, he's been the perfect gentleman ... except for never apologizing."

She turned her head and lifted her lips. Their kiss was tender, lingering. Jim stroked her long neck.

When they parted, she continued. "In case you're wondering, we had painful sex, a few times, and Don's urologist suggested Astro Glide. It made having sex painless for Don, but not for me, physically or mentally.

"When I grew stronger, I insisted we sleep in separate bedrooms. Since then, I've granted him one visit to my bedroom each year ... but not on our anniversary."

She shuddered to a thunderclap. "I've tried to know him in the Biblical sense, but it's never been pleasurable."

Liz leaned her head against Jim's shoulder while he traced the edge of an areola and rolled a nipple back and forth between his rough fingertips.

She moaned. "My lord, the gift you've given me, sweetheart. I've never self-lubricated with Don. Now, I'm an artesian fountain."

Jim pictured something more like the Morning Glory Pool at Yellowstone.

She stroked his arm as she concluded her story. "I haven't let him see me naked since I banished him from my bedroom. During sex, I wear a long nightgown that I pull up ... just enough, before he lays on top of me." She grimaced. "Like I said, my demons haven't left.

"We've been married eleven years now, and I've been the dutiful wife around the congregation. I haven't done all the things minister's wives do, but I haven't lowered his standing in the church, either."

Her look softened. "Thanks for listening, Jim. You're the only one who knows my story. Somehow, I feel better. Cleaner."

He didn't make an outward motion, but inwardly shook his head. Don was married to a beautiful and loving woman. Had he been tender, taken his time instead of raping her on their wedding night....

But most likely Don hadn't received sex education, either. Most boys didn't even though they needed it as much or more than girls to be fully respectful of females and not put the onus on women for the manner and consequences of their relationships. Men didn't get pregnant, have morning sickness, suffer miscarriages, carry a fetus for nine months to give birth, and then sometimes have stillbirths or die giving birth.

Liz was passionate beyond his wildest dreams. She'd undressed for him when it took all her willpower to do it. She was now so comfortable with their relationship that she paraded naked in front of him and had partially stripped in public at the Big Tree.

He worried more than a little about that.

Lifting her in his arms, he somehow weaved his lesser bulk and her long, slender body up the steps, though the narrow passageway, and into the bedroom.

50
Black Skimmers

The storm churned, growling and flashing, out over the Gulf. The dark clouds and dramatic cloud-to-water and cloud-to-cloud lightning presented a flashing display for humans' amazement and animals to gaze at.

Roiling, frothy white caps topped gigantic, dark-green, wind-driven waves. From the west, sunrays pierced the clouds to spotlight dunes, beach, and waves. Arching over the jetty, double rainbows appeared to explode where their ends struck the sea.

Emotions buoyed by their lovemaking, Jim and Liz stayed in bed until the rain stopped and they regained their energy. She rolled off him. "It's time to call Mother. Come sit with me on the sofa. I need your strength."

Helen saw her cellphone number. "Hello, Mary Elizabeth, how are you?"

"Better than you can know, Mother."

"That's nice, sweetheart."

"Mother, could you do me a favor?"

Helen hoped her recalcitrant daughter had become rational and was ready to come home to begin therapy. "Of course, baby, anything."

"Today's sermon was about trust. It was the best I've heard, and I've heard quite a few." Liz paused, waiting for the statement sink in.

Helen wondered where the conversation was going. "And you want to regain my trust?"

"Um, something like that. Are you having me followed by private investigators?"

The phone went silent except for Helen's sharp intake of air.

Liz wouldn't lead her mother into anything.

Helen exhaled. "Yes, and it's for your own good."

"In what way is it good for our trust in each other?"

"Well—"

"Does Daddy know?"

Silence.

"I love you, Mother, and I'll speak with you later, but I need to speak with Daddy."

"About what?"

"You know, very well, about what. There are a couple of investigators spending a lot of time and money following me around, and Daddy has a right to know how much your bloodhounds are costing. It's partly his money, too."

"Let me break the news to him, Mary Elizabeth. I'm sure he'll understand when I tell him why I did it."

In the background, Liz heard her father ask what news needed to be broken. "That's all right," she said, seemingly unconcerned. "You have things to do, Mother, so please hand Daddy the phone. I'll tell him for you. However, if you're refusing to let me speak with him, he'll find out in a couple of days when I return home."

"Mary *Elizabeth.*"

"Yes?"

Liz again heard her father speaking in the background.

"What's wrong, Mama? Has something happened to Mary Elizabeth?"

"Not really, Daddy," Helen said, her hand over the phone's mouthpiece. To Liz she said, "I'll call you right back."

"Mother, if I were you, I wouldn't end this call until I hear you tell Daddy that you hired private investigators. Either that, or hand him the phone."

"You're a horrible daughter," Helen whispered. She looked at her husband. "Daddy, I have a little confession to make."

"What is it, and what does it have to do with Mary Elizabeth?"

"Well, I sort of hired a private investigator to keep an eye on her. She's so fragile and excitable—"

"*What?*"

Helen cupped the mouthpiece. "Can I call you back, Mary Elizabeth?"

"You can now," Liz said sweetly. "And I'd like to speak with Daddy when you do."

Despite sounding calm, she trembled visibly.

Jim held her tightly. *Good. She's crossed another boundary.*

When the call ended, Liz sighed in relief. "Well, that's that. Our PI problems are over."

"So ... where do we go from here?" Jim asked.

Liz pointed at the light dancing on the translucent window shades. "To the beach. The late afternoon sun should be perfect."

Jim decided the diversion would do them both good. Despite their lovemaking, he remained nervous about the day's traumatic events—the pastor's warning and Liz's revealing story.

"Then let's go. I'm still a little discombobulated."

Jack sat in the back seat of Edith's current rental while she prepared to make her afternoon report to Matthews. The RV bug had either died or been discovered, so Edith fleshed out something that would sound plausible.

Removable dark-plastic film obscured the windows, and Jack wore a headset attached to a small, round, dish-shaped sound amplifier. "No more screwing around with those little remote thingies. They aren't worth crap."

The black dish, black hood and clothing allowed him to crack the window without being observed. He became impatient. Their quarry should be leaving Smith's RV due to her penchant for late afternoon sunlight for photos. "Come on. Come on," he muttered.

Edith heard a changed woman when Matthews answered her call.

"I'm sorry I had you follow my child. You can stop now. Please send me your final invoice and add whatever you like for a termination fee."

Edith sat stunned after the call ended. "Jackie, the case is over. Closed."

"We've been fired? Just because we couldn't get proof soon enough?"

"No, that's not it at all. Matthews said she was sorry she hired us to follow her daughter. She said she'll pay what she owes as soon as I send her the bill."

Jack's face flamed. "No way. The bitch screwed with me. She has to pay."

Edith looked pensive. "This case went south after the storm on St. Jo., Jackie

... except for the money, and we've made a ton of that. Why don't we let things drop?"

"The slut owes me."

She shrugged. "You know best."

Five minutes later the RV door opened, and Jim exited. He grasped Liz's hand and assisted her down the steps.

"Let's hope the skimmers are at the jetty, lover." Liz said. "I'd like you to get some pictures of them. They're quite a sight."

Jim grimaced. "I hope so. My muscles are killing me."

Liz smiled sympathetically. "The skimmers will make up for it, and we're running out of time. Tomorrow afternoon, we'll go back to the state park to shoot some least terns, weather permitting."

"What a jerk-off," Jack spouted sarcastically. "Always helping the lady."

Edith smiled wistfully.

He removed his headset. "Well, Edith, what do you make of this *lover* crap? Maybe we have our pair, after all."

"It's a figure of speech. They're bird lovers."

"How can you be sure?"

Jack rubbed his chin as he rolled up the dark window. "Tomorrow at the state park. Perfect. Let's shut this puppy down and go soak up some suds."

Edith smiled in anticipation. Most of her reservations had dissipated with her night's rest. Whatever occurred, it would be good. Well, maybe not so good for Ms. Liz, but it would be for Jack. And with luck, for her.

* * *

Perfect lighting greeted Liz and Jim at the beach. Churning waves tumbled to shore. Yellow sargassum seaweed lined the beach. Lightning flashes in the blackened eastern sky filled Jim with awe. "This couldn't be more spectacular."

Most bird species on the coast were there—pelicans, terns, sandpipers, plovers, cormorants, gulls, skimmers. Liz stood in photographer's heaven, and Jim shared it with her.

They concentrated on the skimmers. The birds' four-inch long, red and black bills glowed in the evening light. The lower half of their bills were significantly longer than their uppers, and the birds fed by slipping them through the edge of the surf while flying low. When they sensed prey, their heads dipped downward, and their upper bills snapped shut in a quick, difficult-to-see motion.

The high tide and grinding waves had surged seawater into long pools, with tire-track dams made by foolhardy souls testing their vehicle's rust inhibitors and four-wheel drives. Out of reach of the tumultuous waves, skimmers stood in those pools. Their reflections created mosaics in the wind-rippled water. Except for the waves, the skimmers would be making their feeding runs that continued late into the night.

Jim studied the oddly majestic birds. Their three-inch long red legs and tiny webbed feet seemed too short and small to support their foot-and-a-half long bodies. Their wings, which could be up to two feet long, extended well past their tails. Their backs, wings, and top half of their heads and necks were black, mingled with dark reddish-brown. The trailing edges of their wings appeared white, like the lower half of their heads, necks, and undersides. In the existing light, their obsidian eyes would be impossible to distinguish from the black feathers were it not for diminutive sparkles reflecting the setting sun.

Unlike Jim's silent camera, Liz's fired burst after burst at the maximum exposures per second.

Two birds lifted grandly into the air and flew down the beach. Jim thought they were leaving, so he was caught off guard when they circled, lowered to inches above the tidal pool, and dipped their lower bills.

Unprepared to take pictures, he examined them instead. Their four-foot wingspans exhibited majestic grace as their wingtips somehow avoided touching the surface. Although he missed the shot, the wondrous sight made him as ecstatic as Liz after an exciting encounter.

"Get ready, Jim. They're starting to feed."

Two more birds lifted into the air and followed the same path. He switched on his camera and thought himself ready. His single-shot setting resulted in a blurred shot. Red-faced, he turned to Liz. "A perfect photo op and I blew it."

"Welcome to the club."

Prepared, he panned the next bird for the entire length of the pool.

The sun's dull-red sphere appeared to balance on the dunes. Its light turned the storm clouds above the Gulf into an artist's pallet.

Liz cupped a hand around her mouth and shouted above the roar of wind and waves. "The clouds. Shoot the clouds."

Jim wondered how there could be any memory left in her camera. She hadn't stopped taking pictures since they arrived. He snapped a few pictures and then admired the changing mosaic of clouds and sea until all turned gray.

Liz pursed her lips in a kissing motion, and he blew one back.

He then mulled the beauty of his world—the scenes he'd just witnessed, the ecstatic vision jubilantly sharing his life. How could anyone keep a butterfly in a jar for eleven years? *Damn Don.* Or for twenty-nine, like Helen had?

He and Liz walked hand in hand to the car as breathless as if they'd made love on the beach. They were in love—with each other and with God for His majestic creation.

"Wasn't that breathtaking? Nature photographers have the best lives in the world," Liz gushed.

"I'll second that," Jim babbled back. "Thanks for inviting me."

She squeezed his hand. "Sexy, isn't it?"

"My world, or the scenes we saw?"

"Yes."

Liz became practical and reminded him they would have to carefully clean their cameras.

She hummed "America the Beautiful" on their slow stroll to the SUV. At least Jim thought she did. The incredible experience might be a dream.

Liz was so thrilled when they returned to the RV that she remained all superlatives. "Jim, look at this photo. It's awesome. ... Isn't this skimmer the most gorgeous thing you've ever seen?"

"Beautiful," he kept repeating. The photos were all that and more, but he suspected that some of her euphoria was from finding the courage to confront her mother that afternoon.

She didn't stop editing until it was late for them, after ten-thirty.

Jim felt fortunate he hadn't taken many pictures. The two he liked best were a skimmer standing beside a pink conch shell in a tidal pool and one streaking a line through rippled water.

When he finished, he called Marsha. "Hi, sweetheart, how was your day."

"Much better. The kids are in bed with me, and I'm reading them bedtime stories."

"Sounds like fun."

"I'm sorry I've been so hard on you, Jim. The kids are being so nice that I'm managing fine without you. Even the house was left clean. How's your leg and the picture-taking?"

"The leg's okay, and I took a couple of nice photos of some black skimmers, this evening. It was after a storm, and the lighting was perfect." He described the birds and promised to send email photos.

"I love you," he said, unencumbered by guilt.

He found Liz fawning over his pictures, but hers were knockouts—brilliant colors, sharp focus, storm-driven waves in the background. Spellbound, he asked, "Can I buy a set?"

He received a mischievous smile. "You've already paid for them, but I'll take a tip."

He appreciated the double-entendre, but the day's emotional roller coaster left him drained. "I'm flat out of tips, tonight. Maybe tomorrow. I'll walk you back to your cabin."

"You'll do more than that. Bring your jammies."

With her helpful determination, he discovered sufficient reserve to tip her, after all.

* * *

Jack and Edith spent their evening in a sports bar, planning to divide and conquer. The brews sharpened their mental faculties.

"I told Amanda I'll be gone for two days, maybe more, and she didn't blink an eye. She doesn't give a darn anymore."

Edith nodded sympathetically and resisted the urge to tell him that she did. "Ms. Liz likes afternoon sun for photos, so that should give us plenty of time to rent a trailer and set it up."

Jack shrugged and took a long swig. "The girl's hot for me. I'll have her in the Party Wagon before you lure doofus into the trailer."

"Why don't you set up a rendezvous for later, like we usually do?"

"Nope. The bitch has got to be punished. Bring the Party Wagon."

"A few days won't make a difference. And with Teddy along, your time will be limited no matter what I do."

"Who's Teddy?"

"Fats. He reminds me of a big, fluffy teddy Bear."

"Just keep him out of my way."

"How much time do you think you'll need?"

"All night."

"And how do you propose I do that?"

Jack stared incredulously.

Edith blinked. "Won't Teddy get a little suspicious when you and Liz disappear? Where should I say you went?"

Jack shrugged. "Tell him we went to a nightclub."

"Pardon me, Jackie, but your plan is dirt stupid."

"Then what do you suggest, Mrs. Genius?"

"Pour me another schooner, first."

She drank most of it before speaking. "If she's so hot for you, make a date. If not, accuse her of having an affair. I'll manufacture evidence you can show her, and if she bites, it doesn't matter if she leaves. She'll show when you tell her to. And if she's innocent, you can practice your seduction skills."

"There's a better idea. Knockout drops will prevent both our problems."

Edith aspirated on the dredges in her glass. "We're going to jail. You know that, don't you?"

"I want my revenge ... now. When we're through with them, we'll leave them naked in her SUV, and the park office will get an anonymous tip that a couple's making out in the beach parking lot. No one will believe their story, and they won't remember what happened."

When Edith gawked, he added, "If that doesn't work, there's the farm in the Yucatan Peninsula. Amanda doesn't know about it."

Edith didn't like the look on his face. She thought his eyes looked weird. "So, it's the trailer?"

"Yup."

"*And* the Party Wagon?"

Jack nodded.

"Did you miss the part about going to jail?"

"The girl has to pay."

"Hey, waiter, this man needs the bill."

51
Endangered Species

"Up and at 'em, lover. You keep telling me how much you enjoy exercising, so we're going to the beach."

Jim tried to focus his eyes. "Can't we have breakfast first?"

"No. We'll eat after we get out of the pool."

"Pool? I thought the fitness center and a two-mile jog were a day's work-out."

"Two-thirds," Liz said, smiling benevolently. "And no one can call your poking along jogging."

Jim groaned, returned to his RV, swallowed his morning pills, grabbed sweats, and headed back to her cabin.

Two friends hailed him.

Billy Carlton, who repaired his pickup when its power steering hose popped off, two years earlier, waved him over. "Morning, preacher," he said innocently.

"Hey, Billy."

"As much time as you're spending at your nurse's cabin, why don't you move *all* your clothes to her closet?"

So, his friends had noticed after all. Jim didn't blush. "Liz and I have a heavy day of birding ahead of us, and we're headed to the gym to get in shape. Care to tag along and see what a real sport's like?"

Billy held out his index fingers in the shape of a cross. "Get thee behind me, Satan! How can you call sitting on a bench, holding binoculars, sport? Bite your tongue."

"Oh, ye of little faith, I kid you not. Come with us, and you won't be able to climb out of bed tomorrow, you'll be so sore."

"Pssh. No way."

John West, the park's premier blue-water fisherman, joined in the conversation. "There's room in the boat for one more today, Jim."

When Jim looked wistful, John sweetened the offer. He held up a long, thin bait fish with inordinately large eyes and jagged, needle-pointed teeth. "This ribbonfish knows a king mackerel with your name on it."

Jim grimaced. "Wish I could, but I'm still under doctors' orders. No fishing. Not till Thursday, and then I have to head home."

"Maybe next year. Take care, Jim."

"You, too, John ... Billy."

Back at the cabin, Jim and Liz tanked up on water and stepped outside into a clear, blue morning. Downed limbs, palm fronds, and bits of debris littered the area. Liz stretched and motioned for Jim to follow her as she led the way to the fitness center. "Gee, no one's here."

Jim yawned. "I wonder why."

An hour later, they were in the tepid air, typical of a Port Aransas spring dawn.

"Beat you to the gate," Liz joked.

She sped to it before Jim took twenty plodding steps.

He walked briskly while Liz ran loops. She ran ahead of him for a couple of hundred yards, circled, ran back past him for half that distance, and repeated the process.

At the beach she jogged in place while he bent forward, hands on his knees, catching his breath.

"When ... did they ... build this mountain ... on Mustang Island?"

"You turkey. I should kick your rear for saying that. Now, get it in gear, or I will."

Jim saluted. "Aye, aye, Captain." He barely avoided her foot.

They changed into bathing suits in her cabin—she to swim, he to relax and watch.

"Betcha can't catch me, sexy." She scooted through the door.

Jim focused on her hips. "What a swing."

Liz stopped in mid-stride, turned, and kissed him. "Great lips. Oh, and thanks for the compliment."

She dove into the cold-water pool without hesitation and swam laps. Jim wondered how and where she learned to execute perfect flip turns, given her previous disposition to hide her body.

When she bounced out of the water like a seal, thirty minutes later, he inquired, "Where did you learn to flip like that?"

"At a private pool." Liz didn't offer an explanation and grabbed a towel. "I'm famished. How about you?"

"Your place or mine?"

"Yours, of course. But we need to shower first."

In her shower Liz took Jim the final mile—with much energetic activity and heavy breathing.

"You're killing me, Liz"

"Shut up. I'm making you young."

After breakfast, they edited pictures. Their time was short, and she wanted to teach him as much as possible. Each time he showed her a photo, she studied it, tweaked it, and saved it under a different name.

She then made him repeat the edits until he memorized the steps. By the time they stopped, mid-afternoon, he'd committed most of them to memory—saving months of trial and error learning.

They ate a late lunch and headed to Mustang Island State Park. The sun bathed the beach in a warm glow. It wasn't the only thing providing warm glows. Liz wasn't wearing a breast band or bra.

She opened her shirt while they sat in the parking lot. "I want you to have something to remember me by, sweetheart."

He fondled her breasts. "How do you expect me to concentrate on birds?"

"I said I wanted to be the most beautiful one you'll ever see."

"You are that." His mouth replaced his hands.

Liz's groin clutched, throbbed. She glanced out the windows. Too many people. "Damn."

When they exited the SUV, Liz pitched an imaginary coin, and they headed south. They were passing a row of short pilings at the edge of the beach area, when she spotted a preferred bird. She grabbed Jim's arm. "A red knot! They're endangered."

It was a lifer, a new bird for him. About ten inches long, with a fairly thick bill, it resembled a plover, but he didn't think it was. He wondered if it was changing from winter to breeding plumage. Red-orange feathers covered its chest and neck, and streaks of orange paralleled its eyes. The rest of its feathers were gray. "Is it a sandpiper?"

Liz nodded. "Time for pictures."

Trailing behind, he took a tenth of the pictures she did, while envying that she could kneel and stand so easily. He could, once.

They spent an hour following it and two other red knots they encountered. She turned frequently and flashed broad smiles. "What a treat."

So, it was. Her smile, long legs—a superb treat.

They walked a half mile before giving up the stalk. On the way back, she told him the sandpiper's story.

"Red knots have one of the longest migration routes of any bird—more than nine thousand miles from their wintering grounds in southern Argentina to their summer grounds in the Arctic.

"A few years ago, they were the most numerous sandpiper migrating through the U.S. Today, their population has fallen from more than a hundred and fifty thousand, to around twenty-five thousand. Miles of tundra where they once nested are now bare.

"The main reason for their decline is their need to eat horseshoe crab eggs on the northeast Atlantic coast to sustain them on the final leg of their journey to the Arctic. Unfortunately, eel fishermen use female horseshoe crabs for bait. Delaware Bay, between Delaware and New Jersey, is the red knot's last stop on their trek north. New Jersey has banned harvesting the crabs for bait, but it may be too late. Researchers don't know the size of the crab population required to save the red knots from extinction.

"Global climate change may play a part, too. The bird's migration timing is changing, and rising seawater may have a further impact. In any event, if we kill them off, we can't complain about our forefathers exterminating the billions of passenger pigeons that were here when they arrived in America.

"Horseshoe crabs are another story. Killing females for eel bait may be depleting their population. The last I checked, scientists weren't sure how long it takes the crabs to reach maturity or how many are required to keep the species from going extinct."

She smiled ruefully. "And we're on that chain. Horseshoe crabs have copper-based, blue blood that's very special. It contains enzymes that create a substance that detects toxic bacteria in medicines. In other words, the crabs protect us while they feed the red knots. Wouldn't it be a kick in the rear, if we decided that we'd rather eat eels than be healthy?"

Jim stared. "How did you find out about all this?"

"Daddy's nature programs. And online research."

A hundred yards before reaching the beach, Liz grabbed Jim's shoulder. "Look up."

Above the surf, a large tern flapped casually, head down, searching for prey.

"A royal tern?" Jim guessed.

"Something better and usually harder to find ... a Caspian tern."

"How can you tell the difference?"

"Note the bill. It's dark red with a black tip. Royal terns' bills are lighter and more red-orange. And the undersides of the wingtips are dark on this bird. They aren't on a royal tern."

Least terns rested within a large flock of mixed birds when they returned to the state park beach. Liz beamed. "This is our lucky day."

The sleek birds were about nine inches long, with thin white wedges on their foreheads. That was about it for distinguishing features, other than their tiny size and black tipped yellow-orange bills. Their legs were mostly yellow-orange.

"Liz, I saw some of these near the jetty the day you took pictures of the snowy egret. They were out of my range, near the water's edge."

Satisfied with their afternoon photo expedition, Liz felt exhilarated—like she always did after a grand shoot. Her endorphins were high, her groin twitched, and she wanted nothing more than to suck Jim's tongue out of his mouth.

"Wasn't that the greatest? It's as if those terns posed for us. And the bonus," she breathed, much like she did under the full crush of Jim's weight. "Red knots."

As they approached the parking lot, a lady sitting in a lounge chair beneath a wide blue and white-striped beach umbrella waved at them.

Liz couldn't believe her eyes. "Jim, it's the PI."

"Come visit a minute," Edith called out. "I don't bite."

Liz looked at Jim. He shrugged.

"Hi, Mary Elizabeth," Edith said, looking pleased. She saved Liz the trouble of trying to recall her name. "I'm Edith Mansfield and, yes, I've been following you." She looked apologetic. "Your mother wanted to make sure you were safe."

She peered at Jim. *My, you've lost more weight.* "Hello, again. That was some mountain in San Antonio, wasn't it?"

Jim nodded ... the woman seemed too friendly, but he tried to treat everyone with respect ... and winked at Liz. "I'm glad someone besides me recognizes a mountain when they see one."

Edith looked back to Liz and spoke in a motherly voice. "It's okay if I call you Liz, isn't it? It's what your companion calls you."

Is the PI real, or am I hallucinating? Liz nodded.

Edith rose from her Texas-orange chair and extended her small, delicate hand to Jim. "We haven't formally been introduced. I'm Edith Mansfield," she said, as if she hadn't told Liz the same thing. She stared appreciatively. "My ... you're *tall.*"

Not having a choice, Jim lightly grasped the woman's hand. It felt soft, sensually so. "I'm Jim Smith." The PI held his hand longer than he preferred, and he decided she was one of those talkative, demonstrative-type women. He noticed her wedding ring when she grasped his wrist. Her lingering touch confirmed his suspicion—and raised his discomfort level.

"Call me Edith." She purposely relaxed her hand in a submissive move, one that aroused a man's desire. Breathing deeply to advertise her more-than-adequate bust, she coyly cast her large eyes down ever so briefly while studying the man's face. He was a novice, nervously sizing her up, and he liked what he saw. *You're Texas toast.*

Jim eyed Edith when she turned back to Liz. He thought her oval, pixyish face, with wide blue eyes, a small, perfectly formed nose, nice cheekbones, and full Cupid's bow lips, quite pretty. Her eyes reminded him of someone's, but he couldn't recall who. Her shorts were much shorter than most women her age could wear without looking ridiculous. She wore them well—rounded hips, shapely legs. He considered her slightly overweight, but by no means obese. Her frilly neckline revealed much of her large, jiggling breasts that appeared exceptionally soft. The sight challenged his heightened libido.

"I'm so glad this nasty business is over, Liz. Your mother was so nice about it, yesterday." Edith gave a look of distaste. "To tell the truth, we didn't much like following you, but my associate and I felt that if we didn't take the case, some other service would."

She caught Liz's frown. "Sorry about Jackie's approach. He uses it to get people's attention while I do the dirty work." She freed Jim and soothingly caressed Liz's arm. "I do hope he wasn't too fresh with you." Her touch again lingered.

Perplexed, Jim and Liz glanced at each other.

Edith looked past them, still stroking Liz's arm. "Here comes Jackie. I sent him for some drinks when I saw you two walking around, kneeling down, and taking all those pictures."

Jack West ambled up, smiling crookedly. He had a swollen, purple nose and a black right eye. He held out a tray

Jim wondered if his condition had anything to do with Liz's actions in San Antonio. Liz just wondered.

"Hi, folks, we've got to stop meeting like this," Jack cracked. "Actually, Edie and I usually come out here to relax after a long, hard job with late hours. The sounds of the wind and surf help us unwind. Sometimes we stay a week." He winked. "And you sure put us through our paces in that wilderness park."

He noted their bemused stares. "In case you're wondering, I did go up to help Edie. It's why I look like this. I tripped on the way down."

Liz failed to detect lust in his eyes for the first time since she met him.

"I hope I didn't damage your opinion of me, too much, Liz," Jack said. He glanced lovingly in Edith's direction. "I play the heavy, so Edie can work behind the scenes."

Edith loved the nickname, Edie, Jack had just bestowed on her. She considered it his first show of true affection, regardless of his reason.

A diet Pepsi on the tray stood out among three regular drinks. Jack held it in Liz's direction. "I figured you'd want a diet soda."

"Thanks, Jack." He'd certainly changed, she thought. "You sure had me fooled."

He gave a quick, embarrassed smile and held the tray toward Jim. "And a regular soda for the big guy."

Jim declined after a stern look of disapproval from Liz. "Sorry, you guessed wrong. A diet drink for me, too."

Able to relax around Jack for the first time, Liz took a long swallow. Just the thought of him made her tense before. She had a quirky thought. *Maybe my subconscious will stop making me have sex with him, now that he's no longer dark and dangerous.*

"Do you go birding often or was that just an act?" she asked.

Jack smiled sheepishly. "Guilty, again. I boned up on bird guides."

"Was that a king rail we saw?"

His crooked smile crooked even more. "To tell the truth, I haven't the slightest idea. It did look like the one in the book, though."

The man was honest. Easy to like. "Thought so," Liz said.

"Let's all go back to our camper, so I can get you a diet soda, Jim" Edith said. "You look like you're dying of thirst.

"And by the way, you two, now that we know each other better we need to stop being formal. Call me Edie."

Nodding, Liz gazed at Jim. "You *are* red, Jim."

He found it difficult to relax around their former adversaries, but he trusted Liz's female intuition—despite the fact she was filled with exuberance from their successful afternoon. "I guess it couldn't hurt."

They followed Jack and Edie to the RV area.

"I'll be right back with your drink, Jim." Edie disappeared into a small trailer and returned with a large glass filled with ice and soda. She cocked her head. "You're too flushed. I'm going to take you inside in the air conditioning until you cool off."

She glanced apologetically at Liz. "There isn't much room. Would you mind sitting out here under the awning?"

Tired from lugging her heavy camera around, Liz plopped into one of the lounges. When she glanced at Jim and Edie, she frowned.

Edie patted Jim's arm as she tugged him toward the trailer. "Has anyone ever told you that you look like a big old teddy bear?" Jim shook his head. "Is it okay if I call you Teddy?" Jim nodded.

Liz sipped her drink, relaxed, and peered around the campground. Being a Monday, more than half of the campsites were empty. Those beside Jack and Edie's trailer were vacant except for the next site over, where a large, windowless industrial van was connected to the electrical outlet. She heard its air conditioner running, so someone must be using it as an RV. The next nearest campers were about seventy-five yards away, on the other side of the wide lane.

Jack reclined in the adjacent chair. When Liz finished her drink, he got her another without being asked.

"Jack, your last name is West, and Edie's is Mansfield. Are you married, like you told us in San Antonio?"

"Yes, but not to Edie."

Liz smiled knowingly. She was essentially sharing a cabin and RV with Jim, and they weren't married.

"It's not quite as bad as it seems," Jack winked. "We have a platonic relationship. The dinette breaks down into a second bed."

Liz laughed and relaxed even more.

He gave her a fatherly look. "What's it like to be a real nature photographer?"

"What was that rig you used at the birding center?"

He chuckled. "Business equipment. I take photos, too. Some might even call it nature photography."

Liz smiled. "I hadn't thought about that. I guess we're in the same business, only my subjects have feathers, fur, scales ... and sometimes ... lots of legs. I find it the most satisfying avocation in the world."

They talked about their adventures as the sun lowered in the sky. People returning from the beach strolled past and entered trailers and motorhomes in the gathering dusk. When the sun dipped below the horizon, all became still. Even the wind died down.

Jack cocked his head and gazed in the direction of the dunes. "There's a shorebird over there. At least it has long legs. It's a cute little fellow." He stood and walked past the van.

Liz rose reluctantly. It felt good to be sitting, and she felt light-headed from the morning exercise, sun, and long afternoon. She wondered if her thirst from trailing birds on the beach contributed.

When she reached Jack, she saw nothing. "Where is it?"

He stared at the nearest dune. "Over there. It has a couple of bands on its neck and forehead. Any idea what it is?"

Liz couldn't locate it but knew what it was. "Yeah. It's a killdeer. A little plov—"

"We're aware your affair and have proof," Jack said, in a calm, friendly tone.

Liz's legs faltered. Darkness blurred her vision. Jim had been correct, the PIs had somehow discovered their secret. Worse, had taken pictures.

Though terrified, she tried to keep concern off her face. "What do you mean?"

"You know exactly what I mean. We have you in stills and on video. Did you think we couldn't?"

Liz's heart raced, but she met his gaze, her blackness replaced by frightening clarity. She made an offer. "What will it—"

Jack again interrupted. "You'll both be ruined when your parents and ..." He paused for emphasis. It was also a risk. "His wife finds out."

Feeling faint, Liz's willpower kept her knees from buckling. Her family, Don, the church would find out about her infidelity. So would Marsha.

Unless she prevented it. "What do—"

The vulnerable woman stared desperately, and Jack pressed his advantage. "You're good. Great even. You scream. Moan."

Liz hyperventilated. "I ... I ... but ..." She stared at the trailer. *Jim. Marsha.*

Jack misread her intention. "That won't do you any good."

Liz's mouth fell open, but her breathing returned.

Jack was in control, his arousal full. The more he rattled the woman, the better. "Edie's an expert, and she uses drugs. By now, Jim's buck-naked. That's a good thing, and you know it. He's out of your hair."

Thank goodness.

Liz tried focusing her eyes on Jack's face—but his bulging pants. She couldn't keep from staring.

When the woman stared at his crotch, Jack became overly excited and broke a rule—made the offer before waiting for her to do it. Edith would be pissed, but he had a better grasp of the situation. His tone softened. "All you have to do to keep the matter quiet is enter the van with me."

Liz managed to raise her eyes and lock them on the beast. She again considered offering money and decided against it. Her body for their silence would have been her last resort, but it prevented having to explain a large expenditure. And most likely, Jack and Edie had been richly compensated by her mother.

"Pictures," she mumbled, intending to demand all copies of the evidence to prevent further blackmail.

"So, you want proof before payment. Good thinking. They're in the van." He reached out. "It's soundproof. If Jim comes out early, we'll wait 'til he leaves."

Dizzy, Liz wondered if her drinks had been spiked, too. Something stirred in the back of her confused mind. *Marsha.*

Jack read the conflict in his victim's face. Liz was the most strikingly beautiful woman he'd ever held in his power. If she came willingly, obeyed his commands, he'd take his time—make the encounter as enjoyable for her as for him.

"Come on," he murmured softly. "Take my hand."

52
As Easy as Shooting Birds in an Aviary

Jim's arm, clamped tightly against Edie's bountiful bosom, gave a new meaning to touchy-feely. The problem was, he felt flattered.

He used the opportunity afforded by opening the screen door to disengage his arm. And brain. "Allow me."

The gentleman felt good against her. Exciting. "Why, thank you, Teddy."

Edie bounced lightly up the steps and grasped his hand to steady him as he followed. His large, rough hand felt great, and she released it slowly. "Have a seat while I pour myself a drink."

She apologized for the small booth. "When you rent a trailer, you take what's available."

The dinette was typical of small travel trailers. Instead of a table and chairs, it resembled a diner's booth. The tabletop sat on pedestals set into metal receptacles on the floor. The pedestals could be removed and the top lowered to convert it into a bed using the seat and back cushions. The tight fit made Jim appreciate the table in his fifth wheel.

"Would you like a shot of bourbon, too, Teddy?"

"No, thanks. I don't drink."

"It'll relax you. If you're like me, stove up from climbing that mountain, you ache all over."

"I hurt, but it's a good hurt. Liz is a good trainer."

Thirsty, Jim quickly drained his soda.

"Would you like another? I found a diet Coke. Which would you prefer, it or Pepsi?"

"It doesn't matter."

"Done."

Jim watched her remove two cans from the small refrigerator and set them on the counter beside the stove. Curious about Liz and still wary, he peered out the window. She and Jack seemed to be having a conversation she enjoyed.

Edie returned carrying two glasses of fizzing soda. "You better hope that pretty bird doesn't kill you with exercise. She's in perfect condition and might overestimate what you can handle."

Jim grinned. "She's testing my limits, that's for sure."

Edie slid into the seat opposite him, brushing his legs in the process. When he tried to move them away, she laughed. "There's no need to be shy. It's impossible in this trailer." She nodded at the sofa. "But if you wish, we can sit there."

Jim stared longingly at the sofa, but it was small. It would be easier to ignore bumping legs, than rubbing thighs with the charming woman. "This is fine."

She stared quizzically at the glasses. "I can't remember which one's which, so I'll let you decide." She pushed them toward him.

Jim sniffed the first glass and made a face. "This smells like bourbon."

"And how would a teetotaler know?" Edie asked, lips pursed, wide eyes sparkling.

"I was in the Marines, and my buddies imbibed."

He sipped the second drink. He was too courteous to tell her that it, like the first one she given him, tasted a little odd. But it was cold, and he needed liquid. "This one tastes okay."

Edie took a long swallow of her drink and relaxed. "Ah, the nectar of the gods." She sighed contentedly. "Jackie will be a happy camper tonight. He likes me a little loose." Teddy's grimace pleased her. Maneuvering people into their discomfort zones impacted their libidos. She would push him vigorously.

She manipulated the conversation, doing things to put him at ease, while filling it with body language, sexual innuendos, and double-entendres.

When her repertoire didn't immediately yield the desired result, she stopped being subtle. Raising her legs above the seat, she made a show of removing her shoes and rubbing her bare ankles. "My shoes are too tight."

Leaning her elbows on the table to sip her drink, she made certain Jim could peer into her low-cut bodice. His failed attempts to keep his eyes on her face delighted her.

Spiking his drinks with grain alcohol helped. Not enough to significantly change the taste. She wanted him loose, not under the influence of the date rape drug Jack obtained from one of his contacts. In fact, she'd conveniently misplaced the drug by tossing it into a dumpster at a convenience store.

She smiled when Jim drained his second drink as quickly as he did his first. "Need another one?"

He nodded. Relaxed and more comfortable, he didn't mind when her knees, legs, and feet moved over and against his when she left the booth.

He glanced outside. Two couples walked past the trailer carrying beach items. Liz and Jack had moved away from their seats and were evidently talking birding, based on their serious faces. With the sun setting, the campground would soon be quiet. He thought it time to return to Palm Gardens but wouldn't hurry Liz. She would let him know when she was ready.

"Are you absolutely positive you wouldn't like some bourbon? Doctors say liquor is good for us. I think even the Bible mentions that." Edie laughed. "You could be like me. I'm feeling no pain whatsoever."

When she handed him the new glass, he held it up. "These Pepsis are relaxing enough. They don't need help."

She bent extra low. "As you wish, master."

Able to see all the way to her navel, Jim executed a bona fide, full-blown, double-eyed ogle. Edie's breasts were larger than either Liz's or Marsha's. Beneath the tan line, they were creamy white like Liz's. They jiggled and swayed hypnotically when she wriggled her shoulders. He couldn't take his eyes off them and breathed a sigh of relief when she sat opposite him and rubbed his feet with hers.

Enough with the visual enticements. Edith wanted this man. She moved to jack his libido to the next level. Adjusting her legs, she touched his crotch. His libido couldn't get much higher. "Oops. Sorry. My leg's falling asleep." Her eyes narrowed when Teddy didn't object and barely flinched at her toe touch.

Glancing outside, her heartrate picked up. Liz was following Jackie toward the Party Wagon. If the woman returned immediately, game over, at least for tonight. If she came back flushed and ready to leave but without complaint, there would be an appointment. If she disappeared into the Party Wagon and didn't come out within five minutes—Teddy time!

There were contingency plans for the latter scenario. If the impossible happened—she failed to seduce Jim and he left the trailer—she would say Jackie and Liz followed some weird bird toward the beach.

If he remained suspicious, she would escort him there to search in vain before returning to the trailer. When Jack and the girl showed up, they would announce that they had indeed done what she'd said.

But her bird wouldn't fly the coop. Afterwards she would use the pager to alert Jackie when he and Liz could safely exit the Party Wagon, and Jim would be so ashamed he'd have trouble facing Liz.

Edie smiled in anticipation. "Teddy, your feet must be killing you. Take off your shoes. I won't bite. Too hard." In a practiced move, she nipped the skin on his ankle using the big and second toes of her right foot.

Jim took a long swallow of his new drink and chuckled. "Ouch."

Edie fixed him with an expression of wide-eyed innocence. "What?"

"My leg's been down too long. I need to elevate it, Mrs. Twinkle Toes."

"Would you prefer to sit on the sofa. I'll get a pillow to place under it. Or I could get a second one to place behind you, and you can rest against the window and elevate your leg here."

"Here's fine."

"Make yourself comfortable while I get the pillows."

Edie sauntered to the bedroom with an exaggerated sway in her hips.

Feeling his Pepsis, Jim couldn't become any more comfortable.

When she returned, Edie handed him the pillows and removed the tabletop before he could move to help her. Kneeling, she took a pillow from him, and positioned it under his injured leg.

Still on her knees, she reached into her bra and repositioned her breasts. "Too confining."

Sipping his drink, staring, Jim uncharacteristically visualized Edie naked—imagined grasping her breasts and fondling them. Giving it consideration, he twisted uncomfortably and glanced over his shoulder. He couldn't see Liz and Jack. *Probably chasing a bird. No matter.*

Warm and aroused, he no longer cared to return to his RV. The woman with him was fascinating to look at, talk to. Intoxicating.

After pressing her breasts into his face while positioning the second pillow behind his back, Edie examined his wound. "Where did this happen? Out on the jetty?"

She walked her fingers over his leg and rubbed. "We have to keep your circulation going. Doesn't look too bad, though."

Jim didn't flinch when she removed his shoe and sock and rubbed his bare foot and ankle with surprisingly strong fingers.

"Does your sweet girlfriend do this?"

The comment gave him brief pause, but the warm hands and fingers massaged the thought away. He shook his head.

Recognizing the longing in his eyes, Edie worked her fingers above his knee.

Fascinated by the sway of her bosom as she knelt before him, Jim trembled reflexively at the seductive touch. He desired to take the plush little woman into his arms, kiss her full lips, and rip open her blouse to release the captivating mounds.

For the first time, he prayed half-heartedly for strength to resist.

And for forgiveness for staring at the large nipple peeking over her bra.

Knowing where her fingers were headed and that the tattered remains of his resistance were in verge of collapse, Jim decided to leave the trailer and rejoin Liz. To bolster his resolve, he drained the rest of his drink.

When he didn't resist, Edie slid her hand under his shorts and up his inner thigh, savoring his shudder and soft moan. Alcohol permeated his heaving breath. He didn't need more.

Smiling broadly, she grasped possession of him.

Jack backed slowly toward his goal. "His wife won't find out, nor will your mother."

Liz's head spun. She clutched his outstretched hand and followed meekly, as if compelled—like a mouse sniffing haltingly forward to determine if the thing flitting its tongue at it was a snake.

Curiosity gripped her. *I wonder if sex with Jack will be like I dreamed it.*

Jack led her to the van and opened the door. "You won't regret this."

53
The Pecking Order

Liz stumbled.

Jack gripped her left hand to keep her from falling, and she put all one hundred and fifty-five pounds behind her straightened right arm and the heel of her right hand. The blow missed his chin and struck the side of his face. When he wasn't knocked out, just disoriented, she kicked at him, slipped on the gravel, and fell.

A foot stepped on her chest before she could scramble up. "So, this is the way you want it," Jack growled, his eyes refocusing.

Petrified, Liz peered wildly about. She only saw one trailer and no people. She'd sized West up as a wrestler at the birding center, and he proved his strength by securing her wrists in his powerful hands as she tried to hit, scratch, and kick. The similarity to her dream added urgency. She struck out blindly.

The woman was strong from exercise but no match for him. Evading a kick aimed at his groin, Jack slipped.

Liz managed a half-scream before his elbow slammed into her chest, knocking the breath from her lungs.

"Enough," Jack wheezed. "You can either get in the van easily or painfully."

He grunted as she used her remaining energy to resist. His forearm ground into her breasts when he tried to regain his feet without lessening his grip. The body contact fueled his imagination. The frown on his face morphed into a smile. Standing, he yanked her to her knees.

Liz jerked back, toppling him forward. Grasping wildly, he gripped her blouse. She twisted away, ripping it in two.

What the hell? Jack had known she was braless, but her reddened breasts were a major disappointment.

He couldn't dwell on them. While he wrenched Liz's arms behind her back, she rotated and tried to kick him in the knee. "Damn you, witch." He ended the conflict by slamming his fist into her solar plexus.

The remaining air surged from Liz's lungs with a rasping sound. Unable to catch her breath, she thought she was dying.

Edie repositioned herself on Jim's lap while leaning to see if Liz had entered the van.

The damned idiot, I'll kill him!

Jack tossed Liz onto the van's heavily cushioned floor.

Barely able to breathe, she saw shackles on the walls. Trying to rise, her arms wouldn't function. Horrified, she rolled onto her back and tried to propel herself toward the door by using her legs.

Jack blocked her escape route. "This was your choice."

Freedom denied and further resistance pointless, Liz struggled to collect her wits and catch her breath. *Marsha. What have I done?*

She'd violated Jim's trust and ruined the opportunity to keep Marsha from learning of their affair. And if Jack was this vindictive for sending him on a wild goose chase to Fort Worth, how much would he punish her, and Jim, for her defiance?

Unless.... She wasn't the person she'd been before meeting Jim. She would protect his marriage no matter the cost. Even follow-on blackmail could be managed.

As she rotated to look at Jack without having to bend her head backwards, she peered at the restraints and devices in the van and recalled the prophetic dream. And though it didn't appear he intended to kill her, the look on his face chilled her. Hiding her fear, she imitated Maggie's smile.

Jack stepped into the van and paused to savor his moment of victory. After his initial disappointment, the rise and fall of her naked chest now beckoned. As did her thighs and long legs. He envisioned caressing them, feeling them encircle his body—after he taught her that messing with him didn't pay.

He thought of Edie. She would be pissed, but Liz had caused her own condition. And by now, Edie would have become so bored by Fat's babbling she would have slipped him the knock-out drug. Innately curious, she would have stripped him anyway and been disappointed as hell. That would add to her annoyance that he let this situation get out of control.

Unable to take his eyes off the half-naked woman, he touched his face, felt the pain she'd inflicted on him. She would experience the same feeling before he was through with her, though it wouldn't be on her smiling face.

Smiling face? Maybe resistance was her form of foreplay. Her mother said she was crazy. He grasped the handle to close and lock the door.

"Hey!"

Jack turned to see who spoke.

A fist resembling a large cantaloupe struck the right side of his face and jaw. The sledgehammer blow slammed him against the doorjamb. His knees gave way as he spun out of the van. He was unconscious before his head and torso slammed onto the gravel.

"Not so fast, there, Teddy."

Looking around, Jim peered into Edie's perturbed face. And at the pistol she pointed at him. Ignoring it, he stepped into the van where Liz was trying uselessly to cover her bare chest with the remains of her shirt. He scooped her up, carried her to the Tahoe, and placed her on the front passenger seat.

Although apparently mute from hysteria and the pummeling she must have received, she didn't appear to be in immediate danger, so Jim grabbed his camera and returned to the van. Moving quickly, he snapped photos of Jack West, the van's shackles and torture implements, the pickup, trailer, and their tags. It was difficult with the telephoto lens, but he couldn't waste time. He hurried back to where Liz sat waiting.

When he passed the trailer, he saw Edie standing in the doorway. He glowered. "If Liz decides to press charges ... and I'm certain she will ... we'll have all the proof we need of your setup here. And if I ever see so much as a hair on either of your heads near her, you won't have to worry about prison."

Edie stared silently, lips pursed, head cocked at an angle.

When Jim reached the SUV, Liz nodded at her fanny pack. She didn't want to talk. She didn't know how to explain to him what she'd done. There would be hell to pay in Edmond, Oklahoma, and Kingwood, Texas. She envisioned photos in the Corpus Christi media, the next morning, and in magazines in the coming week.

"Dawn, a ton of shit's going to hit the fan," she heard her gruff Grandpa Craig tell her.

When they drove past the visitor center, a park ranger's truck left the parking lot and turned in the direction of the camping area.

Edie stayed in the trailer until the ranger parked behind their campsite. Trembling, she ran to meet him. "Thank goodness, you're here. We were attacked."

"What happened?"

"We're private investigators. We were hired to follow a woman with a reported history of violent mental illness. Our client, the woman's mother, changed her mind and terminated our services, but the woman and her giant friend must have found out about us and trailed us here.

"We apologized to them, explained that we were just doing our jobs, and to show we meant well, offered them drinks. The woman had an episode and attacked my associate. When he attempted to protect himself, her companion knocked him out."

Edie wanted the ranger to leave so she could remove the Party Wagon. She pointed at the park road. "They were in the SUV you just passed. If you hurry, you can catch them."

When he didn't respond and looked at van, she urged, "Please go. They're getting away."

Worried about the mumbling man on the ground, trying to push himself up, the ranger ignored her request.

Jack stood, staggered a couple of listing steps, and thudded heavily back onto the gravel drive.

After checking the man's pulse, the ranger peered into the van and whistled. Leaning in, he studied the restraints. "What the *hell* do we have here?"

Edie started to explain, changed her mind, and hurried back to the trailer for her identification.

The ranger called for EMTs and assistance.

An elderly couple approached and identified themselves as Jeb and Sally Makens from Austin, Texas. Jeb spoke first. "Sally's the one who called you. We figured it would be quicker than calling 911."

He pointed at Jack. "A woman tried to kick that guy there on the ground, but she fell down. He stood on her while she tried to slug him, then it looked like he tripped and fell on her. Her shirt ripped when they stood back up. She kicked at him again, he punched her in the gut and pitched her into that van. Then a heavyset man came out of that trailer, over there, and knocked the guy flat."

Jeb peered at Edie. "This woman, here, jumped out of the trailer and waved a gun at the big guy, but he went in the van and carried the lady to an SUV. They drove off as you drove up."

Edie held up her ID.

Sally took up the report. "We didn't hear the commotion over our air conditioning, don't you know. We were playing a card game called Golf."

She gazed admiringly at her husband. "Jeb looked out the window and told me about the fuss. When I looked out, this man on the ground punched a woman smack in the chest. It took the wind right out of her sails, don't you know.

"We're old and small, so Jeb told me to call you. And he's a birder, so he took pictures with his big camera lens. Some are real good."

"Can you give me a description of the car?" the ranger asked.

The couple nodded. "It was a black Chevy Tahoe." Jeb handed him a piece of paper. "Here's the tag number."

"Thank you."

The ranger returned to his pickup and called the Corpus Christi Police.

* * *

The triage nurse immediately escorted Liz to an ER examination room.

Jim Edwards soon approached Jim in the waiting room. "I found out Liz was admitted. What on earth happened?"

Jim looked pensive. "Too much parental care, I'm afraid."

When he didn't explain, Edwards sniffed. "Have you been drinking?"

"No, of course not."

54
Winging It

The exams and lab work began immediately.

"What happened, Mrs. Crane?" the nurse asked.

"I was attacked."

"Sexually?"

Liz nodded absently.

Her arms wouldn't function without pain, and it was mandatory that she change into a hospital gown. She wanted her Jim to help her, but he had to stay in the waiting room until notified. Having a female nurse help her do it added to her discomfort. The gown wasn't designed for her height or hips—didn't offer a shred of decency—worsening an already humiliating experience. She trembled throughout the ordeal.

Jim made a vital trip to the restroom, and twenty minutes later, still waited to be escorted to Liz.

An officer approached and motioned him aside. "Mr. Smith, may I speak with you? Outside?"

"Sure." Jim followed him.

"What were you and the lady drinking? Was it a private party?"

Why is everyone asking me this question? "We weren't drinking, sir. A person we were with was drinking"

The officer looked dubious. "Would you mind taking a breathalyzer test?"

Jim welcomed the opportunity to prove himself innocent.

The result sent him reeling—as did the next line of questioning.

"Mr. Smith, your name came up in our database."

"Uh-huh," Jim said dully, in a state of shock.

"You were involved in a multi-vehicle accident three weeks ago."

Jim shook his head. "I wasn't in the wreck." He wondered where the conversation was heading. Where his whole life was. He was near the legal alcohol limit—from breathing vapors.

"You didn't wreck, Mr. Smith, but you were involved in the chain of events that led to the accidents."

Confused, Jim wondered if he would now be charged on some technicality.

The officer stared. "The vehicle that caused the wreck was a black Chevy Tahoe, and the one you arrived in tonight is a black Chevy Tahoe. It's registered to Mrs. Crane. Was she the one who caused the accidents?"

Blindsided, Jim struggled to maintain a straight face. He desperately thought of what to say while faking a sincere look. "No, Liz ... uh ... Mrs. Crane is ...um ... the safest driver I know."

The officer noted Smith's difficulty in formulating a response before the veil dropped.

"Mr. Smith, according to the investigating officer, you threatened to take the matter into your own hands." He studied his notes. "You said that if you got your hands on the maniac, you'd turn his life upside down.

"Mr. Smith, I'm asking you, again. Was Mrs. Crane the driver of that SUV? Is that the reason you accosted her?"

Before Jim could erase his look of astonishment, the officer was called away.

"Mr. Smith," he said when he returned, "I've received a report from Mustang Island State Park that appears to confirm Mrs. Crane's account of the incident." He still felt Smith was lying about the traffic accident. "However, I may want to speak with you more about the Fulton incident."

"Of course, Officer, but I can assure you, Mrs. Crane wasn't involved. And I no longer harbor animosity for the driver of that vehicle. After dwelling on it, I believe the drivers behind me were tailgating and driving recklessly."

"Driving dangerously and passing where one shouldn't is also reckless driving, Mr. Smith."

Jim had to repeat his version of the evening's events three times before seeing Liz, which added to his concern. He could only assume what she'd suffered. All he'd seen was Jack shoving her into the van. When he reached them, he found her essentially naked to the waist, with her chest abused.

He debated mentioning Edith's distraction, but couldn't. It would be awkward, and he didn't understand it himself.

After her nurse brought warm blankets and they were thankfully and securely tucked around her, Liz expected Jim to come in.

Instead, other ER personnel and doctors entered, and the humiliation began in earnest. Monitoring devices, X-rays, MRIs, and sonograms. Too many doctors and nurses lifted, twisted, prodded, and poked her suffering arms, shoulders, and chest worse than Jack West had. She wished she and Jim had simply returned to the confines of her cabin.

The one time she put her foot down—vehemently—was when a nurse entered with a rape kit. She couldn't risk exposure of her affair.

Jim stood in the darkness, reliving his complicity in the attack. He'd been an idiot not to realize the PIs wanted revenge for San Antonio. The beach encounter was too coincidental.

They'd planned well. Edith used his testosterone as a diversion, and he succumbed as easily as a teenager in lust. Consumed with disgust, he decided to not tell Liz why it took so long to come to her rescue. Unless she asked. Then, would he lie?

"Hey, Jim, I didn't expect you to be outside," Edwards said, holding out a note. "Liz's nurse asked me to give this to you." He gazed sympathetically. "I'm sure sorry for what happened."

"Yeah, me, too."

The note requested that he buy a blouse and bra and provided sizes.

When he returned, he was allowed to see her briefly to deliver them, then told it would be at least thirty minutes before he could see her again.

He used the time to call Marsha. He couldn't tell her what occurred. That would take too long and require too much emotional reserve. Plus, she wouldn't understand.

"How are things?" he asked, when she answered.

Not as well as he'd hoped, but her sense of humor was intact.

"Bucky's been a pill all day. I would've pulled my hair out, if I had any left, but I did that when I babysat Anderson and Taylor. By the way, thanks for the photos of the skimmers. I can't get over their long bills. I showed the pictures to the kids, and they loved them, too."

The diversion provided by the call allowed Jim to relax somewhat for the first time since the incident. He hated Jack West, but as the Lord's Prayer pleaded, "Forgive us our trespasses as we forgive others." He and Liz weren't guiltless in the affair. *Affair, now there's a word.*

The wait became closer to an hour and felt like several more. At last able to hold Liz's hands, he rubbed them gently. "Need your pillows fluffed?" She did. "Are you comfortable enough?" He made sure her blanket was securely tucked in. "Nurse, Liz needs another warm blanket," he requested, when one grew cool.

He frequently kissed her cheeks, forehead, and hands. "I should have trusted my instincts and insisted on going back outside to sit with you and Jack," he agonized more than once.

"It's not your fault, lov ... Grandpa. I should have recognized him for what he was. Like you say, it's difficult for a tiger to change its stripes."

Not as hard as you might imagine. "No, if I'd stayed outside, none of this would have happened."

"Maybe not tonight, but sometime...."

Liz trailed off when Jim kissed her hand. She wished she'd met him when he was younger. She realized it couldn't have happened, not with her mother controlling her life. It wouldn't be happening now, if not for the opportunity afforded when her father was injured. Even then she'd been extremely lucky. Had she taken Jack West up on his offer to go birding, she would have undoubtedly been violated, perhaps brutalized, like she'd been by Don. The van's interior made that seem more than likely.

I wonder if I would have become Jack's love slave. She would have been too humiliated to file charges against him and too disgraced to return home.

She felt sick for destroying Jim's marriage. By now, photos and videos of their lovemaking were in the hands of the authorities. Copies were probably on their way to Don and Marsha.

Why didn't I give Jack what he wanted?

In her right mind, she wouldn't have balked at the offer of silence, and Jim would have been none the wiser. It was a sacrifice she could have easily taken to her grave.

Thank God for Jim.

Reflecting on their relationship, she felt that, in effect, she was his love slave. He'd awakened her sex drive and fine-tuned it with exquisite sensual lessons.

No, we're mutual love slaves.

She could excite him with a touch, a kiss, could will him to satisfy her whenever she desired.

Jim noticed her wisp of a smile. "What're you thinking?"

"How thankful I am that you and I are together."

She wished he could lock the door and climb on the examination table with her, then wondered if her love-filled thoughts were a form of hysteria.

Answering the police questions was as humiliating as anything the doctors and nurses did to her. She'd have to go to the station later that morning to file assault charges and give a statement.

Angry, Liz found it difficult to wait. She wanted Jack hung, electrocuted—his organ sliced, diced, and shredded like a carrot. A lethal injection was too good for him.

But before she was released, the three examining doctors returned to her room, about thirty minutes apart. Each told her the same things—nothing was broken or torn. West's abuse bruised organs, but none were bleeding, and all were functioning properly. The damage would make breathing difficult for some time. Her arms, elbows, and shoulders would be sore for weeks. She could remove the double arm sling when comfortable enough to move her arms.

In response to her questions, they advised her to avoid exercise with weights during the recovery period. Take it easy. A pool would be okay, but no swimming. Liz scrunched her nose. Exercise was her life even more than photography.

To retain full control of her faculties, she made up her mind to not take pain meds but accepted a prescription to shut the doctors up.

Eager to receive Jim's tender care, she listened absently to her nurse's verbal instructions, briefly perused the written ones, signed them and left—happy to have the traumatic experience behind her.

In her cabin, she ignored the pain in her arms when Jim removed her sling and undressed her for their shower. She enjoyed the look in his eyes as he stared at her breasts.

"Aren't you going to touch them?"

"I can't. I might hurt them."

It surprised her when she looked in the mirror and saw them dark with bruises. The pain in her shoulders and arms had masked Jack's elbow torture.

She gazed at Jim with doe eyes she hadn't displayed before. "The only things you'll hurt are my feelings if you don't fondle them. They'll live."

Jim cupped and lifted them gently.

"Caress them."

He did so tenderly.

"Squeeze them."

He kneaded them gingerly.

"Do what I like best."

He suckled and chewed each nipple.

Ah, the power without doctors around.

"Jim, would you like to know what I was actually thinking when you asked why I was smiling in the ER? It was that you were my love slave."

"Oh, how's that?"

"If I'd gone birding with West after he invited me to when we first met, he might have turned me into his love slave, I was so naïve. And after looking in his van, he might have humiliated me so much I'd have been ashamed to return home.

"Then I thought how the same thing happened with you. You made me your love slave. Only you didn't seduce me, I seduced you, so I decided we were mutual love slaves. And you haven't humiliated me."

Liz smiled wistfully. "You sure have tortured me, though."

Jim cocked an eyebrow. "How?"

"By driving me up the wall with your wild sex.

"But, now, you're my love slave. I can make you do anything I want, whenever I want."

A smile played on Jim's lips. His eyes danced. "First, we're not love slaves. Second, our love-making hasn't been wild. Third, you think every bit as much as I do, maybe more."

His words shocked Liz into seriousness. "Not wild? Lord, what have I been missing all these years?"

She squinted. "What am I missing now?"

Jim grinned.

They showered together, and Liz proved her point—directing him where to apply the soap and how.

Her arms didn't hurt all that much during lovemaking.

Afterwards, she found sleeping difficult, wondering how to apologize to Jim for ruining his life.

* * *

After a late breakfast, Liz and Jim drove to a bank, then to the Corpus Christi Police Department. Arriving a little before 1:00 p.m., they told the receptionist they had an appointment with a Detective Jones.

A few minutes later they were escorted to a small room where the officer greeted them. He didn't smile, and both wondered why.

After the introductions, Jones said, "I hope you won't mind if I question you separately."

They didn't have an option.

"No problem," Jim said amiably. "Ladies first."

He ambled out of the room and down to the waiting area, where he poured a cup of gut-melting, heated-all-morning-long coffee and scrounged up a magazine he liked.

As soon as they were alone, the detective spoke. "Mrs. Crane, are you ready to make a statement?"

Liz pulled her notarized statement out of one of her large pockets. "Yes, Detective Jones, and to the best of my memory, this is everything that occurred."

Jones scanned it. "This doesn't mention that you struck Mr. West first. Did you?"

An hour later, Jim passed Liz on his way to Jones' office. She was crying. Without asking why, he gave her a sympathetic hug.

Wearing his widest grin, he strolled into Jones' office and stuck out his hand. "What would you like to know, Detective Jones?"

Jones didn't return Jim's smile. "Are you ready to make a statement, Mr. Smith?"

"You betcha. Do you have someone to take it down?"

"According to Mrs. Mansfield, you told her that if she and Mr. West approached Mrs. Crane, again, they wouldn't have to worry about going to prison. Did you say that?"

"Absolutely."

"Then you admit you threatened to kill them?"

"Kill them?" Jim said, looking puzzled. "Where did that come from? I meant that I'd lock them in that van of theirs and stand outside until they calmed down and promised not to stalk Mrs. Crane again."

The way Smith said it made Jones chuckle in spite of himself. Jack West had claimed the same thing about Mrs. Crane.

An hour and a half later, smiling, shaking hands, and patting each other on the back, Jim and Detective Jones parted.

Besides talking fishing, Jim found out most of what he wanted to know. The private investigators rationalized their actions. They were innocent. He and Liz were guilty. With the exception of one startling revelation—an apology, of sorts—it confirmed his faith in his fellow man.

Everyone's a victim, especially the guilty.

55
Madder than a Wet Hen

Liz quaked. "I can't believe it. That ... that ... turkey!"

Jim was proud that she didn't backslide into cursing.

"He said I hit him first. I did, but—" Placing her face in her hands, Liz again regretted not choosing the proper course of action. "I forgot to put it in my statement, and Detective Jones insinuated I left it out on purpose."

"He did wonder why you didn't return to the trailer and tell me we had to leave," Jim said softly.

"He didn't see Jack's eyes or hear what he said to me. Jack would never have let me walk away," she explained, nailing Jim with her wide, unblinking stare. "And I was confused. My head was spinning. He told me he'd drugged our drinks." She blinked. "Well, maybe not mine ... but yours."

Time to confess. She lowered her eyes, breathed a trembling breath. "Jim," she peered around and lowered her voice to keep the adjacent customers in the Whataburger from hearing. "You were right. They somehow broke into my cabin and installed hidden cameras. Jack was specific. Very descriptive. He said no one would find out if I did what he wanted." Liz' forehead furrowed in thought. "Um ... if I went into the van with him.

"I told you I wasn't thinking straight, and that's true, but I also worried that he might blackmail us and disclose the photos anyway. Looking back, I'm sure the real reason I chose fight over right is...." She couldn't bring herself to admit that. Not yet.

"Now, the world's going to find out about us, compounded by charges of assault and battery. Me for starting it, and you for sneaking up and ending it."

Tears brimmed in her eyes. "I wish I'd gone into the van. Then we wouldn't be sitting here like this."

Jim stared, open-mouthed.

"In the van, before I saw you, I made up my mind to do what he wanted, so you and Marsha could live happily ever after. Oh, Jim, please forgive me."

Jim shook his head. Liz had mentioned doing whatever was necessary to prevent Marsha from learning about their affair, but he never suspected it included allowing Jack to have sex with her.

It was partly his fault. He'd intended to provide his take on Jack's comments in the wilderness park, but the conversation had been interrupted—first by the discoveries at Walmart, later by the falcon. Sunday's trauma followed, and he'd forgotten to mention it again.

"Liz, you did the right thing when you resisted. Even if Jack and Edie have photos and put them on the Internet, two wrongs don't make a right. Letting him get his revenge by submitting to him would have added to the crime.

"That said, I think he was bluffing. If they had videos and pictures, they wouldn't have had to follow us to San Antonio and then chase off after the GPS. They would've sent them to your mother and collected their fee."

"But Jack's descriptions of our lovemaking."

"I suspect he used generic terms to frighten you into doing what he wanted. If we'd been innocent, you wouldn't have gone through the soul-searching.

"And I believe you were right when you said it was a matter of time before they came after you. We evidently made them so mad by the wild goose chase that they set you up for rape ... and who knows what else."

Jim didn't reveal that their plans included him and that it had been a near miss.

Still lamenting her decision, Liz returned to the original subject. "Oh, I could spit nails. Edie told the police that my mother said I had a history of violence. She said Mother hired her because I attacked you at Paradise Pond and Mother wanted to make sure I didn't hurt you or anyone else. Edie also claims to have a tape where I apologized to you for making you my punching bag by proxy."

She bit her lip to keep from screaming. "I swear, Jim, you're the only one I've ever attacked. Other than Jack." She puffed an unruly strand of hair away from her eyes. "Well, maybe I threw some flowers at Mother, once. And destroyed a coffee table."

Jim nodded, recalling how he'd thought of her as Birdzilla after their confrontation at Paradise Pond.

"Now, he's requested a restraining order to prevent *me* from assaulting *him*." Liz leaned forward, took a sip of water to calm her nerves.

Jim thought the safest thing to do was to keep quiet and function as her sounding board.

Liz's normally sleepy eyes narrowed. Her wide lips set in a hard line. Disgusted, she no longer whispered. "Can you believe that *pervert* is a well-respected family man? A deacon in his *church*? A pillar of the *community*?"

Jim nodded. Jack's resume surprised him, but it fit his opinion of people in general. They were human, and that wasn't good. Church leaders, elders, and religious figureheads had stumbled in the past and would continue to do so in the future. He knew that from personal experience.

"That story about locking me in the van until I calmed down was pure bull," Liz continued.

She shook so hard that Jim stood, moved behind her and gently massaged her neck and shoulder muscles. They felt like knots.

She flinched in pain, when he touched her shoulders, but didn't complain. Pain equaled penance.

"And that malarkey about accidentally ripping my shirt when I was kicking and screaming. Jim, if I hadn't been struggling so hard, I swear he would've dragged me to the truck by my breasts."

She paused, eyes on fire, "I'd like to accidentally ... no, I wouldn't stoop to his level."

Jim was glad she no longer felt sorry for her decisions and was mad at Jack. She was the victim and needed to see it that way.

People in the adjacent booths no longer consumed their food. They gaped, gawked, and listened.

Liz squinted in fury. "He tried to rip my arms off. Now, he says he was trying to calm me and that I wouldn't have hurt myself if I'd stopped struggling. And that punch. I saw his fist coming like it was in slow motion and couldn't do a thing about it."

She closed her eyes and shuddered. "Oh, Jim, life's so unfair. The police don't believe me."

He felt obliged to comment. "I think they'd like to, but it's mostly our word against theirs. The couple that saw part of your struggle didn't see you hit Jack, but they saw you fall down when you kicked at him as he stumbled backwards."

Liz winced.

"They couldn't hear you, so they don't know what was being said. And the only thing I saw was him pitching you into the van. Who would a jury believe? Right now, there's no proof either way. Lawyers make great livings from things like that."

"You're right, as usual." She motioned. "Feed me another bite of sandwich." She chewed slowly and swallowed. "Inside that van ... when I saw those cuffs and chains ... I could feel them. I tried to scramble out of there, but my arms wouldn't move."

She recalled her dream while finishing her water, then asked for another bite of sandwich.

"Although I'd made my mind up to do what Jack wanted, I was sure happy when I saw you. He thought I was smiling at him. I'm glad it held his attention."

"I couldn't hear you from the trailer," Jim said. "Edie turned up the air conditioning, talked a mile a minute, and kept blocking my view."

Liz nodded. "Jack told me that our drinks were spiked ... yours anyway ... and now he denies it. He says, since my mother says I'm crazy, I must have been hallucinating. But that's the silver lining. If they had drugged our drinks, we might be waking up about now, hurting all over more than any place else, like you're so fond of saying."

Jim doubted that Edith drugged his drink with anything more than alcohol, although he couldn't imagine how she did it. He hoped it explained the unusual liberties he permitted—and the things he'd done. "I *was* drugged, but the story's confusing. At least convoluted."

"What? Then ... how did you save me?"

Jim noticed the prying eyes and ears around them. "We couldn't talk in the hospital, and we were *recuperating*, afterwards. Plus, I didn't have the information I needed until after I spoke with Jones."

Liz leaned back to listen.

"Everyone in the ER kept asking me what I was drinking, and I kept telling them I don't drink. Then, an officer requested that I take a breathalyzer test, and I jumped on the opportunity to prove my innocence."

"Good. You don't drink."

"That's what I thought."

"What do you mean?"

Jim gave a quirky smile. "Let's say the results were sobering. I didn't flunk the test, but I had a lot of alcohol in my system."

"That's weird."

"It gets stranger. The police found my name in their database for the wreck on the way down here. They somehow found out we arrived at the ER in your Tahoe, put two and two together, and came up with four. The officer asked if you were the one who caused the wrecks."

Liz's eyes widened. "You didn't tell them. Did you?"

"Of course not. But he accused me of getting drunk and assaulting you."

Jim gave a guilty smile. "After the wreck near Copano Bay, I sort of told an investigating officer I'd wring the neck of whoever was driving the Tahoe. Luckily, the couple in the park and Edith confirmed it wasn't me who assaulted you."

He winked. "I had the feeling the officer didn't believe me, when I told him you weren't the driver, but I assured him you're the best driver I know."

Liz's wide smile filled her face. "I took Driver's Ed from an expert. But how did you get drunk? I mean ... how did Edith ... Edie ... drug you?"

"She told Jones she must have done it by accident."

Liz snorted. "An *accident*?"

"She said she became tipsy and must have accidently switched drinks. She asked Jones to apologize to me for her."

"And you believe that bunk?"

"I like to give people the benefit of the doubt. And I didn't get legally drunk, so I can't judge."

"I think she didn't have enough time, Jim. If Jack hadn't been so anxious to chain me in the dungeon, there's no telling where we'd be."

She cocked an eyebrow. "You said there were cameras in the van. I wonder if they would have taken pictures of us naked." She lowered her voice to a whisper. The corners of her mouth tilted up. "Now, I would've paid pretty good money for those."

Jim was happy her sense of humor was still active. "They sure set us up, didn't they? All that, we're sorry we followed you around and let's be friends, balderdash. I was suspicious, but I let my guard down."

"And I was stupid. The minute Jack didn't stare at my chest, I relaxed. He seemed so friendly and normal. I won't be that gullible again. Ever."

Jim recalled how friendly both PIs seemed. "It's probably not good to be too suspicious. Even tigers can change their stripes ... when they want to."

That managed to get a grin out of Liz before Jim again became serious. "But it's probably a good thing to have a healthy dose of wariness, especially when things seem too good to be true. Care for another bite of sandwich?"

Liz nodded

When Jim looked up after cutting off a piece for her, people's heads snapped away. He held it to her mouth, not caring if they listened.

Hysteria and anger waning, Liz envisioned the events at the park. She asked the question Jim had been dreading. "You apologized for not coming to my rescue sooner. Why?"

He mulled the safest things to admit. "I mentioned the air conditioner and that Edie kept blocking my view. She also seated me with my back to the window. One time, when she glanced out the window, she looked startled, and I became suspicious. Even then it wasn't easy. She'd blocked the door with the tabletop."

He didn't mention having to lift Edie off him.

"And I guess the reason she didn't warn him was because she went for the gun she pointed at me."

"That was incredibly dangerous, the way you faced her."

Jim shrugged. "I figured she wouldn't shoot me, and you looked so helpless, all I could think about was getting you to the hospital."

"But you took time to take pictures."

"You weren't bleeding, and I wanted proof of the van. The good news is that the posse was on its way due to the couple who saw you. FYI, the man's a birder, and he must have a camera like yours. He took pictures, although it's unlikely we'll see them since he gave them to the police. Maybe we should go thank the couple."

"I'm not sure I want to go back to the park. At least not this soon.

"You know, Jim, I think it would be stupid to go forward with this thing. It's probably a lost cause ... like fighting windmills. And if there's a long, drawn-out court case, everything will come out, for sure."

She bolted upright. "Isn't there a sign at the park that says firearms aren't allowed?"

"Edie's a licensed PI. She was supposedly threatened, so she has a permit to carry ... even in a state park."

Jim's answer deflated Liz momentarily.

"What about the dungeon van? Surely there's a regulation that would hang Jack for owning it."

"He got away clean on that one."

"What? How?"

Jim realized Detective Jones hadn't told her much. Or maybe she hadn't listened. "It's not his. It's Edie's. She told the police she likes kinky sex and offered a tape to prove it."

Liz's mouth fell open. "That old woman? You must be joking. She's too old for sex."

"She's much younger than I am, and you haven't let that hold you back."

Liz was stunned. Jim was so virile, she'd forgotten his age. And Marsha's. "I'm sorry," she said, smiling weakly. "You mean I have something to look forward to?"

Jim winked. "I've heard it gets better for women as they age. Not so for men, though."

"Oh?"

He returned to the previous subject. "The van's also more an illusion than it appeared. Most of the devices are decorative."

Liz stared in disbelief.

"All the deadly-looking implements are fake and fastened to the walls. There are supposedly things that can smart, though. And according to Jones, it has a love seat, a stereo with satellite radio, a small refrigerator, a stocked wine rack and wet bar. Edie calls it her party wagon."

"Gracious lord." Liz resigned herself to the fact that some fights couldn't be won, no matter how right someone was. She sat back. "So, Edie's a foxy pervert."

Her frown softened to a smile, eyes became dreamy. "If you're this good at almost sixty-eight, I wish I'd met you when you were eighteen."

"That was more than twenty years before you were born."

As they finished their meal, another image materialized in Liz's memory. "Why did you have a bare foot when you rescued me? I bet it hurt on that gravel."

The obvious reason popped to mind. "Oh lord, Edie took your shoe off."

Liz's fertile brain kicked into gear. "Tell me the truth, Jim, did Edie tie you to the bed? Coyotes chew off a foot to escape from a trap. You only had to chew off a shoe and sock."

"Edie removed them. She wanted to help the blood flow in my injured leg and didn't want my shoe to mess up the pillow she placed under it."

Liz lifted an eyebrow in mock disbelief. "That's plausible for the shoe, but it doesn't explain the sock. Or why your belt was unbuckled. Admit it, Edie was stripping you ... just like West said."

Jim maintained an innocent expression. Edie's delay hadn't been only to get the gun. And she'd bound him, just not with restraints. "There weren't any cuffs and chains in the trailer."

"So ... you were lured into the bedroom, after all."

"*No.*"

"Then how can you be sure there weren't any cuffs and chains?"

"You're right. I can't be."

Liz mulled over Jim's comments and the fact that West might have been telling the truth about Edie. "Now that I know more about the van, maybe I misjudged what West intended ... other than blackmailing or tricking me into giving him what he wanted ... but it doesn't make sense. Who uses handcuffs for lovemaking?"

Jim lapsed into stupidity. "Some couples don't mind a little tying up from time to time."

Liz arched backwards. Eyes wide, she shook her head slowly from side to side. "You and Marsha don't do that ... do you?"

Jim winked. "It's more like ropes. And I plead the fifth."

"Oh ... my ... stars."

There was a long pause while she contemplated a vivid dream, a dungeon that wasn't all it seemed, and what Edie must have done with Jim in the trailer. She found her thoughts disconcerting. And strangely titillating. "Feed me that last bite of sandwich."

The people around them sat transfixed, most with unfinished meals. Some took surreptitious photos with smartphones. One scribbled furiously on a note pad.

"One thing worries me," Jim said. "Jack and Edie must have used that van before. And not only for her perverted pleasure, unless I'm misreading Jack. I wonder if women *have* been raped and maybe abused in it. I think he would have tortured you, based on what you've told me."

"By the way, I asked Jones if they were going to run tests on the van and trailer due to West's drug claim. He said they were already on it."

Liz stared in admiration. "I'm so happy I met you."

It was time to set the record straight. "I have another confession to make, Jim. Jack didn't threaten me before I slugged him. He sounded like Don making an altar call."

Jim's mouth gaped open. His agonizingly derived and painfully constructed deductions of the altercation wavered and vanished like a wisp of smoke.

"Jim, what if they find ... you know ... a video."

Still stunned, he shook his head. "If they do, they do." He took a deep breath. "But I'm willing to bet they don't."

"But suppose that happens?"

"I don't know what police do with evidence." Jim studied his water cup. "This is the first time I've ever had a reason to think about something like this."

The sick look returned to Liz's face. "Marsha's going to find out, isn't she?"

Jim finally shrugged off her startling revelation. "Changing the subject, I asked Jones to check with the Walmart service department in San Antonio to talk to the employee who took the GPS tracking device to Ft. Worth. Jack didn't have any bruises when we last saw him, and Edie seems kind of smitten with him, even if she isn't his wife. I doubt that she shoved him down the mountainside for coming to help her."

"Hill," Liz corrected perfunctorily, staring at Jim in amazement. "How'd you find all this out?"

"I had a good teacher in RV debate class. Maybe the best."

"Maggie?"

Winking, Jim nodded.

Liz hadn't thought of the questions Jim asked the detective. Might not have, even if she hadn't been so upset with Jack and herself. Furthermore, Jim acted on his thoughts and appeared ready to accept exposure of their affair. He didn't seem to mind facing assault charges, either. She blew him a kiss. "I love you so much," she said, startling the eavesdroppers. "Let's go home."

Realizing she'd made the same mistake Jim made in San Antonio, she giggled. "Home, it has a nice ring to it, don't you think?"

Jim thought.

56
Caging the Bird

Liz shifted uncomfortably. The awkward sling made it impossible to find a position in the recliner that didn't make her shoulders, hips, or back hurt. She squirmed back and forth, from side to side. It felt like she'd been in the recliner for hours even though Jim had surprised her with a superb supper forty-five minutes earlier—a roasted chicken breast from the IGA and a handmade salad that was a work of art.

The worst thing was doing nothing. Unable to edit her pictures, she could instruct Jim with his, but he was nodding drowsily from lack of sleep.

I'll fix that. "Jim, help me out of this chair so I can help edit those pictures."

He forced himself awake and helped her to the couch. "How's that? More comfortable?"

"Not really. Maybe if I lie down."

He started to lay her lengthwise onto the couch.

"Not here ... on the bed."

"Would you like to go to your cabin?"

"No."

After he helped her up the steps, she changed her mind. "Let's go back to my cabin, I need to use the restroom and it's time to bathe."

Jim grabbed some clean clothes.

"Bring your jammies, too."

Liz surprised him in the shower. For the first time, she didn't make a seductive move or request that he please her in any way.

Afterward, she demanded they return to the RV. Exhausted, he wasn't about to ask why.

She changed her mind again. Once in bed, she lay back, arms folded together across her breasts, looking vulnerable, sexy.

Jim moved to lie beside her.

"What are you doing?"

"I thought I was supposed to spend the night here. Do you want me to sleep on the couch?"

"No, I want you here. But you have to pay the rent first."

"Uh ... pay the rent?"

"Are you an absent-minded professor? You're my teacher. You have to teach me something new every day."

"I've taught you everything I know."

"No, you haven't. You told me so."

Jim wondered what he'd said.

Liz feigned a look of concern. "I hope you aren't getting dementia. Hmm ... maybe I should help you find your way back to Oklahoma. That way, I could meet Marsha."

"Okay, what's going on?"

"Ropes. Handcuffs. Does that help?"

Jim shook his head. "I don't think you're ready for those, especially not in your condition. And what do they have to do with me paying rent?"

"You can't sleep with me unless you make love to me. That's your rent. And my choice of payment, tonight, is to be tied up and made love to."

Liz's eyelids lowered. Her face became sultry, seductive. She lifted her right arm higher, exposing a light-pink areola with a sleepy nipple.

Jim swallowed. Things were getting sticky. Or was that slippery? "Umm ... where can I find ropes? Handcuff stores are probably closed at this hour."

"That's for you to find out. If you want to sleep here, that is. If you'd prefer your RV, be my guest."

Jim made a long face and let his shoulders droop. "I guess I'll have a bed all to myself tonight, but it's sure going to be lonely."

"*What?*"

He pulled on the clean shorts and T-shirt he brought with him. "See you tomorrow."

Liz's head spun as she heard the cabin door close. What happened? Were rope games something Jim reserved for Marsha?

She became jealous. Marsha could have him any time she wanted, any way she wanted. She would only be with him this night and one more.

Tears welled in her eyes. First, Jack lying like he had—at least slanting the information—then Jones believing him and treating her like the criminal. Now, the love of her life just walked out on her.

Liz chided herself. Jim had been nothing but nice. This was his first time to resist a seduction attempt. And in his defense, it had been a long day. She would go to his RV, apologize, and sleep with him there.

When she stood, she realized her arms felt better without the sling. *Yoga and exercise. Don will think it was money well spent when I tell him.*

The thought startled her. Why had she thought of him? And that?

The thick mental curtain she'd erected to prevent herself from dwelling on the reasons for her trip parted. In two days, this world would end, and she hadn't thought of her life past that deadline—other than fantasizing about becoming Jim's mistress.

Her shoulders hurt when she donned her shorts and shirt, but not much more than the pain she experienced after starting a new exercise regimen. As she dressed, she thought about her husband.

After their wedding night and the Biblical, hands-on honeymoon homecoming, he hadn't mistreated her again. Though she limited sex, the thought of it hung over her life like a deathly pallor that soiled the rest of their relationship and their relationships with others. Like having to explain to her mother why she wasn't pregnant. Pretending she and Don were happily married for the congregation. Having to endure rumors and whispers about why she wasn't more active in church activities.

She visualized her home—the way she'd decorated it, the gifts from family, friends and the congregation displayed there. The pictures on the walls.

Her throat clutched. Tears welled in her eyes. Her mother-in-law had personally converted one of their bedrooms into a nursery as a honeymoon gift. "This isn't a hint," she'd said. "There's no need to rush." But the disappointment had grown in her mother-in-law's face yearly.

The curtain slammed shut. Ten years of this charade were too much. One was too many, and she was approaching the end of the eleventh year.

I wish Jim was single. It would make things so simple.

When she opened the door, she staggered backwards. Except for the protruding belly, she would have thought Jack was standing there. Holding a rope.

Smiling Jim, hid something else behind his back.

"You scared me to death, Jim. If it wouldn't hurt my shoulders, I'd slug you."

"I thought you said you weren't violent."

Liz didn't smile. "I thought I was dead. You're going to have to give me time to get my wits back."

They lay on the bed, talked, and it didn't take long. Liz became more than a little disappointed when he remained unready. *How can I change that?* She stood.

Jim feared she would aggravate her shoulder injuries. "You're not hurting yourself, are you?"

"No. My shoulders feel better without the dumb brace."

She fisted her hands on her hips. "We're running out of time. How on earth can you be out of the mood?"

"I'm not sure I ever had it this evening even when you blackmailed me into getting the rope. I'm an old—"

Liz's glare cut him off. "And I'm young and exciting and the best thing you'll have the rest of your life. You should get hard from that."

Jim couldn't argue with impeccable reasoning. "You're getting pushy ... too demanding."

Liz was struck by the realization she was acting like a brat. "I'm sorry. I don't know what's come over me. Maybe it's realizing we only have tonight and tomorrow night left."

Jim felt sorry, too. She was right. She'd hurled his life into a different dimension, and in two days they would have to leave it. "What do you want to know about ropes?"

"How do you do it? Should I lay back and let you tie my hands and feet? Or do you tie me to the bed? And what do you do after I'm tied up?" She visualized the cuffs in the van. "Do you want me to resist? What does Marsha do?"

She was immediately sorry for saying it but apologizing could make things worse.

Jim would have preferred leaving Marsha out of their lovemaking for a host of reasons, but Liz seemed eager to do anything to please him. And his favorite thing about lovemaking was pleasing her. That was more important to him than achieving his own gratification.

"I wish I hadn't been cute when you mentioned seeing those things in the van, because you're going to be disappointed. The thought is more exciting than the doing, and I'm not an expert. A lady on a British TV show mentioned ropes ... with a sexual innuendo ... and it sounded interesting."

He recalled his misadventures. He'd asked Marsha if he could tie her up, and she surprised him by agreeing. He was more surprised when she enjoyed it.

The one time she tied him up, she did so reluctantly. He'd been unable to fantasize, and the event had become a major disappointment, for each of them.

His silence made Liz realize she'd been stupid to mention Marsha.

And why did she feel the need to be bound? After the previous evening, she shouldn't want to ever to see ropes, straps, or clamps again. Was she trying to recreate her fight with Jack and reenact her honeymoon tragedy with Don to give them happy endings? She'd heard it was therapeutic.

Regardless, imagining Jim's huge, rough hands stroking her, taking advantage of her as she lay struggling to move, excited her.

Liz then startled herself by recalling her dream with Jack—its surprise ending. She pictured Edie sitting on Jim's stomach as he lay bound in the trailer.

Jim gathered the courage to relate his experiment in bondage. "My tying up Marsha is something we've rarely done." He didn't mention that their lovemaking was similarly rare. "And we didn't think about her trying to prevent me. She held out her arms and legs, and I tied them to the bedposts. I fondled her until she became excited and then made love to her without untying her. I probably shouldn't be telling you this, but I'm giving you the whole nine yards."

Liz agreed that it didn't seem all that great. Disappointing even. "That isn't what I expected."

She raised her eyebrows inquisitively. "What made Marsha excited?"

"She fantasized."

"About what? Maybe that would help. Make a difference, I mean."

"She ... um ... said something about being captured by a pirate. And she mentioned being a village maiden initiated by an English Lord."

What would make those exciting? *Well, maybe Lord Jim.* "That's it?"

Jim nodded.

Liz recalled being roughly thrown into the van. "What I thought ... imagined ... after you told me some people did this, was you and Marsha..." *Lord, I'm talking about Marsha, again.* "Well, not her, someone more like Edie, struggling until you grabbed her and threw her on the bed."

I'm ruining everything.

Jim was amazed Liz could express her thoughts so easily after suffering a similar trauma the day before. She'd even brought Edie into the picture.

Liz continued. "I figured she'd make it hard for you to tie her up. I didn't picture anything past that. I guess that's why I felt excited. I imagined being your prisoner and having you rub your body all over me while I tried to escape. I figured you'd surprise me with the rest."

Jim reckoned that Liz's way did sound more intriguing.

Liz smiled impishly. "And I kind of want to tie you up, too."

She sighed. "Maybe I do have demons, like Don said. All I think about is making love with you. And the things you do to me ... and have me do for you. My lord."

Jim didn't know what to say. Or do. He'd thought he had when he got the rope and bandana. Now, it seemed pretty lame. He also didn't want to harm her injured arms and shoulders and couldn't see a way to restrain her without doing so.

He didn't have to.

Liz picked up the rope. "Stretch out."

At first startled, Jim became amused. Whatever he'd imagined, it wasn't this. He laughed.

Liz's eyes narrowed.

Jim kept laughing—until the rope smacked a red line across his belly with a loud crack. "*Ow.*" Your arms can't be that injured."

"This isn't funny. I mean it." She swatted him again. Harder.

The wind left Jim's lungs. Two red marks now crisscrossed his stomach. "Stop. That hurt."

"Then do what I say."

He wriggled and spread out on the bed.

No bedposts. Liz placed a hand on her hip and propped her chin on the other, wondering where to secure the short clothesline. It was barely long enough to bind his hands and feet. She managed to tie him to the corners of the bed railing. "Stay here."

"As if I could do anything el—"

Liz pinched him. "Quiet."

The pinch wasn't hard, but sufficient to make Jim jerk. The pain resulted from pulling through her fingernails. He was now more than a little concerned. Liz's demon was alive and in fine form. The bonds proved tight. Would the spider finally consume the fat, juicy fly? If so, there was now more of him to eat.

He heard her moving around in the living area.

"My, my, what do we have here?"

Liz returned, twirling the blue-checkered bandana he brought with him. The one he intended to blindfold her with, if she agreed, since Marsha found it exciting.

He didn't get the choice.

"Was my naughty little boy going to blindfold me? Let's see how you like it." She straddled him. "Raise your head, or I'll bite you where you've bitten me."

Jim made a mistake. "But you asked me to."

Liz scooted back, leaned forward and clamped a nipple between her teeth.

"*Ow.*"

"Did I bite you too hard?"

Jim wanted to say, yes, but the love-nip heightened his desire. "Only when I jerked back."

As she tied the bandana over his eyes, he became fearful. The only sources of lighting were rays of streetlight slipping past the edges of the room-darkening shades. Shadows created by the objects in between gave her a ghostly appearance. Her drying hair stood away from her head, grotesquely and chaotically. Her nose, flared by heavy breathing, was a ghostly white in a thin beam of light playing on her face. Her wide lips curved in a sinister pose. Her eyes appeared obsidian, peering at him like those of a malevolent creature lurking in the dark. The last thing he saw was a demon contemplating his fate.

Vertigo. He was drawn into a vortex.

Liz breasts broke the spell. She rubbed them back and forth across his chest. Across his nipples. The sensation jacked his libido to fully erect.

He felt her breasts slide down his stomach, massage his sex. Bounce against it. He'd been mistaken. He felt himself hardening even more.

Liz moaned at his response. She passed his burning hot sex between her breasts, weaved figure eights around it. Heard his fragmented breathing, felt him shudder. "You're so *hot*, lover."

All Jim could do was gasp. And throb.

His growing excitement stimulated Liz. She positioned herself until they were barely touching, then rotated her hips and slid back and forth. Sex against sex. "This is exquisite."

Her body exploded in orgasmic mode. She moved uncontrollably, gasped as her breathing quickened. Paralyzing spasms left her limp on Jim's splendid shaft, which pulsed against her, still not within her.

"OK, lover," she said, when she could again move, "this is for me since you didn't take the initiative, tonight." She clamped her teeth on a nipple. Chewed.

An electric-like shock blasted through his chest, down his stomach, and into his gut. "*Shit!*"

Liz released his nipple. "My, my, a regular potty mouth." She bit the other one.

Jim grunted as waves of unpleasant sensations gnawed through his body like those from the sound of fingernails scraping a chalkboard. Holding his breath, he somehow resisted the urge to pull away.

Liz nipped hard.

Jerking away, Jim yelped, "Oh, *damn*, that hurt."

"Now, aren't you sorry?"

Liz didn't wait for a response. "This is for you ... for not snitching to the cops."

Kneeling, she positioned him, shuddered as she took him in, and braced her hands against his shoulders. Her attempt to start slowly failed. She was immediately driven into orgasm by his fiery sex.

"I was wrong, lover, that was for both of us," she said after regaining her senses.

Supported by her powerful thighs, her movements became more urgent. Forceful. Jim found it impossible to match her rhythm. Her thrusts were sometimes uncomfortable, but eminently stimulating. "Oh, Liz, darling, I love you."

Driven by his words of love, she became too aggressive. Her alignment failed. Both cried out.

"Sorry, sweetheart."

She rode him through another peak, until her thighs trembled from exhaustion. Unable to stop, she slowed and did what he'd done to her—slowly unsheathed and recaptured him. They convulsed each time their plethora of nerve endings—created solely for sexual pleasure—converged. "Like what I'm doing, lover?"

Jim could barely breathe. He didn't have any fantasies other than the one on top of him stimulating every erogenous zone on his body. And mind. He wanted to caress Liz's body, knead her infinitely malleable breasts. "Please, release me."

"Sorry."

He tried working his hands loose. Unable to do it, he understood Marsha's frustration.

Their lovemaking quickened, became insistent. The room filled with uneven, ragged gasping. When Liz expelled her loud, guttural cry, Jim felt like Mount St. Helens. He thought the pulsations wouldn't end.

"Good. That's it. Fill me, sweetheart."

Moving slowly, Liz deliberately milked him. Another ghost banished. One that sent her into hysterics eleven years earlier. It now completed her, gave her purpose. *Damned birth control pills.*

The constant thunder Jim heard was the beating of his heart. Though exhilarated, relishing sparks and lifts in his groin that should have ended long before, he agonized. Had he released, was he nurturing, a demon of pleasure in

Liz? One she might not be able to control?

Liz's body quaked. Despite the fire of their previous lovemaking, she hadn't experienced such uncontrollable lust followed by such intense gratification.

Tears of joy rained down as she smothered Jim's face with caresses and kisses. She wanted his child. She'd given him her emotional virginity, and for that, would love him forever.

She started moving gently when she felt him start to soften within her. She didn't want to stop. Didn't have to. Her love slave was beneath her—tied to her bed.

Trapped like a bird in a cage.

57
Birds of a Feather

Drenched in sweat from the morning humidity, his task less than half complete, Jim watched Liz jog away from him. The woman was a slave driver, not only for him, but for herself. She must be aching from the pummeling Jack West gave her accidentally, if not on purpose. And last night.... *No rest for the weary. Or the wicked. It had been one hell of a ride.*

Unlike his previous dabbling in the dark side of romance, Liz had provided mind-numbing delight for them both. Had it been her enthusiastic role playing?

After they'd fallen asleep—she on top of him—he'd awakened to the uncomfortable pins and needles sensation in his left arm and called her name. She'd fumbled with the knots, and they'd crashed without showering.

He was now on an early morning walk while she jogged. She ran in his direction, forearms braced against her chest to support her aching shoulders, which mounded her breasts. She wore his T-shirt with the green iguana. Off her left shoulder, it made her look extra sexy.

She blew a kiss when she ran past. "Hi, lover." She stared wantonly. "Looking *good.*"

He was a trooper, she thought, in more ways than one. He'd acquiesced without complaint to her demand that he didn't eat breakfast until after accompanying her on her run. He'd been a super trooper the previous evening—taking her torments and giving her the best lovemaking of her budding sex life.

Besides being sweaty, she was wet. She looked forward to the rest of the day. The rest of her life. She sighed through heavy breathing. Life was incredible, beautiful, wonderful. Jim was her muse, her life force. With him, even the worst things in life could be meaningful, keep life worth living.

The thought brought her back to reality. She stared around and saw nothing suspicious. Jogging once meant freedom, but the incident with Jack left her nervous. He had proven she couldn't count on her strength to protect her from a strong man. Or someone with a weapon. Should he have Edie drive the van beside her, he could attack her, and she could resist only so long. It could be the same with other sex fiends. She wouldn't jog alone or unprotected again, and she would carry her cellphone and pepper spray.

She peered over her shoulder. It was time to head back toward Jim.

When they returned to the RV park, the swimming pool beckoned, after Jim's long, hot walk. The wound on his leg had scabbed over, and the redness had been replaced by a light green cast, so he knew the water posed no danger. Neither did he doubt that Dr. Gutierrez would release him the next morning.

He dove into the pool to see if he could swim a lap but ran out of wind long before reaching the end of the pool—a fifty-yard marathon.

Gasping, he clung to the edge, recalling how he loved to swim in his youth. If he became fit, he'd do it again. Perhaps even compete in U.S. Masters swim meets. That should give him incentive to stay in shape.

They showered together in Liz's cabin. She asked him to soap her body.

Lord, he loved holding her tender breasts in his hands and having them pressed against him. He traced the veins visible in her alabaster chest. Soaped her slippery back and buttocks. Kneeled to wash her long legs.

But this morning she reserved her lower abdomen for herself. She soaped gingerly.

"Anything wrong?"

"I guess I got a little carried away last night."

"We probably need to slow down, huh?"

Liz pushed to arm's length and fixed him with her patented stare. "Are you nuts? Haven't you heard? No pain, no gain."

She laughed and rubbed her tummy against his glistening belly.

They ate breakfast in the RV—same old sumptuous repast, topped off with juice and fruit.

They decided to forego birding and go sight-seeing instead. They wouldn't even take their cameras. Afterward, they would do their laundry to prevent having much to do when they arrived back at their respective homes. Jim imagined Marsha's surprise.

The tour of the USS Lexington in Corpus Christi Bay took longer than they'd expected. The ship was huge, a town with its own airport. Three thousand officers and enlisted personnel lived on it while the ship was commissioned.

They marveled at the planes that once landed on its flight deck, as they checked out the many aircraft displayed there. They entered the ship's gun turrets, climbed up to the bridge like enthusiastic children, and viewed informational videos in the living and eating quarters, ship's laundry, and stores. The mess hall contained beautiful paintings of naval aircraft.

Afterwards, they toured the adjacent Texas State Aquarium.

"I have to pet a stingray," Liz said. Jim did, too.

They posed beside sculptures of whales, sea turtles, and herons. They empathized with rescued raptors, pelicans, and birds forever unable to fly. The dolphin show thrilled them, and they had fun watching divers feed fish.

Liz wore an outfit not unlike her morning attire—another of his Ts that dropped well off her shoulder. It revealed translucent skin and eye-popping cleavage. Her shorts, sports socks, and hiking shoes enhanced her long-legged, Amazonian appearance that magnetized the eyeballs of every man in the vicinity.

Jim didn't see her reciprocate, but knew she had to be aware of the emotions her attire engendered. The thought nagged his subconscious.

Liz was well aware of her effect on the men around her. She was sowing wild oats, and the object of her dreams was standing beside her. He would harvest a crop that evening. She felt empowered. Other men could scratch their heads and wonder what she saw in him that she didn't see in them.

She briefly wondered if she was taking her fury at Jack and Don out on every other man on the planet by tantalizing them with something they couldn't have. She decided she wasn't. She was making use of the opportunity fortune gifted her at Paradise Pond.

She grasped Jim's arm and pulled it hard against the side of her breast. Her heart raced with love, whispering *Go to Oklahoma. Become his mistress.*

They stumbled onto a small park containing colorful dolphin statues. One was a patriot painted red, white, and blue and covered with stars. An astronaut dolphin wore a space helmet. A cowboy dolphin sported a Stetson hat and held a lasso.

Jim stood transfixed. "Aren't they beautiful?"

"I want my photo with each, Jim. Here's my phone."

The park contained a playground. He watched her rock on a seahorse mounted on springs for children to ride. It easily supported her weight, and she laughed happily—like a giant child.

Liz tried to pull herself, hand-by-hand, down a high bar and managed only two, but not many women her age could accomplish that feat, especially someone whose arms had nearly been wrenched from their sockets two days earlier.

They played on the swings and slid down the slide.

"I think it's swaying a bit in the middle there, buster."

It was Jim's turn to stick his tongue at her.

She responded by blowing him a kiss.

"Liz, I wish you could be my personal trainer. I wouldn't dare defy a dominatrix like you," he joked. Instead of the laughter he expected, she grew wistful. Her sadness caused a lump in his throat. It was their last day together. Had three weeks flown by this quickly?

Liz wished they were single. Age didn't matter. She wanted to spend the rest of her life with him, but it was a pipe dream. He had a soul mate. And becoming his mistress was too risky. Thus far, no pictures had surfaced, and she hadn't received a call from her mother berating her for having an affair, but that could end in a heartbeat.

And there was Marsha. She couldn't allow herself to come between them ever again.

They reclined in the grass, talking about what they wanted to do with their lives.

"I wish I could follow my heart and do whatever I wanted," Liz said, meaning going with him.

"And the money to do it with," Jim added.

She slapped his arm. "Stop being funny."

She was right, he realized. It was a melancholy day.

After lunching in the Bakery Diner in Aransas Pass, they didn't arrive back at Palm Gardens until after 4:00 p.m.

The ferry ride across the ship channel was the end of a fairytale morning and magical afternoon. Dolphins surfaced, puffed, and rolled in the clear water. Terns and pelicans dove into a school of fish, bayside of the boat, and gulls feasted on the remains. Their raucous cries filled the air.

Life couldn't be better.

* * *

"What the *hell* do *you* want?" Edith's face contorted in anger, but she resisted hanging up. "Yesterday, you told me to screw myself."

She'd contacted Jack the previous day to apologize for not being able to warn him about Teddy and found Jack in a belligerent mood. She'd suffered a tirade of verbal abuse—been harangued for every disaster in the universe since the Big Bang.

"Aw, it wasn't that bad," Jack said soothingly, sounding like he was holding his nose. "I was just upset. I didn't mean anything by it."

"Bull hockey. You ranted that I messed things up by tossing your persuaders." His actual verbiage would have wilted cactus needles. "Remember what I told you about going to jail? Where would we be if I hadn't saved your butt?

"And it was you the old couple saw ripping off the girl's clothes. What a blockhead. Couldn't you have waited until she was in the wagon to ogle her breasts?"

"Aw, Edie, she hit me. And her blouse was an accident."

"You could have backed off and given her a chance to think things through. What on earth did you do to make her hit you?"

"Nothing. I swear. Her mother's right. I think it was weird foreplay."

"Crap. Pure crap. You pressured her too much."

"She looked guilty, took my hand, and went with me. I thought she was going in the van."

"You scared her, and she was confused. The girl's clean."

"You didn't see her face in the van. She was ready."

"She was ready, all right, ready for Teddy to coldcock you into slumber land. She was distracting you so that you wouldn't see him coming."

"That brings us back to yesterday. I still think you could've warned me."

She'd been mostly naked, delirious from an unbelievable kiss, enjoying bliss. Then mad as hell about the interruption. "I was looking for my pistol."

She had no idea what Teddy did with the condom.

"Oh, well," Jack grumbled, "the good news is that we're home free. We've got her and her dim-witted pet on assault charges."

"That's as dangerous. The girl's parents have money, and sooner or later, one of their lawyers is going to question why we were on the beach ... together ... when you're supposedly a happily married man."

"You're right. I'm sorry. I was wrong." Jack tried sounding as pleasant as he could. At least she was still talking to him. "Please, forgive me."

Edith wanted to end the call but couldn't. "And what was that donkey doodle about me taking the rap so it wouldn't hurt your standing in the community? You bastard! Mr. Big Shot! Mr. Religiosity! If I told the media all the things you've done, you'd be Mr. Little Turd. Your wife would get everything you have except your privates. She'd cut those off and give them to your grandkids for crab bait."

Jack let her wind down, hoping she'd cool off. If so, he'd soon talk her into joining him.

When she ran out of expletives, he apologized again. "I'm sorry and I mean it, Edie. Let's meet so I can make things right. How about the San Juan Restaurant? My treat."

"You *jerk*. You still want a piece of that girl, don't you? You're one dumb butthole, hell-bent on going to prison. Well, you can go without me."

"Come on, Edie." Jack had surprised himself when he called her that at the beach, but it fit.

Even though she knew he was calling her Edie to put her at ease, Edith liked it. And she didn't know why, but she felt the urge to accept. Well, maybe she did. "There are lots of places closer."

"Hey, we can have Mexican and a brew. Kiss and make up. Whatcha say?"

"What time?"

58
Bird's Eye Views

Liz and Jim carried their clothes hampers to the park's laundry, which contained a bank of commercial washers and dryers and a row of stainless-steel tables for folding clothes. Comfortable chairs, a flat screen TV, and a library of magazines and novels were available to pass the time.

They talked instead.

"I apologize for mentioning Edie's name last night. You know, before the game," Liz said apprehensively.

"You mean that was only fun and games? No love?"

"No, it was love. Trust me, Jim. It was love."

"Then why the apology?"

"Well, I haven't seen Marsha. And there was no way I could use my mother for what I had in mind, although she deserves it. No, in my daydream, I had you punish Edie for what she did to you ... trying to get you drunk and into bed. It worked me up. Maybe it was revenge for what she and Jack tried to do to us."

"So, I have Edie to thank for last night?"

Liz looked sheepish. "Yeah. And there's ... well ... from what you told me, she looks something like Marsha, and Marsha refused to come help you."

Jim reflected. Liz was right. Though younger, shorter and less plump, Edie shared Marsha's facial features and curves. And, he hated to admit, Edie had the more pleasant face—seductive. But that was part of her ploy. "Yes, she does, but I didn't think about it before you mentioned it."

"Did you notice her eyes? It made me mad when she dragged you into the trailer, but I didn't know why until yesterday, when I was fantasizing my ... your revenge."

Jim recalled Edie's eyes. They'd made him uneasy when they met on the beach and nervous in the trailer. Make that downright uncomfortable. Maybe that's why he'd remained suspicious. "Yeah, they looked like..." He searched for a word.

"Maggie's."

The name poked Jim in the gut. "You're right. I'll be doggone."

"Looking back, Jim, I should have known they were up to no good. Ms. PI was undressed to kill ... what with that low neckline and shorts unfit for teenagers ... and she looked like she was grabbing a Snickers bar when she grabbed your arm."

Liz tried to imitate Edie's words. "Has anyone ever told you that you look like a big old teddy bear?"

She intended to be sarcastic, but the words came out way too low and way too funny and she snorted in laughter.

Jim belted out laughing.

"Jim, that woman could taste you, and something in my mind warned me to stop her. Thank goodness things turned out like they did. Can you imagine what would've happened if the ranger had discovered Jack chaining me in the van ... after ripping off the rest of my clothes ... and found Edith bouncing on you like a mattress?"

Visualizing her description, Jim burst into another fit of laughter. "Liz, you should feel guilty for accusing me of thinking too much."

But her words forced him to remember. It was pure luck the incident didn't end up exactly like Liz envisioned. He wondered if his frequent lovemaking contributed. Since he'd met Liz, his body hadn't been under his control for the first time since he was in high school.

He rationalized. It had been well more than a month since making love to Marsha when he began this odyssey, so he was in a weakened condition to begin with. But it was still disconcerting to discover his willpower and morals weren't what he believed them to be three weeks earlier.

He left to take his evening pill.

"Sorry, I've been thinking again," Liz confessed when he returned. "Besides worrying about blackmail ... before I belted Jack ..." She wore a curious smile.

It gave Jim pause, but venting could be cathartic.

"It looked like he was hiding a baby elephant in his pants."

The statement conked Jim like a mental two by four. He absolutely didn't want to hear the rest but sticking his fingers in his ears and humming didn't seem like an option.

"His look told me I didn't have another alternative, and I thought you were ... well ... indisposed. It was stay, fight, or flight, and I didn't even think of flight. I'm sorry I didn't, but at the time I thought my only options were doing what he said or resisting."

Jim patted her hand. "All that's in the past."

Liz fixed him with a look of adoration. "Thanks. It's a good thing he reminded me of someone else."

"Don?" Jim asked, imagining the agony she must have gone through.

Eyeing him lustfully, she shook her head.

Addled by the off-the-wall nonverbal he hadn't seen coming, he became stupid, like his friends—especially Bill—chided him at every opportunity.

"I'm not," he sputtered.

"Oh, yes you *are*." She squeezed his knee. "You aren't anything to sneeze at. More like something to write home about."

"But Don? How can you tell in the dark?"

Liz rolled her eyes. "You and Jack. Either way. Lord, what an initiation."

The red glow on Jim's cheeks lighted the laundry room, as he became even more worried about their relationship, its effect on Liz, on him. How things would have been better off left to a professional and that he was the one at fault.

They discussed Jack and Edie. Jim reasoned, and Liz agreed, that they couldn't go through life hating people and plotting revenge. Life was too short, and they were responsible for their own happiness. It didn't have to be a run-of-the-mill, rose-colored-glasses type of happiness, it could be rose-colored-glasses-made-in-Missouri. Sensible, logical happiness. Justice might win out, but they couldn't hold their breaths. And they couldn't deny their own complicity.

They would have to deal with the courts and police for a long time. The incident hadn't made the local media, probably due to Jack's position and influence, but their families would soon become aware of it. The bad news was the authorities were attributing it to Liz's reckless behavior.

59
The Fallout

It was after 6:00 p.m. when they put away their clean laundry. With time for a final attempt at the least grebes, they headed to Paradise Pond. They turned on their cameras as soon as they stepped from the SUV.

A scarlet tanager swooped above a yellow-flowering shrub in the first flower garden, snapped up a wasp, and flew to the nearest tree to dine.

Jim observed it through Helen's binoculars. Other than the tanager's black wings and tail and a slash of white on its sides, it was vivid red—florescent in the light shade. A much deeper red than cardinals., he found it altogether marvelous.

"Beautiful, isn't it?" Liz said.

"It's the reddest bird I've ever seen. It takes my breath away."

Liz squeezed his arm and mouthed a kiss. "Scarlet tanagers are superbly scarlet, but those black wings and tail feathers knock them out of the red bird of the year awards."

"I guess cardinals *are* redder overall."

Jim heard one singing and turned toward the sound. A male sat on the motel fence, singing for his sugar babe.

"Not cardinals," Liz corrected. "The champions are male summer tanagers. Perhaps we'll see some in the willows, eating poor little bees and wasps like this fellow's doing."

Orioles were the birds de jour. Or so they thought when they reached the turn in the sidewalk at the end of the motel fence. Across the narrow pond arm, a myriad of the gold and black birds aggressively jostled and squabbled over the many orange halves pinned on limbs and nails. At least one plucked sweet fruit out of each rind.

Camera clicks reached a crescendo as they took dozens of shots trying to capture the brilliant birds in all poses—eating, balancing precariously, wings flapping, pecking away encroachers.

Baltimore orioles made up the bulk of the diners, but smaller and darker male orchard orioles and mustard-yellow females snuck in when they could. Black-headed and rose-breasted grosbeaks cut in when they desired. Blue indigo buntings and their brown mates took advantage of temporarily vacated oranges. Jim marked them on his bird list and turned right, toward the boardwalk entrance.

Liz tapped his arm. "Jim, there, in the weeds, a golden-winged warbler."

A four-and-a-half-inch bird hopped and pecked in the leaves. Mostly gray, its throat was black like a chickadee's. Jim's eyes were attracted to its yellow forehead and golden wing bars. A black mask bordered in white surrounded its eyes.

Many birdwatchers viewed it through their binoculars or frantically tried to take its picture. Fumbling with his camera, Jim joined them. The bird played peek-a-boo in a thick canopy of short plants with nasturtium-like leaves. Jim shook his head and peered at Liz. "This is tough."

She nodded. "Don't you wish we could shoot something easy ... like an elk?"

They snapped a few photos and left the warbler to other admirers.

They walked ten paces, beyond a mass of trees and dead limbs, to where birdwatchers were focusing their attention on a bird near the water. They eased forward. "What is it?" Liz asked the first person they approached.

"A mourning warbler eating a larva. Over there. On the log in the water."

"Jim, look," Liz said unnecessarily.

He was trying to compose his shot of the dark-headed warbler that had penetrating black eyes. Its olive-green back contrasted with the rest of its body. The yellow-bellied, black-bibbed bird was tenderizing its meal by smacking it against a short nub of a limb. "Incredible, Liz, two more lifers. It's been some trip."

After working their way around the mourning warbler group, they joined the Kentucky warbler, common yellowthroat, ovenbird, and Lincoln's sparrow cluster of birdwatchers at the edge of the Brazilian pepper trees.

Hopping and scratching about in the dead leaves beside and beneath the trees, the well-mannered group of tiny warblers and lone intruder ignored the mass of bird lovers focusing on them with binoculars and cameras.

The day became brighter for Jim, even as the sun dipped further into the trees on the other side of Paradise Pond. He fired away at the olive-backed, yellow-necked and bellied Kentucky warbler. Its black Fu Manchu-looking mustache designated it a male. Unfortunately, its erratic movements and frequent vanishing acts beneath the pepper trees made a good shot problematic.

Common yellowthroats were common this time of year, so they didn't hold his interest. The males looked similar to Kentucky warblers, but instead of whisker markings on their faces, black masks topped with a bluish-white wash were their prominent feature.

Streaky, brown and tan Lincoln's sparrows frequented the woods near his home in Oklahoma, so his second series of shots focused on the ovenbird that bobbed and wagged like a waterthrush. Large for a warbler, at six inches, the ovenbird had pronounced white eye-rings, light-pink legs, and an orange crown sandwiched between dark stripes. Its white breast and belly, splotched with dark-brown streaks, contrasted with its dull olive-brown back.

Jim's wheeled when Liz grasped his arm and pointed. "God is good, and we blew most of the afternoon doing laundry."

"What is it?"

"A chestnut-sided warbler. See the reddish streaks along its sides."

The five-inch bird had a bright yellow crown like the golden-winged warbler, but its back was a streaky brown and black. In place of a mask, its face bore a horizontal Y—if one included its black bill. "Three lifers," he whispered. "It doesn't get any better than this."

A fourth first joined the list of checkmarks on Jim's bird list.

"Maggies!" Liz shouted jubilantly.

"Maggies?"

Busy taking photos, she didn't answer.

"It's a pair of magnolia warblers," said a smiling woman Jim saw frequently at Paradise pond and the birding center. "They're obviously your first. Don't you love fallouts?"

She nodded to her right. "There's a bay-breasted warbler working the willows at the boardwalk, in case you haven't seen one of those, either."

Jim thanked her and began trying to photograph a Maggie. He took several excellent shots of bare limbs and green leaves before nailing one of the bright-yellow-chinned, yellow-breasted, yellow-rumped birds. Its black necklace trailed black bangles down its sides.

"They look like Zorro," he whispered.

A black mask, unbroken except for split white eye-rings, extended into a black cape. A splash of white separated the mask from their blue-gray crowns. The female lacked the black mask and cape.

Dusk hurried them along to Jim's fifth life-bird. The bay-breasted assassin fed at a more leisurely pace, so it became Jim's favorite of the day. He exulted in Liz being by his side. He enjoyed sharing life experiences, and Marsha seldom birded with him.

The warbler's rusty-red crown topped its black face and cream-colored nape. Vivid black streaks graced its gray back and shoulders. A cinnamon band extended from its chin to its flanks above a bright white belly.

"I was wrong," Jim laughed happily. "Now, it can't get any better."

Just then, a male summer tanager lit above him, carrying a hapless bee in its bill. He took a couple of shots and studied the bird through his binoculars. Its wings were slightly darker than the red on the rest of its body, but it was entirely red. "I see what you mean about summer tanagers, Liz."

They observed black-throated green warblers plucking insects from the white, cottony willow fuzz. "That's as close to the golden-cheeked warbler as we'll see this trip," Liz said.

When the deepening dusk made photography iffy, they shut off their cameras and checked the blackboard on the motel fence.

Paradise Pond had lived up to its name that day. In addition to the warblers they'd seen, the warbler list included American redstarts, cerulean, prairie, Blackburnian, yellow, prothonotary, yellow-throated, and yellow-breasted chat.

The flycatcher list included empids, vermillion, scissor-tailed, and great-crested flycatchers, eastern phoebe, eastern wood peewee, eastern and Couch's kingbirds.

Indigo, painted, and lazuli buntings were posted. As were thrushes—veery, hermit, Swainson's, and wood thrushes. Among the vireos were blue-headed, Philadelphia, warbling, red-eyed, white-eyed, and yellow-throated.

Liz pointed out ladder-backed woodpecker, yellow-breasted sapsucker, yellow-billed cuckoo, and bronzed cowbird.

The list seemed endless, and Jim lamented not spending the day there. Many would have been lifers. The list provided incentive for returning the following year.

The sounds of night insects filled the air. Black-crowned night-herons edged forward from their daytime hideaways in preparation to depart for meals of aquatic animals and insects when darkness arrived.

The trip to the parking lot held one last surprise.

"A Canada warbler!" Liz squealed, nudging Jim around her. "Go ahead and shoot with the flash. I know a trick for the eyes."

The bluish-gray bird's eye rings and yellow *spectacles* caught Jim's attention. Black feathers encompassed its face, graced its cheeks, and formed a black, dangly necklace on its lemon-yellow breast.

Liz leaned against Jim and breathed heavily into his ear. Her statement made his camera useless.

"I should have worn Depends, I want you *so* much."

Having just parked in the San Juan parking lot, Jack jolted. His quarry was walking toward him, and he hadn't injured the witch's arms that badly. She was lugging her heavy camera and lens. He slid lower in the seat and watched her and her dimwitted companion stroll by. Awed by her body and hip movements, he vowed to kidnap her, no matter the cost, even jail, as Edie warned.

At 7:40 p.m. he decided Edie had changed her mind about meeting him. Just as he placed the tip on the table, she entered. He hailed her, but she continued peering around the room. He moved to her and gripped her arm. "Didn't you see me over there waving at you?"

She eyed him suspiciously. "Who are you? I'm looking for a Mr. West."

"Very funny." Jack dragged her to the table.

Edie wouldn't let him off easy. "My, aren't you a beauty ... nose taped up, smashed lip, blackened left eye swollen shut. How did your other eye miss out on the fun?"

She cocked her head. "Jackie, with those cute little scrape marks all over the side of your face you should try out for the *Phantom of the Opera*. And you sound like you're talking through a toilet paper tube." She smirked. "What does Amanda think of all of this?"

"As you well know, I was preoccupied, when someone who should have been occupied, blind-sided me."

"Well, if the dunce of the class had promised a mutual acquaintance that no money would change hands and she could choose the time of the rendezvous, I could be home snuggling with a teddy bear," Edie snapped.

"Between the two of you I could start a stable in Kentucky. And, Mr. Always-Has-To-Be-Right, I had him bedded before he jumped up to save his damsel ... who shouldn't have been in distress."

Jack knew he deserved her belittling, so he played the gentleman and bought the enchilada dinner she wanted and all the Mexican light beer he could funnel into her. Then coaxed and flattered.

She gradually warmed to him. "Okay, *Don Quixo*te, what are you after?"

"You can read me like a book, Edie."

"I can read all my third-graders' minds. Now, what do you want?"

Jack lowered his voice. "I want to screw the girl."

"You'll get screwed, all right. After what we've done, they won't have to sit a jury. Jackie, what are you thinking?"

"You can knock on her door and change your voice or something. When she opens it, I'll jump inside, and we'll tie her up."

"You're nuts, if you think I'm going to have any part of this."

"You can join the fun, Edie. You'd like that."

She felt a stirring. "Yes, but what about all those guys and girls in the pokey who are going to enjoy our innocent young bodies? Why do you think they call it the pokey? Or is that one of the perks of this venture?"

"Edie, we'll have our fun and leave the country." He made a frame with his fingers. "Picture it. Me and you ... in Cancún ... like you've always wanted."

"Then count me in. She won't recognize you anyway. Not with that mask you're wearing."

60
A Bird in Hand

Jim and Liz wasted little time on supper their last night together, but they took the time to clean the RV to surprise Marsha.

Liz's abdomen twitched. She lowered her voice. "Time for my cabin, lover boy."

"I'll be over later. After I call Marsha."

She nodded and hurried to her cabin to prepare for their evening. After finishing, she readied for her trip home. When Jim didn't appear within twenty minutes, she wondered what was delaying him. *If he's showering in the bathhouse, I'll strangle him with the stupid rope.*

She was killing time editing photos, when she heard a knock on the door. Reluctant to open it without first checking, she called out, "Who is it?"

No answer.

She saw no one through the peephole and edged to the window to peek out. A park maintenance man, sitting on his utility cart, spoke with someone out of her line of sight. If he was talking to Jim, Jim would soon knock, so she moved to her laptop and shut it down.

She was about to go outside when she remembered that she, too, should call home. No need to risk their evening being interrupted.

Helen answered, her tone cool. "Hello, Mary Elizabeth. Are you coming home, tomorrow?"

"No, Mother, not till Friday. Jim's appointment is late tomorrow afternoon," she lied.

Liz spoke last with her father. He eventually asked the questions Helen avoided. "Has the matter with the private investigators been resolved?"

"Somewhat. We'll discuss it Friday."

"What do you plan to do about Donald?"

"I'm still making up my mind."

"I'll support you, whatever you decide."

Liz's throat tightened. "Thanks, Daddy. I love you."

* * *

Jack lingered with the maintenance man while Edie bristled. She felt sure Jack's bandaged nose and badly bruised face were why the attendant asked if he could be of service. If the girl disappeared now, his description of Jack would lead the world to the obvious conclusion.

Taking matters in her own hands, she yanked Jack away. "Come on, hubby, we'll be cutting it close at that late movie at Sunrise Mall."

"What were you trying to do, make sure that guy could pick you out of the lineup? We're going back to Corpus. *Now.*"

"Un-uh. We'll hang around and come back later. The rope in the back seat has got the girl's name on it."

"Jackie, I'm through putting up with your crap. You know I can spot playgirls, and Ms. Liz isn't one of them. All she thinks about is her camera and those silly birds. That and knocking a few pounds off Teddy." She resisted patting Jack's belly. "You could stand to lose a few pounds, yourself."

"Losing twenty pounds wouldn't hurt you, either," he hissed.

Ignoring the comment, Edie took another approach. "Let's drive around until things settle down."

She kept trying to convince him his idea was flawed. "If the girl sees your rope, she'll pass out. Then, what will you do? That would be like humping a pillow."

Her attempts failed, but the drive around Robert's Point Park, out to the south jetty, and along the beach provided pleasant views.

* * *

Jim's call to Marsha lasted longer than he expected. Then John West and Billy Carlton showed him two huge kingfish and a giant cobia they'd caught. That lead to a long chat.

Liz glared when he arrived. "What took you so long? I'm out of the mood now, so do you want to play cards? How about two-handed Pegs and Jokers?"

Confused by her spitefulness, he followed her to the couch. "I ran into my pals. I told them I was leaving tomorrow, and we talked because we won't see each other until next spring. They asked about you, too."

"A likely story."

"And Marsha felt like talking."

That delay was important. "What did she say? Has she calmed down any?"

"Actually, she has. After all, she's in her element. Keeping her away from her grandchildren and great-grandchildren would be like cutting off her legs. She'll be home on Saturday and says she's anxious to see me."

He omitted Marsha's comment about something much more intimate.

Liz toyed with him a few more minutes. Unable to wait longer, she lit candles and turned off the lights. "Shower time."

She undressed Jim, shook hands with a certain part of his anatomy, and used it as a leash to lead him to the shower. There, she surprised him again. She lathered him into trembling excitement—until he thought he might not make it to the bedroom—and turned her back on him.

Stepping out of the shower, she wrapped a large towel around her and acted like lovemaking was the farthest thing from her mind.

"Have I done something wrong?" he asked.

Inwardly so excited that she thought he could see her heart thumping, Liz pouted. "It's what you haven't done."

This might take all night. Jim decided on the direct approach. "What have I *not* done?"

"You haven't asked where the ropes are. You'll find them under the bed. Tonight's your turn."

Jim grinned and tried to pick her up to carry her to the bedroom. When she pulled away, he figured resistance was part of her game play.

It became a struggle. Trying not to injure her arms and shoulders proved a daunting task. She used them to her advantage. Teeth, too. He was sweating by the time he pinned her to the bed.

Oops, no rope.

As soon as he lessened his grip, Liz slipped beneath him. He felt the tip of her tongue. Her lips. Her mouth.

When she finally cleared his body and bolted, Jim collapsed on the bed. *I need a cardiologist.*

Liz berated herself for acting impulsively. Jim hadn't followed. Was he deciding what to say—how to tell her he was leaving? She would beg his forgiveness.

Jim found the rope cut into four pieces. Liz's demon had a good imagination. It made it easier for him one way, while taxing his strength and determination in another.

And that experiment. Her innate curiosity might be the death of him. He hoped she wouldn't be the death of anyone else. Or herself. He feared she might not be able to control her exponentially expanding sexual appetite.

What could he do about that? Warning her probably wasn't a good idea. Telling people what they shouldn't do, seldom was. Look what he'd been taught in church and read in the Bible about adultery all his life. And here he was—chasing a married woman around a cabin, trying to tie her to a bed.

But his troubling thoughts and doing what was right didn't provide enough incentive for him to quit her game. He secured the ropes to the corners of the bed.

"Lover, come here," he demanded.

No answer.

"Stop being naughty."

He hoped guests in the adjoining cabins couldn't hear him.

"If you make me come get you, you'll be sorry."

Knees drawn to her chest, arms around her shins, Liz huddled happily on the couch.

When he entered the room and ordered her into the bedroom, she shook her head.

"OK. You asked for it."

"No. You can't make me go to bed with you."

When he grasped her, she sunk her teeth into his shoulder.

Jim grabbed her short hair and wrenched her head back—taking care to be as gentle as he could—but he wouldn't risk getting bitten again. He wanted to stroke and kiss her long, delicate neck, but she glared hatefully in the flickering candlelight.

Fearing it the result of Monday's terror, he released her.

Liz fisted her hands on her hips. "Come on, Jim, make it real."

Game on. He manhandled her over his knees and swatted her rump.

"Ow!" She squirmed, trying to get away.

When Jim raised his hand a second time, she managed to place her hands over her buttocks. He pulled them away and pinned them with his leg. "Are you going to be a good girl and do what I ask?"

She shook her head defiantly and received a blistering slap on her reddened cheek.

Gasping, Liz cried out. "I'll go."

To prevent her from escaping, Jim led her by her hair to the bedroom. "Kneel."

He barely avoided the knee rising toward his groin.

"You, young woman, are no lady."

He shoved Liz forcefully onto the bed. Capturing her legs, he grabbed a foot and tickled.

Liz jerked, yanked, and howled in laughter. "I give. I surrender. What do you want me to do?"

"Kneel at the end of the bed and hold out your arms."

Nodding, she obeyed.

Jim tied her wrists to headboard. Knotting the rope above her knees, he drew her thighs tight against the end of the bed.

Bent forward, head and torso on the bed, knees and toes on the floor, Liz breasts were squashed uncomfortably against the hard mattress. She tested her restraints. She wasn't going anywhere. "This isn't fair. I let you lay on the bed."

After making sure the ropes weren't cutting off blood flow, Jim silently patted and rubbed her incomparable derriere.

Naked and exposed—arms and legs spread apart—Liz felt vulnerable. More so than with Don or Jack. "Um … Jim, I've changed my mind. Let me go."

"Now for a hairbrush."

"A hairbrush? You *wouldn't*."

He found Liz's flat, oval-shaped, previously abandoned hairbrush and smacked it loudly into his palm. "This should do it."

"*No*. No!"

Liz struggled against her bonds. The bed squeaked and swayed. "You can't do this. I was gentle with you last night." She felt herself wetting.

"I don't think a jury would believe that my bruised lips and nipples are the result of your gentleness, so hold still."

He's actually going to do it. "Please, lover, no."

The shaking bed sounded like broken bagpipes.

Liz's body convulsed, vibrated with pleasure. "I can't believe this."

Waves of delightful impulses surged throughout her lower abdomen. "Jim, I love you. I love you."

He was caught off-guard by the effect of a threat he didn't intend to carry out. *Is this the same woman I thought couldn't have an orgasm?*

He caressed her rump and slipped his hand between her legs.

Liz thrashed in pleasure as his fingers rubbed, stroked, and plumbed until, shrieking in joy and relishing spasms, she crossed a mountain range.

Jim untied, cuddled, and kissed her until her chest stopped heaving and her breathing calmed. "Get on the bed and lie on your back."

She joyfully spread-eagled herself.

Jim kissed each wrist before securing it to the headboard. He did the same to each ankle before tying them to the bed legs. He then sat beside her and slid a rough hand the length of the left side of her body—toes, leg, to her belly, with a quick diversion to where her legs converged.

Liz shuddered in delight as his hand made the journey. She moaned when his fingers worked their magic. Grunted when a prickly fingertip encircled her belly button. Begged for more as fingers tugged her left nipple. Gasped as the rough hand slid from there to her shoulder, the length of her neck, the side of her face, and forehead.

When he reversed the procedure, she waited in eager anticipation. She was so prepared for her right side to get equal treatment that she pre-anticipated the squeeze of her right breast and squealed—just as his hand bypassed it at the last second.

"Didn't you miss something?"

"Quiet."

Jim toyed with her belly button. The chill shot from her navel to her head and down her legs.

Jim's odyssey continued, but he avoided her groin and caressed her hips.

Tormented, Liz desperately wanted his fingers to reach her goal. "Please come back loving hands."

A loving hand smacked her thigh. It stung sufficiently that she yelped and struggled against the ropes. She thought her mind would fry.

"What did I order you to do?"

"Nothing."

It might be her game, but Jim controlled the game board. He stroked her smooth hip and thigh.

"You're torturing me, lover."

Chuckling evilly, Jim lowered his lips to her belly and kissed his way to her sweet sex.

"Damn it, Jim, untie me and make love with me ... *now*."

"My rules," he said, as her body unleashed itself in a frenzy of movement.

Empowered, he found the places on her body that became rigid, made her shudder and quake, squeal and moan, call out his name. He took her to too many hillocks and mountaintops to count.

Liz drifted in a glorious dream—floating above a field of daisies covered in goldfinches and Monarch butterflies. They swarmed her. The birds' feet and tiny nails sent sparks rippling across her body. The butterflies congregated, fluttering at the junction of her legs, on her mons. She convulsed in pleasure. Squealed in delight.

Though drained, utterly exhausted, her body still wasn't under her control. It did Jim's bidding. When he positioned himself on top of her, she begged softly, "Please, untie me so I can hold you."

He did, and together they achieved throaty, mutual orgasms.

Smothered by his heavy body, Liz was euphoric at the crush on her breasts and abdomen. She would die happy. Comatose from the intense lovemaking, she probably couldn't be revived.

"I'm a fat old man," Jim said after recovering his breathing. "A candidate for a heart attack. What would you have done if I'd died on top of you?"

Eyes closed, smile wide, she whispered, "I already have. I've gone to Heaven."

Jim surmised there was a much more likely destination for what they'd done.

He wondered why he'd never treated Marsha the same, then decided it took two. Liz was his muse when it came to the powers of the flesh, and her lust demon now had a bosom buddy.

They re-showered. While drying, Liz studied her reddened body in the mirror. "Jim, do you think I'm a sex maniac?" She looked over at him. "And, by the way, I apologize for earlier. I don't know why I did it. It was just there."

He let fly from his heart. "I don't think anything a man and woman," he lost his inner battle to qualify the statement as husband and wife, "does consensually is wrong."

Liz's sober countenance relaxed into a dreamy gaze. "Put like that, I don't either."

"On the other hand," Jim continued, "if one of the pair doesn't want to do something and the partner can't convince them otherwise, that's the end of the matter. No sneaking off behind their back with someone else. If I'd refused your ... real wishes, or you mine, we should have respected each other's requests."

She nodded thoughtfully.

"And no going past limits. What we did tonight can result in injury if it's carried too far."

Liz chewed her bottom lip and gave an odd smile. "I can see that. And thanks for being kind. I promise to do it for you next time."

Next time?

They sat naked in the air conditioning to cool down. Despite his body heat, Liz wrapped Jim's arms around her and lifted his hand to her breast.

Something caught her attention. She walked her fingers down his stomach and pricked it with her right index fingernail.

Jim yelped.

"Big baby. You're lucky I don't have long, sharp fingernails."

She raked him again.

"*Liz.*"

"Aw. It's smiling."

Liz's eyes widened. "And it's coming out to play."

Having been given permission, she leisurely satisfied her curiosity.

Jack and Edie sat in his car, startled and aroused. After returning to Palm Gardens, she'd convinced him to make sure the girl was alone. "Unless you want a matching set of eyes. You can't dye the black one white."

Though the RV was silent and dark, Edie had left a listening device on a tire. She placed a second one on the windowsill of Liz's cabin. Their ten-meter range was guaranteed to penetrate aluminum, windows, and concrete walls.

The one at the cabin had. Superbly. They heard every sound, demand, each loud orgasm, the after-shower snippet, the effect of Liz's generosity.

"Whodathot?" Edie said breathlessly. "Way to go, Teddy. Great girl, Liz."

Jack trembled in rage. "I can't believe it. The stupid fart did everything I planned to do. Every damned thing!"

"Buffalo poop. You wouldn't have thought twice when the girl asked to be strapped and chewed."

Edie sighed. Her eyes became starry. She stretched luxuriously. "Teddy played Liz like a Stradivarius violin concerto, Jackie. You should take lessons.

"You know the only thing wrong with what we heard? It's that I wasn't the one sitting in that cabin with the lights turned off. In the dark, men can't tell a twenty-something bud from a full-flowered rose. And we fluffies feel better, softer." She sighed. "I swear. That was like listening to the Kentucky Derby. I think Teddy could have challenged Secretariat. He was kind of chunky, too, as I recall."

"If you say Teddy one more time," Jack howled, "I'll strangle you." Hell, he might as well do it. It would help rid him of his frustrations. "At least now we have what we need to ruin them. I'll send copies to the fat turd's wife, the girl's family, the Media—"

"Jackie, you should be happy, instead of sitting here fuming. You wanted to diddle the girl, right? Well, she's screwed you good and proper. Twice."

When Jack reached for her throat, Edie's voice lost its sweetness. "Touch me, and I'll break both your little fingers. It's game over. We've been fired. Let go. Terminated. That recording isn't worth diddly-squat, now that the police have the Party Wagon. They'll think we cut and spliced their conversations and mixed in love sounds."

Jack had so much trouble breathing, she feared he might have a heart attack. "Sweet thing, you know what you need and it's not that girl ... no matter how experienced she turned out to be."

She lifted his hand and placed it against her chest. "No amount of trouble is worth what you'd go through if you carried out your crazy plans. Her daddy owns a company with hunky plumbers. They work with pipes ... cut 'em, bend 'em, rip 'em out ... if you catch my drift."

She pulled down her blouse and unfastened her bra to allow Jack to get an unobstructed grip on her breasts, so he could savor its generous size and softness.

"Besides, what does Ms. Liz have that I don't? My boobs are larger, probably softer, too."

Jack stared. Squeezed. Nodded.

"My lips are as lush, and I have something that neither she nor Amanda has."
"What?"
"Full-time availability.

"Jackie, the Party Wagon's been confiscated. Our reputations have gone down the toilet. We're pathetic ... two horny idiots who wanted a little sex, now and then. We knew it couldn't last and are lying to ourselves if we think it can.

"And you were getting out of hand, addicted. Maybe I am, too, but at least I worried about you."

Edie offered, "Since I tricked you into this mess, you can take your frustrations out on me. Did you notice the vacancy sign on the motel on Alister Street?"

Jack nodded.

"Then, you can have me, no questions asked. No matter what you do."

She narrowed her eyes and held up a finger. "This one time."

While Jack mulled her offer, Edie strolled around the park like she was the night watchman. She plucked the bugs off the cabin window and RV tire and pitched them into the fish dumpster.

An hour later, Jack ended what she had promised him he could do. He held her soft, plump, shaking body tightly against his. Their tears bathed their chests.

"Edie, I love you. I have since I met you. Please, forgive me."

"Done, Jackie, but if you ever get drunk and mistreat me again, they won't find all the parts of your body."

They satisfied their long pent-up sexual desires.

"You might be crap with a violin, Jackie, but you're a master of the trombone."

Before they fell asleep, Liz asked, "Sweetheart, would do something for me?"

Jim knew he shouldn't agree without asking what, but he thought he knew the question. "Yes. Of course."

61

Morning

5:00 a.m. Friday. A pre-dawn glow brightened the eastern sky. The puffy clouds would soon be bathed in gold and pink. Although Jim didn't need to take an antibiotic pill, he awakened at the same time he had the past three weeks. Liz was awake, too, so he rose, turned on KLUX, and returned to bed.

* * *

Thursday had come and gone like the St. Jo thunderstorm—only without the rain and thunder. They spent the early morning preparing for their trips back home. When they arrived at Dr. Gutierrez's office at 10:00 a.m., the day seemed half-gone.

The nurse again weighed Jim on the way to the examination room. "No, the scales aren't broken, Mr. Smith. You weigh two hundred eighty-six pounds." The former grouch smiled. "Good job." She grinned at Liz. "You, too, granddaughter."

Liz winked. "Good living, smart eating, and some much-needed exercise."

The nurse cocked an eyebrow. They didn't look much alike. *Oh ... my ... lord.* She stifled her ridiculously funny thought.

Not unexpected good news. "Your infection's gone, Jim, but you'll have this scar a long time."

"Thanks, Dr. Gutierrez. I appreciate all you did for me."

"It's been a pleasure meeting you, Jim.

"You, too, Liz. Make sure your grandpa stays away from those jetties."

"No problem, he has a new hobby. And a new will to live right."

"Birding, right?" When Liz nodded, the good doctor gave a thumbs-up.

"Thanks for suggesting I re-read Proverbs and Philippians, Liz," Jim said, as they left the building. "I kind of lost my focus all those years, didn't I?"

She squeezed his hand. "And thank you for your advice. We both did. It's always easier to see faults in others than in ourselves."

Out of habit, they scanned the parking lot for a dark-blue Dodge pickup.

Jim chuckled. "Once paranoid, always paranoid."

"Hey, I did it, too."

They lingered at the Packery Channel to watch the oystercatchers spear and consume more hapless crabs. "The poor little guys don't stand a chance, but they always go down clawing," Liz observed. "Sort of like crab on the half-shell."

Jim empathized. Liz had pierced his heart, and he was still trying to determine what to do about it.

At the scene of the crime in Mustang Island State Park, they met Jeb and Sally Makens.

"I gave a copy of my photos to the police for evidence and deleted my set," Jeb said.

Sally gave a knowing look. "The indecent ones, don't you know."

"Thanks, that was nice of you." But Liz was a different person. She no longer cared if pictures of her half-naked went viral on the Internet. She also had confidence in the police and this sweet couple and didn't expect it to happen.

Similarly, she no longer feared any photos Jack and Edie might have. The world wouldn't end—although the greater Houston metropolitan area might suffer a 9.0 magnitude quake, with a destruction zone that reached more than four hundred miles north to Edmond, Oklahoma.

They drove from the Makens RV to the beach. The brisk wind whipped up large, beautiful breakers. Schools of mullet and other fish flashed in the clear, green water.

Gulls and terns rested on the sand, some on one leg with their heads tucked under a wing. Others noisily scolded their neighbors under the noonday sun. A few preened and scratched. A pair of black skimmers lay flat on the sand. Territorial peeps chased each other off their small patches of shoreline. A great blue heron stepped majestically past.

Liz draped her arms over Jim's shoulders and drew him into a lingering kiss. "It doesn't get any better than this, and it all ends tomorrow."

They breathed in the salty ocean air made pungent by seaweed and the sea creatures in it lining the beach. It would be Jim's last look at the Gulf this trip. Liz might see it further up the coast, depending on the route she chose to return home.

She pointed at a piping plover and sanderling running about in the edge of the surf as if playing together. "Sweetheart, would you take off your shoes and walk in the water with me like that?"

They walked and splashed and shared passionate embraces.

Strolling hand in hand onto the boardwalk for their last view of the birding center, they were startled to find a couple just as surprised to see them.

Jim kept his voice stern despite his friendly smile. "You're off the case, Jack."

Liz scowled. "We're not changing our statements. Or dropping charges."

Jack and Edie looked like mismatched bookends—one large, one small.

The left side of Jack's face and bruised mouth were covered in fresh scabs. Looking wistful and a good ten years older, he didn't say a word, didn't smile. He nodded and turned, noticed white pelicans landing in the distance, and slowly proceeded along the boardwalk.

Edie carried herself as if in discomfort. "We decided to take our lumps."

She chuckled, then became serious. "We've decided life's too short. We'd rather be happy than cause a long court fight, so we dropped all charges. What happens now is your call."

She stared at Jim, tilted her head, and sparkles reentered her eyes.

Seductive? Recalling a private joke? Maybe both? Liz was right, Jim thought. Edie could pass for Maggie's evil twin sister.

She reached out and stroked his arm. "Big Teddy, you put on quite a show last night. And I apologize for the drinks. I'll make it up to you. Promise."

Opening his mouth to speak, he thought better of it.

Edie slapped her rump. "You surprised me, Liz, sweetie. I see a lot of me in you."

She then winked at them. "Don't worry, your secrets are safe with us. Make the best of it."

Speechless, Liz and Jim stared as the tiny woman blew each of them a kiss and followed Jack.

When she caught up with him, she grasped his arm and squeezed his rear. "Jackie, aren't birds lovely? How can people be mad at the world while watching them?"

Nodding, Jack draped his arm over her shoulders.

Jim and Liz gawked at their familiarity with each other and at the words they'd heard.

Liz spoke first. "They spied on us *again*."

She relaxed, grabbed Jim's arm, and pulled him close. Mimicking her enemy, she pinched his tush and led him along the boardwalk.

"Jealous?" he asked.

"No. You're *my* Snickers bar, big Teddy."

Jim gazed at Edie. His closet had become Skeleton Grand Central.

Jack and Edie strolled to the end of the boardwalk, but Liz tugged Jim up the steep steps to the observation tower. The view from the top thrilled her—common moorhens and American avocets graced the large, cattail-lined pond.

She clapped and pointed. A hundred feet away, at the edge of the cattails, Boots and another large alligator—Bags perhaps—were mating. Boots rumbled the water, laid his giant head on the slightly smaller gator's head, and pushed it under. Bags reciprocated.

She clutched Jim's arm with both of hers. "Quite a trip, huh?"

He enveloped her in his arms and kissed her.

At the end of the boardwalk, the two other lovers didn't notice. The small one stood on tiptoe to reach her lover's bruised lips.

A group of girls in the crowd of Boots' junkies pointed at the observation tower. "How gross!"

A mature couple within that group stared at the gators, the tower, and end of the boardwalk. "Must be something in the water," the woman muttered.

Her significant other took the hint and doubled her over with his kiss.

When Jim and Liz arrived at Paradise Pond, the least grebes were swimming at the edge of the boardwalk.

"You turkeys," she scolded. She'd packed her camera for the trip home.

"Hey, be nice. They're part of the reason we're here now, like this," Jim reminded her. "They were the first things I thought of after you electrocuted me."

Liz kissed him. After catching her breath, she mumbled. "Who did you say got electrocuted?"

"It slips my mind."

She blew a kiss to the two little birds paddling about under their feet, kissed Jim again, and they returned to her car.

Not wanting to mess up the clean RV, they drove to one of the excellent seafood restaurants with a deck overlooking the harbor. He chose baked flounder, she the baked snapper. The oysters on the half shell were an afterthought.

At the cabin, Jim went quiet, and Liz let him think. She thought about their day together. Though he'd laughed when she did, been sad when she was, and did what she wanted to do, he'd had something on his mind since they woke up that morning—gazing at her often, before slowly looking away.

It was twenty minutes before Jim found the courage to speak. He struggled with his words. "Liz, I know your honeymoon was literally the honeymoon from hell. I'm happy ..."

Liz worried about his pained expression.

He frowned and started over. "Right this minute, I love you more than anything or anyone in the world, even Marsha."

"Jim, sweetheart, I'm sorry. I didn't mean to—"

"Wait. Please listen."

Liz choked up.

"I've thought about this for several days now, Liz. I can't help worrying about you. I love you and want you to think about this, about what I'm going to say."

Ashen, Liz placed her face in her hands. *Marsha! What have I done?* She felt like throwing up. Although she loved Jim as much as he loved her, she'd never wanted to destroy his marriage.

"I ... I ... How can I put this?" Face drawn, brow furrowed, Jim's eyes brimmed with tears. "I want you to think about your marriage to Don. I don't want you to live a lie for the world."

Unable to speak, Liz choked back sobs. She wanted to spend the rest of her life with Jim, but he and Marsha had been married nearly forty-five years. She hated herself for allowing her demons to control her. And there were so many complications—including her own decision, reached after painful reflection.

"But I don't think you should divorce him yet. For whatever reason, a sense of helplessness, hopelessness ... your mother ... you've lived with Don for eleven years. Those times couldn't have always been bad, and you've assured me that he hasn't abused you again physically, or mentally by having the congregation lay hands on you again.

"I'm not anti-divorce. I don't subscribe to the idea that all marriages are made in heaven. I've seen abusive relationships with either spouse the victim, the far majority being women. I've read about too many women ... even whole families including babies ... being murdered by their husbands and fathers. And vice versa. But please make sure your marriage problems can't be resolved, somehow."

Dumbfounded, Liz shook her head. She'd thought Jim was making a marriage proposal. He was—just not the one she expected. *Lord, I love you.*

Her relief was tempered with apprehension due to the look on his face.

"Liz ... boy, this is difficult ... your sexual appetite is incredible ... voracious ... and you have a lifetime to discover there's much more."

Liz smiled through her tears. "Great minds must think alike, sweetheart. I already made the decision to return home. And yes, what you've taught me is the main reason. I no longer fear sex. Great stars, how I don't fear it.

"And even though Don's eleven years older than I am, he's a prude when it comes sex. He hasn't tried any of the things you've done with me. He basically climbs on and gets off." She chuckled at her unintended pun. "I don't think it's ever taken him longer than a minute since he moved to his own bedroom."

"I can imagine. But what would you have done if he'd tried?"

Liz nodded. "Gone berserk."

"There's danger in parents protecting us from sex education, Liz. You wouldn't believe what my mother told me when I asked where babies came from."

Jim gave a weak smile. "Or maybe you would. Anyway, it generated some serious humiliation from my friends.

"And I've heard it's no different these days, with the Internet. Some studies have shown that more than half of middle school-aged girls are getting their own sex education by watching porn websites." Jim frowned. "Psychologists involved in the research say it can lead to long-term issues.

"As for Don, there's no telling what his preconceived notions were of men and women or of the Scriptures when he married you."

"Trust me, Jim. He'd have a panic attack if he were forced to give a sermon on the Song of Solomon. His forte is the Gospel ... forgiveness, loving thy neighbor. And donating. He's great at convincing people to do that."

Jim stared. "I still have problems with what he did to you on your honeymoon. You told the truth, didn't you? Abuse isn't just physical. There's mental and emotional abuse—threatening harm, bullying, belittling, isolating a spouse from family and friends. Has he done any of those to you?"

"I'll admit I've kept a lot of things from you, sweetheart, but not that."

"I've worried about it, wished you would have forced him into counseling, but with your upbringing, I can understand why you didn't.

"At the same time, please promise me that you'll tell others what he did to you. You need to get it off your chest to someone other than me, and others having knowledge of the incident can be a deterrent."

Liz grimaced, took a breath. "I promise."

Jim studied her look of sincerity. "If you took control of your sexual relationship, why were you so stressed out when I met you? There has to be something else."

"Children pressure," Liz admitted. "From my mother and his. You know about Mother, but not Don's. She's the sweetest woman." She chuckled when Jim fixed her with a silly grin. "You're right. I'm probably the only woman in the world who loves her mother-in-law."

Her eyes grew misty. "While we were on our honeymoon, Lavern fixed up one of our bedrooms as a nursery. It's beautiful. As the years have passed, she's become increasingly sad but never complained ... at least not that I'm aware of.

"Don no longer fears having Satan's spawn, so maybe his mother's sadness affected him, too. But with my honeymoon experience, hatred of sex, and fear of semen, I couldn't stand the thought of his sperm entering me. So, this past winter and spring ..." Liz shook her head. "I don't know. I guess I cracked under the pressure."

"You'll be a great mother, Liz, nothing like Helen. You were wonderful with that little girl in San Antonio. It might be trite to say it, but you're a natural."

"Thank you."

"You're an amazing woman to have allowed Don back into your bed one night a year. I can't picture anyone going through your ordeal being able to do that. And you must have been persuasive, because he obeyed you." Jim smiled. "Like I did when you asked me to stay the rest of today and leave tomorrow.

"You're perceptive, Jim. Yes, I had feelings for him ... love feelings ... not sexual ones. And as strange as it seems, I think our relationship, yours and mine, has changed that." She stared questioningly. "Can you understand?"

Jim nodded. "I believe with all my heart that you're a different woman than you were when you arrived here. I know I'm a different man. You're not weak anymore, you're strong ... super strong, sexually ... and as emotionally strong as your mother. Perhaps you always have been. It's easy to erect mental fences we can't seem to cross without outside help.

"Even the ordeal with Jack and Edie made you stronger. It put you in places and situations that would have made you die of shame three weeks ago." He warped Liz a smile. "Or turned you into a love slave.

"You have your life to live, Liz, and the world isn't going to help you much. It's like what we talked about ... how we're responsible for our own happiness. I think, if you love Don, that you can mold him into the kind of man you want. Make your marriage work. If not, you now have the power to walk away.

"And don't worry about your mother. You can put her in her place. From what you tell me about your sister-in-law, Becky, and your new relationship with your father, you have a support group. You can contact me, too. And don't forget Maggie, she can put a hex on her for you."

Liz chuckled. "In a way, Maggie offered to do that for me the night we played Pegs and Jokers. She sounded like Grandpa Craig ... without turning the air blue. As for the hex, as you put it, Maggie says you just need to say the right words, and people's subconscious work against them.

Jim raised an eyebrow. That was a good thing to know.

He stepped on his soapbox. "Whatever we humans are good at, it isn't being rational."

The last time he started this conversation, she told him to shut up, Liz recalled. This time she would let him finish.

"We have to be the dumbest creatures on the face of the planet," Jim said. "When Adam and Eve bit the forbidden fruit and received knowledge, it's too bad they didn't take a fruit off the tree of common sense, too. Look at us. I'm a fat old man in love with a beautiful young woman. You've shared passionate love with an ugly old man."

Liz sniffled back tears.

"Our unprotected sex was just as irrational. We know that until two weeks ago, neither of us had been in an affair or even seriously considered one, but what about our spouses? What if Marsha found someone exciting while babysitting when I wasn't around? And Don could have been swept off his sex-starved feet by a church member or his secretary. It's happened before."

Liz nodded. "We'd still be safe. Remember the prophylactics? Don changed his mind, but I didn't. There was the semen-phobia thing, so I made him continue using them."

"Then why the pill?"

"Insurance. I didn't want his child."

"And now?"

Liz gave a longing look. "I've fantasized having your baby."

The confession shocked Jim, but he maintained his outward composure.

She nodded soberly. "Yes, I want children."

"Then think about what I've said.

"As for us, we've been involved in an adulterous relationship despite being brought up in church. Even when we found out we were being followed by a private investigator, we did it. We can try rationalizing by pointing at King David. Although he had six wives, he made Bathsheba pregnant, then took steps to make her husband, Uriah, believe the child was his. When that failed he arranged Uriah's murder. Though those were death penalty offenses, God absolved him for them. David and Bathsheba were even Jesus' ancestors."

Liz nodded.

"Another woman in Jesus' lineage tricked her untrustworthy and immoral father-in-law into making her pregnant. And King Solomon had seven hundred wives and three hundred concubines."

"Maybe I'm your concubine," Liz interrupted. "Or I could be Marsha's handmaiden, like Sarah's or Rachel's. I've always thought our love was ordained. Think about our chance meeting at Paradise Pond. Why did I attack you for doing something I've seen thousands of other people do? And look at the luck we've had ... Daddy getting his leg broken, your falling on the jetty and getting an infection, Marsha refusing to come help." When Jim made a face, she clarified. "I didn't say it was all good luck."

She raised her eyes, "And then you rescued me, right after I decided to have sex with Jack."

She kissed Jim, clung to him. "Sweetheart, you released my inner spirit so that I could accept love." She kissed him again.

Jim mulled over her comments, then shook his head. "We can make believe that what we've done isn't wrong, but I worry we'll pay for it. Maybe the ultimate price ... like your mother said would happen when you told her about your reaction when you held Harold's hand in high school. Or maybe our penance will be something different. I know I'll pay with my heart, tomorrow."

Liz gazed questioningly. "At least you can agree that you've been a blessing to me."

"I even worry about that."

"Why, sweetheart? You saved my life."

What he would say next might wreck their relationship, but Jim had to get it off his chest. "I worry that I've taught you too much about sex ... and not enough about self-control."

Liz placed a finger on his lips. "Isn't that what you're doing now? Jim, you don't think too much, you think just right." She leaned her head against his and sobbed happily. "I love you more than the world."

She cried for long minutes then left Jim on the couch. She dug her cellphone out of her fanny pack and tapped an icon.

"Hello, Don. I've made a decision, but my final one will be tomorrow, after we've had a face-to-face talk. Call Mother and Daddy and tell them to meet with us because it concerns all of us. ... No, our house, not theirs. And Don ... um ... I love you. I really do."

After the call, she took a shaky breath, replaced the phone and pulled out a simple white-gold wedding band. Eyes filled with tears, she handed it to Jim. He slipped it on her ring finger, and they kissed in a long embrace.

The red-orange sun met the horizon. Tears trickled down her cheeks as Liz grasped Jim's hand and led him to the back of the cabin. Their passionate lovemaking was searching, experimental, exploring.

"This is the way it should have been with Don and me," she said.

In the afterglow they traced each other's bodies with trembling fingers, memorizing what they would be unable to touch or see again.

"These past two weeks have been the best honeymoon a woman could ever want, sweetheart. No matter what happens, wherever life takes us ... even God's punishment ... you'll always be the first love of my life."

* * *

Friday morning.

Naked lovers entwined in each other's arms listened to the sounds of the dawn and the music on the radio. Jim Ed Brown sang Bill Graham's song, "Morning". Jim hadn't heard it in at least thirty years. Liz never had. They savored its beautiful, poignant words about lovers overwhelmed by a similar relationship.

Liz and Jim had reached the end of their three-week journey. She stared into his soulful eyes and breathed his name as he traced her wedding ring.

When he finished, she touched his ring—Marsha's ring—and caressed it with a fingertip. "Our last time," she whispered, with trembling breath.

Jim blinked. Gulped. "Liz, the poets were masters of understatements. Parting isn't such sweet sorrow. It's ... pure agony." Tears streamed down his face. Unable to say more, he clung to her, felt her heart pound wildly against his own.

"It's ... pure ... torture," Liz gasped, between sobs. "The worst pain ... I've ever felt.

"A type of death."

62
Nesting Birds

Liz steered her SUV onto her driveway in Kingwood. What would Jim say about her home and Olympic-size swimming pool? Or the new Cadillac Escalade, vintage Jaguar, '56 Corvette convertible, and '57 Ford T-bird in their six-car garage—not to mention their bay house and yacht in Kemah?

Don, shoulders slumped, stared apprehensively. At forty, age was catching up with him. Overweight, his face looked fat. His stomach bulged over his belt.

Standing beside him, looking as anxious, were Liz's mother and father—her father in a wheelchair.

Liz took a deep breath to calm her trembling hands and prayed for the strength to say what she'd rehearsed during her drive. She turned the rearview mirror, so she could see herself. Red, puffy eyes and a red-nosed face stared back.

Instead of making her self-conscious and lessening her resolve, the reflection gave her strength. Thoughts of Jim did, too. His strength buoyed hers. Had he asked her to stay and start a new life with him, she would have, would have even become his mistress.

Liz had suffered more than a few misgivings about returning to Kingwood. Jim was warm and kind, thoughtful and insightful. The recollections of his body on hers, driving her insane with passionate fury, meant life would no longer be a drudgery, simply an existence, but a passion.

He was also right about it being filled with difficult choices, and they had made the correct one. They would have their three weeks—the memories of it—forever.

When she stepped from the SUV, Don walked hesitantly toward her, a pained look on his face.

Will he still love me after he and my parents hear what I have to say? Well, he had things to say, too.

But this was her show. Not everything she said would be welcomed. There were things Don and her parents might not be able to understand. Or accept. Things she didn't understand herself.

Don reached her but kept his hands by his side. His red eyes leaked tears. "I'm glad you decided to come back, Mary Elizabeth."

She smiled tearfully and settled her body against his. Wrapping her arms around him, she kissed him. That itself was a new beginning.

It wasn't Jim's kiss. No one could replace his kiss or her love for him, but this was Don's kiss, and it would be their kiss. If things were settled by the end of the evening. And fate, good fate—regardless of Jim's doubts and concerns—controlled her life the past three weeks. Otherwise, she wouldn't be here giving her marriage one last chance. Would the good fate continue?

"I love you, Don," she whispered.

Her father and mother approached. She leaned down and hugged her father, then shuddered at her mother's touch.

"Leave the bags in the car, for now," she ordered, staring at Don. "Let's go inside. I have things to say, and I don't know how things will turn out."

Everyone stiffened. Helen glowered.

In the living room, Liz positioned herself so that the others were in front of her. "Don, Daddy, Mother."

Don stared curiously when she called her father daddy.

"When I left, three weeks ago, I was literally at my wits' end. I'd bottled up too many things from the past and was living a lie. I tried to get away by myself, Mother. But you went with me."

Helen smiled benevolently.

"Well, God, fate, something, stepped in. I became mad at a man at Paradise Pond."

Helen nodded triumphantly at Frank. "*That's* why I hired the private investigator."

Don jolted. "What?"

Liz was glad he didn't know about the investigators. It might make things easier.

She stared her mother and Don into silence and looked at her father. "Then you were injured, Daddy."

She gazed at her mother. "And I took the opportunity to escape from you, Mother."

Scowling, Helen shook her head. "Mary Elizabeth, I'll never be able to forgive you for what you did."

"Hear me out, Mother."

Internally quaking, Liz kept her voice firm. Don and Frank stared in surprise. Even Liz didn't expect the words to flow so easily and without anger. The realization gave her added strength.

Helen started to protest. "Mary Elizabeth—"

Liz cut her off. "I found out that I didn't need to be alone. I needed someone to help me sort things out."

Helen relaxed. "I knew you'd come to your senses. You should've returned home immediately. You don't know how long I've prayed for this to happen. You have an appointment with Dr. Parkman on Monday."

Liz ignored her. "Fate intervened again. I helped Jim Smith recover from a severe infection and helped him with nature photography. Jim is the nicest, most considerate and understanding person I've ever met." She paused. "And he turned out to be a marriage counselor and sex therapist."

Don bolted stiffly upright in his chair but remained silent.

Helen gasped and clutched her chest. "Mary Elizabeth, how dare you say such things in mixed company?"

Frank put his hand on his wife's shoulder. "Please, Mama, let's hear Mary Elizabeth out."

Liz's hard stare made her mother blink and look away. She turned to her husband. "I was ready to leave you, Don, but I didn't know where to go or what to do. Jim encouraged me to give you and our marriage another chance."

Don looked on solemnly.

Helen interrupted. "Mary Elizabeth, I'm sure Dr. Parkman—"

"Daddy, if Mother interrupts me again, will you escort her into the yard and lock the door until she's ready to sit and listen?"

A smile played on Frank's face. "Sure, baby."

"Well!" Helen huffed. Glaring, she crossed her arms. "Such disrespect. I always knew you'd take Mary Elizabeth away from me someday," she hissed at Frank.

"I'm sorry that you feel that way, Mother," Liz said. "I love you, but you're sure making it hard on yourself."

Helen clenched her teeth, tipped her head up and away.

Liz studied her husband. Right now he didn't look like the televangelist preacher of a large congregation. "Don, I won't be frigid any more ... if we can be husband and wife and not lord and servant. There won't be any more laying on of hands on the wrong person."

Three faces stared, two open-mouthed, one smiling.

"You can have a loving wife, willing to have your children, or you can make me leave. I won't stay in the relationship we've had, allowing you to use my body once a year."

Don's face drained of color. "Mary Elizabeth ... your parents."

Helen jumped up snarling. "Mary Elizabeth, your responsibility is to your husband, *not* the other way around." She shook her head. "My God, no wonder you're childless. This is disgusting!"

"Don, should I tell her what happened on our wedding night? Or will you?

She turned and glared. "Or do you already know, Mother?

"And what about you, Father? What did you think when I came home from our honeymoon with bruises on my face ... that I'd been stung by bees? Or had fallen?"

She alternated her gaze between her parents. "What did you both think, when the first thing Don did was hold a prayer service to rid me of demons?"

The three remained silent, each registering different facial expressions.

"Well, those days are past," Liz continued, less forcefully. "Someone else's demons must be exorcised.

"You are the main people in my world. You can either live with me or without me. It's your choice. But if you choose to live with me, then you're going to have to accept me as I am, not as you want ... or demand me to be."

Helen, face hard and unforgiving, muttered loudly enough for the others to hear, "A stranger has ruined our lives. Mary Elizabeth let a complete stranger ruin our lives." She glowered. "Mary Elizabeth, you don't even talk or sound like you."

"No, Mother. Jim's the *only* reason I'm here ... the only reason we might have a chance to be a family, a whole family."

She stared at each of them. Her father looked supportive but afraid of what she might say next. Don appeared petrified. Her mother fumed.

"Mother, Father, Don raped me on our wedding night. He ripped off my panties and beat me into submission. Then he wouldn't let me come home ... wouldn't let me out of our hotel room ... until my cuts healed, and my bruises faded. I'm not sure you noticed or knew, Daddy, but I think you did, Mother."

"Mary Elizabeth, how dare—"

Frank cut his wife off and frowned at his son-in-law. "Forgive me, baby, I noticed your face, but I didn't have the courage to say anything about it. Like I told you the other day, I'll support any decision you make."

Don sat holding his face in hands. "I'm so sorry, Mary Elizabeth, so sorry. I've had nightmares about that day. I can't believe I failed the Lord that way. I've asked His forgiveness over and over."

Liz stood, moved to her husband, lifted his face, and said softly, "You didn't fail the Lord. You failed me, and you failed yourself. God knows we're human, that we're fallible, make mistakes, sin, and seek revenge."

She caressed his cheek. "I failed you, too. Besides being scared, I wanted revenge, wanted you to suffer like I did." Her lips moved slowly to her husband's lips. She kissed him tenderly.

"Then Jim made me see what life has to offer."

Embarrassed, Frank felt disgust for himself and hatred for his son-in-law. At the same time, he marveled at the changes in his daughter in just three short weeks. It reaffirmed his decision to hold firm when she wanted to help Smith. The man must be one of the most accomplished marriage counselors in the state of Oklahoma, maybe in the nation.

Disgusted by her daughter's hateful words and open display of false affection, Helen trembled in rage. God forbid what Satan Smith told her daughter. "Mary Elizabeth, that fat fucking bastard is the world's *worst* marriage counselor. Look at you. You've become completely immoral ... saying things like *sex* therapy in mixed company and demoralizing and humiliating your husband. If you acted this way on your wedding night, you deserved to be beaten, but I think your condition's giving you paranoia. You're delusional." She turned to the others. "Can't you see that she's snapped? We must have her committed."

Shocked by Helen's curse, the men sat mute—Frank stunned by the fact that his wife condoned Don's brutal behavior.

"Listen to me, all of you, I'm not finished," Liz demanded.

She stared at Helen. "Was it my hallucination that you hired a private investigator to follow us, Mother?"

"I did it for your own good."

Liz noted Don's questioning look.

"Was it good that her assistant assaulted me? There's no telling what he would have done if it hadn't been for Jim."

Don and Frank sank back in their seats, staring at Helen, who was momentarily taken aback.

Frank wheeled his chair toward his daughter. Don reached her first. He wrapped his arms around her. Both men spoke at the same time.

"What do I need to do to help you?"

"Mother, you had no way of knowing who you hired. The thing is, you didn't have enough trust in me to let me grow up and live my own life. I don't hate you for what you did. I love you for what you tried to instill in me. But from now on, you'll have to be a mother, not a controller."

Liz extricated herself from Don's embrace and pushed him away.

"You'll soon learn what happened in Corpus Christi. I don't know why you haven't already ... bad news usually travels fast ... but fate may have something left in store in that regard. At least I hope so. I heard encouraging news yesterday."

She put off their questions concerning the details of the incident. "Tomorrow. First things first.

"Daddy, please forgive me for how I treated you all these years. There's no excuse for what I did ... hating you and being disrespectful." She leaned down, kissed his cheek, and they hugged.

"And please forgive me, baby, for not having the strength to give you the affection I should have all your life."

"I love you, Daddy."

Liz faced Helen. "Forgive me for making your life miserable, Mother. And for not having the strength to put you in your place." *Not the best of apologies, but it'll have to do.*

"Mary Elizabeth—" Seething, Helen fell silent.

"Oh yes, about my name, I don't care what y'all call me, from now on, as long it isn't Mary Elizabeth. I don't hate the name like I used to, but I'm tired of it."

She gripped her husband's hand. "Don, I ask your forgiveness for the things I've done to hurt you. I promise to be a good wife ... if you'll be a good husband to me."

Staring at the most beautiful woman in his world, the one he'd desperately wanted to hold and caress for eleven years, the bride he thought he'd lost, Don began crying. "Mary Elizabeth, please forgive me."

"Is that the best short name you could think of," she teased.

Ignoring her parents, she kissed him again. "Why don't we redo those wedding vows? Maybe have a second honeymoon? And this time, let's give them real meaning."

She kissed him in a way that made her parents blush. She wanted to test Don's religiosity to determine if it would stand between them.

He passed the test.

"Mary *Elizabeth!*"

"Daddy, will you please take Mother home. She's bothering us."

* * *

"What are you doing here?"

Darla Seager tried to force the door shut, but Chuck wedged it open. "I'm here to apologize and start our life over."

"I'd hoped the mosquitoes killed you."

"I thought they would. The gator, too. How could you leave me tied up naked in the woods, like that?"

"I wanted to castrate you, but Edith talked me out of it."

"You damn near did with that cane. I'm still swollen and have a blood blister the size of Houston."

Darla glared. "She warned me you'd show up. How'd you drag your lousy behind back here?"

"I flagged down a deputy sheriff, and he let me use his cellphone to call Chip."

"He should have stuck your perverted ass in jail and thrown away the key."

Chuck shook his head. "He said the same thing happened to him."

Darla's mouth fell open. "You're *kidding* me."

"Yeah. Come on, sugar babe, you caught me and taught me a lesson. I won't cheat again."

"I'm done with men."

"That shocked me."

"And you wanted us both."

Chuck wouldn't touch it. "I'm ready for counseling. I did a lot of stupid things, but you're the one I love. And the kids."

"You sure didn't let that stop you before … sleeping around while I took them to their games and dance classes. You even had sex with some slut on Billy's birthday and told him you were fishing. How can I forgive someone who did that to me and to our children?"

A tear rolled down Darla's cheek. "Thank God, you didn't give me an STD."

Chuck didn't offer a defense. "Those are some of the reasons I cried so much this week." He gave a forlorn look. "What did you tell Billy and Cindy?"

"That you were on a fishing trip and might not be back for a long time."

"So … can I come back home?"

Darla used the response Edith gave her. "You have to prove yourself first, get counseling, and give me three months to think about it."

"My counselor says it would be best if we received the counselling together."

Darla took a shuddering breath. "That's what mine said, too."

Chuck hoped to change her mind. "So, it's still three months?"

"At least. And you have to get a job." She shook her head. "I can't believe I paid for you to run around on me."

Shit. Chuck forced a broad smile. "I can do that."

"You'd better. Edith's on retainer."

"Speaking of retainers, whose idea was it to leave me in the swamp?"

"Didn't I tell you I wanted to cut your balls off?"

"And you don't think what you two girls did was punishment enough? That was horrible. I couldn't do anything about it."

"So, you'd have preferred the scalpel?"

"Hell no, but you were inhuman to put me through it."

"Chuck, you haven't changed a bit. Poor baby. *I'm* the bitch for putting you through hell." Darla glowered. "What do you think you've put me through?"

"I'm sorry. You're right. It's my fault. Everything's my fault."

"Daddy! Daddy!" Billy and Cindy raced to the door. "You're home! You're home!" The children bounced and hugged their father.

Chuck picked both up at the same time, kissed them, and spun them around. He glanced at Darla, who scowled and held up five fingers. "I can't stay home, right now, kids, I'm in a real big tournament. But I'll be back soon. I promise."

* * *

The many tears Jim shed on his two-day trip home weren't tears of grief. Nor mixed emotions. They were tears of love.

He fondly pictured Liz's range of emotions during their days in the sun—frustration with the recalcitrant least grebes, ebullience with the photogenic kiskadee. Her wide-eyed excitement while petting stingrays at the Texas State Aquarium. Her innocent joy and throaty laughter when they were children in the park. Tears welled up at the memory of naming clouds while they lay on their backs in the grass in the dolphin park.

He vividly recalled Liz shaking with excitement as the oystercatchers searched for crabs in the shallow tidewater wash, her passionate kiss that destroyed his resistance and united them, body and spirit. Followed by her budding love attempt on Padre Island. Her sultry vision after the storm on St. Jo Island when they celebrated their survival in the most natural way imaginable. He smiled at the thought of her testing his inhibitions under the big tree.

Suffice to say, he would share such memories only with her. They weren't in Marsha's DNA.

Liz had given him purpose, as well. He would think of her each time he edited one of the photos they took together.

Something unimaginable occurred during the past three weeks. He had lived and loved a lifetime and felt no guilt. He simply loved two women.

He also felt comfortable with regards to Jack and Edie. Yes, they'd get away with their transgressions, but he couldn't cast the first stone.

Late Saturday afternoon, he turned onto his street. Thankfully, a car wasn't blocking the curb in front of his home. He could park the rig there overnight to remove the remaining food items from the pantry, the few things that needed washing, and move his ocean fishing gear into the attic.

Marsha heard the loud pickup and rushed out to meet him. When he stepped down, she gave him a weak hug—then braced her hands and arms against his chest when he tried to kiss her more forcefully.

"Boy, you must have missed me, but stop it, Jim. You know we can't kiss in front of the neighbors."

He peered around, saw no one, but backed off. "Your hair looks great, Marsha. Did you have it done for my homecoming?"

"I'm surprised you noticed. Do you like the color?"

Its honey-blond reminded him of Edie's. Endowed with a renewed sexual appetite, he moved against her. "It's beautiful. You're beautiful." He tried to kiss her again. "I love you so much, Marsha."

She gave a vixen-like smile while holding his mouth and abdomen at bay. "I know what *you* want to do tonight."

The smile changed to a glare when he made a final attempt. "*Jim*, you're embarrassing me in front the whole neighborhood. Give me the key to the fifth wheel."

He acquiesced despite the lack of visible neighbors. Marsha would be forever unable to show affection in public. *No matter*. He handed her the keys with the smug assurance that she was going to be surprised.

Two minutes later, she returned carrying the night's sheets and pillowcase, his pajamas, and a towel. "Did you throw everything else away ... or give them to the Salvation Army?"

"We washed most things and cleaned up Wednesday afternoon."

Marsha looked contemplative, and Jim wondered if it was his inference that Liz helped or because he hadn't acted the way she thought he would.

Her next words were unexpected, although he knew they shouldn't have been. "It's book club night. You don't mind if I go, do you? It'll give you time to clean out the RV."

It was an evening Marsha wouldn't relinquish. Why a group of women would pick a Saturday night, once a month, to discuss books, sometimes until midnight, mystified him.

She left for her meeting before he finished unloading his fishing tackle.

After taking off his musty travel clothes and showering, Jim went to the kitchen. A thick, fat-rimmed steak immersed in Marsha's mouth-watering gravy simmered in a covered frying pan. A large pot of mashed potatoes, yellowed by butter and cream, occupied the next burner. A medium-sized pot of English peas sat behind it. Two slices of Texas Toast were ready to be pushed down in the toaster, and a note informed him of the pecan pie in the pie safe and ice cream in the freezer. It requested that he not eat the entire pie. Sarah's family would be dining with them the next day after church.

Peering at the meal and down at his thinner stomach that Marsha either hadn't noticed or chosen not to comment on, he debated what to do. Having not required an antacid since going on Liz's diet, he chose to cheat. He removed the steak from the pan, scraped off the gravy, cut the steak into thirds, placed two of the sections in containers and the containers in the fridge. He ladled a half-cup of mashed potatoes on his plate, added English Peas, and ate the reduced-sized meal.

The small portions of the savory steak and mashed potatoes left his taste buds yearning for more, so he returned to the fridge. He found nothing in the fruit drawer but smiled when he looked in the vegetable keeper. Cherry tomatoes and lettuce. He fixed a salad and splurged with a small slice of pie topped with a dollop of ice cream.

Still hungry, he resisted temptation and made a mental note to pick up nuts, fruit, yogurt, and skim milk. He would purchase those things the next day on his way home from the YMCA.

He put the remaining food in the fridge, cleared the table, and ran the dishwasher. *What have I done?*

Chuckling, he finished drying the last pot. It felt good. Besides, he envisioned bouncing Marsha's plump body that evening, and the book club always ran late. This would save time.

The lack of dishes to put away and the clean pots and pans surprised Marsha when she returned at midnight. She walked to the bedroom and saw Jim reading one of their daughter Deena's novels. "Thanks for doing the dishes, hon."

"Don't mention it."

"By the way, you're looking a little thin. That must have been a pretty bad infection. And I knew you wouldn't eat well."

"Uh-huh."

"I'm sorry. What did you say?"

"I said, you're right. It was a bad infection."

Jim read while waiting for Marsha to bathe and come to bed. His erection became so full he found it difficult to keep from joining her in the shower, but she kept that off limits.

The first ten minutes, he called out twice. "Are you about ready to come to bed?"

"Be right there."

He was asleep when she accidentally awakened him while sliding into bed a little past one. Sleepily, he reached for her.

"Not tonight. I'm tired, and it's late."

She clicked off the lamp and turned away from him. "Besides, we have church in the morning. It would muss up my hairdo."

Hoping to change her mind, Jim rubbed her enchanting derriere.

Marsha pushed his hand away. "Tomorrow."

Sleep robbed him of further desire. He snuggled against his warm wife and contentedly put an arm around her.

It's good to be home.

Epilogue
Birding 102

"Well, the Smiths are late as usual," Charles Danielson grumbled, as three of the four amigos prepared for the first fishing day of their annual Port Aransas trip. "First they call and say they'll arrive late at Thackerville. Then they tell us they'll catch up at Schulenberg. Finally, they say they'll meet us here."

Bill Warner shrugged. "It's more promising than last year, when Marsha didn't come, and Jimmy only made the last week. Then he had the bad luck of falling on the jetty."

Jeff Saunders pished. "You call that bad luck? He made out like a bandit when Liz nursed him back to health. Can you imagine spending two weeks with her? I'm going to his spot and scrape my shin, so she'll take care of me when she gets here Saturday."

Bill smirked. "She's pregnant. She'll have her husband do it."

"Don't that beat all? Jeff said. "Would either of you let your wife run off for three weeks to take care of a man she met on a birding trip?"

Nadine Danielson and Patsy Warner sat enjoying a Port Aransas morning ritual in Maggie Saunders' motorhome—coffee and fruit.

"I'm worried about Marsha and Jim. They should've been here by now. Do you think something bad happened?" Nadine fretted.

"Are you trying to take Marsha's place?" Maggie chided. "She's the worrywart. It's a good thing she's with Jimmy, or she'd have us calling the police."

Patsy and Nadine nodded.

Maggie frowned. "My guess is something bad did happen ... one or more of their grandchildren were in an event or needed being attended to. That *woman*."

"What do you think about Liz and her ... husband ... coming to visit?" Nadine asked. "She wasn't wearing a ring year last year."

"That was a shock," Patsy agreed. "If I'd known she was married, I would've told Marsha to tell Jim to come straight home even if his leg rotted off."

"She's only seven months pregnant and doesn't have a child three months old, so I hoped this would happen. I'm glad she found the courage to tell her mother to get screwed."

"*Maggie*," Nadine and Patsy said in unison.

Patsy stared accusingly. "Why didn't you tell us she was married?"

"Cause of what you just said. The time she spent caring for Jimmy gave her initiative and self-respect, and she helped Jimmy's self-confidence and will power. He's lost more than a hundred pounds. They were good for each other."

All agreed Jim had changed. He no longer seemed to mind when Marsha went babysitting without him. He'd joined an Audubon club, and his nature pictures were receiving attention. Some had been selected for juried exhibits.

"I can't get over how good he looks," Nadine said. "Marsha says he swims and works out every day at the Y. I think he looks like James Garner, but he still thinks he's the ugly duckling because of the extra skin from his weight loss."

Patsy grinned. "He looks more like Clark Gable, to me, but Marsha complains he's become a picky eater. I wouldn't like Bill turning up his nose at the meals I make."

Maggie stared. "Are you kidding? Marsha's into comfort foods, and Jimmy wants to eat healthy. He's so handsome now ... with those heavenly lips and bedroom eyes ... he makes my twat twitch. If I weren't married, I'd be on him like a chicken on a June bug."

"*Maggie!*" Nadine and Patsy shouted in unison.

* * *

Jim and Marsha arrived at noon. While registering, he glanced out the office window and saw Maggie hugging Marsha beside the pickup. *She's got to be psychic.*

In case she was a mind reader, too, he determined to keep his countenance straightforward when he saw Liz on Saturday.

After Jim and Marsha set up their RV rig, Maggie invited Marsha to a light lunch with her, Nadine, and Patsy.

"Marsha, why did you and Jim arrive a day late?" Patsy asked.

"Taylor wanted Meemaw to see a painting she made of Peepaw and me. Jim and I couldn't resist."

She smiled apologetically. "By the way, I'm only staying three weeks. My second cousin Daisy, in Alamogordo, New Mexico, has a job interview in New York. She needs me to babysit her love-struck teenage daughter."

Maggie coughed. "Marsha, I have to tell you something ... and I mean this in the nicest possible way. You're an idiot."

Turning red, Marsha started to explain.

Maggie passed the carrot sticks. "More veggies, anyone?"

* * *

Saturday didn't come too soon for anyone in the group. Jim was as pleased as an expectant grandfather could be. Maggie felt like she was waiting for one of her daughters.

Patsy wondered about Liz's husband. How could Liz leave him for three weeks to go birding with Jim? Those were grounds for divorce.

Nadine, unaware that Liz knew and didn't mind, worried that someone might let it slip that she opposed Liz staying with Jim.

Jeff and Bill had bets on how pregnant she looked.

Marsha awaited her first look at Liz. The girls said she was beautiful. The guys had laid it on thick—claimed they wished they were the ones who fell on the jetty.

The longer she waited, the more apprehensive she became. How could such a woman have donated time to care for her husband?

Jim's cellphone chimed. He glanced at the number. "Hey, Liz."

"Hey, Jim. We're in Fulton. We'll be there in an hour or two, depending on the ferry. Don and I can't wait to see y'all. We'll stop by on the way to the condo. See if you can get everyone together."

"Come straight to the clubhouse. Maggie will tell us when it's time to meet you. And the girls are making a ton of food, so I hope you're hungry."

"We're starved. I figured she'd set something up, so I convinced Don to skip a meal, a few miles back."

"Good move. I can't wait to see you."

Liz choked up. "I've missed you, too. See you in a little while, Love … ya."

"I love you, too."

Glancing at Jim while she sliced strawberries for the angel food cake she made for the potluck lunch, Marsha felt a twinge of jealousy. He'd just told Liz he loved her. That seemed a bit strong on affection. Strange how three weeks could forge bonds as strong as those between her husband and Liz. They emailed each other regularly.

As Liz predicted, an hour later the black Tahoe pulled up to the clubhouse where the gang, led by Maggie, stood waiting. Liz was happy she'd refused to let Don trade the Tahoe for a new SUV. She was working on the rest of Jim's concerns, too.

Jim's heart skipped when she fixed him with her long gaze. The love, the excitement, would always be there. And trim as ever, she barely looked pregnant. He strode toward her. "You look marvelous, Liz. I'm so happy for you."

Her heart pounded. Her lover now looked as young as her father, except for his balding head. He had a handsome face—square-chinned, with a touch of jowls she found incredibly cute.

She hurried to meet him and kissed his cheek after brushing her lips lightly against his and changing her mind. She couldn't risk melting in the fire because the same electricity sparked in their embrace as it had a year earlier. No one could take his place. As her mother might say, when God made Jim, he broke the mold. "It's so wonderful to see you again."

She hoped no one noticed the desire in her eyes.

But someone did. And frowned.

Liz giggled when she gazed at the rest of the group. The men were gawking. Good. She'd selected the right maternity outfit. And they'd never seen her in makeup. Her salon-styled hair was done in a wave. A small, red hibiscus made the light-brown appear gold.

Maggie, hands on her hips, cocked her head. "You sure you aren't making up the part about being seven months pregnant?"

Liz turned sideways and put her hands on her very noticeable baby bump. "Whatcha think?"

Maggie ran to hug and kiss her. "My lord, it's good to see you again, sweetie. You look wonderful."

"You, too."

Eyes glistening, Liz whispered in Maggie's ear. "Mom changed the minute I told her I was pregnant … like you expected."

Jim led Marsha to Liz and announced proudly, "This is my Marsha."

Liz studied the plump, pleasant-faced lady she'd imagined for the past year. E-mail photos didn't do her justice. If she were one of Marsha's grandchildren, she'd love being rocked against her bosom and bounced on her lap while having stories read to her. She looked like the grandmother she always wished she had. She beamed, kissed Marsha, and gave her a hug. "Hi, Marsha. It's wonderful to finally meet you."

Marsha had thought surely the others had exaggerated Liz's beauty. She couldn't picture someone so young and beautiful helping Jim so selflessly. *This will take getting used to.* Flustered, she hugged back.

After the hugging gauntlet, Liz introduced Don. Tall and trim, his full head of dark-brown hair ragged from the wind and humidity, he looked something like the picture of her dad she had showed Maggie, Jeff, and Jim the previous year. He seemed embarrassed by the attention.

Unusual for a minister, Maggie mused.

Don looked young for his age, and Jim wondered if living a year with a changed Liz had anything to do with it. She'd mentioned he was overweight and showing his age, during one of their many discussions after confessing she was married. He gave a prayer for their unborn child.

As if reading his thoughts, Liz smiled demurely and flicked her eyes in Don's direction.

Jim nodded. He could tell she was in love. And in absolute control.

Bill and Charles tried to keep from staring. Jeff couldn't take his eyes off Liz for most of the two hours she and Don lunched and visited with them.

In those moments when Jeff tore his eyes away to look at the transformed Jim, he marveled at Maggie. She'd reached a new height in the art of meddling. She looked so smug he figured her indigenous side had added mental eagle feathers to her bouquet of merit—one for Liz's mother and one for Marsha. She would be hard to live with.

Don watched his wife interact with the people who changed their lives. He studied the man to whom she attributed to her dramatic changes. She'd become every man's dream—her aversion to intimacy gone, their sex life full. Well, she might not be every man's dream. She was dominant, demanding—in church, at home. In bed.

She called Jim Smith her sex therapist. Old and balding, the man didn't appear to have a worldly bone in his body. Don found that comforting. He'd retained doubts about her faithfulness the entire year, wondering how she could lose monumental, seemingly insurmountable fears in three short weeks. She'd returned home far more knowledgeable than he and enthusiastic, even frightening, at times. That made it hard to believe Jim's email pictures were real. He pictured someone who looked—at least much younger. It felt good to finally put that fear to rest.

The first time they were alone, Don approached Jim and held out his hand. "I want to thank you."

Jim accepted it with an inquisitive gaze. "What for?"

Taken aback by the question, he found it difficult to articulate. How did one thank a person for kindling love and passion in a wife on the verge of filing for divorce? "For saving my marriage."

"All I did was suggest that she not leave a marriage of eleven years without giving it another try, after she assured me ... since your honeymoon ... that you had never mistreated her again."

Don winced at the knowledge that Liz had told all, but it had been for the best. Still, how was Smith able to make his wife lose all inhibitions and not only in the Biblical sense? She was proving adept in developing new missions for the church and even teaching a Sunday school class for single women. "That's it?"

"Pretty much."

"But what about...." Don couldn't find the nerve to voice his questions about the sex therapy.

Liz had described her encounter with the private investigator. She'd said she may have misunderstood his intentions, so she struck him, and he retaliated. "I also need to thank you for saving Liz during the incident."

Jim nodded. "I'm thankful all charges were dropped and that it's behind us."

Don recalled Liz's revelation that her shirt ripped during the struggle and that someone took photos of her bare breasts. He suddenly realized that Jim, being there, may have seen them. The thought disturbed him, but Jim had prevented matters from becoming worse.

"Me, too."

The two men shook hands while holding each other's elbows throughout the short conversation.

"Thanks for everything, Jim."

"Don't mention it, Don."

* * *

Mr. and Mrs. Jack West celebrated their anniversary in San Antonio. Their love began to blossom there a year earlier, so even though it was technically their honeymoon, they considered it their anniversary.

This year, as last, they spent much of their day at the Friedrich Wilderness Park. That time, they were following a woman suspected of having an affair. Now, they were indulging in their new pastime—bird and nature photography. Specifically, they sought Texas's famed golden-cheeked warbler.

The previous year their physical conditioning had been so poor it had been a devastating experience. Their new passion had made them fit. They considered it more of a sport, actually. Jack stood five-feet-nine-inches tall. A year earlier he weighed two hundred twenty-five pounds. Today he was a trim and muscular one hundred sixty-eight, with a body mass index of 24.8. Edie had trimmed down to one-hundred-ten pounds and gained outstanding stamina.

They watched many golden-cheeked warblers drink and splash in the tiny pools below the windmill in the park, but the heavy shade made good photographs iffy. In addition, Edie found the area too crowded for her taste.

They hiked up and over the four-hundred-foot hill and down to the Fern Del because brochures claimed it offered views of the warblers equal to the windmill area. Unlike the previous year, they didn't work up a sweat during the trip.

Not until effervescent Edie made an irresistible suggestion that had absolutely nothing to with birding.

"Faster, Jackie. Ooh. That's it."

She heard a call she'd memorized in preparation for the trip. "Wait. Did you hear that? Hold up. There it is. Quick, hand me my camera."

Legs wrapped above Jack's hips, his strong hands grasping her satiny rear for stability, Edie took a photo they would treasure for the rest of their lives.

"A golden-cheeked warbler," she exulted. "In the sunlight."

Their excitement and the words golden-cheeked warbler attracted two other couples who were astonished by the couple's unusual birding method. They backed silently away without being seen.

That evening Jack reclined in bed in their motorhome while Edie readied herself for bed.

"We received a thank you note from sweet little Darla Seager," she called from the bathroom. "Hunky Chucky couldn't stop fishing posted water. Their divorce is final, and your photos of him with the judge's wife kept Darla from having to divide the community property equally.

"He still received too much, considering he didn't contribute a penny to the marriage. And he's already found another sugar mama he's cheating on. Tough on the kids, though."

"I told you we didn't have anything to worry about," Jack called back.

"Mm-hmm."

Edie went silent, so Jack glanced back at his e-book but didn't read it. A year ago, the woman they were surveilling tricked him into driving hundreds of miles on a wild goose chase. In the process, he received a beating and snapped—became obsessed with revenge.

He often reflected on the incident with Liz Crane. Because their client, Crane's mother, hadn't been up front with Edie, they hadn't known Crane was married or even her last name.

He still didn't know what he'd have done had Jim Smith not restrained him after Crane attacked him. Looking back, any of several scenarios might have played out—all bad.

At Edie's insistence, he'd dropped all charges after telling the authorities he had overreacted. Liz Crane did the same—after insisting he and Edie close their investigative practices.

Had it not been for a crime reporter who printed a short summary a month after the incident as part of her weekly column, the altercation would have amounted to nothing more than a one-line entry on the daily police log in the newspapers. The article had resulted in a few calls from some surprised friends. His minister asked him to step down as an elder in the church and advised him to seek psychiatric counselling. He couldn't say no, and the counselling helped immensely.

Humiliated by the beach incident and infuriated by Edie's presence, Amanda had filed for divorce. She'd kept meticulous records of his out of town business trips, and her divorce petition included adultery, abandonment, and emotional abuse. She requested a disproportionate share of the marital estate—seventy-five percent. Although Texas was a no-fault divorce state, he agreed, considering it penance for his behavior of the prior three years. Plus, he had all the money he could ever use, and it continued to flow in.

He and Edie married thirty-one days after the divorce finalized. Jack chuckled. He would never forget her loving words when she proposed.

"I'm not about to shack up with some lonely old reprobate. And while you're at it, stop your damned cussing. I won't have a potty-mouthed husband."

Surprisingly, she remained celibate until shortly after their wedding vows, when she asked him to check out the broken lock on the ladies' room door in the reception hall.

The rocket scientist of the boudoir kept his life on a fast and delirious pace.

"Use it or lose it," she frequently reminded him.

The corners of his mouth tipped up. Would using it as often as Edie required it result in it being worn down like a wooden pencil?

Being incorrigible, she has also suggested they join her old swingers club. "You'll be the star."

He'd refused. No need to risk falling off the wagon. Besides, he was a one-woman man again. Anyone married to Edie would have to be. Tireless and infinitely experimental, there wouldn't be time or energy left for anyone else.

They were on an open-ended honeymoon, with a bucket list of destinations—swimming in the cold spring at Balmorhea State Park, hiking in Guadalupe Mountains National Park, using flashlights to explore Slaughter Canyon Cave in Carlsbad Canyon National Park, walking barefoot in White Sands National Monument. Life was good. Much better than he deserved.

Suddenly having the feeling he was being watched, Jack placed his e-book on the nightstand.

An hour later, he staggered to the bathroom. There were more marks on his ears, chest, and neck. Additional toothmarks on his newly trim belly?

Looking at his reflection in the mirror, he shook his head and smiled. His honeymoon had already become a trip of a lifetime.

Returning to the bedroom, he stared at Edie. She looked like a sleeping angel.

He slid gently into bed, put an arm around her, and fell contentedly asleep.

About the Author

When on vacation, E. M. Williams enjoys this marvelous orb by hiking, birding, and nature photography, especially along the Texas Gulf coast. At home, there's too much weeding and mowing and stuff.

Humanity, what a track record. We have a great capacity to love, to help others in time of need, but unlike our animal brethren, we humans typically do strange things. We seldom appear rational, but we are infinitely rationalizing. Why else build homes and cities in known harm's way, take limb-, love-, career-, and life-threatening risks?

Great material. It's why thinkers think, writers write, musicians compose, and people read and listen. Plus, stories, poems, and songs with happy endings are supposedly cathartic—at least for their authors.

Or we could savor the sea breeze and bird antics as we stroll along Malaquite Beach in Padre Island National Seashore. Watch from the Port Aransas jetty as pelicans and gulls trail shrimp boats. Try to photograph dolphins leaping and splashing in ships' bow waves. Go birding at the sites mentioned in this novel.

9781943313013